The Albion

Derryl Flynn

First published in 2008 by

Authorhouse

This edition published in 2014 by

Grinning Bandit Books

http://grinningbandit.webnode.com

ISBN 978-0-9575851-6-4

Cover design by Derryl Flynn

Early praise for The Albion

"This book is so well written it will take you on a roller coaster journey of a working class man trying to make a difference in life. A must read for anyone who appreciates a story with a social comment." M Wood

"What a brilliant read. Don't think that this book is just for men! It is a heart-rending, funny, gripping, superbly written story which once you pick up, you just won't be able to put down." S M Coleman

"It will make you smile, laugh out loud and cry. You will be exhausted by this roller coaster of a story, you will be unable to leave it alone. Don't expect it to be 'sweetness and light' reading, this is a story about hard folk in hard times demonstrating their love of life, their love for others and with a good dose of the bloody funny side of life." Alex James

Also by Derryl Flynn

Scrapyard Blues

DEDICATION

For me mam.

Acknowledgements

Much love goes to: Jane, Ami, Liam, Joely, Phoebe, Ava, Richard and Jane.

For their unwavering faith, support and encouragement: Sue Coleman and Martyn Wood.

For unconsciously planting the seed: The Pendleburys and the Rapers.

Special thanks to Roman "Hawkeye" Laskowski for speed of light editing, formatting and general level headedness.

1

With two hands the youth raised the bloodied spade for the final time. Poised in ritual fashion, features void of emotion, he watched the terrified rodent scamper to the four corners of its pen, squealing in terror, scrambling over sticky red sawdust and the bodies and severed heads of its siblings in a futile effort to escape. The youth, unhurried, calmly chose his moment. His timing was deft. The squealing ceased abruptly. Nearby, he heard the sound of glass being smashed regularly and systematically. He turned his head and craned his neck toward the joyous noise. Without ceremony he let the crimson spattered tool fall to the floor, and, as if being led by sirens, wandered off in the direction of the dissonance. It appeared his mates were having better fun and he wanted in on it. There were no more animals left to kill anyway...

* * *

Terry Gallagher was going back to school. He wasn't looking forward to it. It wasn't for a reunion or anything. It had been almost twenty-four years since he was last there. He'd hated it then and the thought of having to set foot inside the place again, even after all this time, gave him an uneasy feeling in his gut. It wasn't the actual thought of his schooldays that made him feel like this, they had been okay; it was more about the institution of school itself, that authoritarian thing if you like. He couldn't quite explain it, nor had he ever tried to, but during the course of his thirty-nine years he had developed and harboured a particular resentment for those who were in charge of things, be it schoolteachers, bosses or bank managers. To him they were of the same breed, and he'd never met one he didn't trust as far as he could throw. He railed against officialdom and those fuckers who had got themselves a little bit of power and let it go to their heads; socially inept sycophantic misfits who arse-licked their way to the top, your jobsworths and your little Hitlers; grey men in grey suits or pillocks in uniform like traffic wardens who swaggered around thinking that wearing a striped hat and a badge made them better than everyone else. And at the other end of the scale, worse still, came the untouchables: the judges, lawyers, politicians, and the ones whose nests are feathered from birth, the old boys network, the secret societies, Masonic rituals, dodgy handshakes and all that. He wouldn't go so far as to label it illuminati, all that shit was a bit too deep for him, but it was definitely all wheels within wheels, not what you knew but who you knew; a closed shop and that's how it had always been and those who wielded the power would make sure it would stay that way.

Terry passed old Mr. Johnson's house near the end of his street, all vandalised and boarded up now. Six months ago he'd been robbed, severely beaten and left for dead. The image of the old guy's battered and bruised face, spread across the front page of the local rag, came back to him. Words couldn't describe the picture; he was unrecognisable. Up to now no one had been charged. While he'd been in hospital the house had been systematically ransacked and stripped bare, all the old man's worldly possessions along with his memories gone, and for what? Maybe a few wraps of smack.

Giving the place a backwards glance, Terry felt a pang of guilt. *'Where was I?'* he thought. *'I was his neighbour for God's sake.'*

Nobody seemed to give a shit anymore. The whole fucking world was apathetic and Terry supposed he was as bad as the rest, although he would love to get his hands on the bastards that did it. But who'd be a have-a-go hero these days? Was it really worth getting maimed or murdered for your troubles? What was the point of being a Good Samaritan when you risked getting sued by the criminal; when you faced a jail sentence yourself just for trying to do the right thing. To him it was all wrong. The bleeding heart Liberals held sway, political correctness was in the driving seat and the silent majority were either too scared, or too brainwashed to speak out.

Caroline Goulding had travelled half the world, back to the town where she grew up, back to oversee her father's transfer from hospital to the Garden Springs nursing home. She hadn't recognised him when the nurse had first pointed him out, and he would never recognise her.

The tears had welled up and spilled down her cheeks as she'd tried to spoon-feed soup into the living vegetable that had once been her father. She'd gazed into his face while trying to stifle the sobs. Herbert Johnson stared back, right through her, soup spilling from his mouth and down his chin. Soon she would have to return to her own life, ten thousand miles away. Who'd be there for him when she'd gone? She was his only living relative – who'd be there? Her guilt was massive.

Herbert Johnson was a real life hero. He had been a Chindit during the Second World War, and had fought alongside the Ghurkhas in the jungles of Burma as part of the first expeditionary force named Operation Longcloth under the command of Major General Orde Wingate. Terry had often tried to coax the old man to regale him with tales of battle over a pint down at the Working Men's Club, but Herbert showed his reluctance at dredging up the past and had always humbly declined. Then, one day, right out of the blue Terry's persistence paid off. From his wallet, and with a resigned sigh, the old guy had produced a battered and faded sepia photograph and, in between sips of his IPA, began to dip deep into his memories...

During one skirmish deep inside North Burma in 1943 the whole of Herbert's section, which consisted his own unit, 142 Commando, and men from the 32nd Gurkha Rifles, had been pinned down for three days by mortar fire and a heavily armed Japanese machine gun post. Several attempts at storming the fortification had ended in failure with heavy losses. Snipers were also wreaking havoc. The situation had become desperate. Supplies and morale were low and the list of casualties of both sick and wounded was growing by the hour.

On the third night twelve volunteers, Herbert amongst them, set out under the cover of darkness to locate and take out the snipers and create diversions to allow one last assault.

The Ghurkhas and their kukris did their job on the snipers, and on a pre-arranged signal all hell broke loose. Despite the carnage all around them Herbert and a Ghurkha were the first to the machine gun post. Herbert had two bullets in his leg and one in his shoulder. The Ghurkha had one arm blown off but this didn't stop him tearing pins out of grenades with his teeth and lobbing them as he screamed forward, Herbert in his wake firing his bren gun from the hip.

Operation Longcloth and the campaign that succeeded it, Operation Thursday, was hailed a success by Churchill and the other allied leaders. The campaign showed that British troops could take on the Japanese and win. The Japs had been thought to be invincible jungle fighters, the Chindits proved otherwise, and the legend of the Japanese superman was dealt a savage blow.

For their bravery in the face of overwhelming odds and enemy fire, Herbert and the Ghurkha were awarded the Victoria Cross.

The photograph showed Herbert and his Ghurkha mate looking fit and tanned in their uniforms, proudly showing off the medals and the Brigade standard that depicted the Chinthe, a half-lion, half-griffin mythical beast. In the photo the void in the sleeve of the Ghurkha's tunic could clearly be seen, somehow confirming the reality of it all. Herbert was only twenty-four when the snap was taken.

Terry wondered what might have happened to the medal and the photo. If it wasn't something the burglars could flog in the pub for a few quid like a telly or a DVD player it would have been useless to them. Would they have even known the value of something like the VC? He doubted it.

He imagined them laying into the old man and wondered what must have been going through his mind as boot after boot landed, turning his face into pulp. He wouldn't have been able to put up much of a fight. He was eighty-five, really bad on his pins because of the wounds sustained in the war. He tried to picture the old lad fighting them off with his stick. The Japs couldn't put paid to him but these cunts had. He felt sick thinking about it. Feeling the anger well up inside him, Terry kicked out at a coke can lying in his path that went rattling away into a gutter. He quickly shook himself back to reality realising he was getting too deep, annoyed with himself for getting so agitated, especially today of all days.

Despite the way he felt, Terry had never been politically motivated. He certainly wasn't a socialist. He hated doctrines and labels. He wouldn't be pigeonholed. He'd come to realise that they were all tarred with the same brush, communist, fascist, you name it; to him they were all the same with the same hidden agendas: manipulate the masses, feed on their fears through the media and the like, gain power and self-serve. What he couldn't understand was how people allowed themselves to be brainwashed so easily. Nobody questioned things anymore. Don't upset the status quo, anything for an easy life. But the way he saw it, it wasn't an easy life, far from it.

Terry turned a corner at the end of a terrace to be met with a cold blast of wind. It was already May but any spring weather seemed to have by-passed this northern city. He reached for the zipper on his jacket only to get it stuck in the lining. Jan, his missus, had bollocked him for not wearing something smarter, especially as he was going to see the headmaster. *'Fuck that,'* he had said. *'They tek me as they find me.'* Jan knew it was futile to argue.

He passed the working men's club with its heavily grilled windows and graffiti daubed walls. Take-away cartons and fish-and-chip paper danced to the tune of the wind around the car park. Opposite on some waste ground a freshly burnt out car, still smouldering, sat alongside another already rusting heap, the aftermath of an evening's entertainment on the streets of West Broughton. Night after night the police chopper would drone over and around the rooftops, searchlight scouring the avenues and rat-runs, clocking up the increase in next year's council tax by the hour, while the joy-riders and ram-raiders, slumbering by day, came alive at night to play catch-us-if-you-can, fearless and frenzied, whooping and hollering, hand brake turns and burning rubber in somebody else's hard-earned pride and joy. Twenty-first century outlaws fuelled with amphetamines and crack.

Terry passed oblivious, still struggling with his zip and cursing to himself.

A few avenues on, he sidestepped a pavement full of broken glass and nodded a *'mornin''* to the guy working on the door of the latest burglary victim. *'Academy Locksmiths – 24 hour emergency service – Free quotations'* was emblazoned across the side of his brand new Mercedes Sprinter van. *'Can't be bad; I'm in the wrong bleeding game, me,'* Terry thought to himself as he went on his way. *'Security: that's the one, the new growth industry for sure, especially round here.'*

He knocked on the door of the stone-built terrace then tried in another vain attempt to free his zip. Nobby was at the door almost immediately.

''Sup mush?'

'Got me fuckin' zip stuck,' Terry muttered without looking up. 'C'mon, we're late.'

Nobby Clarke and Terry Gallagher had been mates for as long as either of them could remember. They had grown up in the same street, gone to the same schools, started out on the parks working for the council together and were now equal partners in their own landscape and gardening business. They were an unlikely pair, both in their physical appearance and general outlook on life, yet their looks certainly mirrored their characters. Terry was about five-ten with a wiry build and features that said *'fools not suffered here'*. His eyes had grown cold over the years and his forehead had a semi-permanent frown, a fact that had not gone unnoticed by Jan. She would often lift the framed wedding photo off the sideboard when the house was quiet and gaze at the image of the good looking, happy-go-lucky guy she had married. The struggle to bring up a family and keep a roof over their heads had made him intense. She understood why and had tried to be a calming influence over the years but he wouldn't always listen to her and would often escape to the bedroom and bury his head in a book.

She could trace the start of the transformation in her husband back to when the kids were born, Joe, thirteen years ago, and Rory almost two and a half years later. The change had been gradual. He had started to act more responsible, most right-minded dads would of course, but it was more than that with Terry, he had begun to care about the things that went on around him. He would start to air opinions about local and global issues, something he had never done before. He had even graduated from buying '*The Sport*' and '*The Sun*' to the more highbrow broadsheets. He had finally put away his brother's old comics: *The Victor, The Valiant*'; the implausible Captain Hurricane laying waste to whole platoons of Hun single-handed and disabling enemy tanks and armour plated vehicles like they were kids' toys, and began to read books; not just novels but history, mythology, you name it; great volumes of work strewn about the bedroom. At first she had been quite pleased with the thought of him feeding his head with all this knowledge but lately it had become a pain in the arse for her, mainly because of the lack of space. They only lived in an ex council semi. When the shelves he had built became full any available spot in any room would end up home to a pile of books. When Jan had suggested he join a library Terry had screwed his face up and said '*Sod that - don't like libraries*'.

Sometimes Terry's opinions would turn into rants, especially if you got him onto something he felt passionate about. Jan had learned to pick her topics of conversation carefully, more so when the kids were around because when Terry went off on one the air could be filled with four-letter expletives. Occasionally, he would get a little bit too far up his own arse with it all. In bed once, she had asked what the book he was reading was about. He had turned to her and with a hint of a smirk had replied '*It's esoteric.*'

'*Oh well, balls to you mate,*' she had thought at the time. '*No need to get all intellectual with me. Don't forget I know who you are and where you come from - cheeky bastard.*' She was going to remind him that it was her who was in the 'A' stream all through school while he was one up from remedial, but she couldn't be bothered, same as she couldn't be bothered to look up esoteric in the dictionary.

John 'Nobby' Clarke was a gentle giant. He stood about six foot two and had muscles in all the right places. His nature was the antithesis of Terry's. Nothing seemed to faze him, not even when he got into serious scrapes. Terry couldn't ever remember him being angry. Even the scariest situation would become a big laugh to Nobby. When they used to go to football, back in the old hooligan days, Terry would often be genuinely shitting it while Nobby was there taking on all comers with a big grin on his face. Despite his size, overwhelming odds would sometimes get the better and after a good kicking he would emerge battered, bloodied and bruised but somehow would always manage to crack a joke.

They had become inseparable from day one at school. Nobby had never been academically bright. He struggled, especially with reading and writing. Terry had always been there for him, helping and encouraging, letting him copy stuff, even writing things out for him, trying to disguise his hand. Subsequently, he'd fall behind in his own work and he often got into trouble from the teachers for it. '*Fine,*' he had thought, '*then why don't you wankers help him?*' Much later Nobby would be diagnosed dyslexic.

Terry hated the idea of anyone fighting his battles for him, but sometimes needs must and having Nobby Clarke as your best mate could get you out of, as well as into, a lot of trouble. From early playground scuffles to full-blown grown up Saturday night brawls, Nobby was usually at Terry's side. No one seemed to know how he came to be known as Nobby. His real name was John but apart from the teachers at register nobody ever called him that, he'd always been Nobby. Terry's old man had said that everybody who had Clarke as a surname was called Nobby. '*Oh...*' Terry had said, none the wiser, and thought better than to ask why Nobby's mam was called Doreen. He had liked Nobby's mam, she always had a cheery smile whenever he went round, always made him feel welcome as though he was part of the family. Even through adversity the smile never seemed to leave her face. He thought her and Nobby were very much alike.

Factory grime and chimney smoke. Faded images in monotone: shunting yards and hooters heralding knocking off time. A hunched figure cycling home from work: Nobby's dad, regular as clockwork, half-five every tea-time on the dot, passing them in the street as they played footie. A whistled tune, a greasy old knapsack slung over his shoulder with the top of his thermos sticking out the side. A shout from the boys and a friendly wave in return without taking his eyes off the road or interrupting his whistled tune, all in shades of grey. Then he didn't come by any more. '*Me dad's on t'sick*' is all Nobby said, but they never saw him on his bike whistling away ever again. He'd contracted an asbestos-related disease of the lungs from the factory where he worked. Terminal.

Nobby's dad took a long time to die. Terry would call round and Mrs. Clarke would still greet him with that warm, loving smile, but Terry could see sadness in her eyes, while upstairs, confined to his bed, Terry could hear the coughing and the rasping as Nobby's dad fought for his every breath. Eventually they brought his bed down into the front room where Nobby's mam could tend him better. Terry didn't call round so much then.

After Nobby's old man died the sense of loss and the long drawn out battle for compensation in the ensuing years took its toll on Nobby's mam's health. She never lived to sign the settlement. She died three days before Nobby's nineteenth birthday. Five years later the company paid up. Nobby, being their only child and next of kin, got the money, and he used it to buy the house from the council when he got wed to Kath. Soon after, the factory folded and was eventually demolished. Council flats now occupy the site.

Inside Razi's Mini Mart, Razi Ahmed was counting the cost of the previous night's attempted break in. Four times in two months was the count on this latest spate and, save staying awake through the night in shifts with his two sons armed with knives and baseball bats, he didn't know what else he could do. Ten years he'd spent grafting to build up his business. He'd bought the rundown old corner shop at a knock-down price, obtained a spirits licence and eventually built an extension turning it into a thriving, open-all-hours convenience store.

The pitfalls of owning a shop on the Broughton estate were no more than he'd expected, but over the last couple of years, and despite the small fortune he'd spent on security, the situation had become intolerable. He was at the end of his tether.

Terry and Nobby barely noticed the boarded up window as they entered the shop. In the back they could hear raised voices, it sounded as though Razi was rowing with his missus. Eventually he emerged from the back room looking flustered and agitated.

'Alrate Razi, what's up mate?' Nobby greeted him cheerfully.

'What's up? What's up? I'll tell you what's bloody up; them bastards have tried to do me again. Look at my bloody window!'

Terry and Nobby looked over at the broken glass and the large square of chipboard shutting out the morning light.

'I thought yer had metal grills up at night.'

'I bloody do! Look at this.' Razi disappeared into the back and re-emerged with a large metal security grill. He held it up to show the lads. A neat circular hole had been cut from the centre of the criss-cross bars. It framed Razi's distraught face and the lads couldn't help but smile at the bizarre image in front of them. 'Don't you bloody laugh, it's not funny,' Razi remonstrated and put the grill down. 'The bastards are using bolt cutters now. Bolt cutters! I ask you, where is it all going to end?'

'What you need is them metal roller shutters Raz. They won't gerrin to them,' Nobby offered helpfully.

'I wouldn't like to bet on it. These buggers will stop at nothing. No matter how many thousands of pounds I pay for security, they always come back. They try to destroy me. I show the police the tape from the CCTV and the bastards are showing their arse to the camera. I ask the policeman, what is the point? They all have masks. What are you going to do, have an identity parade of arses?'

The lads glanced at each other with this image in their heads and tried not to smirk. Nobby bought a paper and Terry a packet of Rizlas while the shopkeeper whined on about police inertia and indifference. It was hard not to be sympathetic but it was the same old stuff, they'd heard it all before. You just had to bat on as best you could.

The alternative was to take the law into your own hands, become a vigilante. The portent for mass social unrest grew stronger by the day. The prisons were full to overflowing and the C.P.S. had their orders from on high; put the buggers back on the streets wherever possible.

As they left the shop, Terry and Nobby could hear Razi resume his row with the wife, a torrent of Urdu fading into the background as the door shut behind them.

The school had only been open a few years when Terry and Nobby had first gone there. It was intended to be a proud flagship in the new fleet of Labour's comprehensive dream, the future of education. Terry could remember back to the day of the official opening. It had been a scorching hot afternoon in August and the education minister of the time was doing the officiating. There had been a crowd of around fifty or so folk among the Mayor, future head, and other dignitaries. Terry and his mates were still at the junior school then, but on the day had been buzzing around the newly paved inner areas of the school grounds on their choppers and grifters, weaving in and out the bike sheds, round the sports hall, then bombing down the main drag, pulling skids just before the ornamental fountain in front of the main entrance, and generally being a nuisance.

God it was hot. Tee-shirts stuck to sweaty skin and the pillock making the speech droning on and on. The crowd were getting restless. The area in front of the still-unveiled plaque consisted of freshly-laid tarmac that was beginning to melt in the heat. Women's stilettos were starting to sink into the black goo and the carpet at the town hall reception would take a right pasting.

'*Get on with it!*' some bloke at the back of the crowd had piped up, much to the amusement of the lads who took it as their cue to launch the verbals.

'*Gerron wi' it, yer silly old bastard!*' Nobby had shouted. The rest of them had fallen about laughing. They had ridden off into the distance hurling the most childishly crude insults back at the gathering. As a parting shot one of the boys had launched his empty pop bottle high into the air. As it hit the ground the resulting explosion had prompted three other empty bottles to go the same way. Back in the crowd most heads were turned toward the disturbance as the minister struggled to hold their attention to his rambling monologue.

'*This post is going to be a challenge,*' Walter Dodds, the new head, thought to himself as he stared at the distant pool of broken glass shimmering and winking in the midday sun.

Terry wondered if Nobby could remember back to that hot August day all those years ago, but his mate's head was buried in the sports section of his newspaper, so he decided to keep quiet. Strolling through the school grounds he thought the place looked tatty and rundown and smaller than he remembered, but that was always the case when you went back to somewhere you knew in your childhood.

The ornamental fountain was now a flowerbed, home to a few battered old shrubs, crisp packets and pop bottles. The fountain itself had ceased to work before he and Nobby had gone there, and the resulting dirty, stagnant water would become the alter of initiation for hundreds of new boys, for a few years at least, until one poor little sod nearly drowned by having his head held under for a bit too long.

As they approached the entrance Terry got that butterfly feeling in his stomach again. Nobby folded his paper under his arm and pulled open the door. As they entered, Terry glanced over to the wall where the plaque commemorating the opening had been unveiled. Only the wooden base remained, the brass inscribed plate having been nicked long ago and weighed in for scrap.

A large, peardrop goblet of spittle dangled precariously from the youth's mouth before dropping onto his outstretched fingers. With a deft flick of the wrist he sent the slimy projectile hurtling towards its target. Bullseye! Straight between the teacher's shoulder blades. The saliva blob began to make its way down the back of the jacket, slowly catching up to the other three or four direct hits. The youth turned to his mate and they mimed a high-five celebration before doglegging it up the nearest staircase, while the teacher, still oblivious to his malaise, continued down the corridor. Observing the scene, Nobby shook his head and laughed to himself. Terry curled his lip before ringing the bell at reception.

'Hello love, we've got an appointment with Mr... Mr...' Terry couldn't remember the head teacher's name.

'Mr. Swallow?' the secretary helped.

'Aye, that's it, Mr. Swallow. I knew it had summat to do with birds.' He nodded and smiled.

The secretary's face didn't slip an inch. 'And you are?'

'Mr. Gallagher and Mr. Clarke, love.'

The secretary bristled. She wasn't from round here and she hated that condescending term, '*love*' that all northerners used. She wasn't his '*love*' and never would be. It was the same when she had worked in Nottingham, it was all '*duck*' this and '*duck*' that. '*Yes me duck, no me duck, three bags full me duck.*' She stared hard at the two peasants in front of her.

'Er - appointment with Mr. Swallow, ten o'clock,' Terry repeated.

She glanced over her shoulder to the clock on the office wall, slowly looked back at the pair of them and raised her eyebrows. The clock showed fourteen minutes past ten.

'Aye, sorry we're a bit late, love; got delayed.' Terry gave Nobby a look as if to say, '*Hey up, we've got a right one here.*' He smiled back at her with the most falsely apologetic look he could muster.

They sat and they waited. Nobby buried his face back in his newspaper while Terry ground his teeth, slowly winding himself up, reliving the events that led to them being here this morning.

The images of headless rodents and the bloodied spade that had been used to decapitate them made Jan Gallagher recoil in horror. DC Dave Knowles spread the photographs slowly and deliberately across the Gallagher's kitchen table with a sanctimonious-cum-grave expression on his face that a lot of uniformed policemen seem to have. The damage would run into thousands. Broken windows, smashed cold frames, gas taps turned on full in the chemistry lab, a small miracle the whole school hadn't gone up. And the rural studies department littered with the severed heads and bodies of rabbits, guinea pigs and gerbils.

Joe sat with his head on his chest, answering the policeman's questions in little more than monosyllables: No, he had nothing to do with this he sullenly confirmed having been forced to lift his eyes and look at the distasteful pictures being thrust at him. Human excrement had been daubed around the walls of classrooms and Joe knew this to be the hallmark of East Broughton natives but he was keeping shtum: yes, he'd been on school premises at the time; no, he hadn't seen who'd done it. In the background Terry had been silently seething. He knew his lad wasn't a saint, but he knew he wasn't a sadist either and there was no way he could have been responsible for something like this.

Joe and his mates had been playing footie on the school field at the time of the incident; trespass, technically, but that wasn't the issue here. The rest of them had fled in all directions as soon as they had heard the police siren, a natural reaction for the sons of West Broughton even if you'd done nothing wrong, but Joe and his best mate, Young Nobby had stayed put. They were playing keepie-up headers and had already managed a hundred and twenty-seven when the two out-of-breath officers finally got to them, annoying really 'cos it looked like being a record breaker.

The frustrated Detective Constable closed his notebook and got up to leave. Fingerprints would need to be taken down at the station along with more statements.

'*By the way...*' Terry had shouted at the back of the policeman as he returned to the panda car. '*...Any nearer catching the bastards that did old man Johnson?*' DC Knowles turned and slowly shook his head before getting into the vehicle. '*No - thought no*t,' Terry muttered under his breath.

'This cunt's tekin' the piss,' Nobby hissed from the corner of his mouth after finishing the newspaper and stretching out a yawn. 'We've been here ages. He's getting his own back for us being late.'

'I'm getting deja-vu sitting here,' Terry hissed back. 'It's like waiting to get t'stick off Doddsy.'

They both chuckled at the thought and started regaling each other with remembered misdemeanours that had ended with a visit to Mr. Dodds and a taste of the old willow stick he called '*Savage Henry*'. One stinger across each palm for general misbehaviour, two for more heinous crimes. The pair of gobbers they had met on the way in would certainly have been up for a double taste of '*Savage*', even expulsion in their day. Corporal punishment had been banned in their last year at school and '*Savage Henry*' had been retired. Terry could argue a strong case for bringing it back. It had never done him and Nobby any lasting harm. At least it taught them where to draw the line, a benchmark as to how far you could go. Now the kids were untouchable and they knew it. The teachers had lost control and the good ones among them, the ones who had the kids' interests at heart, had their hands tied with PC and beuracracy, so they left in droves to become plumbers and call-centre operatives and what remained was a naive liberal elite who arrived with their heads full of doctrine and spin but after six months of harsh reality ended up on long term sick through stress and intimidation.

There had been eight heads at the school since the inimitable Mr. Dodds; some had lasted longer than others, but taken as a mean we were talking of an average residency of no more than three years.

Gerald Swallow had been in the job a little over eighteen months. It was his first Headmaster post and his rise had been quite meteoric, not because of any particular teaching or leadership skills. Quite simply he had been the best out of a bad bunch that had bothered to apply for the job. Even he had been surprised when he was offered it.

Mr. Swallow looked edgy and nervous as he took his seat behind his desk, eyes flitting from side to side as if looking for something important that he had mislaid, eventually settling on a fountain pen which he awkwardly fiddled with while deciding on his opening gambit. He hated this bit, not knowing how to start off proceedings. He wanted to appear assertive but quite often that tack had earned him an immediate punch on the nose from an irate parent. At the same time he didn't want to look weak and indecisive, something he realized he was doing right now. He offered a pale smile by way of greeting to the two men sitting opposite him. Terry and Nobby stared back at him, expressionless. He began to think he should have seen this pair separately. Terry had already picked up on Swallow's sense of unease and could well imagine what the poor guy had had to put up with in his year and a half reign at this place. He looked as if he should be running a small bookshop in some quiet backwater somewhere, not trying to control thousands of mainly dysfunctional kids in one of the biggest comprehensives in one of the most lawless and deprived housing estates in the north.

Terry glanced up at the framed photo on the wall behind the head. A fresh faced young Gerald Swallow smiled back at him bedecked in cap and gown and clutching a scrolled B.A. Hons. His graduation day hadn't been all that long ago, it only seemed it. He was still only forty-seven but he looked and felt ten years older. Terry looked from the photo to the man. He wouldn't be long in this job, he thought - maybe another twelve months or so, tops.

Terry ducked his face inside his knackered jacket to shield his roll-up from the wind as he lit it. He hadn't spoken a word since they had left Swallow's office. His mind was buzzing and Nobby knew better than to start a conversation when he was like this. Best to let him stew on whatever was going on in his head.

The upshot of the meeting had been that Joe and Young Nobby were to be suspended for two weeks pending further police enquiries. Terry, predictably, had gone up the wall, ranting on about so-called British justice, being innocent before being proved guilty and all that. Swallow had reasoned that the decision to suspend had been made by the board of governors based on the trespass issue. He had conceded that the pair weren't what he called bad lads, and that their disciplinary record, although not exemplary, was above average, nevertheless in the circumstances the governors felt…blah, blah, blah… Terry accused him of doing a Pontius Pilate. Nobby had looked across at his mate and thought '*What the hell is he going on about?*' Basically, Nobby didn't give a shit. The way he saw it suspending the lads meant that they got a bit of cheap labour for the fortnight. He assumed that they would come into the business when they left school anyway so what was the problem? He knew Terry would have to have his say so he kept quiet and let him get on with it, in fact Nobby had found it hard to keep awake at all during the proceedings, Swallow's droning voice sending him into that daydream, twilight zone state where voices become distant and start to echo, only his mate's occasional sharp retorts snapping him back to reality.

Terry didn't like the way Swallow had continued to make veiled insinuations about the boys' guilt, so he went on the offensive. One topic that got Terry really passionate was sport, in particular the lack of it. He had argued that half the problems Mr. Swallow and his colleagues were facing now were caused by the dismantling and discouragement of competitive sport in schools.

'Why don't you have school football teams anymore?'

'Because games with other schools ended in mass brawls'

'Why?'

'I'm sorry…?'

'I'll tell you why, because you've lost the will and the power to discipline. Also your teachers are so bogged down with unnecessary paperwork they've no time or inclination for extra curricular activity.'

'Well…'

'Okay, forget other schools, what about inter-house sport? What's happened to all the football, rugby and cricket pitches that used to be here?'

'I do believe the goal posts got burned down'

'Try metal posts'

'We did, they were stolen I'm afraid'

Terry was undeterred. 'The kids are bored. They've nowt to do and nowhere to go. You have a duty to provide amenities for 'em. Is there any wonder you have these problems. You lot and your daft policies bring it on yourselves. All our lads were doing was playing a game of footie on the only decent piece o' grass there is around here and you go and suspend 'em for it. What d'yer think they're gonna gerrup to while they're off school? Me and the wife can't afford time off work…' Swallow was finding it hard to get a word in. '…And don't give me all this - *The governors have decided* - bollocks. Why aren't they here now? Why have they left you to do their dirty work? Just how much clout do you have in your own school?'

'Mr. Gallagher, I do assure you that a great deal of time and consideration has been given to this matter. We don't take these decisions lightly, but when certain policies are put in place we have to be seen to uphold them. The democratic process is….' It was blah, blah time again. Politik speak. Swallow had the politicians' knack of talking for ages without saying anything. Terry had heard enough. Joe and Young Nobby had been stitched up good and proper by the faceless ones. An example had to be made and the boys were the scapegoats.

Nobby had woken up with a start as Terry nudged him out of his slumbers.

'C'mon, we're off.' Terry marched out of the office. Nobby stumbled after him still half asleep, then, remembering where he was, turned back into the room to offer the headmaster a dozy smile and a wave goodbye.

Terry took a long pull on his roll-up as they walked past the end of the science block. At last he broke his silence.

'Look at that…' He gestured over to the vast expanse of green that used to be the school playing fields; acres of grass that they had both played on as kids and maintained on their tractors when they worked for the schools and parks department. Nobby followed his gaze but wasn't sure what he was supposed to be looking at. '…Warra fuckin' waste.'

'Yeah...' Nobby agreed, still not entirely certain what his buddy was talking about.

2

''Sup wi' me dad, Nobby?'

'I dunno know, Joe. He's been a miserable old get all week.' Nobby plucked a pickled egg from his lunchbox and popped the thing into his mouth in one go. Chewing on it slowly, he looked over to his grumpy mate who had taken himself off to eat his lunch alone in the pickup. Nobby looked back at Joe who couldn't understand why his dad had been acting like an arsehole all week. He'd said he believed their story, didn't think for one minute it was them who had done all that stuff at the school, so why was he giving them a hard time? 'Listen, don't worry about it, fella,' Nobby consoled, 'It's not you he's mad at really. You know what he's like. Tell yer what, I'll have a word with the silly old sod tonight over a few pints.' Nobby gave Joe a wink and patted him on the shoulder. 'It'll be alrate. Here, do you want one o' these?' Nobby pulled another pickled egg from his lunch box and offered it to Joe.

'Nah, they make yer shit stink, them.' Joe backed off and screwed his face up.

'Your shit stinks anyway, I had to fumigate that pick-up last night after you'd been in it.'

''Ere, that weren't me, that were your Noberto, old Johnny fart pants. He was at it all day yesterday.' Joe pointed an accusing finger at Young Nobby who was sitting on a piece of rockery a few feet away. Young Nobby smiled back, his face full of flaky pastry and custard from the vanilla slice he was devouring, quite happy to be guilty as accused.

Mrs. Gladstone appeared from the house with a tray of four steaming mugs of tea. She placed it on the patio table and shouted 'tea up' to the boys. Young Nobby wiped his mouth with his sleeve and went up to retrieve the brews. This was the life. Despite Terry's moods, the lads had loved every minute of their two weeks in exile.

Most of the jobs had been off the estate, out of the city, and into the country to the posh developments where the real money was. The weather had improved at last, the winds had gone and it had got warmer during the course of the week.

Young Nobby collected the tray of tea then paused to survey the scene. From this elevated position he could see down the impressive rockery, boulders and rocks of all shapes and sizes, the spaces filled with heathers and alpines, subtle hues of mauves and lilac, leading onto the gently sloping lawn, freshly cut and striped, rolling away down to a copse of silver birch trees and a stream which marked the boundary, then beyond; fields and hills right to the horizon, a million miles away from the West Broughton estate.

Mrs. Gladstone re-appeared.

'Would you like some of these, young man?' She brandished a tin full of chocolate biscuits and waved them tantalizingly under his nose.

'Ta,' said Young Nobby grabbing a handful.

'Not at school this week?' enquired the old lady.

'Nah, work experience,' he replied, parroting the line his dad and Terry had told them to say if asked.

'Oh, work experience. I see...' she said, thinking that they looked a bit young for that. '...Well, I have to say you're doing a lovely job and I'll leave these biscuits over here in the shade if you want some more.'

'Ta,' Young Nobby said as she went back in the house. *'What a nice old dear,'* he thought to himself.

The smell of freshly cut grass wafted up from below and a big fat bumblebee buzzed past. He looked down at the tray: Kit-Kats, Penguins and Clubs. Marvellous. Life didn't get any sweeter than this.

'Hurry up with that tea, it's gonna go bloody cold!' his dad shouted up from below.

Emily Gladstone actually *was* a nice old dear. She had been a widow for almost ten years now. Her husband had been big in wool; a business that had been family run almost from the start of the industrial revolution and had helped to shape the prosperity of the city at the turn of the twentieth century. She was old money and down to earth with it, not like your nouveau riche; Thatcher's children living in their half a million pound shoe boxes thinking that they're better than everyone else. She was one of Terry and Nobby's oldest customers and she had looked after them; regular maintenance as well as some big profitable projects including ornamental ponds, patios and decking, and the pièce de resistance, the rockery. It had been their biggest single project to date and had taken months to complete. When it was finished Mrs. Gladstone had been ecstatic and the lads had been rightly proud. It had been Mrs. Gladstone's niece who had first put her on to them. They had been cutting the grass verges on her estate one day and she had come out and asked them if they would cut her lawn for a few quid. They still worked for the council back then, but they often got folk approaching them asking if they were willing to do the odd guvvy job. This of course they were more than happy to do, anything to earn a few extra quid. Most of the council lads did it anyway; you just had to be careful not to get caught. By the time they did get caught they had a thriving little moonlighting enterprise on the go, working evenings in the summer and most weekends. Terry knew the scam wouldn't last forever, and he cleverly persuaded Nobby that they should plough the money they made into buying their own mowers and machinery so that when the shit did hit the fan they would at least have a ready made business to fall back on.

The day the shit did hit the fan was to be a sweet moment of revenge for Eric Smales, a.k.a. 'Trotsky.' He was the Clerk Of Works down at the Council depot, a little weasel of a man and a despot to boot. Although the nickname suited him down to a tee, he had actually acquired it from the peculiar way he moved around the yard, haranguing drivers who were late out on their rounds, homing in on someone, usually Terry or Nobby, he would break into this strange little trot, a sight hilarious to behold, especially in winter if there'd been a sudden heavy snowfall and all the gritters were late out. Trotsky had been the butt of some wildly funny practical jokes over the years, nearly all at the instigation of the pair of jokers he had come to hate. He knew that the two of them were always behind these pranks; he had just never been able to prove it.

Horace the road sweeper had learning difficulties and was what some would term mentally challenged. He wasn't a complete dimwit but Trotsky used to treat him like one. He'd swept the City's roads for almost thirty years. It was all he knew. For most of that time Trotsky had made his life hell, bawling him out whenever their paths crossed, threatening to take his cart away and send him down the road. Some of the lads had even witnessed Trotsky physically abusing him. Nobby never got angry at anyone, but he had a special hatred for Trotsky and he secretly promised himself to personally make sure that he got his comeuppance one day.

Horace had a morbid fear of toilets; some sort of irrational terror that probably stemmed back to his childhood. As a result he would do his business wherever the fancy took him. When asked why he never shat in a toilet like normal people he would just clam up and go rigid with fear. Trotsky, in typically sadistic fashion, would sometimes try and make him clean out the bogs at the depot, trying to corner him into a cubicle, threatening him with the sack if he didn't get to work with the bleach and bog-brush. He took great pleasure watching Horace in a blind panic go off his head as he tried to escape his torment. Often, these scenarios would result in Horace having to be sectioned for weeks at a time, having his body pumped full of pills and chemicals until his head got over the trauma.

Terry and Nobby would use Horace's strange habit to get back at Trotsky.

'D'yer wanna get yer own back on the bastard, Horace?'

'Yeah, - yeah,' Horace had nodded enthusiastically.

'Right, here's what you're gonna do…

The wail of disgust could be heard all around the depot. Trotsky had just stepped into his council issue Wellingtons into which not ten minutes before Horace had deposited a steaming great turd. After this, Trotsky had become obsessive, almost paranoid, checking clothing, gloves, footwear, drawers, everything he could think of ritualistically on a daily basis. He viewed everyone with suspicion, and Terry thought he was developing a nervous twitch.

Trotsky never ate in the canteen, not that he would be welcome anyway. He had a little Belling cooker in his portakabin office, and his ritual meant that every Friday at twelve-thirty he would fry sausages for his lunch. One particular Friday while tending his sausages he had been called away as a matter of urgency. He had trotted out of his office cursing and swearing at having his lunchtime interrupted. This of course had been merely a diversion for the mother of all pranks. Horace might have been a sausage short, but Trotsky certainly wasn't that day!

The frying stink that greeted him on his return almost knocked him off his feet. He knew almost straight away what the bastards had done, but his curiosity prompted him to clutch his hankie over his face and go and count the sausages in the pan. Sure enough, there they were, four bangers sizzling away where there had previously been only three. He turned and retched violently into his waste-paper basket before staggering out into the yard, trying to compose himself before heading towards the canteen, his stagger turning into that determined, stupid little trot. The door of the canteen had flung open and simultaneously a dozen heads buried their smirks into their sandwiches. Everybody had been in on it and the restraint they had all needed not to fall about the place in hysterics had been excruciating. Only Horace had sat at the back of the canteen, his face beaming in open glee, oblivious to the consequences. Along with the twitch, Trotsky had all of a sudden developed a stammer. He struggled to get any words out and his head looked as if it was about to explode. He clocked Horace wearing his triumphant grin at the back of the room, and letting out a strange, strangulated scream hurtled towards him. Nobby had jumped up from his seat blocking the gangway, stopping the demented Trotsky in his tracks. As he fumed and spluttered, Terry had calmly stood up beside him and warned him off.

'Now that's not a good idea, is it Eric?' Terry reasoned, 'assaulting an employee in front of all these witnesses?'

Trotsky spluttered a bit more before venting his rage on the two men barring his way. 'I know you two bastards are behind this,' he spat. 'I'll have you. You mark my words, I'll have you.' His eyes bulged and narrowed alternately as he screamed at the pair of them. 'You won't fucking get away with it, I'll make sure of that. Your days are numbered, you fucking, filthy, disgusting pair of bastards.' Trotsky had retreated uttering oaths and threats as he went, the sudden release of laughter from the canteen ringing in his ears as he trotted back across the yard to disinfect his office.

Every dog has its day, Eric Smales thought to himself as he leaned back in his chair at his desk, his hands clasped behind his head in a most smug, self-satisfied way. The eight-page report sat neatly in front of him, enough to hang, draw and quarter that pair of cunts good and proper. He couldn't wait to see the looks on their faces as he told them to collect their P45s.

Terry scanned the note pinned to his clocking in card. 'Fuck! — What's that little twat want?'

'What's up?' Nobby asked as he punched his card.

'We've been summoned by the almighty.' Terry screwed the piece of paper into a ball and threw it over his shoulder. 'Trotsky wants to see us in his office.'

The door to Eric's inner sanctum swung open unceremoniously. Terry and Nobby sauntered up to his desk. 'What?' was all Terry said without trying to hide the irritation in his voice.

'Haven't you pair ever thought of knocking before you enter an office?'

'Cut the crap and get on with it, Eric. What d'yer want? We've got work to do.'

'Well, that's just where you're wrong, you see. I think you had better pull up a chair each, I've got something to show you.' The lads took a quick glance at each other.

'We'll stand if it's all the same to you.' Terry tried to remain defiant while wondering what it was Trotsky had up his sleeve.

'Recognize this?' He slowly turned a page of the report and with great deliberation aimed at maximum effect placed it in front of them. He cocked his head to one side and raised his eyebrows waiting for the reaction. He was absolutely loving this moment and would milk it for all it was worth. The lads peered down at the page in unison. In the top corner was a Polaroid of their council pick-up parked up a drive. Terry turned the page, another Polaroid taken from a distance. Through trees and bushes they could just make out an image of Nobby mowing a lawn. And so it went on; eight pages of Polaroid snaps and text containing details of streets and avenues; days, dates, times and even statements from residents. There was no getting away from it. It was all there in black and white, and even colour. *Touché*, Terry thought to himself and for a fleeting moment felt a touch of admiration towards Trotsky and his detective work.

'Well, we have been a busy little boy haven't we, Eric? You're in the wrong game mate; you should be working for MI5.'

'You can make all the smart-arse comments you want. Fact remains you two are up shit creek without a paddle.'

'So? Sack us. What do you expect us to do, get down on us hands and knees and beg for us jobs?

'Oh, no. - No, you don't get off that lightly. What you've been up to constitutes fraud, deception and possibly one or two other misdemeanours: moonlighting, misuse of council property. There's plenty in here for the police to have a birthday with. We could end up suing you for thousands. With a bit of luck we might even get custodial sentences.' Trotsky was starting to get excited and his facial twitch had begun to put in an appearance. Nobby, as usual was keeping quiet, letting Terry take the lead but he didn't know how his mate would get them out of this one. Inside he was raging and he didn't know how long he could restrain himself from knocking Trotsky's smug little head off his shoulders. The ball was in their court. Nobby looked to his mate waiting for the riposte while clenching and unclenching his fist. Terry was already thinking on his feet. He'd heard rumours but he didn't know how true they were, just the odd innuendo from some of the lads. Maybe he was clutching at straws but it was worth a go, after all, they had nothing to lose now. Terry went for the bluff.

'Well now, Eric, if we're talking fraud and deception here I'm sure the boys in blue would be interested to hear how certain council contracts were placed with certain companies over the last few years.'

Eric's expression changed from smug to shock in an instant, but the twitch remained.

'What the hell are you talking about?'

Bingo! Terry had hit a nerve, but he was fishing in the dark. He went on the attack regardless.

'Come on, Eric; don't treat me like a complete idiot. Where is it you live? Easby Park? Not much up that way under three hundred grand is there? And what are you driving these days? Brand new Lexus, in't it? Big car that for a little guy like you.'

'What's your point?'

'Point is, Eric, big house, big car, oh, and I nearly forgot the holiday villa. Costa del Sol, is it? - Clerk of works? - Don't get me wrong, it's not a bad job but it doesn't really add up, does it now?'

'You just keep your fucking nose out of my business. My affairs have got fuck all to do with you.'

'I aren't the slightest bit interested in your affairs, Eric, but I know of one or two people who might be. Like a certain builder friend of mine who wants to know why the Blakeys Mill project never went out to tender like it should have.'

'You're barking up the wrong tree, I've got nothing to do with building conversion tenders.'

'I know that, but you're an important part of the team all the same. I've heard all about those cosy little rendezvous in Parkers restaurant; you and your mates from the planning department and a certain director from I.D.L. Construction.'

Trotsky's eyes widened and he swallowed hard. Just how much did this pillock have on him? Terry couldn't believe his luck, all this stuff had been just hearsay but with an element of truth if Trotsky's reactions were anything to go by. If Terry kept the accusations ambiguous he might just be able to pull off the bluff. He batted on.

'Funny how you see all them I.D.L. construction vans all over the city these days, isn't it? Must be some nice juicy, fat contracts floating about for those who are willing to grease a few palms.'

'Now l-look here... ' Trotsky stammered, his cockiness beginning to evaporate. '...You'd better watch what you're saying. You - you can't go around making wild accusations like that, you might end up in more trouble than you already are.' He slackened his tie and flicked open the top button on his shirt, letting loose a couple of twitches as he did so. Damp patches were beginning to appear in the armpit region. Terry leant over the desk and leered into Trotsky's face.

'Finding it a bit warm are you, Eric? Shall we open a window for you?'

Trotsky was unsure how to react. Harry Bairstowe from planning had already been moved to another department because somebody had been writing letters and asking too many questions. He daren't try and broker a deal with this cocky sod because that would leave him open to all sorts of blackmail, plus that would be an admission of guilt and he wasn't entirely sure just how much he knew. He became aware that he was squirming in his seat. Here was a little runt of a guy who loved the power he yielded because it made him feel big. Now he felt that power slipping away, while Terry's sneering mush hovered menacingly above him making him feel smaller than he already was. Instinctively he went for the cornered rat routine; he jumped to his feet sending his chair crashing into a filing cabinet behind him. 'Don't you fucking dare come in here and try and call the shots with me,' Trotsky screamed. 'I know people who'll crucify the likes of you.' Terry backed away from Trotsky's flailing arms and observed his rant with mild amusement on his face. 'You've got nothing on me you fucking no-mark, so back off or I'll make sure you're sorry you ever crossed me.'

Terry tut-tutted and shook his head pityingly. 'Really, Eric, all this heavy gangster talk; it just isn't you, is it?'

The veins on Trotsky's temple pulsed, the now familiar narrowing of the eyes and the twitch were both present.

'Get out,' he hissed before building into a crescendo. 'Get out of my fucking office now and take that big, stupid cunt of a mate with you!'

Nobby's features snapped alive. In an instant he reached over, grabbed Trotsky by his tie and lifted him clean off the ground, knuckles pressing hard into his windpipe.

'Who d'yer think you're calling a stupid cunt, yer little shit?'

'Kyychh—yerchh!!' Is all Trotsky could say as his feet flapped about wildly in mid-air, his face turning purple. Nobby calmly looked over to Terry who slowly gave him the nod. The big lad drew his head back slightly and flexed his neck muscles. In a flash Trotsky's nose was spread across his face. Nobby let go and Trotsky fell to the floor in a crumpled heap. The eight-page report on the desk was spattered with crimson. Terry peered over the desk to where the prone Trotsky lay gurgling and groaning, curling his lip with distaste at the sight, before motioning to Nobby that they should obey the man's request to leave his office.

'Bastard's bled on me,' said Nobby wiping his jacket with his sleeve as they departed.

The ringing inside Eric Smales's ears changed a couple of octaves as his bruised throat tried to cope with the mix of air and blood being gasped into his lungs. Nothing inside his head seemed to be working. He was unable to compose a rational thought, or make sense of the distant voice deep inside his brain, which seemed to be repeating over and over. - '*No more practical jokes - no more practical jokes...*'

They were on two totally different trains of thought as they walked back across the yard. Nobby was buoyant. He had just realised the ambition of his working life, and he felt like turning round and doing it all over again. He'd waited all these years to give Trotsky what he deserved, and now he had finally got to twat him one, the feeling of satisfaction had been great, it just hadn't lasted long enough, so he thought of Horace and the lads, and the big laugh they would all have when the word got out what had happened. More than anything, he had done it for Horace; a small piece of retribution for all the years of misery the poor guy had suffered under that bastard. He felt vindicated, a self-satisfied smile spread across his face.

Terry's thoughts were all over the place. What would he tell Jan? Would Trotsky dare go to the police? Had the bluff been enough to keep him quiet? They were out of a job, shit! Could they find enough work to keep them both going? All this stuff faded away to the back of his mind as his mood turned to anger. Trotsky was as guilty as fuck. That much had been obvious. Christ knows what scams and fiddles he was into, but Terry didn't really care, what really pissed him off was the hypocrisy. The cheeky cunt sat there all high and fucking mighty with his report and his Polaroids. Sure, they'd been at it, he'd held his hands up to that, but it seemed like Mr. Smales and his councillor buddies had their snouts in the trough big style. And that's how it was across the spectrum. The world ran on corruption and dodgy dealing, and the higher up you were, the more likely you'd be to get away with it, right to the top, from multinationals to governments but as soon as the guy on the bottom rung tries for a small piece of the action, it's a case of no-way-Jose, get back into the mire with the rest of the scum where you belong.

They were on their own now. Him and Nobby against the world, at least that's how Terry felt at that moment in time, a little bitterness creeping into his thinking. '*Fuck 'em all,*' he said to himself. From here on in they would answer to nobody but themselves. No more jumped up bosses harassing and ordering them around. The anger slowly gave way to determination and resolve. Whatever happened now, they had a business to get up and running. He was sure they could make a go of it. He had to be, the alternative was the scrap heap.

'I won't be a minute,' Nobby said, clearing out the last of his belongings from his locker and slamming the metal door shut. 'I'll see yer back at the car.'

He left his mate swapping his council issue rigger boots for his trainers, wondering where he was off to. An eerie silence descended on the room as Terry took a last look around. Twenty-three years of memories. There was no emotion.

Walking back to the car he got that all-too-familiar butterfly feeling in his gut. 'What's in the bag?' he asked as Nobby climbed into the passenger seat.

'Oh, Trotsky forgot to give us our leaving present for long service, so I went back for it.' Nobby opened the bag to reveal a nearly new, council owned petrol strimmer; the only vital piece of equipment the lads had been really short of. He beamed a smile.

'You bad lad,' Terry smiled back, shaking his head and starting the car.

The trouble with landscape gardening is it's a luxury. First thing to go when times are hard is the guy who cuts your grass and maintains your garden, plus the fact it's a seasonal thing, and almost inevitably they had struggled through the first winter after they had gone on their own. They'd been forced to sign on when the work had dried up and Terry had hated that - oh, how he fucking hated that. He'd never been out of work since he'd left school, and having to go join the queues with the great unwashed down at the pan-crack hurt his pride.

Despite the two hour wait and the form filling, despite having to sit amongst the smack-heads and the single mums with their screaming brats who were having cheap sweets forced down their throats in a vain effort to keep them quiet, building up the E numbers and making them worse, despite the acrid cig smoke haze and the general air of desolation and despair, despite all this Terry had been determined not to lose his cool. He would remain calm whatever came his way - wrong.

The girl had visibly winced as Terry's fist came crashing down on the other side of the counter. She should be used to this sort of thing but was still grateful for the re-enforced glass screen that separated them.

'How the fuck d'yer expect me to run me business if I have to sell me vehicle an' equipment?' Terry had raged at the screen.

The girl let out an exasperated sigh. 'I've told you, Mr. Gallagher, you've listed these items on the form as assets of your business therefore you would have to sell those assets before you would become entitled to any benefit. And if you don't stop shouting and swearing I shall be forced to call security.'

Terry had started as if to rant at her again then turned away in utter frustration only to see Nobby sitting among the scumbags with an inane grin on his face. They were enjoying the entertainment.

This was the very thing guaranteed to give Terry a thrombosis, bureaucracy at its best. He would love to meet the wankers who made up these rules. Little boxes on forms that need a tick or a cross but the question can't be answered with a tick or a cross – so tough luck mate, you're screwed. The job centre want to know what you're doing to find work and you say I'm building up my own business but it's winter and there's not much work about, so they send you up the social and you tell them the same thing and they say sorry, you're classed as employed and the only way you can get benefit is to sell your assets and declare yourself unemployed. Catch 22, so much for enterprise, so much for paying your stamp all these years. He wanted to work. He'd filled in all the forms as best he could, played it by the book, told the truth and look where it had got him.

Terry had helped Nobby fill in his forms. This time there were no assets, no equipment, no nothing; just tick the boxes. Make it up as you go along. 'Sod 'em,' he had thought, 'If that's what you get for being honest, they could go bollocks, it's the black economy for us in future.'

Terry threw his pen down, stretched out his arms and cracked his fingers. He hated doing estimates, but he preferred to do them on his lunch break rather than eating into his evening at home. He popped the last bit of Kit-Kat into his mouth and swilled it down with the dregs of his now cold tea.

Nobby was playing footie with the lads on Mrs. Gladstone's freshly cut lawn. He watched them through the open window of the pick-up. Nobby had been a good player in his day, an uncompromising centre-half who took no prisoners. But he was a big lad and nowadays he turned like a battleship. Terry laughed to himself as Joe and Young Nobby ran rings round him, taking the piss, through his legs, nutmegging, and occasionally leaving him on his arse. The lads were good. They looked really sharp and had some nice touches. Terry loved to see good football, and watching the lads play began to lift his spirits and snap him out of his mood. Since the boys had been suspended Terry had been morose and he knew it, he just found it hard to be a pleasant guy when he was stewing on something. Joe had probably borne the brunt of his capricious mood swings and for that he felt a touch of shame, but for the B.M.W. driver who happened to cross him that morning on the way out to Mrs. Gladstone's he felt nothing but contempt.

They had been sitting on the Bergenstrasse; a snarled up stretch of dual carriageway that led on to the ring road; stupidly named after a piece of tarmac in southern Bavaria that some idiot on the council with nothing better to do had pointlessly twinned with its German counterpart, no doubt costing your unsuspecting council tax payer thousands in the process. They were going nowhere fast, about two hundred yards in twenty minutes. Joe was playing snakes on his mobile. Young Nobby was snoozing, while his dad had his nose in the newspaper as usual. The road was notorious because the two lanes became one near its end and despite the long tailback, cars would fly down the outside lane then force themselves into the front of the queue when the road ran out; subsequently those in the near lane, pretending to be patient, weren't moving much at all. After suffering about half an hour of this, Terry, who wasn't in such a good mood anyway, had decided he'd had enough.

The A.B.S. on the B.M.W. three series had to prove its worth as Terry slewed the pick-up into its path across the outside lane. A screech of brakes, a blast of horn, and the smell of burning rubber rent the air, and the surprised, simultaneous, exclamations from Nobby and the lads all contained the word *fuck*! The guy in the B.M.W. kept his hand pressed to the horn while Terry reached for the long-handled sledgehammer under his seat and was out of the pick-up in a breath. B.M.W. man's anger soon turned to fear. His hand relaxed and the horn fell silent. His arsehole began to twitch and he instinctively reached for the door lock as the hammer-wielding maniac approached. Terry didn't rant and rave at the poor bloke, he didn't need to, the manic look in his eyes was enough. He rested one booted foot on the car's front bumper and swung the hammer to a poised position above his head.

'Toot your fucking horn now, you cunt!'

Terry hated flash, executive types who swanned around in their company cars, taking the arrogance and power of the boardroom onto the roads, thinking they had a right to be in front of everybody else; bullyboys in Armani suits clinching million pound deals on the mobile while carving up some poor sod on a roundabout. B.M.W. drivers were the worst; stupid gits with personalised number plates like **5TUD.1** that basically equated to **TO55ER.** So far up their own backsides, they had to be up yours as well.

The bloke didn't respond; his face had gone almost as white as his shirt, his eyes transfixed to the fourteen pounds of iron ready to come crashing down on his gleaming bonnet. With his free hand, Terry pointed to the line of stationary cars and their open-mouthed occupants. 'This is a queue,' he gestured. 'These people aren't sat here for the good of their health. You get in this queue now if you value yours - savvy?'

Terry didn't wait for a response. He let the shaft slip down through his fist then lowered the hammer to his side before slowly turning back to the pick-up. He gave B.M.W. man one last look of contempt, slung the hammer back under the seat and climbed into the cab.

'I fucking hate B.M.W. drivers,' was all Terry said. The lads looked at each other in awestruck silence. Nobby just shook his head with a knowing smile and carried on reading his paper.

Terry made a mental note to remember to tell Joe not to say anything to his Mam about that morning's incident, not that he regretted it or anything, he just didn't want Jan giving him a lecture for flying off the handle in front of his son and Young Nobby, setting a bad example and all that. Anyway, he would make it up to the lads big-style soon. Watching them kick that ball around at lunchtime had sown the seeds in his head. A near fortnight of anger and frustration began to give way to a feeling of alacrity as his thoughts began to take shape. There was no point in going around with all that acrimony inside you, the bitterness eating you up, making you not a very nice person to be around. That had always been one of Terry's faults. He couldn't help it. It's just the way he was. He despised injustice and it seemed to him that injustice was everywhere. No, the way to do it was to turn all that malevolence into something positive, focus the resentment and prove the bastards wrong. Acting like a twat made you no better than them. It was a hard lesson that Terry inwardly promised himself he would have to learn.

When they had started grafting again that afternoon, Terry had suddenly become all chirpy and chatty, and it was nearly all football talk; what was happening in the transfer market, was so-and-so worth twenty million? Who would stay up next season; who'd be for the drop? Then he got all reminiscent about him and Nobby in their playing days, immodestly spouting on about how good he used to be, and how a cartilage op' had prevented him from turning pro. Of course, the boys had been sceptical about these claims.

'I'm tellin' yer, lads; if they'd have had keyhole surgery back in them days the world could've been me oyster. You ask Nobby, he'll tell yer.'

But when pressed, Nobby couldn't remember which clubs were interested, nor could he keep a straight face. At least it had brightened up the afternoon, and knocking off time had come much quicker. But this change of mood had only served to torment Joe's emotions even more.

On their way home a car had carved them up, another B.M.W. ironically, causing Terry to slam all on. The lads had cringed in anticipation of the inevitable outpouring of rage, but it never came. Terry just tutted and sighed the word '*Wanker*.' under his breath.

Joe watched his dad with a bemused look on his face. He wished he knew what went on inside that head of his. How could you love someone and hate them at the same time? That's how he felt and he didn't like it. Why couldn't it be one or the other? His emotions were all over the place especially since the suspension. He wanted to be believed, because after all he was telling the truth and his dad said he believed him, but sometimes he wondered if he really did. He'd overheard his mam talking about the onset of adolescence and changing hormones and all that, and although he didn't fully understand what she was going on about he thought maybe that was it. Maybe it was all *his* fault. Maybe he was turning into a wrong 'un. But he knew plenty of wrong 'un's and he knew he was nothing like them. He took a sideways glance at Young Nobby and his dad. He wanted to ask his mate if he loved his old man, but that would be a soft thing to do, and he knew the type of response he'd get if he went around asking questions like that. Anyway you could tell that he did, and you could tell that his dad loved him back. There were no issues with those two. Joe actually wondered if he loved his mate's dad more than his own. Nobby was approachable. You could talk to him and ask him anything; okay, he tended to make a joke out of everything even if you were trying to be serious, but that's what made you like him even more. Joe looked back at his dad. Terry had pulled up at some traffic lights and had become aware of his son's attentions. He turned to him and without saying anything, gave him a big, warm smile. The lights turned green and they set off again. Joe wanted the feeling that he had in his chest at that moment to last forever, but he knew, eventually, it would be replaced by one of doubt and confusion.

'Tell me mam I'm staying at Nobby's for tea,' said Joe as they pulled up outside the Clarkes'.'

'Oh aye; why's that?'

'He's got t'new Championship Manager game for t'Playstation. We're gonna set up a league.'

'Oh, right. I might have to come and have a look at that, get some tips - see yer later.' Terry drove off leaving him standing there with that same bemused look on his face. His old man must be cracking up, Joe thought to himself. What the hell was he on about - *get some tips*?

3

'Are yer serious?' Nobby asked, setting down the pint of Guinness in front of his mate.

Terry eagerly took a couple of inches off the pint and wiped the froth from his mouth with the back of his hand before replying. ''Course I am.'

'A football team?' Nobby queried again, wanting confirmation that he'd heard right the first time.

'Yeah, a junior football team.'

Nobby settled into his chair and started into his lager before inquiring further. 'What, an' you're gonna manage 'em?

'Yeah, well, you and me both - you know, a sort of manager, coach arrangement, like say, Revie-Cocker, Clough-Taylor, Shankley-Paisley type thing.'

Nobby looked at his buddy dubiously. Normally he would go along with anything Terry said or came up with, but this, a kid's football team? He had to be joking. But he could tell from the look in his eyes that he wasn't. Nobby's heart sank. What did they know about running a football team? They'd just got the business up and running nicely. Life was steady. There was no need to add distractions and complications. Why was he doing this to him?

Nobby didn't say anything; he just pulled a face, hoping that would be enough to let Terry know what he felt about the idea. It didn't matter. Nobby knew that when Terry had set his mind on something that was it. He would see it right through to the end. Right or wrong, there would be no going back. And as the night wore on and the more Guinness he got inside him, the more enthusiastic he became. Nobby tried his best to dampen that enthusiasm but to no avail. Terry fielded every one of Nobby's reasoned arguments against the venture. Terry the pessimist had become Terry the optimist.

The Fusiliers had filled up steadily during the course of the evening, and now the atmosphere was buzzing with small, noisy groups of young lads and lasses gearing up for the regular Friday night assault on the town.

Nobby pushed his way to the bar, taking in the heady aromas as he went, not sure if the varied scents were coming off the birds or the blokes; unavoidably pressing against nubile tits and arses, not that he was complaining. He glanced around the heaving throng and almost wished he were twenty years younger. It was a different generation now, all hair gel and Alco pops. Nobby drank lager, always had. His mate used to be your original Tetley bitter man until the Aussie conglomerates took over the breweries and turned everything into cask conditioned chemical crap. Now you had stuff called 'smooth-flow'; a pretend, headache inducing 'traditional ale' pumped full of formaldehyde and the like. Terry drank Guinness now, at least it was universal, and you rarely got a really bad pint of the stuff. Nobby would tease Terry and tell him that the water they used to make it came directly from the Liffey, the most polluted river in Europe. That's why it was so black. In reality it was probably brewed somewhere in Warrington.

Nobby shouted his order to the barmaid and clocked old Arthur sitting on his stool at the end of the bar. He waved to him and Arthur responded with a friendly nod. Old Arthur was one of those characters who always seemed to be a permanent fixture. He'd been a regular at the Fusiliers for what seemed like forever. He'd been there when Nobby had first started drinking and always on the same stool in the same corner at the end of the bar. The thing was, he never appeared to get any older, but Nobby couldn't remember him looking younger either. He'd always looked the way he did now. He looked over again and took a wild guess, sixty-five? Seventy? Eighty even. He would ask him one day. At least he knew that his capacity for ale had never diminished. He was doing between twelve and sixteen pints a day when the licensing laws were tighter, so God knows what he was doing now they were open all day and night. But the other thing was you never saw him drunk, okay, a bit unsteady on his feet now and again after all he was an old man, but you never saw him rolling around absolutely plastered. He liked his fags as well. Forty a day Capstan full strength and he didn't even have a cough. Blokes like him were an anomaly, a freak of nature. He indulged every vice under the sun but never ailed of anything in his life. He reckoned that the only time he'd ever seen a doctor was when he had to have his medical when he enlisted in the Navy. He was a salty old dog who'd sailed the world. Been there, done it, bought the teeshirt. He'd seen it all, from the donkey shagging women of Cairo, to the ping-pong poppers of Bangkok. A whore in every port, from Portsmouth to Kuala Lumpur, and he never caught a dose, or so he said. Nobby believed him. He wasn't a bragger or the romancing type like your Uncle Albert character in Only Fools and Horses. And he'd only relate some weird or wonderful tale if you bought him a pint and pressed him on the subject.

One of Nobby's favourite stories was the one Arthur used to tell about a stoker mate of his who copped for some African tart in the port of Zanzibar. The bloke had been on the rum all day and had fallen unconscious on the job, pissed. Insulted by this, the lady, for want of a better word, decided to turn him kosher, and set about his knob with an old razor blade. She then invited two of her colleagues in on the act, and they had taken it in turn to shit on him. Mixing blood and faeces together, they had smeared him from head to toe with the foul paste then rolled him outside into the gutter to bake in the afternoon sun.

They'd found him covered in flies but still alive. Back on board ship they'd had to hose the poor guy down from a distance before the doctor could take a close look at him. Apparently the blood and shit had formed some sort of poultice around his impromptu circumcision and had prevented him from bleeding to death.

Not everyone believed Arthur's exotic stories, but he didn't care. He had a hundred such tales to tell if you were interested, all told as a matter of fact and with a straight face, a face that was etched with world-weary knowledge and wisdom. Knowledge that had been learned the hard way; practical knowledge, the type you only learn by going places and experiencing things firsthand. Arthur had studied at the University of Life. He had a fair idea of how things ran, what made the world tick. He'd seen enough depravation, starvation and human exploitation on his travels. He'd seen the great global grinding machine in action. Coming back to his home town and living on the East and West Broughton estates with their own levels of expropriation must have paled into insignificance compared to the sights he'd witnessed around the world, but he understood that it was all intrinsically linked. The world as he saw it was a giant melting pot, and the hands of crooked governments and the multinationals would keep stirring it. Organised chaos was the key. Covertly create conflict then offer solutions to the conflict, thereby controlling and exploiting any given situation whilst playing the saviour to a gullible outside world. '*Ordo Ab Chao*' the Freemasons called it.

Arthur didn't have any solutions. If that's how the world was, so be it. He avoided getting into deep debate about that sort of thing. He'd heard Terry in the past give some political idealist an ear bashing at the bar, and had just sat there without offering an opinion, a knowing smile on his face. He liked Terry's train of thought, and perceived him as a well-read young man, but he could see that he was angry with it. Arthur's advice to Terry would be, '*It's a short life lad, try and enjoy it.*'

Nobby wouldn't need any such advice. Those were his sentiments exactly. Anything for an easy life, but no, Tel had to come along with his crackpot ideas and balls it all up.

He edged his way back to their table. The Fusiliers was really heaving tonight, must be the warm weather. A couple of girls got a lager shower down the backs of their blouses as he struggled past, and the collar on Terry's Guinness was a bit thick now it had settled, but sod it, he wasn't about to fight his way back through that lot just for a top up.

Terry's attentions were so divided he didn't notice the short measure.

'What are yer gonna call this 'ere football team then?' Nobby tried to sound interested.

Terry had already thought of this one. 'What about - West

Broughton Albion?' he offered enthusiastically.

Nobby mulled it over for a few seconds. 'Sounds like West Bromwich Albion.'

'Yeah, I know it does a bit, but it rolls off the tongue don't it? Anyway, we can abbreviate it to just The Albion if we want.'

Terry had been reading about Mythological Britain. Albion, the ancient Greek and Roman word for Britain kept cropping up and he liked the sound of it. To him, West Broughton Albion fitted perfectly. He knew Nobby wouldn't argue the toss.

'An' what about a kit, a pitch, nets, balls, equipment an' all that?'

'Don't think I haven't given that some thought,' Terry said reassuringly. 'One-step at a time my friend. We'll cross those bridges when we come to 'em.'

'Have yer told the lads yet?

'No, I thought it best to run it past you first. Mek sure I had your approval and everything. No point in building t' lads hopes up if you weren't in full agreement.'

Nobby saw straight through this bullshit. 'Bollocks!' he said indignantly. 'Don't you try and use the lads as emotional blackmail to get me on your side with this one. You'll go through with this no matter what I think, and I'll get dragged along in yer wake like I allus do.'

Terry grinned sheepishly. It was true. He shouldn't underestimate his amigo like that.

Nobby wagged an admonishing finger. 'You've been brewing this for ages. I'm not fuckin' stupid. O'course I'll go along with it, if only to stop you being such a miserable twat.'

Terry's sheepish grin broadened to a Cheshire cat one. He knew his mate would come through. He wouldn't bore Nobby with the real reasons for wanting to do this. He wouldn't want to know about giving some of the lads off the estate some esteem, a goal to aim for, maybe a bit of pride in what they were doing and learning about the potential to achieve things. Above all it was about fun; having a laugh with your mates as opposed to being chased from pillar to post by the law; being seen as potential villains on every street corner 'cos there was nothing else to do and nowhere to go.

Terry and Nobby had played for three football teams at the same time back in the day; the school team, the church team and the youth club team. It had helped keep them out of any major trouble, and the fact that they were good, that they actually won cups and titles, made it a great time in which to grow up.

Because of council cutbacks and overspent budgets the youth club they had gone to back in their day that bordered the two Broughton estates had closed down in the early nineties as did many others across the City. Yet now, that very same building had been totally refurbished and was being used as a day centre for asylum seekers. But the only asylum seekers Terry ever saw were young Albanian types in designer gear, making drug deals on expensive looking mobile phones.

The influx of heroin and crack into the area had gone up by thirty five percent in the last eighteen months according to latest figures. You didn't have to be a rocket scientist to join the dots. Terry laughed when all the bleeding hearts came out of their ivory towers to express shock, horror and dismay on your telly 'cos the B.N.P. had won a few seats in the local bi-elections. What the hell did they expect? They should take time to come and spend a few days in the real world.

Terry was under no illusions. He knew getting a football team off the ground wouldn't be easy, especially around here. There would be more folk pulling strokes against him rather than for him, but he was up for the challenge. Thinking about faceless school governors and their ilk had given him all the incentives he needed. And with his reluctant buddy in tow they would show 'em.

Come half-ten, the pub had started to empty, the crowd thinning out as people caught buses and taxis into town. All over the City and surrounding districts the pattern was the same, local boozers spilling forth hundreds of half-cut punters heading for the noise and buzz of the nightclubs; birds and blokes all done up in their Friday night finery, everybody on the pull, eager and ready to strut their stuff, each on their own brand of high-octane fuel: alcohol, ecstasy, speed, crack and smack; anonymous but deadly. Heading on deep into the night, the preening and the posturing. Bravado. Stand offs. Confrontations. Cat fights. Fist fights. Sweat and pheromones mingle and dilated pupils connect. This was human courtship twenty first century fashion. Then after the chase, a knee trembler around the back of the taxi rank for the lucky ones. Frantic fumbling. Fleeting, forgettable. A Technicolor yawn for those who tried hard but failed; mam's tea and twenty-five quids worth of Jackie Daniels and coke spread across a municipal pavement, looking like an early Jackson Pollock painting. And of course, what evening would be complete without the nightly tour de force from the company of players who perform for the CCTV; from pure farce to full-blown horror shows, Keystone Cops to Clockwork Orange. It was all there in grainy black and white, a sick and sad testament to a fucked up society. But hey, the boys in the bubble had an erase button, no crisis of conscience here. Staring at monitors night after night showing sickening acts of violence numbed the senses after a while, and videotape was expensive anyway. It became a soap opera where the victims were just actors on a T.V. screen.

Nobby always had the feeling he was missing out on something when the pub loosed on a Friday. They were both turning forty this year but Nobby had never quite been able to let go of his youth. On the odd occasion he would persuade Terry to venture into town but if they were honest with themselves, neither enjoyed the experience. Times had changed. You couldn't hear yourself talk in the pubs. Walls and taprooms had been knocked through to create vast open areas to cram more and more punters in. Garish colours and lighting assaulted the senses, with hordes of fresh-faced young things bobbing along to the cacophony, pulsing along to a drum and bass beat, oblivious to the pair of middle aged blokes standing bewildered, looking awkward and out of place, trying to protect their pints from the heaving throng. And inevitably the evening would usually end up with Nobby threatening to punch the lights out of some cocky young wazzock who'd got a bit clever and fancied his chances.

Terry had moved on. Those days were behind him. He neither liked nor pretended to understand what went on inside the heads of the following generation, nor did he want to. Today was for them; it was their time, best leave them to it. The late seventies and early eighties had been their era. They'd only caught the back end of the punk thing, and after, when fashion and music had started to turn shit, they'd gotten into the football big style.

Mick, Terry's older brother had been a die-hard Leeds fan. He'd grown up during the glory years of the sixties and seventies, watching Don Revie's magicians in all-white carve a niche for themselves in the annals of the modern game. He'd followed them home and abroad, tasted the glory and the heartaches, the near misses, the major upsets and the injustices. He'd gone to Paris in seventy-five for the big one, the European Cup Final against Bayern Munich; gone without a ticket, but managed to blag his way into the Parc De Prince as did hundreds of others to watch the game of their lives, only to be robbed by a bent referee, resulting in riots that would earn the club a five year ban from all European competitions.

Terry remembered Mick's face as he walked through the door the following day, his blue, white and old gold CHAMPIONS OF EUROPE banner draped forlornly around his shoulders, his features weary and drained. Terry was only twelve at the time, but even then he understood what it was his older sibling was going through. He knew all about the passion and dedication it took to be a true fan.

Mick had reluctantly taken his young brother to a few home games and he had been instantly hooked; the noise, the smells, the atmosphere charged with raw excitement and a strange undercurrent of danger. It was that veiled hint of fear that enchanted Terry more than anything. The chanting and goading from rival supporters, the threat of violence in the air captivated him as much as the game itself.

Mick shut himself away in his room and didn't go to work for a week after Paris, only venturing downstairs for his meals, red rings around his eyes like he'd been crying constantly. Terry marvelled at his dedication to the cause. He wanted to get inside his head and share the sorrow, feel the bitterness eating him up. Later, when he'd come round a bit, Mick had told Terry about the rioting, about ripping up the seats and hurling them at the triumphant Bayern players taking the piss, parading the cup in front of them. What the papers had reported as just a minority of mindless idiots chucking things about was anything but. Mick had witnessed everyone around him tearing the place apart; middle aged family men, some in suits and ties, older blokes in their sixties and seventies and even women, all launching hate and vitriol towards the pitch. Those who couldn't rive the wood and plastic from the fixings flung coins and bottles, anything they could lay their hands on. A decade of frustration and injustice came to a head on that balmy May evening in seventy-five.

Terry understood what it was all about; His older brother's near fanaticism had left a lasting impression. He knew what made normally law-abiding people behave this way; the feeling that started in the pit of your stomach and surged upwards into your chest making it fit to burst. People who expressed disgust at such behaviour, especially over something as trivial as football, would never understand.

After Paris the glory days were well and truly over. Revie had already left for his ill-fated spell as England manager, and the team went steadily into decline. When they were relegated, Mick had already started a family and couldn't bear to watch his beloved club in the old second division. The baton passed to Terry.

Neither he nor Nobby were bona fide members of the Service Crew, but they *were* nearly always in the middle of the action. Nor did they subscribe to any particular dress code. They couldn't see the point of togging up in designer gear just to avoid the attentions of the railway police, only to have it ripped to bits in a ruck with a bunch of Chelsea Head-hunters. Plus the fact that the London clubs always did it better, bigger wages, better shops, the best labels. The northern clubs couldn't quite carry it off somehow. Nobby insisted on travelling everywhere in his old Harrington and Doc Marts which made him stick out like a sore thumb.

Football and its hooligan culture had grown more sophisticated since Mick's day when hundreds of young head-the-balls would steam into each other en masse. The Police had finally caught up and had better methods of control now. Proper segregation and C.C.T.V.

meant doing battle away from the grounds and stations. Staying one step ahead, dedicated nutters would use inter-city-service trains instead of the football specials and travel in small groups or firms, hence Leeds' Service Crew, and West Hams' I.C.F. (Inter-City-Firm). Craft knives and calling cards were also a new and sick innovation.

Terry shuddered at some of the memories and images that came flooding back. He felt shame now whenever he thought back to those times; the stabbings and the slashings, the acts of mindless violence that him and Nobby had been party to; the youth laid out on a pavement outside St. Andrews, face slit from under his eye, right down his cheek and across his neck, the blood pumping and pulsing into the air in time to his racing heart; a bizarre image that lasted for a few fleeting seconds as they raced by, but would stay with him forever; didn't even know if he was Leeds or Brummie, just another poor unlucky sod; wrong place, wrong time, reactions not quick enough. And the mere thought of the many near death experiences with Millwall and the like, still invoked sudden bowel movement to this day. Thank fuck he usually had Nobby by his side; just a small crumb of comfort when confronted by a team of Bushwhackers.

Terry passed those times off as a phase, a rite of passage if you like. They were young and stupid; no excuses, it happened. He wasn't proud and he didn't like to dwell on it, the images were too disturbing, the excitement and the adrenalin rush gone and long forgotten. But there were still plenty around from those times who couldn't let it go, who became addicted as if it were a drug. For some it became a way of life. Mobile phones and the Internet added a new dimension; ultra violence, covert and ever more sophisticated, highly organised and super efficient, any which way for a new kick, metaphorically and literally.

When they had started to get serious with the girls the away days had become less frequent, and after they returned from one particular torrid trip down the smoke, where Nobby had got glassed and collected the prize scar that still sat across his forehead, and Terry had spent the night in Vine Street nick, the ultimatum had been delivered. Jan and Kath were deadly serious; it was football or them. Thinking back, they both realised that the women had been their saving grace.

Bournemouth, the scene of Leeds's triumphant return to the top flight had been their last hurrah and it had been a brilliant weekend. Not much aggro, just plenty of ale and mass celebration. It drew a line under an era for them, and what with the rave scene and a new, little white happy pill on the circuit, times were a-changing again; things would start to chill out - for a few years at least.

The bell rang for last orders, not that that meant much to the die-hard regulars in the Fusiliers. Arthur still had room for another two or three yet. Norman the landlord would serve the faithful until they dropped or staggered out of the side door and into the night. Ringing the bell was merely a ritual; there was no official closing time here.

The lads had one more for the road. Neither could remember if they were on their ninth or tenth pint. Whatever, it was at least a couple more than they usually had and Terry in particular was feeling a little fresh.

Nobby wasn't really listening to Terry's drunken chatter, it was his good mood that was infectious, and he sat there with an inane grin on his face happily nodding or shaking his head at what he thought were the appropriate moments, just glad that his mate had got over the nonsense from these past few weeks.

Those last drinks took longer to shift and it was well after midnight when they left the pub. Nobby said he was starving and suggested they go for a mucky curry. Terry said he was too pissed to be arsed, and he'd settle for fish and chips, and anyway mucky curries were to be avoided after closing time on a Friday night 'cos you never knew what you were getting after the Asian waiters had been subjected to a night of insults and abuse from groups of blathered white punters. A few quick ones off the wrist and into the pot and you could end up downing a mélange of Kashmiri bred D.N.A. with your jalfrezi and he didn't fancy that, pissed or not.

The regular chippy was shut when they got there so they settled for a kebab from Denero's, overdid it with the chilli sauce, a mistake they would both regret the next day while contemplating on the lav'.

They walked through the precinct in silence, both concentrating on keeping the contents of their supper inside the flimsy paper wrapper as they ate it and failing miserably as bits of kebab meat and onion fell to the ground in their wake. Terry had chilli sauce dribbling down his fingers and round his mouth, but he didn't care. Right now it was the best meal he'd ever had, there just wouldn't be enough of it. At least it would soak a bit of the Guinness up. It was the only time he'd been quiet all evening.

The sound of shoe leather on concrete amplified by the dark, hollow caves of shop doorways echoed back at them as they walked along. Remnants of meals and packaging from earlier Denero customers littered the floor. It was as if people had suddenly sobered up, realised what it was they were eating and had thrown it down in disgust. Or maybe it was the overpowering smell of stale piss that seemed to ooze from the fabric of the buildings and permeate the air that had put them off the food. At least there would be no waste from these two tonight.

Heads down, chewing on the last morsel of pita bread, footsteps slowly fading into the night; a couple of dogs barking defiance at each other and a police siren, way in the distance, the only other sounds.

Terry woke with a Gobi desert gob. The smell of frying bacon had aroused his senses and brought him out of his slumbers. From the mists of sleep, and barely conscious, he became aware that his head was banging - and he had a hard on. What the fuck was all that about? Was it God having a laugh or what? It was one of life's great mysteries; an unexplainable phenomenon that only someone like Dr. Robert Winston could probably shed some light on. Anyway, at that moment in time both were unwelcome. He wished he'd remembered to take some aspirin and some water to bed with him the previous night. In fact, he wished he could remember coming to bed at all. He looked over at Jan's side of the bed. Empty - No, he couldn't remember - but she could…

The banging about downstairs had woken her. She had switched the bedside light on briefly and looked at the clock. It was half past one. He was a lot later than usual and, by the sound of it, drunk. She had resisted the temptation to turn the light back on and bollock him when he had staggered up the stairs and crashed into the bedroom. She had feigned sleep and maintained the pretence throughout the pantomime of him getting undressed. When he had finally crawled into bed and snuggled up to her she had cringed. She had hoped he wasn't going to start. Their sex life hadn't been brilliant lately, and she didn't fancy a booze-soaked, fumbling shag at this time of a morning. He whispered her name and breathed lustily down the back of her neck. The reek of Guinness and kebab made her wince but she still managed to stay 'asleep'. He put his arm round her and cupped a breast while manoeuvring his penis into the cleft of her bum. After a few adjustments and contented moans and groans his breathing fell into a steady rhythm and as he slipped into unconsciousness it became a full-blown snore. Jan breathed a sigh of relief and went to sleep for real.

Erection slowly subsiding, Terry kicked off the quilt and got out of bed; too quick. Blood roared through his ears and made his head pound. God, he felt rough. He made his way to the bog and emptied his bladder, letting loose a couple of rasping Guinnes inspired farts as he did so. He remembered the kebab from last night and water came into his mouth in an instant. He swallowed hard a few times and tried to take a few deep breaths. He hated being sick, he wasn't the type who could stick his fingers down his throat to get shut. He flushed, got a quick wash, dressed and made his way slowly downstairs. The smell of cooked breakfast stopped him in his tracks. Rory looked up from his plate and nudged his brother with his elbow. Jan stopped tending the eggs that were sizzling and spitting in the frying pan and looked on, spatula in hand. All three of them stared expectantly at the pathetic spectacle that stood before them in the kitchen doorway. Any remaining colour drained immediately from Terry's features and his glands went into overdrive, filling his mouth with water again. This time he knew he wouldn't be able to hold it back. Without a word he turned quickly on his heels and shot back upstairs, reaching the bog and letting fly into the pot just in time. Beads of sweat popped out all over his forehead as he heaved and retched, while he clung on to the porcelain as if his life depended on it.

Back downstairs the boys pulled faces while Jan uttered oaths under her breath.

'I think me dad's gorra hangover,' said Joe as a matter of fact.

'He still looks pissed to me,' said Rory.

Jan gave him a sharp clip round the back of his head. 'You just watch your mouth and get on with your breakfast.'

'Can we have his?' Rory asked.

'No you can't.'

'Why not?' he persisted, 'me dad's not gonna want it is he?'

'I don't want any of it,' said Joe. 'It's puttin' me off me own, listenin' to him throw up.'

Muffled rolphs and barfs could be heard from upstairs. Jan tutted, contemplated for a moment while listening to the sound of her husband being sick, then relented. 'Well, I suppose it'll only go to waste, here you are then,' she said sliding the spatula under the freshly fried egg and onto Rory's plate. 'But don't be coming for owt else now 'till tea time.'

'Don't forget the bacon mam,' he said cheekily.

Joe pulled a hateful face at his younger brother. 'He's a greedy little get.'

'I'm a growin' lad aren't I, mam?' Rory said with a cocky air.

'Yes, you are, love,' his mother said, laughing at his cheeky quip. She put the three rashers of what had been Terry's bacon next to the egg and gave his hair a ruffle; a little guilty about the clip she had administered a moment before.

Joe and his younger brother were chalk and cheese. Joe was a fairly quiet, thoughtful lad. Not entirely shy, just guarded. He observed a lot but tended to keep his opinions to himself. He was a lot like his mother. Apart from that, he was like any other thirteen year old; loved his sport, especially football, and as family tradition dictated, he had to be a Leeds fan. Although he and Young Nobby were best mates, just like their dads were, they both tended to have their mothers' traits and personalities. Physically, it looked as if they were going to be Terry and Nobby clones.

Rory was something else. He had it all off. He possessed cheek, charm, confidence and knowledge way beyond his tender eleven years. He was streetwise as well; so clued up on what was going on around him, he often left Jan and Terry open mouthed with some of the stuff he came out with.

Rory's gran, Jan's mum, was supposed to be a bit psychic. She had watched him closely growing up and would say, knowingly, 'He's an old soul, that one; he's been here plenty o' times before.' Terry didn't know about any of that, he just thought that he probably spent too much time in the company of older lads, hanging about with Joe and his mates, showing off with newfound phrases and swear words. Although everyone around him tended to laugh at his roguish antics, both Jan and Terry knew they would have to keep a close eye on the little bugger if they were to keep him out of any major trouble.

A month or so before he was born Jan and Terry had been bandying around potential names for their new offspring, girls' names mostly.

'What if it's another boy?' Terry had said. Jan admitted she hadn't given much thought to having another boy. 'I like Rory,' he'd said, fully expecting hoots of derision from his wife, but she'd liked it immediately, clearly oblivious as to who Rory Gallagher was. He gave a little smirk to himself and decided to keep quiet. If Jan had known her second son was about to be named after a blues legend and one of their Mick's all time guitar heroes she'd have no doubt changed her mind. After eleven years she still hadn't twigged and in all probability had still never heard of the bloke.

Jan gently shook her sleeping husband awake. He was laid on top of the bed still fully clothed but he felt cold. He shivered and stretched himself back to the land of the living.

'How are you feeling?'

Terry looked up to see his wife holding a steaming mug of tea and a plate of toast but not much pity.

'Better than I was, still got a bit of a headache though.'

She placed the tea and toast on the bedside table then sat at the foot of the bed and watched him in silence as he sat up and composed himself. Sometimes it was like looking after three boys Jan thought to herself and she couldn't decide which one gave her most trouble. At least he had cleaned up after himself - after a fashion.

'What?' Terry said with a mouthful of toast, becoming aware that she was staring at him.

'Nothing,' Jan said nonchalantly.

'You're looking at me as if I've done summat wrong.'

'Well, have you?'

'No,' Terry said defensively.

'That's all right then. What were you celebrating?'

'Nowt,' he said, feeling the hot tea slip down his parched throat.

'You don't usually come home that roaring drunk on a Friday night.'

He shrugged his shoulders and bit into some more toast. 'I wasn't that bad was I?'

Jan cocked her head to one side and gave him that look. Terry could tell she was fishing for something but there was nothing to fish for. He was only celebrating the clearing of his mind; putting things in order, so to speak. He couldn't tell her he was celebrating forming a junior football team, that would sound daft, but in essence, that's all he'd been doing. He supposed he'd tell her, but he'd wanted to tell Joe first. He shrugged his shoulders again.

'Where's our Joe?' he asked

'Over at Nobby's I expect, why?'

'Oh, just had a bit of news for him, that's all.'

'What sort of news?'

'Bein' a bit nosey, aren't we?' Terry said, shovelling down more toast and feeling better already. 'Just a bit of father and son stuff, you know.'

'*Ooh*, right,' Jan said with a sorry-I-asked look. She got off the bed and headed for the door. 'Oh, by the way, Mrs. Evans phoned; you were supposed to be at her house for eleven to give her an estimate for cutting down her leylandii. I told her you weren't feeling too well this morning.'

'Shit! What time is it now?

'Ten-to-one,' she said casually and skipped off down the stairs.

Laying out full stretch on the settee, newspaper folded at the racing section, picking out horses ready for a steady afternoon of sport on telly was the best way to deal with the remnants of a hangover in Terry's opinion. But when he heard the sound of thundering feet tearing down the garden path, he guessed that particular cure was about to be rudely interrupted.

Joe and Young Nobby burst into the room and stood before him breathless and exited. 'Is it rate, dad? Or is he just winding us up?' panted Joe.

'What? - Who?' said Terry, sitting up and throwing down his paper.

'Yer know, what Nobby says about yer startin' a footie team.'

'A footie team?' said Terry, acting all bemused. Joe and Young Nobby looked at each other exasperated.

'Yeah, a footie team,' Joe implored with a tone in his voice that said: *Please don't mess about, dad.*

A slow, sly smile spread across Terry's face. Confirmation.

'Yes! – Yeess!' The two lads pogoed and high five'd in front of the telly until the ornaments on the mantelpiece rattled. Terry looked on, grinning from ear to ear, a nice warm glow suddenly enveloping his whole body. He was happier than he'd been in weeks.

'What's all this about, then?' Jan was standing in the doorway, hands on hips, alerted by the commotion. Rory had joined her and was trying to push past, eager not to miss out on whatever was going on.

'We're gonna start a team, a footie team,' Joe exclaimed.

'Oh, so that was the big mystery, was it?' Jan said, unimpressed.

Rory squeezed past his mam into the room and tried to join in the excitement. He leant on the arm of the settee and jumped up and down. 'Am I gonna be in it, dad? Am I in t'team?'

'You're not in it, yer little sod. Is he, dad?' said Joe.

'Ah, you won't be old enough for this team, I'm afraid, son,' said Terry, suddenly realising that he'd not taken into account the reactions of his youngest.

Rory stopped bouncing up and down, his excitement evaporated. Terry saw the disappointment in his face and tried to retrieve the situation. 'You could be t'mascot, though.'

'I don't wanna be a bloody mascot, I wanna play.'

'You won't be able to, son,' Terry reasoned. 'It'll be an under fourteens side, in a league; there are rules, you'd be too young.'

Rory's bottom lip came out and quivered. Terry looked into his eyes and hoped what he saw wasn't hate. He tried a weak smile.

'Bastard!' he aimed at his dad. 'Bastards!' he aimed at his brother and Young Nobby before pushing past his mam again and slamming the back door on his way out so that the whole house shook.

Arms folded across her chest, Jan gave Terry that old familiar look and slowly shook her head. Untouched by Rory's outburst, Joe and Young Nobby were still fervently jabbering away to each other.

Terry watched his wife turn and leave the room. The happy feeling had been short-lived.

4

Nobby painstakingly read the note pinned to the club notice board, face screwed up in concentration.

'Hey, it's club trip to Blackpool next month,' he said. 'Are we having us names down, or what?'

'Not this year, Nobby lad,' said Terry as he lined up a red on the snooker table. 'We'll be in full trainin' by then, no time for trips.' The red rattled the cushion a few times before disappearing down the pocket. He moved round the table and lined up the black, decided it was too tight, and plumped for the blue.

'This 'ere football lark is gonna bugger up my social life, up an' right,' moaned Nobby turning away from the board and leaning on his cue.

In the concert room, Jan Gallagher and Kath Clarke were waiting for the next bingo session to start. Jan was having a little moan and grumble to her best mate about the present state of her marriage. Their biorhythms were all out of kilter. He didn't want it when she did, she didn't want it when he did, and when they both wanted it the kids always seemed to be around. It was a vicious circle. But it wasn't just the sex. They didn't seem to talk much lately. Terry didn't like sharing his problems with her. If she tried to persuade him to open up, he would feel that she was nagging him. She felt that they were pulling in different directions. He wouldn't even argue the toss over the telly now. The other night, Jan had been watching, '*I'm a Big Pop Idol Celebrity Brother on ice Get Me Out Of Here,*' or some such banal but perversely voyeuristic reality TV show. Terry had sauntered into the room, sneered at the screen, sauntered back out without a word and had gone upstairs to watch a documentary about The Great War. They were operating on different planes and she was worried that they were drifting further and further apart.

Kath lent a sympathetic ear and made comforting noises at the appropriate moments, assuring Jan that all relationships had their ups and downs. It was probably just a phase they were going through. Even she and Nobby had the occasional slanging stand up. Maybe they needed to throw a bit of crockery around, a sure-fire way of bringing things out into the open and getting stuff off your chest. Jan let out a wry laugh knowing full well if she used that tack Terry would just shake his head and walk out the room. They were firmly in a rut and Jan thought the only way out was to break the monotony of routine. What they needed was a change of scene. None of them had been away on holiday since Terry and Nobby had worked for the council. She desperately needed a break or she would go bloody mad.

The caller switched his microphone on. 'Laydeez an' chenelmen, please take your seats, the next session is about to begin,' he announced above screeching feedback. 'Your next card is for a full house – A bit of hush if you please – Dabbers at the ready – And it's eyes down...' All chatter in the room died, the lights dimmed slightly, balls popped and danced and Jan put her marital problems to the back of her mind for the next half hour. '...And your first number is...'

Nobby was sulking. He wanted to do the club trip; they always did the club trip, it was tradition. He didn't want to miss out on the biggest piss-up of the year; the afternoon session in the Bier Keller; all the lads from the club, all on one giant table, pissed as rats, swaying from side to side, steins held aloft singing '*Ein Prosit*' along to a German oompah band who were dressed in silly hats and lederhosen. He didn't want to miss out on a potential punch-up with a bunch of paralytic jocks, or the capers they got up to like when they dragged poor old Bobby Saunders into the sex shop, pulled his strides down, lobbed his knob on the counter and asked the startled assistant if she had any leeches for this? He felt like telling Terry to stuff training with a bunch of kids. It was only one weekend, once a year. Surely he could make that concession. He felt defiant; wanted to say '*Sod it, my name's going on t' list.*' But he could see Terry's response in his mind's eye; it would be a wry smile, a shrug of the shoulders. '*Okay Nobby, you go on the trip.*' And he knew that Terry knew that he couldn't do it. He wouldn't enjoy it without his mate. He hated having to admit it but it was true. They were as one, whether sometimes he liked it or not.

Nobby turned from the bar with two fresh pints just as Terry was sinking the black. The twat had won again. He always won, and Nobby wasn't just thinking of snooker.

* * *

It was an impressive turnout, at least in terms of numbers. A rough head count showed about twenty-seven, twenty-nine if you counted the two dogs that had come along with their thirteen year old masters. Joe and Young Nobby had done well putting the word about.

Terry and Nobby scanned the motley looking gathering.

'This is gonna be a bloody challenge,' muttered Nobby under his breath.

A kaleidoscope of colour they weren't. The array of kit and club colours on display, although varied, certainly wasn't up to date. Some were sporting tops faded and baggy like they'd been boil-washed a million times. Others in gear that was either so tight it was obviously a Christmas present from days of yore, or so big it had been purloined from an older brother's wardrobe. Others weren't in what you could describe kit at all and even a couple of kids had turned up in school uniform. The footwear was even less impressive and Terry's heart sank a little as he looked at what some of these kids had to walk around in. For some, what they had on their feet now was all they possessed, be it a shoe, a trainer or a boot. Those who wore Nike's or Addidas gave themselves away as being skilled shop-lifters rather than affluent.

This bunch of lads looked as grey and depressing as the background from which they came. Terry knew his job was to bring a bit of colour into their lives. He was under no illusions. He knew it wouldn't be easy. He looked around the scruffy little band of oiks, who despite their raggedness seemed keen enough. No, he thought to himself, it wasn't going to be easy, but it all starts here.

Nobby broke the ice: 'Right,' he announced. 'Anybody wearing a Man U shirt can sod off now, 'cos yer won't be mekin' this team.'

'Fuck off, yer Leeds scum,' was one of the more choice comments from around half a dozen dissenting voices.

'What's that thing you're wearin' anyway? *Top Man* went out wi' t'fukin' ark.' piped up a little ginger haired kid wearing a Liverpool top that had *Candy* emblazoned across the chest.

'Don't diss the shirt, kid,' said Nobby, lifting his top to kiss the old badge, revealing his slight paunch as he did so.

After a few minutes of light-hearted banter quite a few of the lads had already warmed to Nobby. Here was a bloke they could have a laugh with. You could take the piss and he would just give you some back. The big kid in Nobby was coming out; he was one of them.

'What we gonna do with this lot, then?' he asked breathless after escaping an impromptu kick about with some of the lads.

'Separate wheat from chaff first,' said Terry. 'Tek 'em on a two mile run then time 'em on some sprints. Fitness assessment. Gather 'em round.'

'Right lads,' Terry opened, 'sit down; watch out for the dog shit, shurrup and listen. For those of you that don't know us, I'm Terry and this is Nobby...' A few boos rose up from the gathered. Nobby loved it. '...I'm the manager and Nobby's my assistant and coach...'

Terry launched into a speech, talking about his aspirations, but the lads were full of questions and kept interrupting.

'When are we gonna play football?'

'All in good time.'

'Where we gonna play?'

'Don't know yet.'

'What we gonna be called?'

'West Broughton Albion.'

'West Bromwich Albion? – They're shite.'

'What's us colours?'

'Don't know yet.'

Terry wanted to say a lot more but cut his talk short seeing that the boys were getting restless, so he took this little ragbag army of hopefuls and two dogs, jogging and jabbering along excitedly onto the streets and avenues of West Broughton; him, Nobby and Rory, who had come along to prove a point, up at the front, leading the way.

They hadn't gone far when they began to attract attention. Two lads on BMXs pedalled up alongside.

'What yer doing, Gallagher?' one of them asked.

'Swimmin', what's it fuckin' look like?' replied Joe sarcastically.

'We're footie training,' piped up a breathless lad from the middle of the group.

The two BMXers shadowed them for a while, pulling wheelies and stunts before becoming bored.

'Yer all fuckin' mad,' one shouted before they both peeled away and pedalled off. The kid had a point: twenty-odd youths jogging round the roads of West Broughton, *not* being chased by the police was a peculiar sight.

At the end of the run, back on Soldiers Field, Rory was easing the hurt of not being part of the team by trying to prove a point. 'Bunch o' fuckin' lightweights,' he taunted as he stepped among the flaked out bodies that were spread across the grass, some with heaving chests, wheezing and rasping for breath, others bent double, coughing up and expelling phlegm. It was easy to spot the smokers among them. All and sundry were doing their best to ignore him as he paced around apparently none the worse after the two and a half mile run. 'Footballers? I've shit 'em,' he scorned.

The two adults weren't faring much better. 'Jesus,' gasped Nobby. 'I didn't think I was that unfit.'

'I know,' said Terry pausing for air. 'I'll have to start going easy on t' roll-ups.'

Sweating profusely he surveyed his fatigued troops. Out of the twenty-seven that had started only nineteen remained, and only about eight of those seemed to take the run in their stride, plus Rory of course. Terry dropped to his haunches and one of the dogs, a Boxer, sauntered over and started licking the sweat from his face.

'He likes you,' said his young master calling the dog to heel.

'He's a grand dog,' said Terry. 'What's his name?'

'Colin.'

'No, I meant the dog's name.'

'Colin,' repeated the lad.

Terry looked up. He noticed there was something odd about this kid. One eye was looking at him, but the other seemed to be gazing somewhere over Nobby's left shoulder.

'Oh,' said Terry after a long pause

'My name's Pete, but everyone calls me One Eye.'

'I see,' said Terry cringing at the very moment the words left his lips. 'And what position do you play?' he asked, quickly changing the subject.

'I'm a goalie...'

* * *

'Mr. Pearson will be with you in a moment, please take a seat,' said the smiling young girl behind the desk. Terry smiled back, said 'Thanks, love' and went and sat in a posh leather number that made farting sounds when you moved about in it. He reached out to the glass table in front of him and picked up a glossy brochure that had the words *"Moving Forward Together"* printed across the front in bold. Ten vignette portraits of council officers and their job titles framed the cover. They grinned up at him looking ever so sincere. He quickly turned the page. The booklet was full of self-congratulatory articles on seemingly useless or quirky projects that wasted council tax money. Terry didn't dwell, he didn't want to put himself in a bad mood for the day. He skipped most of the pages, only stopping near the back of the brochure where there was a section for situations vacant. He looked at some of the posts available and his eyes nearly popped out at the size of the salaries that were on offer: Community Liaison Officer £50,000 - £75,000 per annum; Combined Projects

Co-ordinator £65,000 - £80,000 per annum; Communications Director £85,000 - £110,000 per annum. 'Jesus!' he thought, no wonder the bastards on the front cover were grinning at him. This was the council taking the piss big style. Terry wondered what exactly it was that a Combined Projects Co-ordinator did to warrant such a pay packet. And a Community Liaison Officer, what the hell was one of those? He'd never seen anyone liaising with his community. What about the person that made up all these stupid names? Maybe there was someone in this very building with a sign on their office door saying, '*Job Title Creation Department*'. Most of these pretend posts were no more than fronts for un-elected quangos, jobs for the boys. It was nepotism gone mad. He sighed inwardly. These things didn't surprise him anymore but they still managed to make him feel depressed. The Community Liaison Officer post would more than likely go to a middle class southerner with a sociology degree who'd come up north to take advantage of the cheap house prices and decent curries. Stereotype? Maybe, but Terry knew this was all to do with the gravy train. What the hell did these people care about the community? They didn't even understand the colloquialism, the culture or the history. They were no more than parasitic aliens in an extraneous environment. He would love to lead them by the hand into the real world and show them what a real Community Liaison Officer should be doing. He doubted if they would last a day.

Terry threw the pamphlet back on the table in disgust just as Mike Pearson breezed out of his office.

'Tel! – You old bugger. How the devil are yer?'

'I'm fine, Mike, how are you?' Terry got to his feet and shook him warmly by the hand.

'Oh, buggering on, you know,' said Mike cheerfully. 'Hey, it's good to see yer; you're looking well. Come on in, I'll get you a coffee and we'll have a chat.' He ordered two coffees from the young girl and ushered Terry into his office.

Mike Pearson was head of recreation down at City Hall. He was a really likeable, bubbly character and him and Terry went back a long way. They sat and reminisced about the good old days over their coffee and Terry had a jokey dig at the lush interior of his office saying now he knew what happened to his council tax.

'Y'know,' said Mike 'you and Nobby were the best team I ever had on parks and pitches.'

Terry laughed.

'No, it's true, seriously. Your work on pitch preparation was second to none; perfect in fact. You should see the teams we've got on the job these days, arseholes the lot of 'em. Talking of Nobby how is the big fella? Are you still working together?'

'Yeah, I've just sent him for a load of turf. Got a big job on up Queensgate.'

'Ah, it'd have been nice to see him again. Still, good to know you're keeping busy. So, to what do I owe the pleasure?'

'We're starting a junior football team, Mike, and among other things we need a pitch.'

Mike nodded and dipped into a drawer in his desk, pulling out a thick list.

'Most clubs just phone up for pitch lettings,' he said, leafing through paper, 'but I'm glad you called in person. What area are you looking at?'

'West Broughton,' said Terry hopefully. Mike perused his list for a while, mouthing 'West Broughton' under his breath before slowly shaking his head.

'Nearest thing I've got is up at St. Mary's; Sunday afternoon letting.'

'St. Mary's? That's over four mile away from West Broughton.'

'I know,' said Mike. 'That's the nearest unfortunately. Trouble is, Tel, pitches are becoming scarce; I'm losing around five a year now. You know how it is; building land at a premium, developers come in waving big wads of cash around, the powers that be get greedy and lo and behold before you know it, another thirty houses where a pitch used to be.'

'It's all wrong,' said Terry

'Tell me about it. It doesn't make my job any easier.' Mike looked at Terry sympathetically. 'You know, most junior sides are affiliated to senior clubs and a lot of them have their own pitches. Have you thought of going down that road?'

Terry shook his head. 'I wanted to keep it local, Mike. I want it to be a West Broughton team for West Broughton lads; that's the whole point.'

'Sorry I can't help you further, mate.'

'How much is the St. Mary's pitch?'

'Fifty quid.'

'I don't suppose that's too bad for a year.'

'That's per game, Tel.'

Terry looked like he'd been zapped with a stun gun. 'Per fucking game!' he exclaimed. 'You *are* joking.'

Mike shrugged. 'I don't set the charges, Terry, I just implement 'em.'

Terry thought long and hard. 'What about Soldiers Field?' he finally asked.

'Soldiers Field - you mean West Broughton rec? There hasn't been a pitch on there for years. It's not even on the council list anymore.'

Terry pondered a bit more. 'So, as far as you and the council are concerned West Broughton rec. doesn't exist?'

'Well, of course West Broughton rec. still exists, but officially there's no longer a football pitch there.'

'But what if there was a football pitch there?'

Mike smiled. He knew exactly where Terry was coming from. He thought about it, rubbed his chin a bit and let out a deep breath. 'Look, Terry, I might be sticking my neck out a bit on this, but as long as my name isn't mentioned, you go and do what you have to do. As far as I'm concerned, there isn't a council run football pitch on West Broughton rec, and until somebody above me tells me otherwise, that's how it will stay.'

Mike accompanied his parting handshake with a nod and a wink. 'Really great to see you again, Terry; pop by any time you like and make sure you bring Nobby with you next time.'

'Thanks a lot, Mike; will do.' Terry headed for the door. 'By the way,' he said, turning back. 'Is Trotsky still at the depot?'

'Trotsky? – Oh, you mean Eric Smales. No, he took early retirement sometime last year I do believe.'

Terry nodded and said his goodbyes. He descended the wide, Victorian, stone stairs and smiled to himself. So, Trotsky eventually cut and run. They really must have put the wind up him that day. He smiled even more broadly as he recalled the memory and the indignant look on Nobby's face as he had wiped the Dictator's blood from his jacket. The bluff must have worked because the threat of bringing the law in had never materialised. About a week after Nobby had put him on the floor they had received their P45s through the post. No letter of explanation, nothing, and that was the end of it. Old Eric must have been shitting it but Terry thought the pressure must have been on him from other quarters for him to take early retirement. Still, no doubt the little shit got a good severance for his long and 'loyal' service to the council. Terry imagined Horace dancing a jig around his dustcart, and maybe taking a celebratory dump in Trotsky's briefcase, the day he cleared out his desk.

It was drizzling with rain when Terry emerged at the top of the stone steps outside City Hall. Thirty yards away Nobby was arguing with a traffic warden, the pick-up parked on double yellow lines with a ton and a half of rolled up turf on board.

Perhaps it had been the wrong time to discuss the pitch situation with Nobby. He stood in the middle of the garden in his mud-soaked waterproofs holding a large, sodden square of turf, glowering at Terry. It had rained all afternoon and showed no sign of letting up.

'Soldiers – fuckin' – Field?' he said, letting go of the turf that slammed into the mud at his feet. 'Have yer gone totally fuckin' mad?'

Terry didn't say anything. He stood facing his mate, arms full of rolled up turf, raindrops falling from his waterproof hood in quick, regular patterns, slower ones off the end of his nose. Nobby snatched the topmost piece from Terry's arms, catching him under the chin as he did so, leaving a smear of mud that made him look as though he'd grown a goatee. Nobby unceremoniously dumped this piece next to the other. He was steaming. 'You're beginning to tek the piss now...'

Terry opened his mouth to say something but Nobby was in an unusually bad mood and he wasn't going to be interrupted.

'...First, you leave me to load over a ton o' turf on me own, then I nearly have to smack a traffic warden to stop him givin' us a ticket; half the day's gone and we haven't even laid a quarter of it. I've had ten minutes for me dinner, it's pissing it down an' then you come an' tell me I've got to create a football pitch out of a dumping ground and a bleedin' dogs toilet?'

'We've no alternative,' Terry tried to reason. 'Footie pitches cost fifty quid a game. We haven't got that kind o' money.'

Nobby stopped pounding the newly laid turf with his tamper and rounded on Terry again.

'We haven't got *any* fuckin' money! Look what happened when you asked the lads for a pound a week for subs. We've collected four quid, and two o' that was from Joe and our lad.'

Terry let the rest of the turf fall to the ground. He slowly trudged back to the pick-up.

'I told you it were a daft idea from the start,' Nobby shouted at his back, 'but you never listen to me do yer?'

The two of them hardly spoke a word for the rest of the afternoon. Nobby had insisted that Terry should unload the turf from the pick-up on his own seeing, as he had had to load the stuff up. Nobby laid the pieces like a man possessed and Terry had struggled to keep up with him.

Come knocking-off time they were both knackered and soaked to the skin. Steam rose from their sweating bodies, through damp clothes, misting up the windscreen as they drove home in silence.

It had been a twat of a day, and Terry was looking forward to a hot bath and maybe a good read in order to take his mind off things - no such luck. Jan was on the warpath when he got home. First it was a bollocking for getting mud all over the door handles and kitchen floor, and then there had been a letter from school. Rory had landed himself in detention for the third time in two week and what was he going to do about it? And finally, and totally out of the blue, she wanted a holiday, she deserved a holiday, she was having a holiday; with the kids - and with him if he wanted - but she was having one whether he came or not.

* * *

Nigel Addenbrook was an entrepreneur, an Old Etonian who'd been about a bit and dabbled in lots of things over the years, from managing rock bands as a young man in the sixties, to nightclub owner in the seventies and eighties. He now owned a string of nursing homes throughout the north of England. Terry and Nobby had just won the contract to look after the grounds of three of these homes, locally.

Nigel had warmed to them both on their first meeting. He had liked their down-to-earth attitude and the fact that they didn't put on airs and graces in an effort to impress. He had no hesitation in giving them the business.

The now slightly balding, but immaculately groomed Nigel was paying a flying visit to The Garden Springs Home coincidently as the lads were grafting there one afternoon.

'Ah, Terence, there you are. Glad I've caught you,' he said, approaching in his Armani suit.

'Alrate, Nige'. What's up, mate?' said Terry by way of reply. He quickly wiped his palms down the side of his jeans before shaking Nigel's outstretched hand. The guy smelled as good as he looked expensive. Whatever it was he was wearing it certainly wasn't Old Spice.

'Nothing at all, dear boy, on the contrary,' he said. 'Just thought I'd take this opportunity to congratulate both you and Nobby on the splendid work you're doing. The grounds of all three homes have improved no end since you took them on.'

'Thanks,' said Terry. 'We do us best, y'know.'

'Indeed,' said Nigel, placing his hand on Terry's shoulder and leading him slowly round a flowerbed. 'I only wish we could spread your wings a bit and let your talents loose on some of the other homes.'

'How many have you got?' Terry asked.

'Errm, nine I think altogether - or is it eight now?' He paused and thought a bit 'Yes, eight I do believe. We recently sold one off.' Nigel stopped himself in his tracks as he saw the flowerbed Nobby was working on in the near distance. 'I say, just look at those bedding plants,' he enthused. 'Don't they look magnificent?'

'Yeah,' replied Terry. 'The petunias and begonias look like they're gonna be especially good this year.'

Terry wallowed in Nigel's praise for a bit as they continued to small talk, and then decided this was too good an opportunity to miss. 'Ever got involved in sponsorship, Nige'?'

'Of course, dear boy; why do you ask?'

Terry told Nigel about The Albion, about his hopes and aspirations for some of the local lads on his estate. He laid it on thick, maybe a bit too thick.

'How much do you need?' asked Nigel, producing cheque book and gold pen from the inside pocket of his suit jacket with a certain flourish, like he'd done it a million times before. He looked at Terry expectantly as he clicked the ballpoint ready for action. Terry was visibly taken aback. He was speechless for a few seconds. *Shit!* He was asking him how much? *Think, you idiot, think...*

'Err... four hundred?' Terry said with a rising inflection in his voice that made it sound like faint hope rather than a statement.

Nigel just smiled and began writing. Terry stood there feeling awkward. '*Four hundred*?' said a voice inside his head. '*You cheeky bastard.*' He felt his face flush, and he let out a stifled cough for some strange reason.

Nigel continued smiling. He tore out the cheque and handed it over. 'I've made it out for five,' he said matter of factly. 'I don't know who you want it made payable to, so I've left that bit blank. I hope that's alright.'

Terry didn't know whether to doff his cap, tug his forelock, or fall to his knees weeping. 'Oh... that's great... Thanks,' he managed in a weak voice. He stared at the cheque in disbelief. His hand wouldn't stop shaking. 'Err... what would you like puttin' on the shirts?'

'Oh, don't worry about that,' Nigel dismissed. 'Just make sure you get the boys some decent kit.' He glanced at his Rolex. 'Well, Terence, I'm going to have to dash, unfortunately. If you would be so kind as to let me have some form of receipt for that, for the taxman, you know. Keep up the good work. Bye for now.'

And with that, he was off, over the grass, between the flowerbeds and into his waiting Jag.

Nobby strolled across. 'D'yer think old Nigel's a bit gay?' he asked over Terry's shoulder as they both watched his car disappear down the drive.

'Dunno, but I could have kissed him meself, just now,' replied Terry, passing the cheque over his shoulder for his mate to look at.

Terry found it hard to keep his mind on the job for the rest of the afternoon. Good old Nigel coming up trumps like that. Talk about being in the right place at the right time. Now they could really start to get things organised. They were back on track. He felt giddy think-ing of how they were going to allocate the money. He had been ready to sack it. All those negative vibes coming from Nobby and Jan had done him down. He had almost admitted defeat, his marriage and his friendship tipping the balance.

He thought of Joe and Young Nobby and the rest of the lads. He'd built their hopes up, and now he wouldn't have to let them down. The dream was still alive.

Terry planted out tray upon tray of Marigolds, Busy-Lizzies and Pansies that afternoon, happily talking to himself, occasionally let-ting out a joyous expletive, any passing visitors thinking he was a loony.

Nobby had mixed feelings when he saw the cheque. Yes, of course the money was welcome, but it wouldn't go that far, it would soon be swallowed up; it wouldn't last forever is what he tried to say to an excited, un-listening Terry. It also meant that if The Albion had risen again, so to speak, then there was still the matter of the pitch that had to be fettled and got ready. That meant a lot of hard, un-paid graft, and he, for one, wasn't looking forward to it.

The sun had arced its way over the poplar trees and the nurses were wheeling out residents from the day room onto the patio in front of the conservatory, lining up the old dears in their plaid shawls and tartan blankets, looking like a starting grid for a geriatric grand prix.

In his buoyant mood, Terry looked up from his flowerbed and gave them all a cheery wave. Those who still had the strength and faculties, or could actually see him, waved back. Then, something or someone made Terry look up again. He slowly scanned the parade of old folk warming their weary bones on this pleasant mid-June after-noon. His gaze stopped on a wheelchair-bound figure near the end of the line. An old man; he looked familiar, but he didn't know anyone in a nursing home. He studied the still, vacant looking old chap for a few seconds, then, all of a sudden, the realisation hit him in a wave and he dropped his trowel - it was Herbert Johnson.

5

West Broughton Rec., or Soldiers Field, as it was known locally, was a run down recreation ground that had been neglected and almost forgotten about by the council. In days gone by it had been a well used area where the local kids used to play. It boasted swings, a roundabout, a slide; all the usual rides you would find in a park, and a football pitch that had been in regular use every weekend. Nowadays it resembled a battlefield. It had become a dumping ground, a racetrack for motorbikes and quads, an animal toilet, and a short cut from one part of the estate to another. It was bordered on three sides by houses and a snicket, and on the fourth side, by the perimeter wall of Broughton cemetery. The swings and roundabouts, out of use for over a decade, now stood smashed and vandalised, the rusting skeletal framework testament to the decay and neglect. The slide daubed with tar and faeces, rendering it useless.

Further back in time, long before Terry could remember, it had been a parade and drill ground for soldiers who were billeted in barracks nearby, hence the colloquialism. The barracks, now long gone, were on or around the site of the Fusiliers pub, which must have taken its name from the regiment that was billeted there.

The fifteen lads, who had become regulars at training, grafted hard that Sunday. The stuff they cleared and shifted included two burnt out cars, one motorbike frame, two pushchairs, a supermarket trolley, three smelly mattresses, half a dozen milk crates, a settee, some old carpet, four T.V. cabinets, numerous bicycle components, an ironing board and twenty, heavy duty bags that Terry and Nobby normally used for garden waste that they filled with bricks, stones, glass, bottles, dog shit, used condoms, hypodermics and other various specimens of nasty looking crap.

At the end of the day, having managed to locate faint markings where the perimeters of the old pitch used to be, they all stood back to admire their handy-work. Apart from the well-worn path that now diagonally bisected the field it didn't look too bad; a damned sight better than it had, anyhow. There was still a hell of a lot more work to do but at least it was a start.

Nobby was still feeling sceptical about it all. 'You're never gonna stop folk walkin' across it,' he said. 'It's been a path for at least ten years now.'

'Yeah, but it won't be for much longer, once we've got t'rotivator on it and seeded it,' said Terry.

Nobby shook his head just as a noisy trail bike roared out of the snicket and onto the field from the estate, belching out clouds of blue smoke from its tail; the rider winding open the throttle making the two-stroke engine scream like a demented hornet while his helmetless pillion shouted words of encouragement in an effort to make the straining machine go faster.

'An' how d'yer think yer gonna stop those idiots?' shouted Nobby above the din as the two youths rode straight across the freshly cleared field.

'Ask 'em nicely to go away,' said Terry.

Nobby looked at him. He knew he wasn't being serious. 'Don't be so fuckin' fes – fetich – fecee…'

'Facetious,' helped Terry.

'That's the one,' said Nobby.

Terry called over to Joe and little Ginner. 'Tell Nobby what we've come up with,' he said to the two lads.

'Ginner lives in that house over there,' said Joe pointing to one of the semis overlooking the field.

'So?'

'He can see all t'field from his bedroom.'

'Oh, I see, so every time some pillock decides to plough across on a motorbike, or wants to dump a settee, Ginner here's gonna stop 'em by shouting out of his bedroom window is he?'

Joe looked at his dad. Terry nodded. 'Ginner's got a .22 air rifle,' said Joe.

Nobby paused a moment to allow this little revelation to sink in.

He looked down at Ginner who beamed back a smile and nodded enthusiastically in confirmation.

'What, you're gonna shoot people?' exclaimed Nobby in disbelief.

'Only as a deterrent,' said Terry in all seriousness.

Nobby had heard it all now. His mate had lost it big style. This was an obsession that had gone too far - kids taking pot shots at folk in order to protect a footie pitch? Where would it all end? What wouldn't he stop at? He had visions of queues of people in outpatients down at the infirmary waiting to have pellets removed from their anatomy, while he and Terry and a bunch of thirteen year olds were all stuck in cells down at the bridewell. What the fuck had he gotten himself into? If there was still a spare place left on next week's Blackpool trip, Nobby was seriously thinking of being on it.

* * *

Training had been going well. Six or seven of the lads were what Terry would call half decent to good. The rest, not so brilliant, but they were triers, and Terry was enjoying helping them improve their skills. His own fitness levels had shot up over the last month or so and he felt good in himself.

It was a warm, light summer evening, and he had a healthy sweat on as he jogged the half-mile from Soldiers Field to home. He glowed inwardly just from having a sense of purpose, and outwardly from feeling physically tuned. Everything around him seemed to have a resonance; the noises on the street, the smells; everything appeared amplified. He couldn't explain it, but it felt good, sort of comfortable. It was the feeling of being alive.

Terry came home to a lounge full of golden, sandy beaches and azure, sparkling oceans. Jan and Kath were sitting surrounded by an array of holiday brochures.

Indoors, his perspiration levels rose while his spirits sank. He knew it was confrontation time, and he also knew that Kath was there to lend Jan some moral support.

'Hi, Terry,' Kath said in a half-cringing voice that was accompanied with a weak smile.

'Alrate, Kath, love,' he replied wearily.

Still breathing heavily from his excursions, Terry looked at his wife. She looked back at him with defiance in her eyes.

'I'll go get a shower,' he said after an uncomfortable pause.

'*Clever cow that wife o' mine,*' he thought to himself as he let the refreshing water fall on him, washing away sweat and soap suds. She knew that he wouldn't kick off when Kath was there and as a team they were formidable and persuading. She had planned this well. He would have to be at his diplomatic best. He tried to form a strategy in his head as he towelled himself dry.

'What's all this, then?' he asked, looking sparklingly clean and fresh in his shorts and tee shirt. He was developing a nice even tan through work and training, looking pretty good for a bloke about to turn forty; he could pass for someone ten years younger than that, easy, and right now Jan fancied the hell out of him, but she would have to put those feelings aside as she prepared to do battle with her husband.

'You know what it is,' said Jan, calmly. 'We're looking at holidays.'

'Hmm…' muttered Terry, and went into the kitchen to fetch a can of lager from the fridge. Kath looked at her mate and pulled a face while he was gone. Jan's features remained defiant.

'So, where are you thinking of going then, you two?' Terry pulled the ring on the can and the lager fizzed into life. He took a long drink.

'Not just us two,' said Jan, 'we're looking for all of us.'

Terry stifled a burp and sighed. 'Jan love, we've had all this out before. You know we can't take time out for a holiday.'

'Can't, or won't.'

'Look, if we could, we would. Anyway, I bet they're bloody expensive,' he nodded at the brochures strewn across the coffee table.

'It's just as cheap to go to Majorca as it is to stay in England. In fact it's cheaper.'

'But it's us busiest time,' Terry tried to reason. 'We've got work booked in all through summer.'

'So what's the point then?' said Jan, starting to wind herself up. 'What's the point of you and me going to work day in day out? What's it all for? I thought we were supposed to work to live, not live to work.'

'Yeah, I know, but we've got two new big contracts up and running, we can't just bugger off and leave 'em.'

'They're one day, twice a month. They're still going to be there when you get back.'

Kath decided to put her tuppence-worth in. 'It'd be only for two weeks, Terry. You and Nobby have grafted so hard these last couple o' years to get to where y'are now. You both deserve a break. Alcudia's so nice, and the kids'll love it.'

Terry was silent for a moment, thinking about his response. He had to make sure he said the right thing without backing himself into a corner. He looked from his wife to his mate's wife, one hard and immovable, the other reasoning and imploring. How the hell was he going to get out of this one?

Rory stepped out neatly into the middle of the road and held up his arms, palms facing outwards as if he were a traffic policeman, bringing cars to a sudden halt in both directions. One or two sounded their horns and gesticulated angrily at him. He calmly looked around, checking the coast was clear before waving a come-on in the direction from which he came. Slowly, out of the shadows emerged what looked like two columns of munchkins. There were eight young lads in total, all about Rory's age, split into two lines of four, all evenly spaced and walking in tandem with what looked like long lengths of metal tube on their shoulders. Rory made sure his team were safely across before airily nodding a thank you for being patient to the bewildered motorists and waving them on their way.

The holiday debate was fast turning into an argument, and Terry was losing it.

'Right then, Terry. You do what you want, but me, Kath and the kids are havin' a holiday and that's final.'

Jan knew what his response to this statement would be and then she'd have him; he'd play right into her hands. She'd seen through his bullshit. She'd known all this crap about work commitments was a load of bollocks.

'You can't tek the kids,' Terry said sharply.

She could read him like a book. 'Oh, why?' she asked with a smug expression.

''Cos – you can't...' he said, his voice petering out to a mutter, realising that she'd rumbled him.

She now had him at her mercy and was just about to rip into him about his selfish ways and his stupid obsession with this bloody football lark when the phone rang. Saved by the bell, so to speak, Terry lifted the receiver. It was Joe on his mobile.

'Dad, you'd berra come quick.'

'Why, what's up?'

'It's our Rory.'

'Christ, what's he done now?'

'You'd best come see. We're still up at Soldiers Field.'

'I'm on me way,' said Terry, replacing the receiver. He headed for the kitchen.

Jan got up and followed him. 'Well?'

'It was Joe,' said Terry squeezing into his trainers, 'sounds like our Rory's been up to summat.'

'Oh God, what's he done now?'

'Soon find out,' he said moving to the door. 'See yer in a bit.'

The door closed behind him and all at once Jan felt deflated, frustrated and sick at the thought of what her youngest might have been caught up in this time. She stared blankly at the kitchen cupboards. The carefully prepared tirade she was about to launch at her husband and his intransigence ran through her mind and then evaporated.

By the time Terry got there he had a sweat on again. Nobby was already on the scene, giving it verbal with the gang of lads that were gathered round the pile of scaffolding that lay neatly on the ground.

'What's appertaining?' asked Terry as he approached the group.

Rory stepped forward, eager to put his dad in the picture before his brother got the chance to open his gob and condemn him. 'Got yer some goalposts dad,' he said enthusiastically pointing to the lengths of metal.

Terry looked at Nobby who was wearing his familiar non-committal grin. He shrugged.

'Where the hell have they come from?' Terry demanded.

'Ask no questions, tell no lies,' replied Rory, sagely tapping the side of his nose.

Nobby chortled at that while Terry shook his head in despair.

'He's swiped 'em off a building site,' Joe said in a loud voice.

'Pipe down yer muppet,' retorted Rory.

Terry told them both to button it as they sneered hateful expressions at each other. He studied the heavy-duty scaffolding for a few seconds before turning to Nobby. 'What d'yer think?'

'Well, we can't very well ask 'em to tek it all back, can we?'

Terry studied the haul once more.

'You can stare at 'em all you want,' said Nobby, 'they ain't gonna bleedin' disappear.'

'We've even got yer some elbows, dad,' said Rory helpfully holding up a canvas sack full of metal bits. 'Ashley's dad's a welder; he sez he'll purrem together for us an' even grind 'em down smooth. You just have to tell him what size they need to be.'

Terry looked from Rory holding up his bag of bits, to Nobby, to the scaffolding. 'Bit thin for goalposts; might not be regulation,' he said eventually.

'Ah, a few coats o' paint'll soon thicken 'em up; they'll be rate,' said Nobby positively, while casually taking a tug on his roll-up.

In the distance a familiar sound; the muffled, staccato like machine-gun rhythm offering warning to those up to no good, making all present a little edgy. He would have to make a decision quick.

'Right, let's get the bloody things outta sight quick.'

'We've got some tarpaulin in our hut,' said Ginner.

'Good lad,' replied Terry. Ginner scurried off. Terry looked daggers at Joe and Young Nobby. 'Don't just stand there.'

'We aren't touchin' 'em,' said Joe all surly.

'Don't be such a pair o' lemons,' interjected Nobby before Terry could blow his top. 'C'mon, lend a hand; it's for your benefit; they're gonna be your goalposts.' Nobby took the lead, gathering up three poles at one end. Rory's chums jumped into action while Joe and Young Nobby slowly and reluctantly did as they were told under Terry's watchful stare.

They soon had the contraband neatly tucked away down the side of Ginner's garden fence, camouflaged by the dirty, green-brown tarpaulin.

'Well done, lads,' said Terry. Rory grinned triumphantly, trying to catch his brother's eye, smacking his hands together to rid them of the rust and dust. Joe kept his head down, him and Young Nobby messing around with the football at their feet.

Joe felt resentful of the fact that Rory could go on the rob, get up to all sorts and not get into trouble; get praised for it almost, for fuck's sake. While here he was keeping his nose clean yet getting accused and punished for things he didn't do. Both he and Young Nobby were still being persecuted at school. Certain teachers had markedly changed their attitude and seemed to have it in for them, especially the Rural Studies teacher. It was all bloody wrong, not fair at all. He almost wished he had it in him to be a bad 'un, at least then he wouldn't have that feeling of guilt every time somebody pointed an accusing finger even when he'd done nowt. It seemed to him things were more black and white if you were a scally. You did stuff and you took your chances. Either you got away with it or you didn't. The secret, he knew deep down was not to have a conscience, but he had and sometimes it made him miserable.

He glanced up slyly from his kick-ups. Rory was laughing and larking about with his munchkin mates, revelling in the glory of a job well done. As well as being miserable, Joe also felt envy.

'You lot had better make yourselves scarce,' Terry said to the lads that were left mooching around. 'And you, Amerigo...' he singled out Rory, '...straight home.'

Rory looked shocked and hurt all at once and was about to protest until he saw the widening of his dad's eyes. Knowing exactly the implications of that look he adopted his most put upon face before hunching his shoulders and turning to walk away with his buddies. This time it was Joe's turn to catch his brother's eye and sneer at him. It didn't have much effect.

'Huh, just no pleasing some people, is there?' Rory said loud enough for everyone to hear.

The daka-daka-daka sound got closer and louder until the full, dark, bug-like shape of the police helicopter rose above the nearby rooftops silhouetted by the cobalt to orange to crimson backdrop of the mid-summer evening sky.

'...And if I find you're the reason for that thing being out tonight, you're a dead man, Vespucci,' Terry shouted after him before he disappeared up the snicket.

He had an array of nicknames for Rory, all inspired by whatever book he was reading at the time. At the moment it was Early European Explorers.

Rory *was* the reason for the copper chopper taking to the skies that balmy summer evening. As well as nicking the scaffolding he'd hot-wired a dumper and, egged on by his droogies proceeded to wreak havoc all over the building site. Rory loved an appreciative audience but his show-off antics finally caused him to lose control of the machine, jumping clear just in time before it ploughed through a column of breeze blocks, smashed into some concrete culvert pipes, flipping onto its side and ultimately coming to a halt in a pile of building sand. With the whoops, yee-haas and thunderous applause ringing in his ears, Rory's ego burst through the top of his head. And for an encore and finale, in a flash of inspiration, decided to snaffle the scaffolding. Acting as un-elected leader and using the respect now afforded to him he quickly marshalled his troops and, ten minutes before the law arrived on the scene, the lengths of scaffold lay neatly tucked away in a garden in a corner of Soldiers field.

Back on the building site two officers shone torches and surveyed the scene of devastation created by Rory and his chums. The coppers wouldn't have much sympathy; the place had no security. The builder had done his best to get a firm in, but trying to find a security company who were willing to patrol sites on the Broughton estates was a bit like trying to find a virgin in a brothel.

Above them the helicopter searchlight turned its attentions towards East Broughton and completed a few futile circuits of the estate before returning to base.

6

Noel Reid was a face from the early seventies, an original Northern Soul boy who, back in those days was known throughout the City. He used to be a bit of a legend on the two Broughton estates with his good looks and his trend setting panache for fashion. Noel, along with Mick Gallagher and their crew were stalwarts of the Ian Levine all-nighters at Blackpool's Mecca and the early Wigan Casino days. Myths grew up around this group of pill-popping speed merchants. And their cool, cocky aloofness only served to inflate those myths. They were fighters as well; untouchables; Gods to the likes of Terry and Nobby who looked up to them in awe and juvenile admiration. Even the nutters off East Broughton gave them a wide berth and didn't mess with the likes of Noel.

Terry remembered back to the days when the geezer would call round on his L.I. to see their Mick, and two snotty-nosed ten year olds would slaver around him and his pristine Lambretta with its sparkling array of mirrors and flashing chrome, waiting in hope for him to catch your eye, ruffle your hair and say: '*Hop on then, young un.*' Then he'd take you for a blast round the estate and even tear it up into East Broughton, Apache territory, totally fearless, flash as fuck in front of the heroes; snarling no-marks on street corners looking on in hate and envy who couldn't have even afforded the down payment; rubbing their noses in it as if to say, '*Look at us, arseholes. We're going somewhere. We're gonna make a life out of all this shit while you're gonna wallow on the pan-crack and methadone until you die.*'

Young Terry felt like a king; invincible sat up behind his brother's mate, laughing like a maniac around the streets and avenues while Noel sang *Run For Cover* by The Dells at the top of his voice. Life was good when you were ten.

An age gap of a decade is an almighty chasm when you're young, an insurmountable distance between youthful naivety and the perceived cool, in the know of your peers. As you get older that gap somehow diminishes, grows smaller and eventually closes up altogether.

The hero-like status Terry used to give Noel Reid seemed laughable to him now as he walked through the doors of The Royal Oak to meet the one-time untouchable. The ultra-smart suede-head haircut now gave way to a still neat, but massively receding number two crop. The once chiseled, sharp features transformed to jowls and a double chin. Pallid complexion probably brought on by over a decade of substance abuse, replaced in later years by a lager diet that now accounted for the well-established beer belly. Despite all this, Noel was still one of Terry's brother's mates, a West Broughton lad through and through. Pushing fifty; married, two point four kids, steady boring job; in fact, your regular stereotype; the conformed rebel; tamed, stamped, labelled and pigeonholed. Had he gotten anywhere? Halfway up the ladder maybe. Did he make a life out of all the shit? Hard to quantify. All Terry knew was it had something to do with that youthful spark, that kick of puberty and adolescence that surged you forward into manhood. It acted like a booster rocket propelling you onwards through life's experiences. It just depended on how much fuel you had in your rocket. Terry likened that energy to the amount of ambition you had. Around here though, ambition was never enough. You had to have the breaks as well.

Noel Reid's booster rocket had fallen back to Earth in the gravitational pull of conformity sometime in his late twenties, early thirties. At least the exuberance, defiance and determination he had displayed in his youth had kept him out of the mire. Now you had to be grateful for what you'd got. Noel had his family, his two weeks holiday abroad, his mates, his football and his lager, and as Terry approached him at the bar the guy seemed content enough.

Noel's playing days were well behind him, but he'd run the senior Sunday side at The Royal Oak for years, and Terry and Nobby had kicked their last ball in anger under his guidance at The Oak a few seasons back. Noel was no Alex Ferguson, the side usually picked itself and they were always a mid-table team, but he had good organisational skills; he was an excellent fund-raiser and had always managed to keep the club afloat on a tight budget. Terry was hoping to pick up a few hints and tips, and their Mick had said he thought he might have a spare pair of nets going begging.

Terry bought the drinks and Noel tried to give him an appreciation of running a football team. He painted a grim picture. Basically, it was a thankless task and he couldn't really explain to Terry why he'd done it all these years. ''Cos no bugger else would,' he supposed.

The fiver a week the lads paid in subs didn't cover costs and he had to run domino cards, raffles, and organise race nights on a regular basis. Unbeknown to his missus, Noel had baled the club out on more than one occasion, dipping into his own pocket to pay County F.A. affiliation and registration fees. He held a special contempt for the County F.A. 'Greedy set o' bastards,' he called them, with reference to the draconian fines they had to pay out for yellow and red card offences. He noted the opulence and the seemingly endless refurbishment that went on at County headquarters every time he was summoned on disciplinary matters. 'The whole fuckin' place is swimming in money,' he griped.

Terry listened impassively. He wasn't surprised or put off by the tales of woe Noel was relating about his dealings with the old duffers at the County F.A. It was just another example of an inefficiently run hierarchical organisation full of dinosaurs and blazers who squandered bulging coffers while the grass roots, backs to the wall, suffered and struggled for survival. He'd seen it so many times before. It just made a change to hear someone else doing the moaning.

Noel got his round in, then eased himself off his bar stool and went in search of the old, spare set of nets he thought might be still kicking around in the pub's cellar.

Terry walked through to the taproom where Nobby was sitting talking to a face he hadn't seen around West Broughton in a long time.

Smiffy-No-Teef was an old lag; an ex-borstal boy; a car thief, burglar, fraudster, drug dealer, receiver and fence. In short, a villain, but a likeable villain if there was such a thing. He'd spent more time in H.M prisons in his life than he had at liberty, so you couldn't really say he was a successful criminal.

Smiffy didn't notice Terry approach and stand behind him as he excitedly spun some sordid sexual story to Nobby.

'…I swear to God, Nobby, she warra right dirty cow. She'd had it in her gob for ten minutes, merrily noshin' away, ven all of a sudden, out o' ver blue, ver mucky bitch asks me to piss on her…'

Nobby was grinning over Smiffy's shoulder up at Terry who smiled and shook his head in pity, taking sips of Guinness while listening in.

'So…did yer?' asked Nobby.

'Well, I warra bit shocked at first, I mean, I didn't even need a fuckin' piss.'

'So, what did yer do?'

'I said, whoa, love, you'd berra chomp on vis a bit more 'till I've finished me special brew, ven we'll see what we can manage.'

Terry nearly choked on his pint but Smiffy still didn't notice his presence.

'And…?' urged Nobby.

'Oh, I gave her a golden shower in't end up, but I wa' concentrating so hard trying to piss, I lost me boner an' went all floppy, proper put me off me stride it did.'

'Did yer let her have a go then?'

'What, let her piss all over me?' asked Smiffy indignantly. 'Like 'ell I did…'

'Urolagnia,' said Terry.

Smiffy spun round on his seat. 'Tez! - You old bugger,' Smiffy happily exclaimed in his thin, rasping voice that sounded like he'd been smoking too much saltpetre-based prison snout. His gob opened into a bottomless black chasm that Terry took to be a welcoming grin. Apart from one or two dodgy looking molars at the back, Smiffy's mouth was devoid of any teeth. They'd been removed violently some years back while on remand by some lag who'd lost out on one of Smiffy's shady deals. His thin, dark, lanky hair lay plastered to his skull, barely covering the crudely carved and badly faded cross that he'd had tattooed to his forehead as a youth. The two swallows either side of his neck, although professionally done, were also naff looking and faded. Four or five days growth on his face didn't enhance the overall impression, and viewing him at close quarters like this, Terry thought that the story he'd just been telling Nobby had to be pure fantasy, 'cos nobody blessed with sight would surely entertain this ugly bastard sexually. More than likely it had been a scene lifted directly from one of his recently viewed porn videos, of which he was renowned for having a vast collection. Smiffy-No-Teef was also a romancer; anyone who knew him well would take everything he said with a pinch of salt.

Terry gingerly took his outstretched hand then endured his 'Hail fellow well met' embrace. Apart from the halitosis and sour body odour, Smiffy was excreting another pungent, musk like stink; familiar and not entirely unpleasant, Terry couldn't quite place it.

'Uro – what?' said Nobby as Terry pulled up a stool.

'Urolagnia. It's the correct term to use when people get their kicks by pissing on each other, like felatio means blow-job, or cunnilingus means muff-diving.'

Nobby gave him the look. 'Trust you to know that,' he said, emptying his glass and getting up to go to the bar. He nodded at Smiffy. The black hole opened up in a wide grin again and he gave Nobby the thumbs up, displaying a fist full of gold sovereign rings as he did so.

Smiffy began at once to spin a yarn full of exaggeration and improbability. Terry switched off. He sat and studied the ragamuffin jailbird, oblivious to his jabber.

Smiffy was sporting a dirty, grey shell-suit that had once been white, a dubious piece of fashion wear at best. His out of date wardrobe evidence that he'd spent quite a length of time at Her Majesty's.

'*By Christ, this pillock can talk for England,*' thought Terry while Smiffy rambled on. Maybe it had something to do with being banged up for so long, the routine and monotony of confinement sending him a bit stir-crazy; months and months of stagnant conversation with screws and cellmates in Armley and Strangeways effectuating the need for stimuli in conversation and the urge to relate fantastic stories upon release.

Nobby came back from the bar with the drinks and interrupted Smiffy's diatribe. 'So, what new scam are yer on with now then, Smiffy?'

He frowned while eagerly relieving Nobby of the pint of lager. With an unsteady hand, he downed almost half of it in one go and let out a satisfied growl before replying. 'No more scams for me, lads,' he said with a determinedly serious expression on his face. 'I'm on t'straight an' narrer veese days.' He looked at Terry and Nobby in turn. They offered no response. 'I swear to God, I'm never goin' back inside.' He paused, reflectively. 'I couldn't hack it - it'd kill me.'His features, all of a sudden took on a haunted look. The lads gave each other a quick, knowing glance like they'd heard it all before.

Smiffy looked up, like he could read their minds. 'I'm serious, boys. I've been off ver skag for nearly two years now. I'm gerrin' me shit togever. I'm goin' legit.'

He'd only started using heroin while inside, just to numb the pain; help get him through the days, the weeks, and the months. It was only meant to be a crutch, a chemical sanctuary where he could escape the daily mental drudge of prison life. But he ended up with a state sponsored habit, a ten-year addiction courtesy of a compliant and complacent system that unofficially turned a blind eye. In return they got compliant inmates; deferent like zombies who rarely caused grief and were unlikely to rock the boat. Back on the streets, and now institutionally criminal, they became society's problem and with a habit to fund and feed, the whole vicious circle ground on. Like Terry often thought; the powers that be were either incredibly stupid and naïve, or they were following a more sinister, hidden agenda.

Smiffy had the classic drug-ravaged demeanour; skull-like features, dark, sunken eye sockets, semi-permanent D.T's, and that thin, rasping voice that sounded like his vocal chords had been shredded.

Terry was glad to hear he was off the smack. He could sense the determination in his voice, but his body shook with a kind of nervous agitation. One of his legs was going ten to the dozen and he could still see fear in his eyes.

With a furtive glance around him, Smiffy beckoned the boys in close, all conspiratorial. 'I've got meself a great little business up an' running,' he whispered, 'an' it's gonna pay off big-style in a week or two.'

Terry and Nobby looked at him expectantly.

'Hydrotonics,' he said finally.

The boys frowned and looked at each other, puzzled.

'Y'know, ver old stuff; I'm growin' it.'

'Growin' what?' asked Nobby, still none the wiser.

'Y'know – shit, weed; ver old herb – fuckin' *ganja*, man!'

'Ahh,' the pair of them said together, leaning back.

'You mean Hydroponics,' said Terry.

'Vat's what I fuckin' said,' replied Smiffy, sharply.

Terry's brain clicked and he at last twigged what the sickly sweet aroma wafting across from Smiffy's direction was.

He told them all about his secret dope factory, how it was nigh on impregnable and about his staff, the lads he employed to check and tend the plants regularly. Terry was about to counter him and say, 'I thought you said you were going legit,' but then stopped himself, because he realised that Smiffy must have genuinely thought he was doing no wrong, that he was actually running a bona fide business. In his eyes, the growing and supplying of marijuana obviously wasn't a crime. He was being a good citizen, providing employment and paying good wages.

Terry and Nobby listened and learned at length about his entrepreneurial venture.

'…Oh, aye, I've forked out a small fortune for all t'gear; seven hundred an' fifty quid just on lightin'. But I'll be seein' a nice, fat, juicy return for me investment when vat first crop's ready. Won't be long now,' he said, rubbing his gold-laden hands together.

Terry asked how he'd come to learn about Hydroponics and Smiffy told him about how he'd shared a cell with a guy, a dope grower who'd been busted and who'd told him there was big, easy money to be made if you went easy on the product and didn't get careless like he had.

It was the time when Smiffy had been determined to wean himself off heroin, so, in an almighty effort to concentrate his mind, in between bouts of cold turkey, he spent the hours picking his cellmate's brain, gleaning the techniques and knowhow. He even started visiting the prison library seeking out books on horticulture, much to the astonishment of the librarian who had assumed that Smiffy was semi-literate at best.

His seemingly newfound interest had come to the attention of the governor who, sensing some sort of reform in one of his more regular patrons, albeit late in the day, had been happy to encourage his request to work in the prison gardens and greenhouse. Here he learned about cultivation; how to take cuttings, when to feed and when not to feed; about nutrients, male and female plants and hybrids.

On his release, Smiffy had all the Knowledge he needed. A quick trip to Amsterdam for the best seeds; top drawer strains of 'Northern Lights', 'White Widow', and 'Skunk no.2'; a cash input from a couple of investors, discreet, out of the way premises, and after a month or so he was up and running.

'…Oh, an' I've bought a greyhound,' said Smiffy, going off on a tangent.

Nobby looked at him daft. 'A greyhound's no good,' he said. 'You need an Alsatian or a Rottweiler, summat fierce an' nasty.'

Smiffy gave him an equally daft look in return. 'No, yer silly bugger, I haven't bought it for a guard dog; it's a racer - Ballymoney Boy, out of Ireland.'

'Is he any good?' asked Terry.

'Oh aye, he's from good stock. His favver won plenty.'

'Have yer raced him yet?'

'Yeh, just ver once.'

'How did he do?'

'Came second to last,' Smiffy said without altering his expression.

The lads frowned and looked sideways at one another.

'I thought you said he were good,' Nobby snorted.

'Oh, he is.'

'Fuckin' sounds like it.'

Smiffy shook his head, and his mouth opened up into a wide, black grin again. Nobby wished he'd stop doing that.

'No, Nobby lad, va don't understand. It's like vis va sees,' Smiffy explained. 'He's got form. He won his first four races in Ireland; absolutely pissed on ver opposition. I've bought ver bugger to mek me money, so if he starts winnin' over here, he's gonna be odds on straight away, does va see?' Nobby slowly nodded his head. 'So, gerrim to finish near t'back o' t'field for a few races, wait for his odds to lengfen, pick a big meet, lay off plenty o' big bets, Ballymoney Boy romps home, an Smiffy has yet anuver big juicy return for his investment.' He tipped the rest of his lager down the black slit, wiped his whiskers with the back of his ringed hand and sat back contentedly.

'Hang on,' said Terry, 'If he's so good, how d'yer stop him winning?'

'Ah,' said Smiffy, leaning forward and drawing the pair of them in close again, even though there were only three other punters in the taproom and they were glued to *Football Focus* on the telly. 'Sleeping tablet crushed into half a gallon o' milk an hour before t'race,' he winked.

'You sneaky fuck,' said Nobby.

'Don't they test 'em?' asked Terry.

'Vey do on t'national circuit. Veese are Flappin' tracks, not as keen, yer see. Yer can gerraway wi' it if yer pick yer meets carefully.'

'Won't feedin' him all that shit knacker him up for when he needs to win?'

'Oh, no, I train ver fuck out of him in between races. Me an' Pikey George tek ver Terriers up into Baghall Woods, cop for a few live rabbits, choose a nice, steep hill, set up a drag line, connect it to a twenty-four volt battery, tevver t'rabbit an' off yer go.'

'Is it dead?' enquired Nobby.

'What, ver rabbit? Is it fuck,' laughed Smiffy.

'You cruel get.'

'Fink about it, charver,' reasoned Smiffy. 'What's gonna get ver dog racin' up vat hill quicker; a piece o' dead meat on a line, or a squealin' shitein' rabbit fightin' for its life?'

The lads stewed on the image for a second or two before reluctantly agreeing with Smiffy's reasoning.

'It's ver fear he smells, yer see,' continued Smiffy. 'He goes absolutely fuckin' barmy. Teks me all me time to hod him back. Ven, when I lerrim go - foom! He's up vat hill like greased lightnin'.'

'Does he ever catch it?' asked Nobby, not really wanting to know the answer.

'Oh, aye,' enthused Smiffy, now revelling in Terry and Nobby's discomfort at the thought. 'Yer should hear it scream.'

'Does he eat it?' asked Terry.

'Nah, just rips it to fuckin' bits, ven Pikey George lets t' Terriers go, an' vey join in.'

'Jesus.'

'Oh, he has to do or vey'd strangle on ver chokers.'

Noel walked in and dumped a tangled set of nets and a bag of deflated footballs on the floor by the bar. 'I'll leave 'em here for you, Terry,' he said. 'They're not in bad nick, just might need a bit o' sortin' out. And I've found a bag of old practice balls you can have; just need some air in 'em; might put yer on for a bit.

Terry was thankful for Noel's interruption. He'd heard enough of Smiffy's dog and rabbit story.

'Nice one, Noel, thanks a lot, mate; I owe yer.'

'No problem, see yer later. See yer later, Nobby.'

'Cheers, Noel.'

'How's it goin', Noel, mate?' grinned Smiffy.

Noel stopped at the door and stared. 'You're no fuckin' mate o' mine, yer scruffy lookin' cunt,' spat the former soul-boy before making his exit.

'Nice fella,' said a bemused Smiffy, trying to rack his brain as to what he might have done over the years to upset the one time local hero.

Terry felt pleased. They'd got themselves a pitch, some goalposts, a set of nets and some balls and they hadn't even touched Nigel's cheque yet. 'Sorted,' he said to Nobby. 'All we need is a kit, now.'

Smiffy's ears pricked up, and Terry had to tell him all about The Albion.

'So you're after a footie kit ven, are yer?' Smiffy asked.

'Yeah, why, can you gerrus one? Cheap?' enquired Nobby.

Smiffy shrugged, trying to look disinterested now he had their attention. 'Dunno, mebee. Depends on how much yer wanna spend.'

'Two hundred quid; cash on delivery,' said Terry straight away.

Smiffy blew out his cheeks and tugged at the bristles on his chin. 'Well, I'll have to mek some enquiries, see what we can do,' he said eventually, while rattling his empty glass on the table and eyeing it expectantly. Terry took the hint and headed for the bar.

'For that, I want fifteen full strips, a goalie kit, training tops an' four sub-suits,' Terry demanded on his return, setting down three fresh pints.

'Jesus, yer don't want much, do yer?' protested Smiffy.

'An' they'd better not be knock-off.'

Smiffy pulled a face and pretended to be all hurt at the suggestion. 'Boys, I've told yer; I'm all legit now. Fully guaranteed, ex warehouse stock; no problems.'

Terry wasn't daft. He knew that for two hundred the gear would definitely be a bit warm, but buying an over-the-counter kit would take most of their money and leave them skint again, and they still had to budget for things like referees, registration fees and the like.

'But I won't be able to guarantee what colours yer get, chor,' Smiffy added.

'That's okay,' conceded Terry.

'As long as there's no red in it,' said Nobby.

7

Cross hairs slowly scanned the field searching for a target, a sea of empty green, meandering into a garden, pausing briefly on an empty milk bottle, then, quickly upwards, a blur of red brick and grey roof slate, settling finally on a twitchy looking blackbird perched atop a ridge tile. Back down at ground level, noise and movement: a large, paisley pinafore-clad backside danced into view and filled the telescopic sight. Betty Lightowler was pegging out her washing.

'Betty Swollocks – yer big fat mare,' Ginner breathed silently to himself. His heart raced a little and his finger tightened over the trigger. Betty bent over her washing basket and the target became tantalisingly taught. The cross hairs steadied centrally on a piece of paisley design and Ginner's trigger finger squeezed.

A dull thwack, followed a nanosecond later by an ear piercing scream broke any calm. Joe and Young Nobby who had been deeply engrossed in *Grand Theft Auto 2* on the Playstation spun round in unison just in time to see Ginner duck down under the windowsill and grin mischievously up at them.

'What the fuck have yer done, Ginner?' Joe asked approaching the window.

'Gerraway from t'fuckin' window,' Ginner hissed. 'I've just shot Betty Swollocks up the arse.'

Joe and Young Nobby bobbed down sharply and joined Ginner under the window.

'Was she on t'pitch?' asked Young Nobby.

'Nah, she wa' peggin' out her washin.'

'What the fuck d'yer shoot her for then, yer gloit?' demanded a nonplussed Joe.

''Cos I wa' fuckin' bored,' Ginner rasped, trying hard to keep his voice down.

Betty kept calling for her husband with great distress in her quivering voice. Harold Lightowler eventually emerged from the house, slippers on his feet, fag drooping from a corner of his mouth, braces dangling and clutching his newspaper, annoyed at having his ablutions so rudely interrupted.

'What the bloody hell's going on? What's all t'shouting about? What's up wi' yer, woman?'

Betty was shaking, red in the face and rubbing her ample behind. 'Oh, Harold - oh, my God, I've been shot.'

'Shot?' he said with dubiety in his voice. 'What d'yer mean you've been shot?'

She tried to forget the immense pain she was in for a moment while still gingerly caressing her stinging backside in order to formulate an adequate response to her dopey spouse. What did he think she meant?

'Are you alright Betty, love?' said a voice from over the fence. 'I just heard all this screaming.'

'Oh, June, love…' said Betty, fawning over to her next-door neighbour, silently thanking the Lord for a saviour and a sympathetic ear. '…I've just been shot.'

'Shot?'

'Shot – just there…' Betty pointed to the wounded area and began to intimate the incident to her open-mouthed friend.

The boys sat huddled, listening in through the open window, stifling giggles. Harold Lightowler stood scratching his head not really knowing what to do, so he walked to the end of the garden, took a tentative look around, shrugged his shoulders and shuffled back indoors while his wife was being ushered next door for a soothing cup of tea and a closer inspection of the injury.

School was out for summer and the lads had formed a pitch protection roster that was pinned up in Ginner's bedroom; all the boys in pairs, round the clock shifts, four hours per shift. They'd formed a league on *Pro Evolution Soccer 3* to try and relieve the boredom and One Eye had quickly assailed a nine-point lead at the top of the table.

The endless procession of pubescent bodies would cause the atmosphere in Ginner's bedroom to become a little funky over the next couple of months and Ginner's mum would give it a wide berth, only daring to push open the door enough to administer a few quick blasts of air freshener before beating a hasty retreat.

The air rifle ruse had proved to be an effective deterrent. Potential fly tippers and dumpers soon got the message, as did the motorbike boys. They'd be the last to go complaining to the police about a hidden maniac sniping at people. Those who ignored the police barrier tape that the lads had acquired and had circled the pitch with, or the odd polite notice that said please keep off the grass, were given a warning shot across the bows and if they persisted, a pellet up the posterior. The folk who still used Soldiers Field as a thoroughfare now did so nervously and a new path had begun to be worn around the perimeter.

The dogs of West Broughton weren't the type to be led around on leads by their owners, they were free spirits, left to roam their chosen domain and patrol their territory solo or in packs. Now, there were at least a dozen poor, confused mutts, licking their wounds, trying to get their heads round this new, unseen adversary while looking for pastures new in which to do their toilet.

The pitch itself was beginning to look fantastic. Terry and Nobby had seeded or turfed where necessary and they fed it with their own special batch of fertilizer made from old, mulched grass cuttings that produced a thick, brown-coloured smelly goo oozing all the right nutrients. The old path that cut across the field had all but disappeared and a lush carpet of deep green was beginning to develop.

Betty peeled away layer upon layer of undergarments. She undid and let fall to the floor an old-fashioned type corset, a sight that even made her friend raise her eyebrows, amazed that there were people still wearing such things, but then again, this was Betty Lightowler who still wore a paisley pinafore, who pre-soaked her washing in *Dolly-Blue* and steeped her peas in sodium bicarb overnight.

Betty finally got down to flesh, and in the middle of one cheek of her sizeable derriere was an angry-looking red welt. June, her neighbour, audibly drew breath at the sight, but immediately thought that it could have been a lot worse if it hadn't been for the body armour Betty was sporting. She prescribed zinc and castor oil in order to draw out any bruising, and they discussed the sniper menace while June rooted around in her medicine cabinet.

Betty was a professional moaner, not happy unless she was complaining about this or the other. Her griping had become habitual over the years; it had become a way of life and she probably no longer knew she was doing it. Shopkeepers and tradesmen dreaded her, and poor old Razi Ahmed often bore the brunt of her acid and sometimes-racial tongue-lashings. She lived in a time warp and neither understood or cared about the concept of political correctness. To call her a bigot would be unfair. She just lacked tact and believed in calling a spade a spade. She belonged to a bygone era.

When the lads tended to get a bit vocal during training, she would come to the end of the garden and give them a rollocking for using bad language. This only made them worse. They called her Betty Swollocks but she never understood the spoonerism. Terry would try and apologise for the lads and would go through the motions of moving them away and chastising them. She said he wasn't fit to be in charge and that he was no better than them. He resisted the temptation to tell her to fuck off, and would nod his head in obeisance and smile diplomatically. She reminded him of the Ena Sharples character that used to be in Coronation Street.

Harold Lightowler had learned to switch off over the course of their forty-nine year marriage. He lived in a self-imposed cocoon, oblivious to his wife's querulousness, caring only for his beloved racing pigeons now that he was in the twilight of his years. As long as the snipers left his birds alone they could shoot who they bloody-well liked, and seemingly, that included his missus.

Betty's pride was beginning to hurt as much as her arse and she was gearing herself up to go on the warpath.

'I know who it is; it's that little ginger haired kid o' Sheila

94

Thompson's. There's folk going in and out o' that house all day long; it's like Briggate on a Saturday afternoon.'

'Now, you don't know that, Betty.'

'Oh aye, you mark my words; it's him all right. Him and his mates are forever giving me cheek. And the language - well, you've never heard anything like it; it's disgusting. They wouldn't have gotten away with it in my day, I can tell yer.' Betty paused to blow a foghorn-like sound into her hankie and reflect on long-gone halcyon days. 'They're dragged up, no manners, no respect,' she continued bitterly while June busied herself with tidying the bathroom. 'Of course, I blame the parents - well, I suppose if you can call 'em parents. She's had more fellers than you and me have had hot dinners that one, and that lad's not his. There's no ginger hair in that family for a start. And they've all got different surnames,' she tutted in disgust. 'What a carry on.'

'But you've no proof it was him, Betty,' reasoned June. 'Nobody saw him do it, so you can't go round accusing.'

Betty wasn't listening. 'I bet that useless lump of a husband o' mine won't have bothered to phone the police yet, he leaves everything to me, you know. He's like a great big kid himself sometimes. He'd be happy to let me wipe his backside for him if I offered.'

'What good would phoning the police do? They'll take hours to respond, if at all, and like I've said, you've no evidence. It'd be a total waste of time.'

'They'll have to get a search warrant,' Betty persisted. 'They shouldn't be able to get away wi' these things; it's criminal. There'd be none o' this if they did their jobs properly. I've paid my taxes all these years. I'm entitled to some protection...'

June raised her eyes to the heavens while Betty droned on and silently prayed to God that she wouldn't start bringing the blacks and Asians into it. She laid Betty's garments neatly side by side over the edge of the bath noticing that curious mixed smell of potato peelings, stale lavender and wintergreen that went with them.

'...Rene Hepworth got shot coming over t'field t'other day y'know.'

'Did she? I never heard that.'

'Oh, aye – carrier bag full o' shopping – the evil little swine shot her – her leg was covered in red.'

'What – blood?' asked June, shocked.

'Well, no, it was chopped tomatoes, but it could have been blood if that can hadn't stopped the bullet.'

June let out a sigh of relief and shook her head. 'They're not bullets, Betty love. What you've been shot with is an air rifle, they fire pellets not bullets.'

'Bullets, pellets, what does it matter? They could still have somebody's eye out, and you shouldn't go around mekin' excuses for 'em, any road up.'

'I aren't mekin' excuses for 'em, I was just saying....'

'That's the trouble these days, yer see,' Betty interrupted. 'Too many do-gooders; too many folk mekin' excuses for 'em all the time; give 'em an inch and they tek a yard. It's a slippery slope we're on, you mark my words; it'll all end in tears....'

June gave up. She gave Betty a sympathetic, yet pitiful smile and handed her acres of dull, brown hosiery that was the first layer of her many layers of clothing. Betty felt like she needed a lie-down, that in itself was going to be difficult. She felt angry and helpless, and the combination was making her bilious. She was a strong, spirited woman, but deep down she knew that her morals and her social principles didn't count for much any more. Common decency was a rare commodity in people nowadays and she lamented for what she still perceived were the good old days. She'd had her name down for a new hip for the past eighteen months but she felt sick at the thought of how the pending operation might debilitate her. Always fiercely independent, Betty looked forward with mounting trepidation to a future where her reliance on a state that didn't give a damn about good, honest, hard working folk, in a world that was fast becoming alien, would be her living hell.

She looked at herself in the bathroom mirror; face still flushed and flustered, her pounding heart still not willing to slow down as she fastened up her paisley pinafore. She didn't want to admit it to herself, but she felt scared.

It was Young Nobby's turn for sniper detail while Ginner showed Joe his favourite porn site on the net. A few of the lads had a Playstation 2 or an X Box, but Ginner, he had the lot: latest P.C. with flat screen monitor, *and* broadband. His room was littered with all the latest games, gadgets and gizmos. The Thompsons certainly weren't affluent, but his mam's current fella was forever coming home with the latest state-of-the-art gear; microwaves, hi-fis, mobile phones. They even had a massive plasma screen telly in the front room that looked and sounded fantastic, although oddly out of place as it filled an entire end of the lounge in the small ex-council semi. Ginner never bothered to ask what he did for a living, nor did he care, as long as the goodies kept rolling in. His mam's chap seemed to know a lot of people and could call in plenty of favours, like the guy who fixed them up Sky for free.

All the lads were envious of Ginner and the material stuff he possessed, but he had become blasé about it. He just shrugged his shoulders and took it all for granted. The main thing for Ginner was that the bloke treat his mam well, at least he wasn't a bastard like plenty of the others she'd had in the past. He looked after them, and in Ginner's book he was all right. To him, the material stuff was just a bonus.

'Hey up, she's back out,' hissed Young Nobby all of a sudden.

Joe and Ginner abandoned *Lusty Lesbian First Timers* and edged along the bedroom wall to the window, S.A.S. fashion. Cautiously, they peeked round opposite corners of the window reveal while Young Nobby tentatively stuck his head up above the sill, clutching the rifle, feeling like a trench soldier sticking his head above a parapet.

'Harold!' boomed Betty's voice.

Simultaneously, and as quick as lightning, the three heads ducked back out of sight.

'Harold! Have you phoned the police yet?' she bellowed loud

97

enough for the whole estate to hear. 'June says I'm going to have a bruise the size of a dinner plate!' She ambled down her garden path shouting after her husband who was probably still sitting on the bog reading *Fur and Feather* trying to get a bit of peace and quiet.

Joe and Ginner slid down the wall trying to stifle the sniggers. When they finally heard Betty's back door slam shut, all three of them exploded with raucous guffaws; full-on belly laughter; rolling and kicking around Ginner's bedroom floor, smashing C.D. covers and sending D.V.Ds flying.

'Size of a fuckin' dinner plate!' wheezed Ginner.

'A fuckin' dinner plate!' repeated Joe, holding his hands out to emphasize the magnitude.

The image made Young Nobby convulse and choke at the same time, which caused him to involuntary let fly with a giant snot-bog, the three and a half inch tail of which was left dangly, swingy from his nose. The ensuing mixture of hilarity and disgust manifest itself with strange, animal-like howling noises from Joe and Ginner, their faces contorted with the pain of extreme mirth. Joe was holding his stomach with one hand and pointing like an idiot at Young Nobby with the other. Every time he dared look at his mate he just cracked up and had to look away again. Ginner was trying to say something but he couldn't get the words out, in fact he could hardly fucking breathe. He was laughing so hard he thought he might die, but this wasn't funny anymore, it actually hurt. Something had to give and Ginner eventually dropped his guts: a S.B.D. Young Nobby was busy cuffing his slimy appendage as the lethal aroma reached Joe's nostrils. He reeled away, repulsed, mirth-mood evaporating fast.

'You mucky ginger twat!' exclaimed Joe while cupping his nose and mouth.

The gas attack soon reached Young Nobby.

'Fuck! That's evil,' he conceded with authority, him being a renowned fart connoisseur and master artisan.

'I can't help it,' whined Ginner 'It's all t'excitement and adrenaline what does it.'

There was a loud knock on Ginner's front door and his guts instinctively responded again. 'Who's that?' he whispered scared to Joe and Young Nobby.

'It's the Feds,' said Joe.

'Bloody 'ell, they were quick,' said Young Nobby.

'Are yer gonna answer it, then?' Joe looked at Ginner.

'No – you go,' pleaded Ginner.

'Go get yer face fucked – it's your house.'

Ginner looked at them both, afraid to move.

'I'll go,' Young Nobby said eventually.

'Yo,' said Joe as his mate headed for the door. 'Don't yer think you'd better leave t'rifle?'

Ginner snatched the weapon from him and hurriedly slung it in his wardrobe. Young Nobby headed off downstairs. Ginner looked at Joe nervously. Joe stared back at him distastefully.

'You've gone an' shit again, 'aven't yer?' he said.

Joe tried to appear nonchalant as the sound of feet on stairs got closer, while Ginner, in a blind panic, hurriedly shut down the porn site. There was an overly loud knock on the bedroom door and both lads froze.

'C.I.D.,' said a voice. 'Open up in there, we have a warrant.'

Ginner's eyes widened. Joe relaxed, pulled a face knowingly, went to the bedroom door and flung it wide open. Peycos, Sasquatch and Young Nobby were all stood there with big, stupid grins on their faces. It was time for their shift.

'Peycos, yer numpty,' said Joe with a sneer.

'Alrate, lads – had yer goin' there, didn't we?'

'Yer bollocks need to drop a bit more before you sound owt like a policeman, yer girl.'

The lads entered the room and knocked their heads on the stink.

'Jesus, a bit ripe in here, innit?'

'Has summat crawled up your arse an' died, Ginner?' enquired Sasquatch.

With the exception of Joe, who played in midfield, the rest of the lads in the room would become The Albion's back four: Jon Pejkozovic (Peycos) right back. John Clarke (Young Nobby) centre back.

Ben Neary (Sasquatch) centre back. Darren Thompson (Ginner) left back.

Peycos was of average weight and size, not much of a footballing brain but he liked to get stuck in.

Young Nobby was a cool and commanding centre-half in the Beckenbaur mould. Not blessed with great pace but could read the game well. Him and Sasquatch (so named because of his unfeasibly large feet; he already wore a size eleven boot) were around five eleven in height and both were still growing.

Little Ginner was small but quick; his low centre of gravity made him tricky and elusive.

Joe liked to think of himself as a midfield General. He had plenty of skill and good vision, but Terry, always his harshest critic, thought that he sometimes held onto the ball too long and failed to play the options quickly enough.

The lads took five minutes to exhaust their repertoire of fart jokes and phrases and generally give Ginner some stick before relating the morning's events to the afternoon shift. Joe had a quiet word in Peycos's ear before him and Young Nobby removed themselves from the rank surroundings of Ginner's room.

'Are we gerrin' t'league up on t'computer then?' asked Sasquatch.

'Sod the league,' said Peycos. 'What's this *Lusty Lesbian Lovers* I'm hearin' about?'

Joe and Young Nobby left them to their filth.

8

Rory carefully and gently removed the snail from the underside of the Hoster leaf. He brought the mollusc up to his face and studied it closely.

'Hey, how *you* doin'?' he said in a Joey from Friends Brooklyn accent. He inquisitively poked at the two stalky eyeballs and watched them retract into the snail's head. He poked and prodded a bit more until the creature got fed up with this treatment and squirmed and slithered until its slimy body had retreated safely into its shell. He put it in the bucket with the others.

Since the onset of the six-week holidays, Rory had been working with his dad and Nobby. Both Jan and Terry had agreed that, in order to keep him out of trouble, he should do three days a week. For this he would get a tenner a day. Joe and Young Nobby would work the other two days and would get fifteen quid a day. Initially, Rory had protested loudly. He sulked and had been reluctant to graft for most of that first week. Terry had been patient with him, doing his best to make the days varied and interesting, but inevitably it had been Nobby who had coaxed him out of his mood; having a laugh and a joke and the occasional rough and tumble, winding him up and generally taking the mick.

Just two weeks into his enforced tenure, a change had begun to take place in the youngster. Even Jan had noticed and remarked on it. The cocky, stubborn streak, which was definitely a Terry trait, had all but disappeared. He no longer walked around with that cheeky swagger that he copied from some of the older lads. Being away from his mates meant there was no longer a need to brag or impress. And slowly he started to take a genuine interest in the work and in his surroundings. All of a sudden he was full of questions.

'What's that word again, dad?' Rory shouted up to Terry who was busy forking over some soil.

'Hermaphrodite,' he replied, pausing to lean on his fork and study his son.

Rory nodded, taking the word on board and repeating it to himself under his breath as he went in search of more snails.

Terry couldn't quite believe the transformation in his lad, more to the point he couldn't believe how quickly someone heading down the wrong path could be steered straight with just a bit of time, patience and loving attention. Because he had taken time out to teach and explain things to him, Rory's curiosity and newfound thirst for knowledge knew no bounds, and although Nobby would eventually get fed up with his constant '*What's this for?*', '*Why are you doing that?*' and '*How's this work?*' Terry actually loved passing on his knowhow, explaining how a bulb worked, the difference between annuals, perennials and biennials. He also loved to watch Rory's face, fascinated as he learned and grasped something new, watching his expressions as he tried to assimilate things in his head.

This teaching lark ought to be a doddle, Terry thought to himself. But the system said otherwise. It was too preoccupied with league tables and SATs, whatever they were. Constantly changing curriculum and half-baked policies meant generation after generation of kids were being let down by the educational mandarins.

It was true, Rory's reading and writing hadn't improved at all over the last year, but he had learned how to hot-wire a car, forge a tax disc and spring the bolts on a five-point mortice deadlocked patio door. School environment had certainly provided an education of a sort, but it wasn't the type his parents had had in mind.

Terry lit a roll-up, took a breather, and watched his eleven year old slowly fill his bucket with garden pests. Rory was a survivor, however he turned out, good or bad Terry knew he'd be all right.

When he was five, Rory had come running into the house with his thumb all smashed. He'd been breaking up wood for a bonfire with his older brother and some other lads. His thumb had got in the way of a lump hammer and was a bit of a mess. It had caused him a great deal of pain and discomfort throughout the night and by morning the little guy's throbbing digit had swollen to nearly three times its normal size. Jan thought it might be broken, so Terry had carted him off to the infirmary. Having sat around in casualty all morning, the youngster was gnawing his lips raw with the pain and Terry, inevitably, had taken on his agitated, angry persona.

An overworked, foreign intern who somehow managed to determine that the thumb wasn't broken just by looking at it eventually saw them. Terry, at once had doubts about his capabilities. The student donned rubber gloves and produced an alarmingly large needle that brought on shock and instant fear in both father and son. The guy grinned broadly at their reactions.

'Just to relieve pressure, you understand.' He approached the scared lad who had instinctively backed away and clung on to his dad. Terry tried to calm and reassure Rory while at the same time gritting his teeth and resisting the urge to punch the lights out of the advancing junior. He urged Terry to hold the boy's wrist down firmly, which he did, reluctantly. The shaky, latex covered hand came in close and pushed the needle deep into the base of the nail. A despairing little whimper escaped from Rory's lips, and his dad's heart sank to his boots. A fountain of the deepest, dark red spurted into the air and Terry couldn't help but let out an audible moan. The intern withdrew the needle and slowly and deliberately repeated the process down the other corner of the nail. As he did so, Terry caught a whiff of garlic and B.O. He hated this bastard who was hurting his lad, and so badly wanted to kill him. Withdrawing the needle for the last time, he then squeezed the base of the thumb and more bad blood pumped itself to the surface. Terry watched the agony on Rory's face and felt so guilty that he couldn't take the pain for him. He felt the tears welling up in his eyes but fought hard to keep them back, noticing that through all this, Rory had done just that. Apart from a little groan or whine he hadn't cried at all, and Terry's heart surged at his boy's bravery.

As the man in the white coat prepared a dressing, dad grabbed son and hugged him close. It had been a defining moment for him, and he would never forget it.

Since that incident Terry had never been able to trust so-called professionals. He still didn't know to this day if what that raw intern had done to his lad was right or wrong. It may have been correct medical procedure but he would never be sure. From dentists to garage mechanics, he distrusted them all and hated being reliant on other people's so-called expertise.

That visit to casualty five years ago also told him a lot about his boy. He knew it was okay to cry, but he hadn't. He was a stubborn little sod, just like his dad. From that moment on, Terry knew that whatever shit was thrown at him in life, Rory would be okay.

When Jan removed the dressing two weeks later, the little nail came away with it. Rory marvelled at the reddy browns and purple colours that were now engrained and he vowed to keep it forever. It still sits on the mantelpiece at home inside a small, brass jewellery box that belonged to Jan's grandmother.

'So, it's not a girl, an' it's not a boy?' puzzled Rory.

'That's right – or, they can be both,' affirmed Terry.

Rory did his best to get his head round this information while chewing on his meat paste sandwich. 'So, how do they have babies then?' he finally quizzed.

'Well, they're able to change sex when they want, so one of 'em becomes the dad, and t'other ends up being the mam.

'Who decides who's gonna be which?'

Terry looked at Nobby knowing he would be smirking behind his meat and tatie pie, thinking '*Let's see you get out of this one, David Attenborough.*'

'Err… well, that's down to nature, innit? One o' life's little mysteries. Scientists don't have the answers to everything, you know.'

Rory nodded and fell silent for a bit, munching thoughtfully on his sarnies. 'I'm glad us humans aren't like that,' he piped up eventually. 'I don't fancy turning into a girl.'

'I allus thought yer warra girl,' teased Nobby.

'Fuck off, Norbert!'

'Hey Vasco, less o' t'lord mayorin'. Remember what your mam said,' warned Terry.

'You two do it,' Rory protested.

'Yeah, but not when we're in somebody's garden; you've to show a bit of respect when you're on other people's property – now, say you're sorry to uncle Nobby.'

'Bollocks!' Rory retorted disdainfully. The two adults laughed.

Terry knew he shouldn't be taking his eleven-year old's foulmouthed outburst so lightly, lord knows Jan had told him off about it often enough, but he had firm views when it came to swearing. His condoning of Rory's bad language didn't stem from any disregard for common decency or polite behaviour; it was to do with the whole hypocrisy surrounding it. Rory was exposed to four letter expletives as soon as he was big enough to toddle beyond his garden gate, and more so when he started school, as was Joe, as was Terry, ad infinitum. Swearing was part of the culture, engrained into the everchanging English language. Highbrows might argue that it was the culture of triumphant ignorance, that bad language was proof of a poor vocabulary. Maybe so, but whose fault was that? As far as Terry was concerned, the word '*fuck*' was just an old fashioned, expressive Anglo-Saxon word, the connotation and literal meaning of which didn't matter anymore as it was rarely used in context anyway. More often than not, it was used as a springboard for emphasis, and as Terry said to Jan, "It's only a word, love; it never fuckin' killed anybody."

'Tell that to the headmistress,' his wife had said, showing him the letter from school urgently requesting a meeting.

'Not again,' Terry groaned.

Rory had been swearing in class. It wasn't the first time, just another incident in a catalogue of minor misdemeanours that would have inevitably led to his suspension if it hadn't been for the summer holidays looming. It was becoming a familiar theme, but if the crimes fit, as they undoubtedly did with Rory, Terry was quite prepared to see justice done, that is, until he heard about the lad who had his skull fractured in an unprovoked attack by another kid at the school during a break period. It turned out that the boy doing the head cracking was a refugee and the school would be taking no action against him in case it jeopardised his family's application for asylum.

That slid straight into context for Terry; sledgehammer to crack a nut sitting cosily alongside political covertness, and he wasn't having it.

He had sat in the office, him and Jan, listening impassively to the charges; that familiar grave, monotone; that same condescending crap that Gerald Swallow had spouted months ago. *'Must have gone to the same bleedin' charm school those two,'* he thought to himself.

When the headmistress had finished lecturing, he had laid into her fine style; full on, both barrels, and just to prove a point, he didn't ease off on the language either. She winced at his every expletive, so he did it all the more.

Terry hadn't been too concerned about the consequences for Rory, but Jan had. She didn't want him starting the big school with a damning report, another Gallagher on the scene with a bad reputation and a nose for trouble, as well as volatile parents.

When Terry had finished showing his contempt and had left the office in disgust at the head's tartuffery, Jan had calmly got up from her seat and looked hard at the shell-shocked, speechless woman before addressing her.

'I'm sorry for my husband swearing like that,' she said in a soft voice that was in direct contrast to Terry's rant. 'I don't like bad language, especially when it's directed at women. He did it to show his anger at your double standards. He has strong convictions about this sort of thing and that was his way of making a point. I think it was the wrong way, and if I'd have been given the chance, I would have argued the issue without the four letter words but my sentiments would have been the same.' Jan paused but continued to fix her with a stare. 'Let me ask you a question,' she said finally. 'How many parents that you request to see actually bother to show up?'

'Well… er… I haven't got the actual figures, but…' Jan held up her hand and stopped her dead.

'I don't want you to quote statistics at me; the point I'm trying to make is that we're here because we care about our son. My husband's angry because he cares. You may not think it, but he's a damned good dad to both our kids, despite the bad language; probably the most caring parent you've ever had through these doors.'

The head teacher raised her eyebrows. Jan allowed herself a sardonic smile.

'Oh, yeah – you had us boxed and judged before we even walked in here, didn't you?'

'Of course not.'

'No? Then why did you refer to us as Mrs. Gallagher and partner instead of Mr. & Mrs. Gallagher? You assumed I was a single mother who'd brought along her latest live-in to shout and swear the odds.'

'That's not true, I…'

'You stereotyped us without bothering to ask or find out the facts, and you did exactly the same with our Rory.'

'I don't understand.'

'Did you know the last time you put him on detention for swearing in class he was being threatened by three lads, and that one of them was brandishing a Stanley knife? And, to quote, he was going to: "slash open his ball-bag and shove his gonads down his throat".'

Head teacher's eyes widened. 'No, I didn't, and no evidence has come to my attention of such an incident.'

'Of course you didn't, and of course it hasn't,' Jan said, hoping that the penny would finally drop. 'Nobody asked why he was swearing, and nobody cared. It was just that little foul-mouthed Gallagher kid disrupting class again, let's put him in detention for the umpteenth time. It didn't come to your attention because lads have this stupid code about grassing people up, not that anyone would have believed him anyway.'

Jan looked at the woman in the hope that there would be a glimmer of understanding; she was supposed to be a head teacher, surely she had a small grasp of child psychology. She found it hard to look Jan in the eye and started shuffling some papers. She wasn't used to having the tables turned on her, having her regime criticised like that. She was supposed to be the one doing the admonishing and meting out the punishment. These two had taken her by surprise and deep down she knew that some of the things they'd said were right, but she wasn't about to acquiesce and allow guilty feelings to surface. She would stew on some of the more stinging comments later at home over a hot bath and a G and T. But right now she couldn't allow herself to concede any shortcomings in her school and its policies to this woman.

'All my kid's doing is looking after himself the only way he knows how,' Jan continued. 'Like I've said; I'm sorry for the bad language, but if he can put down bullies with a few verbals and swearwords - well, I'd rather have him do that than him open up somebody's head. That's all I wanted to say.'

Jan made her way to the door.

The smallest pinprick stabbed at the head teacher's conscience and she dragged her eyes up from her papers. 'Mrs. Gallagher…' Jan paused and turned. '…In view of the comments you've made, I shall review Rory's report before he goes to his new school, but if he's reluctant to talk about any of the incidents you've raised, there is very little I can do to pursue the matter.'

Jan nodded wearily and left the office.

She hadn't really thought about it before but, as her heels clicked along the empty school corridor, Jan felt like a freak. Despite their recent spats, she and Terry were still together. They'd stuck at it over the years. Her and her three boys, they were still a family unit, and round here that was rare. They were a minority in a society that was littered with broken marriages and broken homes. Apart from Kath and Nobby, Jan struggled to count on one hand couples and families she knew that were still together. The headmistress had encountered something out of what was now the norm and both women thought hard on it that evening.

Jan click-clacked into the school foyer where Terry was sitting on a chair, head bowed, deep in thought, tugging on a roll-up while a cleaner busied herself with a mop around his feet. Jan stood in front of him and he slowly raised his eyes without lifting his head, which made him look a little sheepish.

'I don't think you should be smoking in here,' she said.

They'd both walked home hand in hand and in silence that evening. An almost telepathic understanding of each other's feelings and emotions meant it wasn't a time for words. A full two weeks went by before the issues of that school meeting surfaced again.

* * *

Rory was curled up in a chair watching T.V., chortling away at the crazy antics of the Japanese contestants on *Takeshi's Castle*. Terry was reading aloud to Jan a report in the local paper, the banner headline of which read, *Vigilantes on West Broughton streets*.

'It says here that, "the unnamed twenty-one year old thought to be of Albanian extraction was set upon by at least eight white men armed with sticks and baseball bats. Assuming the victim to be a drug dealer, they robbed and beat him before nailing him to a fence and daubing him with paint…"'

'Bollocks!' interrupted Rory.

Jan and Terry stared at him for different reasons. Rory's face reddened and he made an unsuccessful attempt to look interested in the telly again.

'Have you heard him?' Jan said, expecting Terry to reprimand Rory for the language.

'What d'yer mean, Bollocks?' asked Terry suspiciously.

'Nowt,' muttered Rory.

'Do you know summat about this?' said Terry, flicking a finger at the newspaper.

'Nah, do I heck,' he said unconvincingly.

'What's bollocks then?' his dad persisted.

'I dunno,' he said with a shrug, trying his best to concentrate on the screen.

'Will you stop repeating it?' Jan interrupted. 'He's never gonna learn with you slamming it back at him all the time, is he?'

'You don't know?' said Terry, totally ignoring his wife. 'You don't just come out with "bollocks" as a statement for no reason.'

Rory had to think of something fast, so he did; another trait he got from his dad.

'I know,' he said in a flash of inspiration. 'It's Tourette's, that's warrit is. I can't help it. It just comes out – bollocks. Just like that.'

Terry looked hard at him. Bollocks is exactly what it was.

Rory knew he wasn't convincing his dad so he pleaded to his mam. 'I think I must need to see a doctor or summat, mam. Honest to God, I don't even know I'm doin' it sometimes.'

Jan looked at her son, nonplussed. She just didn't know what to make of him; face full of innocence and sincerity appealing up at her like that. She was at a loss as to where all this stuff in his head came from. Terry knew only too well: documentary on the telly a few months back; Tourette's Syndrome, the swearing disease. He'd taken it all in, clever little sod.

Jan went over and knelt down beside Rory's chair. She put an arm round him and stroked his hair with her other hand.

'You've not got Tourette's love,' she said soothingly. 'Whatever makes you think that?'

Terry peered over the top of his newspaper at the sickening spectacle. From over his mam's shoulder Rory beamed that cheeky grin up at his dad while wallowing in the comfort of maternal love and concern. Terry wasn't in the mood for domestic confrontation so he didn't pursue the matter. He didn't say anything but gave Rory a look that told him, in no uncertain terms, that he knew he was hiding something.

The newspaper story was indeed bollocks, just like Rory had stated. There were no vigilantes, or sticks, or baseball bats.

Rory and a bunch of his mates had been mooching around the estate. They'd fallen into knocking around with one or two older lads from the East side. One of them, a feral lad who went by the name of Asbo, was self-styled leader and Svengali. He was up for any kind of mindless mischief and the younger ones tended to follow him around in a mix of awe and fear.

That particular night, Asbo had acquired a cordless nail gun that he fired at any potential target they came across including cats, dogs, and other kids, and when they'd got bored with that they'd taken it in turns to shoot it at each other.

A shady looking dude who'd been watching them from over the street, approached. 'Want some stuff?' said a foreign-sounding voice from a face well hidden beneath baseball cap and hood.

The lads stopped what they were doing. It was unusual for dealers to be seen on West Broughton streets, they usually stayed on the East side. This guy obviously didn't know the turf and he seemed a bit unsure of himself.

'What yer got?' asked Asbo, looking around to make sure they weren't being watched.

'E's, coke, crack, H.'

'Let's 'ave a gander,' said Rory, pushing his way to the front and taking charge. The hooded one stared down at the little kid, not understanding.

'Show us,' said Asbo.

The dealer partially unzipped his coat and reached deep inside pulling out a handful of his wares. The lads huddled round Rory and the dealer and peered in at the merchandise. Rory looked up at his mates on either side of him. They were on the same wavelength. After a pause Rory flashed into action. With a quick, upward stroke of his hand he sent the cocktail of drugs flying high into the air screaming 'Gerrim!'

Before the gobsmacked bloke had time to react, the lads had pounced, pinned him to the floor and were rifling his pockets. There was a sound of tearing cloth as he desperately tried to squirm and kick himself free.

'Hold the bastard down!'

'I'm tryin'.'

'Sit on his fuckin' legs!'

'Stop strugglin' or we'll brek yer fuckin' legs, yer cunt!' threatened Asbo.

He seemed to understand that and struggled all the more.

'Let's crucify him,' said Rory who was standing aside, directing operations.

'Yeah, crucify the bastard.'

The totally de-bagged and dishevelled victim was dragged kicking and screaming to a nearby wooden fence. His baseball cap came off in the mêlée revealing a shorn head and a pair of wide, terrified eyes. He was forced, spread-eagled against the fence while one of the lads went to work with the nail gun. Every *chu-gung! chu-gung!* sound was met with a corresponding yell of terror along with a stream of oaths in some foreign language as he was attached to the fence via his baggy threads.

'Will somebody shut the pillock up?' demanded the kid with the gun.

His hood was dragged round the front of his face, across his mouth and nailed against the fence at the other side of his head.

Crucifixion complete, one of the lads produced a can of spray paint and wrote - **DRUG DEELER** - across fence and body with the letters **UG** sitting square across the hapless bloke's midriff.

They departed the scene laughing and taunting, taking turns to fire nails at him from a distance; muffled screams confirming direct hits.

That had been the last time Rory had knocked about with that lot. The following weeks he'd gotten into working with his dad and Nobby and at night he'd been either too knackered or simply couldn't be arsed to go seeking them out on the streets. The next time he saw them there was alienation. He'd made himself an outsider and he could sense the hostility towards him.

'Yer muvver's saggy tits, Gallagher!' shouted one of the kids from the other side of the street.

'Yer granny's mouldy fanny!' Rory responded, not bothering to stop.

''Sup Gallagher – aren't we good enough for thee anymore?' shouted Asbo from across the street. 'What's tha scared on?'

'I aren't scared o' thee,' Rory shouted back while keeping to his side of the road. He noticed Asbo had what looked like a miniature crossbow in his hand and he was levelling it at him.

'There's a contract out on thee tha knows. Tha's gorra price on thee head.'

'Ask me if I'm fuckin' bothered,' he replied over his shoulder while walking on his way, all the while trying not to cringe as any minute he expected a bolt to come flying at him. He knew the kid was capable, he was crackers enough. Tonight, though, Asbo had his reasoned head on. He knew Rory's connections, his brother Joe, Young Nobby and Rigger. He knew all about Danny Mortiss and his hard–boy reputation, and although he liked to think he was scared of nobody, he didn't fancy making enemies there.

'Bunch o' tossers,' Rory muttered under his breath. He was best away from that lot, he thought to himself. It was ironic that when they mugged the dealer he hadn't taken anything. He didn't really know or care what happened to the drugs, but he knew that the rest of them had divvied up at least two hundred and fifty quid of the guy's illicit earnings between them, but he hadn't wanted to know. To him it was just a lark, a bit of fun. Humiliating that tosser like that was enough for him. What the rest of them did was up to them. He took a good guess that some of the drugs went with them as well, to flog or to use, he couldn't say. There was no way he was going down that road. He'd also noticed that some of his so-called mates, the ones that were his age, weren't saying much. He guessed that some of them secretly wanted out, but were too scared to jump ship because of Asbo and the older kids. 'Bottlers,' he said to himself with a sneer. He couldn't say what had exactly steered him away, or when and where he made a conscious decision not to seek out their company anymore, but inside his eleven year old head he felt he'd made an adult choice and he had walked away feeling a little taller for it.

* * *

'…And they can grow up to twenty five thousand teeth, and they breathe through their feet,' said Terry.

'Oh yeah, as if,' said a disbelieving Rory.

'It's true, I tell yer.'

'Anyway, snails don't have teeth, or feet.'

''Course they do. How d'yer think they munch their way through all these plants? They're just tiny that's all. You'd have to get a microscope to see 'em.'

Rory looked up at Nobby to see if there was any sign that they were having him on. Nobby nodded seriously in agreement with Terry although he didn't have a clue himself if it was fact or fiction.

'What we gonna do with 'em all?' he asked peering into the almost full bucket of gastropods, a few of which were making their way up to the rim in a painfully slow bid to escape.

'Find a field and lerrem go,' said Terry.

Rory screwed his face up and looked from his dad to Nobby who just shrugged his shoulders as if to say '*Don't ask me, yer dad does these strange things.*'

'Why don't we just kill 'em?'

'Why would yer wanna do that?'

'I thought yer said they were pests.'

'Well, they are to the garden, but everything's here for a purpose. Birds and frogs eat 'em; they're part of what's called the food chain; if we start interfering with nature, using poisons and such, it affects everything down that chain. That's how species can become extinct.'

'What's species?'

'Groups of animals is species; like, birds are a species, insects are a species. Humans are a species.'

Rory nodded that he understood. 'What's extinct?'

'*Oh, shit,*' thought Nobby. '*Here we go; he's started him off again; twenty bleedin' questions.*' He put the lid back on his lunch box, got to his feet and stretched. He let out a rasping fart and looked over at Rory expectantly. To his disappointment there was no reaction. The kid was too preoccupied. Terry was becoming more like a tree hugger every day. Who gave a fuck what a dodo was.

On their way home that evening Terry stopped the pickup and

Rory released the bucket of snails carefully down a grassy embankment.

9

Terry settled himself in his usual spot on top of the stone steps that led on to the sun terrace at the Garden Springs Nursing Home. He undid his Thermos, poured himself some tea and waited for the daily procession of old folk and their carers to make an appearance. Now, whenever they worked at the home, Terry would take his lunch late and spend the hour chatting away to Herbert Johnson. It was a one-way conversation but Terry enjoyed it. It had become a bit of a ritual and it provided some sort of therapy, a chance to get things off his chest and put certain matters in perspective. Nobby sometimes joined them but Terry preferred it when they were on their own. He didn't know why; maybe he liked to think that Herbert was lending a sympathetic ear; that he understood what he was talking about, although that was unlikely.

'Your friend's here to see you again, Herbert,' chirped a voice. Terry looked up to see the young nurse manoeuvring the old man into position like she had done on every available fine, summer day since he arrived at the home. She applied the brake on his wheelchair, adjusted his tartan blanket, smiled at the pleasant but strange gardener and skipped off for a stint in the sluice room emptying commodes.

Terry had nothing but admiration for these young lasses and the thankless, sometimes degrading duties they had to perform, all for very little reward. If he were in charge of things, these angels would be right at the top of the pay scale, no danger.

He couldn't understand why we didn't look after the elderly better. To the powers that be, the old were a costly burden; a drain on resources a one-time taxable commodity that had outlived their usefulness to society and their legion were in ever-increasing numbers. We were in the epoch of '*Do not resuscitate*'. Euthanasia by the back door. That old sci-fi film, *Soylent Green* starring Charlton Heston, came to mind. At least we hadn't stooped so low as to turn our dying elderly into processed food yet, thought Terry – then again – he shuddered at the possibility and quickly dismissed the notion from his head. But he wouldn't have put it past them. Nothing our so-called leaders got up to would surprise him any more. He hoped that the decision makers and the bastard politicians would never have to endure the indignities and suffering that their policies had inflicted on so many vulnerable old people in the twilight of their years – who was he kidding? That's exactly what he hoped they would suffer, and the rest. He'd like to see them all end up in the hands of some un-qualified head-the-ball; a minimum waged, un-vetted, sadistic nut-case with a massive chip on their shoulder. Now that would be sweet retribution.

Garden Springs was one of the better-run nursing homes. Good facilities and reasonably well-paid staff. Nigel Adenbrook knew how to do things right but you had to pay top dollar for a place here. Good care didn't come cheap and many a son and daughter had to forgo their inheritance in order to make mum or dad's last few days a bit more bearable.

Despite its pleasant and sedate surroundings there was a sad and melancholic air about the place. A resignation born of the feeling of finality, and it always put Terry in a reflective mood. As nice a resi-dence as it was it made him quake at the thought of ending his days here or somewhere like it, after all it was still a sanatorium, a form of institution, and institutions were the one thing he'd always had a deep foreboding of.

'Hey up, Herbert. How are you today, mate?' he said in a cheer-fully overloud voice.

Herbert wasn't deaf but that's how the nurses spoke to him, in loud, condescending tones as if he were a child again and Terry in-voluntary found himself doing the same. Nor was he blind or dumb, but his eyes stared unseeing straight ahead and his lips remained still and his voice silent.

'It's no use talking to him, love, he can't hear you,' the young nurse had offered to Terry on that first meeting back in June.

He had left his flowerbeds and walked slowly up the steps to the patio that day just to confirm that the old guy in that vegetative state was indeed his former neighbour, Herbert Johnson.

'Are you a relative?' the girl had enquired when he had ignored her opening line and had continued trying to talk to the old man.

'What? Er... no, no, just an old friend – you don't mind me chatting to him, do you?'

The nurse had given him a strange look. 'Please yourself,' she shrugged. 'But like I say, you'll get no response, he can't hear you.'

'I'll just sit with him for a while, if that's okay.'

She had paused, unsure how to respond to the gardener's odd request. She had seen him talking to Mr. Adenbrook earlier, so the guy must be all right.

'Whatever,' she shrugged again and took her leave.

Terry had taken the old man's grey, dead hand in his, that same hand that had held the small gold band that had been gently placed on the petite finger of his new bride with all the tender love the optimistic twenty-two year old could muster, sixty-three years ago to the day. That same hand that had been calloused and blistered, hacking his way through the dense Burmese jungle, that had taken life for King and Country, certain in his young mind that what he did was duty; for freedom and liberty so that future generations could live without fear in peace and prosperity.

What a fucking sick joke, Terry had bitterly thought to himself as he gazed into Herbert's stone-like features.

He had wondered what had become of the ring, the treasured memory of his beloved wife that he had worn on a chain round his neck that the burglars had so violently torn from him. He had wondered about the medal, the V.C that Herbert had so gallantly won, and the self-effacing, genuine modesty that he showed whenever he was pressed to talk about it.

Terry had unashamedly wept there and then; his warm, soiled hands moving over Herbert's in a gentle but frustrating caress as if he was desperately willing life and movement back into them. Wave after wave of emotion had welled up inside him. He didn't know where it was coming from and it wasn't particularly welcome. He didn't want to embarrass himself in front of Nobby or any watching nurses. After all, the old man wasn't blood, just a nice guy and a friendly neighbour who had enjoyed the odd pint and a chat down at the club.

Terry had felt slightly stupid; sat blubbing like a kid while Herbert stared expressionless at nothing, oblivious to everything around him. But something had been purged from within him that afternoon. A whole gamut of emotions had been rent from deep inside him; from the euphoria of Nigel's benevolence to the shock and utter dismay at seeing Herbert like that.

When the nurses had appeared at the time for them to go back indoors, Terry had quickly said goodbye and had gone straight back to his flowerbed, not wanting Herbert's carer to see him with red eyes. When Nobby had asked what was up with his mince pies, he had muttered something about accidentally flicking soil up into them.

Visiting Herbert at lunchtime had become a fortnightly pilgrimage, and with each week that went by he looked forward to it more and more. Although the conversations were one way, Terry didn't see it like that. He found it easy to open up and talk about things he wouldn't have even discussed with Jan or Nobby. What was weird was the fact that he seemed to be getting answers to his dilemmas and rhetorical questions. He'd reflect on this or the other, and in a breath he seemed to know what to do. Solutions to perceived problems appeared glaringly simple and his thought process was becoming much clearer.

'I see they've done the dirty on your old mates,' said Terry, looking up at Herbert as if there might be a slight flicker of acknowledgement.

He was referring to the government's refusal to allow the Ghurkhas full pension status, a move that disgusted Terry. Just another shameful example of usage, exploitation and rejection by faceless Whitehall top-brass sat in cosy seats of power at the M.O.D.

Terry gave Herbert the lowdown on the story, glancing up at the end of every sentence or point made in the off-chance he would catch a slight shake of the head, in the hope of a frown or a grunt of displeasure at the news of the plight of his former comrades. But there was nothing.

What had happened to all those memories? Sad times, happy times, faded childhood adventures, youthful optimism, dark days of war, doubt and uncertainty, the defeat of evil, a child's birth, the joy of fatherhood, first steps, girlish laughter, the "You've never had it so good" years, a bright new dawn, the short-lived promise of a post war utopia.

Terry wondered whether those images and connecting emotions were somehow still locked inside Herbert's head just waiting for a key to unlock them, whether they just needed a catalyst or a spark, something to trigger the process; a name, an event, a smell even. Or were they gone forever? Evaporated into the ether in a flurry of kicks and punches; inside the old man's head a vacuum; a sea of emptiness, a mass of dead, grey cells just managing to respond to the electrical signals that kept him breathing.

When he had asked the young nurse what Herbert's medical condition was, she couldn't really tell him save to say he had suffered a massive subdural haemorrhage during the attack. The statement was followed by that sympathetic look of no hope and he could tell what she was probably thinking as she had turned and walked away. *'You're wasting your time, fella. I've told you you'll get no response. The old guy's a living vegetable. Give it up.'* But he wouldn't give it up. Although he had mellowed of late, Terry still had that stubborn streak in him whenever he set his stall out. He felt it was his duty, a philanthropic gesture, perhaps subconsciously brought on by a feeling of guilt that he hadn't been there for him. He hadn't been able to prevent the attack, and worst of all, the poor bloke had lain there for almost a day before he was found lying unconscious in a pool of his own congealed blood.

Terry tried to be upbeat and positive on their little get-togethers, but it wasn't easy. He glanced at his watch. He would have to be getting back to work in a minute. The hour they had together seemed to pass so quickly and he always came away with a mix of feelings, often sanguine for himself, spirits lifted after his outpourings, but always tinged with frustration at his failure to connect.

He let out a sigh and looked into Herbert Johnson's sedentary features. A bloodstained scrap of tissue was stuck to his chin where his nurse had nicked him while giving him a shave, somehow confirming that he was still a man, not a vegetable, a man, a human being – Terry would never give up hope.

10

'*eegal as landed. c u in oak at 11 – bring lowry*' read the text. Smiffy's timing, as well as his spelling, was shit.

'I don't need this - I don't need this - do I not fuckin' need this,' Terry muttered to himself Graham Taylor style as he climbed into the pickup scuffing the leather of his brand new Sambas in his haste. Agitated, he gunned the engine into life, grated the gears and floored the accelerator. The over-revved motor roared down the street, not fast, the old bus didn't do fast, just cranky and noisy as if announcing to the whole estate: '*Terry's in a mood again folks.*'

Annoying thing was, he hadn't been in a mood for ages, not for two or three weeks at least.

Out of the blue, and as if by warning for slipping back into his old ways, a reservoir of stomach acid refluxed and surged up his oesophagus, rasping at his tonsils. He managed to choke out a surprised: 'Bastard!' and fumbled for the pack of Rennie that lay amongst the sea of rubbish on the pickup's dashboard.

It was turning into a shitty morning, but for the dog he was about to hit it would cap what had been a shitty few weeks.

He never even saw it. He just heard the bump and the yelp.

'Aww, shit!' Terry yanked up the handbrake and jumped from the cab just in time to see the Heinz 57 finish its triple salco and limp away into a garden. He called to the mutt but it only gave him a scared and bewildered '*fuck you!*' look before sloping away to lick its wounds.

He felt bad. He wouldn't have minded if it had been a cat; he hated cats. Any other time he'd have gone after it just to make sure it was okay, but he was late. He should have been at Nobby's over an hour ago - sod's law. Every time you're late and you're rushing about, shit happens. Smiffy was going to cop a right ear-bashing for this.

As for the dog, he'd had enough of humans lately. His owner had been trying to force some little, foul tasting white things down his throat. He'd even tried to hide them in his food. He was forever hungry and his arse itched like mad whenever he tried to take a shit and you couldn't even do that in peace these days. His old toilet territory was a no-go area; too painful to take a dump there now. The three lesions on his flanks were testament to that, and now this. He checked that the bastard in the road machine wasn't following him before flopping down under a shady hedge to try and recover his senses. He was panting as hard as a paedophile in a playground; rasping, rhythmic dog-breaths, pausing only for a tentative lick of the painful bits and a gnaw at his itchy, mangy coat.

The grinning black hole was waiting to greet him in the taproom at the Royal Oak. Smiffy-No-Teef was still wearing his grey-white shell-suit. At his feet were three large black bin-bags full of 'ex-warehouse stock' footie kit. He looked and smelled exactly as he had on that first meeting, his cavernous smile still hideously disagreeable.

'Tezzer – how's it goin', charver?'

Terry made sure he kept a safe distance. He gave Smiffy a look that told him perfectly how it was going.

Contentment was never a feeling that sat well with Terry. He'd always been happy not being happy with his lot, that's what made him who he was. Shit, conflict and upset flew to him like iron filings to a magnet and that's what he'd forever been used to. Occasionally he'd wonder what it would be like to be Nobby; blissfully ignorant of what went on around him, totally insular and not a care in the world. But he didn't really envy him. Those were the cards fate dealt you. He could never be like Nobby. And all this business with Herbert Johnson; the purging of his innermost thoughts, the subconscious voice talking to him, straightening him out; it was all very well, but deep down there was something in him that didn't trust it all.

For well over two weeks things had been going well, too well. Work was good; bricks were up at home. He and Jan had been building bridges all over the place, not least in the bedroom. Rory had seemingly turned over a new leaf. Training was going great and having the craic with the lads was a laugh. More evident had been Terry's willingness to compromise. He had agreed to a holiday, much to Jan's astonishment. It wasn't to be Majorca, and it would only be for a week, not a fortnight, but for him to accede like that was a major shift. And the rewards that this change of heart had brought about were self-evident. Joe and Rory were great to have around; they grafted their socks off at work and were almost civil to one another at home. His wife had become his lover again, and what with his general level of fitness now, his biorhythms had gone soaring. He couldn't ever remember feeling this good as a twenty year old.

And that was the trouble; it was all too good. There was something deep inside Terry's head that kept saying it wouldn't last. He was scared; waiting for the fall, and that prevented him from truly enjoying the moments for what they were. It wasn't life as he knew it and he didn't quite know how to handle the amenity around him.

With the fall that morning came the mix; the cynical, pessimistic part of him that was glad to get back to normality. The voice that sneered: '*Fuckin' told you so. No one likes us, we don't care.*' It was safe. It was familiar. It was what he knew, and he knew how to deal with it. But the other part of him, the new, naïve part of him didn't know what to do; didn't know how to react. It felt like a punch to the solar plexus, and that emotional mix probably brought on the acid attack. The conflicting voices weren't helping either. The muttering under the breath and the silent mouthing of scenarios was becoming a bit disconcerting. Even now, as he faced a nonplussed Smiffy, an annoyingly calm voice inside his head was reasoning: '*You just need to learn how to be happy.*' He found himself glancing out of the corner of each eye just to check there wasn't a devil and angel perched on either shoulder.

Smiffy was to be the scapegoat. He was partly to blame for the crappy start to the day and was about to bear the brunt of Terry's irascibility until the angel, that Terry had decided was perched on his left shoulder, told him to go easy on the ex con, after all he was doing him a favour. He'd made the effort and had come good with the strip. Terry relaxed a little. It was true; Smiffy was too easy a target, standing there among the bin-bags looking slightly bewildered.

Terry's mobile buzzed an incoming text. It was Nobby: '*ware the fuck r u?*' He tried to remember if Nobby and Smiffy were in the same English class at school. He turned the phone off.

'Couldn't you have dropped it off at our house?' asked Terry.

'Ah, I can't really be seen down your way at ver moment, chor.' Terry looked at him. 'Don't ask,' said Smiffy.

'Well, t'club then.'

'Barred.'

'Fusiliers?'

'Barred.'

'Christ's sake, Smiffy, I could've done without trailing all t'way up here today. Couldn't it have waited 'till I got back off holiday?'

'Sorry, Tez, lad. I've had to shell out for vis little lot an' I need ver readies.'

'This is me bloody' holiday money, I'll have yer know,' said Terry, peeling twenties from a roll.

'No problem; vere's hole in t'wall just round t'corner,' Smiffy said helpfully.

'Don't use 'em,' muttered Terry.

'Yer what?'

'I don't use cards,' he said, annoyed at having to explain himself. 'Don't trust 'em.'

Smiffy pulled a face while Terry handed over the money. 'Don't blame yer,' he said, checking the notes with an expert hand and eye. 'Too many villains around here veese days,' he followed without any sense of irony. 'Don't know who might be lookin' over yer shoulder.' He tucked the wad safely inside his shell suit and beamed a satisfied grin. 'Oh, nearly forgot, charver,' he suddenly remembered, dipping back inside his top. 'Got you a pressie for yer hols; just a little summat to say fanks for yer business.'

He surreptitiously handed Terry a plastic sandwich bag full of dried, green-brown buds.

'Latest batch o' Norvern Lights,' said Smiffy enthusiastically, while pursing lips over gums trying to form a pout in an effort to convey the value of the gift. 'Veeery nice.'

The stink coming off the bag of weed was so pungent it lingered like shit on a sewerage worker's wellies for the rest of the afternoon in the taproom at The Royal Oak.

Kath's sister had a static caravan on a site somewhere between Skegness and Ingoldmells that she'd let her and Nobby use for the week. Jan had managed to rent another one a couple of pitches away, and that's where they should have been headed more than three hours ago.

Terry hadn't noticed just how black his hands were. He glanced down at his new tee shirt and pants. They were smeared with oil and grease and his Sambas were scuffed. He sighed with resignation at the bollocking he knew was waiting for him. One day he'd listen to her.

Two minutes. He'd be as quick as a Ferrari pit stop, he'd said, ignoring her pleas for him to change out of his holiday duds before he swapped the punctured back wheel on the pickup. An hour and a full can of WD40 later the seized wheel nuts were just beginning to yield to the thirteen stone of pressure being forced on them as Terry bounced up and down on the brace. Sweat, grease, frustration, a severely grazed anklebone and incessant text messages from Smiffy and Nobby served to tip him over the edge. Then there was the dog; the poor fucking dog. He hoped it would be okay.

His own welfare would be of more concern as he pulled up and saw Jan waiting at the front door with a face like thunder. He knew the script. He could second-guess the lines to the reproachful onslaught coming his way before the words had left her lips.

Joe and Rory came running to meet him at the gate. 'Where've yer been, dad? Nobby's been tryin' to get yer. Your mobile's switched off.'

'Been to get the new kit lads,' Terry said in an upbeat fashion, trying to put a brave face on it and hopefully deflect a bit of flack.

'New kit – yess!' said Joe, diving into the cab to rifle through the bags. Terry offered a pale smile to Jan from a safe distance. He could tell from the look he got back that the bricks were well and truly down. She stormed back inside, slamming the door behind her. Terry let out another sigh. He fumbled for his mobile and turned it on. There were five new texts. The last one was from Nobby. It read: *'Got sic of wateing - make yor own way ther – yewsless cunt!'* he'd added as an afterthought. *'Charming,'* thought Terry.

He told the lads, now was probably not a good time to go through the new strip.

'Phoo – yer not kiddin',' said Rory. 'She's in a right old strop; you're in for some megga grief there, dad.'

Terry ruffled his hair with an oily hand. 'Cheers, fella-me-lad,' he said philosophically.

A sudden thought came to Terry as the Gallaghers trundled along seemingly endless miles of long, straight, flat Lincolnshire road, and it wasn't the fact that they were lost, although they were. With all the palaver that morning he couldn't remember whether or not he'd padlocked and set the alarm on the garage. It was a big worry because that's where the tools for their livelihood were stored. The crime rate always shot up over the holiday fortnight and usually rapacious burglars were to blame. There was a saying in their part of the city: *When West Broughton's away, East Broughton will play.*

There would be a fire sale in the dens and dives of East Broughton over the next couple of weeks; tellies, videos, D.V.Ds, jewellery; all at knockdown prices. It was a buyer's market; local fences, twenty-first century Fagins, all rubbing their hands together with relish as desperate punters touted their ill-gotten wares and haggled and pleaded for the cost of a few wraps.

Terry nearly asked Jan if she could remember whether the garage had been secured and alarmed, but then his stubborn side prevented him. They hadn't spoken a word since she had accused him of getting them lost and he had accused her of being a shit navigator.

It was nearly five o'clock when they finally drove onto the site.

They were attracting a lot of attention as they slowly meandered up and down the park looking for the Clarkes and their pitch. Jan felt embarrassed and did her best to hide her face from the stares. She felt like they were a family of travellers looking for somewhere to squat. The smoky, old, green-painted transit pickup looked a little out of place amongst the shiny Volvos and 4x4s. People came out on to their posh looking balustrades and immaculately coiffured lawns to gawp as they chugged by. It didn't help that a windswept Rory, perched up on the cases at the back of the pickup, was nodding and shouting a cheery '*Alrate,*' to everyone they passed.

Jan had pleaded with Terry to splash out and hire a car for the week.

'I aren't wasting money hiring a car,' he'd said indignantly. 'There's nowt wrong wi' t'old Trani'. They can tek us as they find us.' It was one of his favourite sayings whenever dealing with snobbery. Jan had never learned to drive, but now, she vowed to herself that the first thing she'd do when they got back would be to book some lessons.

When they finally met up with the Clarkes, a football appeared as if from nowhere. Pandemonium ensued.

'Goal!' shouted Rory as he curled a shot that rattled against the aluminium side of a neighbouring caravan.

'Naff off, yer dullard,' said Joe. 'That's not the goals.'

An almost speechless, dapper little fellow with trim tash and spectacles came to the door of the caravan. 'What on earth do you think you're doing?' he demanded, aghast at the sight before his eyes. 'Have you people a right to be here?'

'Aye,' said Nobby. 'We're gonna be your neighbours for a week.'

'I'm sorry, but you can't play ball games here,' piped up the Nancy Reagan look-alike who had appeared at the shoulder of her husband.

'Find somewhere to play away from the caravans, lads,' said Jan.

'There are no ball games allowed *anywhere* on this site,' stated Nancy, stiffly. The pair of them looked the Clarkes and Gallaghers up and down with unconcealed distaste before shutting themselves back inside.

Terry had barely finished his third can before a flustered site manager came and sought them out, clutching a list of park rules and regulations. He'd already had five complaints from residents who had crossed paths with the lads.

After the day he'd had, Terry couldn't believe he was sat there taking a lecture on happy holiday etiquette. What with the Himmlers next door, he felt sure this was going to be a week of pure, undiluted misery. The devil popped onto his right shoulder. *'Fuckin' told yer so,'* it said.

II

He hadn't given much thought to turning forty. He didn't know why everybody seemed to attach so much importance or trepidation to it. To him it was just another birthday. He gave no consideration to the onset of middle age. Apart from a slightly receding and greying hairline, or the annoying tufts that had started to sprout out of his ears and nostrils, or the odd bout of acid indigestion, he felt no different from when he was a youth. Physically he was in fine fettle and he couldn't understand why people felt they had to change once they got to a certain age. He couldn't decide whether or not it was some sort of psychological trigger that shifted people into what they became or if it was genuinely a chemical, hormonal thing that occurred in the brain that he and his mate lacked. Maybe it was simply down to lifestyle. He had a feeling him and Nobby would always be eighteen in their heads, and that would be fine by him.

Although Terry thought that turning forty was no big deal, other people obviously did. The array of gift-wrapped presents that awaited him as he was called for breakfast took him aback. He ploughed through the cards that nearly all had a jokey, but to him, slightly disconcerting reference to age. '*Old bugger*' this, '*Silly old sod*' that. With each freshly opened envelope, the word '*old*' leapt off the card and slapped him round the face. Even the senders had tried to match the card's printed wit with their own post-scripted ditties that all contained the word, '*old*'.

He was silently chuffed with all the gifts, especially the expensive looking dressy watch from Jan that he proudly displayed on his wrist, but the best present of all was when she wrapped her arms around him and gave him a warm, heartfelt kiss that sent a tingle all the way up his spine. He looked into her eyes to check if the last four days of not really speaking to each other was finally over, and it was.

It was daft, really. Nearly all their arguments and falling-outs were petty and trivial if they looked back and analysed, but they both could be stubborn if they set their minds to it and that always prolonged any conflict, but it did tend to make the reconciliation all the more sweet.

The flying Frisbee cut through the air, silent and sleek; a flash of red, intersecting alfresco breakfast table, missing toast and teapot mid-pour by inches, gliding gracefully to grass a few yards away.

'Mornin' Mr. Himmler – Mrs. Himmler,' greeted a cheery Rory as he retrieved the plastic disc. The 'Himmlers' stood transfixed, staring wide eyed at Rory as though he were an alien; statue-like teapot and half eaten toast poised between hand and mouth as if frozen in time. 'Strange people,' said Rory as he walked back towards Joe and Young Nobby.

'They don't call 'em Mr. an' Mrs. Himmler, yer doylum,' hissed Joe.

'Yeah, they do. I've heard dad call 'em it.'

'That's just summat he calls 'em. It in't their real name.'

'What's he call 'em that for then?'

'I dunno; he just does.'

Rory looked back. The Himmlers hadn't moved. Their eyes burned into him.

'Gimmee the creeps, they do,' he muttered.

It was just as well they were all going out for the day. Jan and Kath were going into Skegness to do a bit of shopping and get some grub in for Terry's birthday barbecue that night. The boys had hard cash burning holes in their pockets from working over the holidays and they were going to invade the rides and arcades at the pleasure park in Ingoldmells, while Terry and Nobby would spend a leisurely afternoon in the pub.

'*Shell-suit City,*' Terry thought to himself as they strolled amongst the holiday throng. Smiffy would feel at home here. Whole families resplendent in forty odd quid a time replica shirts, from Grandmas to little Kylies in their pushchair buggies managing to get ice cream everywhere but the orifice it should go in, all proudly displaying their loyalties while fat, cigar-chewing football club directors sat in their boardrooms laughing their cocks off and made sheep-like bleating noises.

Terry felt like climbing to the top of the highest ride with a megaphone to wake folk up to the brainwashing, but looking around and listening to the discourse he realised that a good percentage of these people were Trisha and Jerry disciples, England's equivalent to America's trailer trash and that the word exploitation would have very little meaning in their lives.

He laughed to himself because he knew that what he was thinking could be explicated as a form of snobbery, ironic really given his own feelings on the subject. He thought of the Himmlers and their ilk; how they looked down on him and his own and he supposed there were those who thought themselves on an even higher plane and would look down at the Himmlers with as much contempt.

He laughed even harder to himself at those who said we now lived in a classless society. The divisions were there all right. Although the days of knowing your place, doffing your cap and tugging the forelock were long gone, the divides were stronger than ever, it's just that they were more numerous and, as such, less definable.

'Happy days' read the chalkboard sign. *'All beer & lager £2:00 a pint – 11pm. – 7pm. – Pool – Sky T.V. – New plasma screens'*

''Ere, this'll do,' said Nobby. 'C'mon, we're in. Your birthday, your round; gerrem in, you old bugger.'

Terry forgot his musings. He was glad to escape the kitsch and the junk. He was sick of dodging human waste disposal units with equatorial girths and listening to the tantrums of their hyperactive brats as they maintained E number levels with cheap, fizzy pop and candyfloss. But if Nobby didn't pack it in with the '*old*' shit he would have to give him a slap, big as he was.

Warmed by an afternoon of alcoholic refreshment, Terry and

Nobby were eagerly flexing their hunter-gatherer, machismo instincts by taking charge of the barbecue. Jan and Kath were busy buttering baps pondering why men always managed to appear pathetic in these situations, especially when they were half pissed. The girls had forgotten to buy firelighters so Nobby wobbled off to get the can of lighter fluid he remembered was in the pickup. He returned with a big happy Stan Laurel type smile all over his face, clutching the Zippo and the bag of weed that Terry had hurriedly stuffed in the glove box as he left the Oak.

'What's all this then, yer bad lad?' said Nobby swinging the bag of Northern Lights in front of his nose.

'Shit, I'd forgotten about that.' Terry looked up, already wearing a smudge of charcoal across his face.

While his mate attempted to light the Barbie, Nobby lost no time in sticking papers together in the construction of a big fat one.

'What's that?' Jan asked suspiciously on her way past.

'Mixed herbs,' said Terry.

'Put this on yer burgers an' you'll know about it,' Nobby chuckled, putting the finishing touches to the mega spliff.

Jan looked to the heavens and silently appealed to the Gods. It wasn't her place to bawl out Nobby, so she left Terry with her most menacing daggers before storming off to let Kath know what her husband was up to.

Kath tutted. 'I don't know; they're just like big kids, aren't they?' she sighed, barely glancing up from her pile of buttered bread, making Jan's reaction to the dope seem a bit melodramatic.

'…All I'm saying is they shouldn't be doing it out here, it stinks like hell, and what if them nosey buggers from next door come home?' said Jan, slicing a tomato with extra vigour.

Kath told her mate to relax and reminded her that they were on holiday. She glanced over at the biggest of her big lads enjoying himself and smiled, thinking that she might stroll over for a crafty little toot herself after she'd finished her chores.

Stress was an alien concept in the Clarke household. Crisis simply washed over Kath and Nobby. Nothing ever seemed to faze either of them. They were soul mates who took everything in their stride with a philosophical smile and a shrug of the shoulders. They both had a *Shit happens, get over it* attitude to any grief that came their way. Even when they fell out, which was rare, they'd have a ten-minute blazing stand-up, everything off their chests, out in the open, kiss, make up, laugh and forget about it. Jan and Terry had never been able to get their heads round the Clarkes' laid-back lifestyle. They were all best of friends, almost family, yet so different. The Gallaghers were also a little envious of the concordant amity that seemed to run through every aspect of their relationship. What Kath and Nobby had was unique and somewhat discomposing to be around for long periods such as a week's holiday.

The more stoned Nobby got the more he sat taking the piss be-tween fits of giggles at Terry's increasingly frustrated attempts to master the barbecue. The more he took the piss the angrier and more frustrated Terry became. A heavy smell of burnt meat and butane filled the air. Stressed sweat dripped from Terry's head onto charred burgers and red hot charcoal which sizzled and spat sending up acrid smoke that stung his eyes and made them water. He looked more out of it than Nobby and he hadn't even had a toke.

'*One more dig, you cunt; just one more,*' Terry thought to himself squinting over his shoulder at his chortling mate. Nobby duly obliged.

The flaming saveloy flew through the air like an exocet and bounced off the head of its surprised target who was too smashed to react to that or the follow-up assault. Terry threw down his tongs, ripped off his girlie apron that had been much the focus for Nobby's jibes, and launched himself at his startled mate.

The canvas and tubular steel patio chair Nobby had been sitting on collapsed and disintegrated under the combined weight of himself and his assailant. As he fell backwards, Nobby somehow managed to shift his weight, bringing his feet up into Terry's chest and, using his momentum, flicked him over his head, remarkably without spilling a drop of his lager, which he expertly clung on to. Terry sailed through the air and crashed into the side of Kath's sister's caravan. The sound of reverberating aluminium alerted the girls just as the Himmlers were returning. Jan couldn't believe the timing. She turned away and covered her face with her hands, too embarrassed to face the haughty neighbours.

'Helooo…' Kath greeted them cheerily as if the scene they were witnessing fifteen yards behind her wasn't actually happening.

Mr. and Mrs. 'Himmler' evacuated their Mercedes with the same gob-struck expressions they wore whenever they encountered these awful, disagreeable people, which wasn't at all surprising as they peered aghast beyond Kath and Jan to where Terry was now sat astride a hysterically giggling Nobby, trying to forcibly stuff the charred, smouldering sausage down his throat.

Once the Himmlers were out of sight, Jan elevated herself to her bollocking best, shouting at and shaming the warring pair while they stood there, heads bowed like a pair of naughty schoolboys, Terry breathing hard and still silently fuming, Nobby with tears in his eyes from laughing so much. Jan ordered them both indoors and they both skulked off to their respective caravans to get cleaned up and changed. An absolute must in Nobby's case as he'd been laughing so hard that he'd pissed himself.

Kath slapped Nobby's hand as it hovered tantalisingly over the table of mouth-watering food. 'Wait 'til everybody's here.'

'I'm starvin',' said Nobby as the munchies kicked in.

The girls had had the good sense to keep some of the best cuts of meat, pork and chicken fillets, away from the barbecue to cook indoors so that Terry's birthday meal wouldn't be a complete disaster.

'Oh, let him have a sandwich if he's hungry,' Jan relented.

In a breath, Nobby had fashioned a meat doorstep and was busy devouring it when his mate appeared, looking all clean and fresh - and still annoyed.

'Alrate, bud?' Nobby winked up at him with cheeks like a hamster's preparing for hibernation.

'You've broke me watch strap, yer twat,' moaned Terry.

'Don't you start again,' Jan intervened. 'It's your own fault. You shouldn't have been wearing your new watch to barbecue in.'

'Or fight,' added Kath.

'Or fight,' agreed Jan.

Nobby sat nodding in full agreement with the girls and he reminded Terry of that Argentinean pillock, Batistuta, in the nineteen ninety-eight World Cup when Beckham got sent off for kicking out at Simeone; stood there like a sanctimonious nodding dog as the Dutch referee brandished the red card.

Batistuta eventually caught the Gallagher stare and soon stopped the nodding. He looked up at Terry, his features inquisitive, innocent. Biting another huge chunk from his sandwich he immediately became Nobby again. 'What?' he tried to say with a mouthful of bread and meat.

Terry regarded the ravenous glutton for a while before dryly remarking that he'd better watch out for his fingers the next time he took a bite.

When Joe, Young Nobby and Rory returned they clocked the tantalising table of food and descended on it like a swarm of starving locusts. Jan and Kath shooed them away and ordered them indoors to get cleaned up. A spit and a cat lick later the lads re-emerged and resumed their raid on the birthday banquet.

'There's plenty o' stuff to go at on t'barbie,' said Terry, pointing in the direction of the portable crematorium that was still smoking away to itself a few yards away.

'Aye, an' best left there if yer ask me,' added Nobby.

'Well, no one's asking you – goghorn,' said Terry. 'Go on lads. Fill yer boots.'

The boys armed themselves with bread cakes and went to taste the wares.

'You'll need asbestos gloves,' warned Nobby

'It's all burnt,' complained Rory, peering down at the crozzled meat.

'Only on t'outside,' Terry reassured. 'It'll be just rate in t'middle.'

The blackened state of the food didn't seem to put Young Nobby off one bit and he soon had a burger and three sausages in between his bread and was heading back for the ketchup.

'Now there's a lad with a healthy appetite,' said Terry.

'Aren't you havin' any, dad?' asked Joe, eyeing the burger between his bun warily, and then trying to disguise it by smothering it in brown sauce.

'I've had one,' Terry lied, 'anyway, too many burgers gimme heartburn.'

'Urrgh! – Mine's all pink in t'middle,' said Rory after he'd took a bite.

'See. I told you they weren't overcooked,' said Terry.

'Don't eat it if yer don't want it,' Jan interrupted while giving Terry the look. 'There's plenty of other stuff here for you.'

Joe and Rory gladly ditched the burgers and refilled their baps with slices of tasty looking pork and chicken.

'Don't eat it, love,' said Jan to Young Nobby the human dustbin, 'you don't want to make yourself poorly.'

'Be rate,' he said carelessly, having already devoured two-thirds of the double-decker.

'I don't know where he puts it all,' reflected Kath, seemingly unconcerned about the likely prospect of her only son contracting salmonella.

The girls had put on a worthy spread and a good do was being had by all, even Terry, who'd started to come round a bit once he'd got some decent food inside him. He hadn't wanted his fortieth birthday marking in any way, but secretly he was chuffed at the efforts put in by Jan and Kath. The angel was in the driving seat of his psyche and he even managed to laugh along with everybody and take the piss out of himself as the topic of conversation came round to his failed culinary exploits.

Everyone had eaten their fill, except Young Nobby who was doing an expert job in seeking out and clearing away any remnants of pie or cake that had been left on the table, and the beer and wine was flowing. Nobby had sensed the gradual mood change in his volatile mate and took the opportunity to spark up another spliff.

The boys announced that they were going to camp out under the stars in the tent that they'd borrowed from One Eye, and do a spot of night fishing in the lake that belonged to the site. They started to get their gear together.

Kath had manoeuvred herself behind Nobby's chair. She put an arm around him and relieved him of the joint. She took a long, slow pull while massaging her husband's neck and shoulders. There she spent a good quality ten minutes with her man, forming a picture of contentment, sharing the smoke before gliding off to help Jan tidy up.

Terry wasn't really into smoking dope. The shit they used to use when they were younger was more often than not rocky soap; poor quality resin mixed with old melted down seventy-eights and other carcinogenic substances that used to make him edgy and sometimes paranoid. This Northern Lights, though, was something else. He observed his mate through piggy eyes. He knew he would have to work ten times as hard to achieve that laid-back demeanour. Fact was, Nobby didn't have to work at it at all. It just came effortlessly and naturally. For most of the time, inside Terry's head was a maelstrom of thoughts, ideas, insecurities, doubts, and notions all pinging around like a bally in a pinball machine. Inside Nobby's head was a millpond; a sea of becalmed waters, so still they were almost glasslike. Any distractions coming his way could be likened to the Marie Celeste breaking cover briefly through a bank of sea mist, then disappearing again as quickly and as silently as it came.

Jan sniffed the air and peered hard at Terry whose eyes were now beginning to resemble piss-holes in the snow. 'Are you smoking dope again?'

'What d'yer mean, again? This is the first I've had,' he protested, bringing the spliff into view from under the table, taking a pull and passing it on to Nobby.

'You'll make yourself poorly,' warned Jan in a tone that was normally reserved for Rory when he wouldn't listen to her.

'It's only a one off, love,' he said, finding it hard to keep the broad grin that wanted to break out all over his face in check. Although there was stuff still pinging around in his head, it was all happy stuff now and for the life of him he couldn't have wiped the smile off his face even if he'd wanted to.

'Yeah, chill out Jan, love,' drawled Nobby. 'It's his birthday. Lerrim have a laugh. Don't forget, I have to work with him every day being all serious an' miserable.'

'Fine, but don't come crawling to me when you throw a whitey, and you're chucking up all over the place.' Jan fired the warning at her husband then fired her glass of wine down her throat.

Kath and Nobby's easy closeness hadn't gone unnoticed by Jan as she flitted back and forth, tidying up after the meal. She felt a touch of envy and, as the effects of the wine took hold, a little guilty about her stolid reactions to the marijuana.

She began to reflect on what Kath had said. She watched her husband and his best mate getting slowly pissed and stoned. They were halfway through the holiday and Terry was beginning to enjoy himself at last. There he was with a big, silly grin on his face, and although it had taken drugs to make him unwind, she realised she should be grateful both for that and to Kath and Nobby for setting the mood. She inwardly chastised herself for acting like a prig and a killjoy and she was even more annoyed at allowing Terry to steal a march on her in the happy stakes.

Jan pondered the merry pair, sitting laughing and joking amongst themselves while she finished wiping the table clean. '*You silly cow,*' she thought to herself. This holiday was her idea. What she had here was exactly what she had wished for. What the hell was up with her?

Joe, Young Nobby and Rory took their leave and happily trudged off, laden with camping gear and fishing tackle. Jan watched them out of sight into the gathering dusk. The feeling that she normally would have whenever they left the house back in West Broughton was gone. The lack of trepidation was tangible. It felt safe. It felt good. She was beginning to feel a little fresh with the wine she had already drunk, but looking at the other three she still had a bit of catching up to do, so she drained her glass and went indoors for another bottle.

Terry looked a little apprehensive as his wife approached. The laughter stopped. What had he done now? Was he in for another bollocking?

'Open us this, love,' she said breezily, producing bottle of wine and corkscrew. There was an almost audible sigh of relief.

'Hey up, tha's givin' that wine some stick, lass,' observed Nobby.

'So? – Are you the only one that's allowed to get pissed then?'

Nobby held up his hands. 'Woah – you feel free Jan, love; knock yerself out.'

Terry and Nobby exchanged glances and gave appreciative nods. Things *were* looking up.

Terry eagerly opened the bottle of Australian Shiraz and filled glasses all round, him and Nobby unwisely mixing grape and grain.

As dusk slowly gave way to nightfall the conversation became more animated. The male voices got louder, and the Himmlers' curtains twitched constantly.

Terry began to feel sorry for the transient neighbours. He wondered if they'd ever been young. If they'd ever had a laugh, if they'd ever found a dirty joke funny. Then his mind went off on one and a disturbing image popped into his head: Mr. Himmler, naked except for SS hat and red swastika armband, skinny white legs squeezed into shiny leather jackboots and brandishing a riding crop; Mrs. Himmler, perched on all fours, handcuffed to the pull-out divan, Nancy Reagan ass in the air ready to be taken roughly from behind.

Terry quickly tried to banish the image from his head but he couldn't. It kept popping back in only more perverse and bizarre than before. He thought about telling the others but it had become too sick to relate. Jan snapped him back to reality.

'What are you smirking at?' she asked.

'What? Nowt,' said Terry, 'mind's wandering, that's all.'

By the time they were halfway down their third spliff a lot of crap was being spouted, but everyone was either too stoned or too pissed, or both, to even realise or care. Topics of conversation were flying off on tangents and no one seemed able to hold a train of thought for more than a couple of minutes. It didn't matter. Despite the earlier events and the falling out they were now all in good spirits, all except maybe Kath who was moaning that she'd eaten too much. The dope had started to make her paranoid about her weight. She'd always been a bit on the heavy side, more so after falling pregnant and giving birth, but Nobby wasn't complaining. That's how he liked his women and had always discouraged her from dieting.

'I feel all fat and ugly,' she announced miserably.

'Don't talk soft, woman. You need a bit o' meat on yer. I can't do wi' these skinny birds. I need a bit o' summat to grab hold of.' Nobby put his arm around his missus, reached down and in his own brusque but affectionate way, squeezed a handful of her behind.

The beauty of it was Nobby was telling the truth, bless him. He wouldn't have her any other way and she knew it. '*You bet it does,*' would be Nobby's lusty answer to the question: '*Does my bum look big in this?*' And that assertion reassured her and brought a smile to her face. Kath's aim was always to please her man and if that meant not worrying too much about the calorie intake then so be it.

Nobby was feeling nicely out of it and the smoke was definitely having an aphrodisiac effect. Copping a feel of his wife's arse had got him going and had sent him all tactile, touchy-feely.

That last joint had sent Terry a bit light-headed, and not wanting to throw a whitey and have Jan tell him '*I told you so*', he suggested they go for a midnight stroll in order to bring him round and get out of the way of the Clarkes before they ravaged each other in front of them.

Nobby whispered something dirty into Kath's ear and she let out a wicked laugh as they retired to their holiday love nest, abandoning the banks of empty beer and wine bottles, safe in the knowledge that the boys were out of the way for the evening. The van would be rocking on its axles tonight.

It was a warm, still night and the silence was deafening save for the sound of their own footsteps on gravel as Jan and Terry left the regimented rows of statics behind for the leafy lane that led down to the lake.

'We haven't done this for ages,' said Jan.

'What?'

'Held hands.'

Terry smiled and squeezed.

'Have you had a good birthday, then?'

'Yeah, it's the best fortieth I've ever had,' he joked.

They smiled at each other. Terry put an arm round Jan's shoulder and kissed her on the head.

It probably *was* the best birthday he'd ever had although maybe he'd overdone it a bit with the weed. He couldn't really put into words how he felt, but a swirl of pleasant emotions kept on welling up, making him want to yell out loud with a joy he wasn't able to explain. So he suppressed it by taking deep breaths and transforming it into the broad grin that now seemed fixed to his face.

Was it love he was feeling, or was it just the effects of the dope and alcohol? At forty years old he couldn't quite recall or describe the notion of love. After all, wasn't it a transitional thing; a feeling that morphed and changed, as had their relationship over the years; an acceptance and understanding of all those little quirks, foibles and habits, which were either funny or annoying? And those really testing times as young parents, when it was no longer just about the two of them; the routines, the hard graft, the times when they took each other for granted; not much time to speak and then nothing to say, like two ships passing in the night. The scrimping and scraping, the pettiness and the bickering; their love had survived it all, come through it, stood the test of time. Okay it wasn't the love they had when they were younger, but it was a mature love, a hard love; a love that went unspoken. When was the last time either of them had said those three words to each other? He couldn't remember. Was it so important? He liked to think that what they had and what they'd been through together over the last sixteen years transcended mere words, even though he had the urge to say them to her now. Somehow, and for some reason – maybe because he was aware that Jan was aware that he was stoned and pissed – he managed to stop himself.

'Are you okay?' she asked as they left behind the subdued lighting of the park perimeter for the eerie darkness of the lane.

'Yeh, but I need a slash, badly,' said Terry

'Don't leave me here,' panicked Jan as he headed for some nearby bushes.

'I won't be long. I'm only over here,' he said disappearing into the opaque undergrowth.

'Keep talking to me,' she said nervously.

Terry unzipped and started to empty his bladder. Funny how taking a leak was much more satisfying when you were pissed and/or stoned. It was almost orgasmic, especially when you were bursting.

He let out a satisfied sigh as his stream hit grass and leaf and a fine urine based mist rose in front of him. His head tilted back in divine relief until his eyes settled on the vast inky blackness of the summer evening sky. Stars were out in force and seemed to go on forever; a multidimensional canvas; a sparkling blanket that drew him in to the depths of space, where distant suns and planets dwelt amongst a cosmic soup that was thick with life, he was sure of it. It was a sky less polluted than in his home city, allowing him to see orbiting satellites, occasional flashes, shooting stars, maybe a U.F.O. if he was lucky.

As his imagination wandered, the vastness of it all suddenly overwhelmed him. All at once he felt a revelation. It was the realisation of infinity, a fleeting moment of perspective that sent a shudder through his entire body. He felt weightless, like he was floating ten feet above the ground, and an energy, a force he would never be able to describe, seemed to course through his veins. With it came a strange feeling of empowerment but at the same time, one of total insignificance in the grand scheme of things.

'You're not talking to me!' Jan's concerned voice broke the spell and snapped him straight back to reality. He shook himself dry, zipped up and made his way back.

As the evening had cooled, warm air from the earth was rising and evaporating into zillions of atoms, each carrying scents and sensations gleaned from the multi-varied vegetation. They were aromas that evoked memories of his childhood, when the sprawling estate of

East Broughton was only half-built and there were still fields and lanes and water-filled quarries, places of intrigue and adventure, places that even then felt like they belonged to a bygone era; a ruined building in the middle of a corn field that must have served some purpose back in the throes of the industrial revolution, spent and abandoned having outlived its usefulness long ago; generations of kids filled with destructive curiosity adding to its decay as it doubled for The Alamo or a hideout to play doctors and nurses where pre-pubescent boys and girls discovered each other's naughty bits, or for the older ones, just a place where they could go for a quick shag; decades-worth of rotting, used condoms testament to that.

Terry smiled to himself. In that instant he realised just what it meant to be forty.

'*So this is what happens,*' he thought. '*You spend the rest of your life getting out of it on stuff you should have outgrown years ago. Have mystical illuminations that only old hippies should experience, and end up reflecting and reminiscing on things that probably weren't half as cosy as you remember them anyway.*'

He thought of what now stood on the site of that old Victorian ruin that had become part of East Broughton in the late sixties. The image was there immediately: a piss-soaked block of three story flats, two thirds of which were empty and boarded up, the other third occupied by single mums on heroin and social security, trapped in some nightmare shit – how much was of their own making, Terry couldn't say.

He knew he'd had a tough upbringing. There had been plenty of shite and squalor around when he'd been a kid, but his childhood memories were positively halcyonic compared to what went down on his old turf these days.

'You were supposed to talk to me so I didn't get scared,' said Jan as Terry's shadow came into view. She took hold of his arm and im-mediately felt safer. They continued cautiously down the lane.

'Could you live out here?' Terry found himself saying out of the blue.

Jan paused before replying. 'Why do you ask that?'

144

'Dunno, really.'

'Well, you must have been thinking about it to ask it.'

He had, and still was. He was weighing up the roaring silence and the heady scents of nature that were all around him, as powerful and intoxicating as the skunk hybrid he'd been smoking all evening, against the noise, the stress, the pollution, shouts of rage, screams of fear, breaking glass and the wail of police sirens – his home of forty years.

It had only been four days since he'd left all that behind. It seemed a lot longer than that and a million miles away to him now, almost a different world. He didn't miss it.

In reality it was only seventy odd miles to the northwest and in three days time he would be headed back to it. It was a thought that depressed him slightly.

'I think I like it out here,' he said

''Course you do. It's the first holiday we've had in years. You were ready for it, I could tell.'

'No, I don't mean just 'cos it's a holiday. We could've gone to Majorca and enjoyed that, but it would have just been a holiday. I mean I actually like this place – I like it out here.

'Yeah, it's okay. A bit flat and boring, a bit quiet.'

'I'm not sure, but I think that's partly what I like about it; the peace, the tranquillity, the pace o' life.' Terry paused to try and formulate his words, to try and explain himself better. 'I don't remember ever feeling like this, not since I warra kid, anyway – Christ, that seems a long time ago now. Where did all those years go?' He posed that last question reflectively, to himself, then, fell silent.

Jan tried to make out her fella's features in the waning light of the half moon. She'd never heard him talk like this before and it scared her a little. She hoped he wouldn't be making a habit of smoking that Northern Lights stuff.

'What are you saying?' she asked a bit worried. 'That you'd up sticks and leave all your family and friends and come and live out here?'

'No...' said Terry, pausing. '...I dunno...' Longer pause.

'…Yeah, you know, I think I could,' he said all of a sudden and feeling somewhat excited at the thought. 'Couldn't you?'

'Don't talk daft,' said Jan, laughing at the very idea.

Terry didn't laugh. 'I'm serious,' he said. 'I think I'd do it if I could.'

Now he was really scaring her. She didn't like it when he got ideas into his head. They could lead to God knows what. The football thing was bad enough, but selling up and moving out to the sticks? She didn't think so. Jan put the notion down to drink and drugs and hoped he'd have forgotten about it all in the morning.

In the near distance, lights bobbed about out of the gloom. They could hear voices and there seemed to be a commotion of activity. As they got nearer they could make out the shape of One Eye's tent silhouetted by the light of a Tilley lamp and torch beams flashing in all directions.

'Odd it fuckin' still, yer numpty!' Rory's unmistakeable tones pierced the quiescent night air.

'You'll land it yerself if you don't shurrup, yer little shit!' Joe's voice snapped back.

Jan and Terry carefully picked their way down the slight gradient to the peg where the lads were pitched.

'Ooh Chihuahua, lads, what transpires?' said Terry, stepping into light.

'Dad! Mam!' exclaimed Rory excitedly. 'Come an' see what I've caught.'

Terry led Jan down the last bit of banking to where Rory was knelt removing the hook from the most beautiful, large mirror carp.

'Vasco De Gama – fella-me-lad!' Terry exclaimed at the sight of the fish.

'It's a beauty, innit dad?'

'It is that; fourteen-pounder I'd say.'

'Nearer fifteen,' said Young Nobby, who, along with Joe was guiding his torchlight at the multi-hued fish.

'At least,' added Rory, proud as punch and happy as Larry to have everyone there to witness the biggest fish he'd ever caught.

'Have yer seen it, mam?' he said, eager to get Jan's reaction.

'I have, love. It's a smasher – you're not going to kill it are you?' she added, a little worried at the distressed look of the fish with its startled eyes, flapping gills and gasping mouth. She felt a bit sorry for it laid across the landing net on the banking there, totally helpless and out of its environment. The boys laughed.

'Mam, don't be daft. I'll purrit back in a minute. It'll be alrate. Don't worry.'

Rory was the centre of attention again only under better circumstances now. He still enjoyed the buzz. Under the moving torch lights the colours of the carp shimmered and altered constantly and reflected up as jewels into Rory's shining eyes that sparkled with happiness. Jan and Terry watched the unconcealed euphoria in his face. He was a different kid now, unrecognisable from the son they had known a few weeks ago.

It was just after one in the morning and there was a faint chill and dampness in the air that made the scents of nature even sharper to the senses. Terry could smell the earth beneath his feet, fish slime and still water, the grubby-sweet smell of adolescence reeking from the boys and the warm, perfumed breath of woman as Jan wrapped her arms round him from behind and brushed his face with her hair.

It set him off again and his spirit seemed to ache with a yearning for something he just couldn't describe or comprehend because he didn't know what it was. His mind was grasping for words that could pin it down but the feeling he had was ineffable anyway.

The sensations always sent him back to another time, imagined or otherwise, he wasn't sure.

A passage from a book he'd once glanced at came to mind. He couldn't remember what it was or who it was by but it had somehow stuck with him and although he couldn't remember it word for word he did his best to recall it. It went something like, *"There exists in the human imagination an instinctive wish to break down the barriers of time and mortality and extend the limits of consciousness beyond the span of a single life. That instinct is akin to that aroused on those autumnal days when there is wood smoke in the air and a strange, disordered nostalgia pervades the mind or to the emotions inspired by distant church bells on a calm Sunday morning."*

That was as near and as good a description of how he felt right now. Here he was, Terry Gallagher, West Broughton lad. Forty years old. Crossroads.

He turned his face towards Jan and they smiled at each other, two proud parents. The perfect end to a great day.

Terry opened one eye and glanced down at his watch at the side of the bed. Just after nine-thirty. He opened his other eye, lay back on his pillow and stretched. 'Not too bad,' he thought; bit of a thick head but no real raging hangover. Not bad at all.

The surreal events of the previous evening came back to him as if he were recalling a dream but he knew they were real enough and they brought the smile back to his face again. It had been a strange night and he hadn't enjoyed himself as much in such a long time. He could hear Jan rattling around in the kitchen. He would get up and give her a hand with the breakfast and take bacon sarnies down to the lads, see what they were up to today, maybe suggest taking a ball down to the beach for a kickabout. He felt in a good mood, kicking off the duvet like an excited kid and jumping into his strides, not giving the fuzziness in his head chance to take hold.

He rubbed the condensation from the glass of the caravan window and peered out. There was a low mist outside; a bit of a sea fret that the sun would soon burn away as it got higher in the sky.

Looking out across the way Terry noticed that the Himmler's Mercedes was gone and he could see a sign stuck in the window of their caravan. He rubbed at the glass some more and could just make out the words '*For sale or to let – Apply at site office*'

'Bloody hell,' he said flippantly. 'Nowt to do with us, surely.'

Terry's pipe dream musings from last night came back to him and he pondered once more. He made a mental note to call in at the site office before they left on Saturday – just out of curiosity.

12

The committee of The Junior District Football League were ploughing through the minutes of the last meeting as Terry and Nobby burst through the double doors of the old ballroom at the Victoria Hotel. True to form, they were late and received the full on clichéd, abrupt silence and stares, like strangers walking into a Wild West saloon full of locals.

An ancient looking bloke sat at a desk near the door looked up at them with watery eyes. 'Name?'

'Er, Gallagher. Terry Gallagher.'

'Nay lad, the name of yer club,' the old guy said, wearily.

'Oh, aye – West Broughton Albion.'

The old chap took what seemed like an age to peruse a list, hands trembling, finally donning a pair of bi-focals in an effort to locate the name.

Nobby noticed that people were sitting at the tables with drinks, so he sloped off to the bar, leaving Terry standing there looking like a lemon.

'What age group?' the bloke asked eventually.

'Under fourteens,' said Terry, 'We're a new team.'

'Ah, why didn't you say?' He picked a pile of forms off the table and handed them over. 'Go fill these out while they're getting on with the minutes, then bring 'em back here.'

The forms were more involved than Terry had anticipated.

'Club Secretary – Club Treasurer?' Terry looked at Nobby in dismay. Nobby shrugged, disinterested, paying more attention to his lager.

Terry was beginning to realise that there was more to running a club than just turning up every Sunday and playing football. When he returned the forms to the old guy Janice Mary Gallagher had become West Broughton Albion's Treasurer and Katherine Clarke the Secretary.

The proceedings were a drag. The minutes went on for ages and the agenda was three pages long, registrations and any other business coming at the bottom of the third page. Nobby wasn't too bothered, Terry was driving and he was enjoying a good slurp, although the beer was a bit pricey.

The whole meeting was a bit of an archaic pantomime really. There was a strict, formal protocol and all questions had to be addressed through the chair. The nine members of The Committee holding court up on the stage were an odd looking bunch. The Chairman, head down, scribbling endlessly away, pausing occasionally to lift up his head and peer over the top of his glasses at someone who had raised a contentious issue, was wearing a dark, tired looking old blazer with some sort of crest on the pocket; shirt and tie, and brylcreemed grey hair swept back in an effort to look the part, but there was a seedy grubbiness about him that didn't quite allow him to carry it off. Seated to his right was the fixtures Secretary: thick Arran sweater and wild, Don King hair, looking like he'd just come off a North Sea trawler. To the left of the Chairman sat the Hon. General Secretary, slightly balding, knitted cardy, ruddy complexion and tugging on a pipe, looking most content and at peace with the world. Terry wondered if he might be wearing his carpet slippers under the table. The rest of the committee and representative officers were spread away from the Chairman in hierarchical importance, all with their own unique repertoire of facial expressions that they used from time to time in an effort to convey interest in the proceedings.

New admissions to the league had to be proposed, seconded and then balloted by the other clubs. When, finally, it came to their turn Terry would be left feeling totally perplexed at the asininity that was to follow.

'...Now, following St. Botolph's resignation from the league a vacancy has arisen in what will be the under fourteens section this season, and I understand a late application to join has been made by...' The Chairman shuffled a few papers before leaning across to the Secretary to get confirmation. '...By West Broughton Albion.'

150

Heads turned to check out the new faces. Terry squirmed a bit at the attention. Nobby grinned his grin. 'Can I have a proposer?' the Chairman enquired. A hand was raised a few seats to the front and left of the new boys.

'Blackbank proposes, Mr. Chairman,' stated the gravely voice.

'Thank you, Blackbank,' said the Chairman who then ordered the minutes Secretary to let it be noted in the minutes. 'Can I have a seconder to this motion?' asked Mr. Chairman. There was an uncomfortably long pause, a bit like being at an auction when the bid has reached its limit and the auctioneer is looking round for one last offer. A few heads turned here and there and any minute now, Terry thought the doors would open and a piece of tumbleweed would roll across the room. Finally, and so it seemed to Terry, reluctantly, a hand was raised in a corner of the room.

'Farshaw Juniors second, Mr. Chairman.'

'Thank you, Farshaw,' said the Chairman and it was duly noted. Then, Terry and Nobby were asked to leave the room while the ballot was taken. Nobby didn't really know what was going on and wanted to go back for his pint under the realisation that they would be out in the foyer for a few minutes. Terry had to drag him back.

'You can't go back in, they're voting, you plant pot.'

'What, you mean we're not in yet? What was all that propositioning bollocks then?'

'That was just to agree to vote.'

'It's a load o' shite if yer ask me.'

Terry concurred.

The old guy with the watery eyes ushered them back into the room. They were asked to remain standing. It felt like they were on trial.

'Gentlemen, by a majority vote the members of The Junior District Football league have agreed to accept the proposal put forward by Blackbank and seconded by Farshaw Juniors to allow West Broughton Albion a probationary period of one season in the under fourteens section of the aforementioned league. Welcome to the league, gentlemen.'

'Why are we on probation?' asked Nobby when they were seated again. 'We've done nowt wrong.'

'Dunno,' said Terry, 'I'll have to ask somebody.' Out of the corner of his eye, he soon became aware of someone staring at them. It was the bloke from Blackbank who had so readily proposed them. 'Don't mek it obvious,' mouthed Terry, 'but there's a proper ugly lookin' geezer eyeballin' us over there.'

Terry should have known better than to ask Nobby to be discreet as he immediately returned the guy's stare with interest. Terry was right, this bloke was your original missing link: shaven head, multiple rolls of skin where a neck should have been, a nose that looked devoid of any bone or cartilage, a few choice scars and an array of tattoos and a few pounds of bling as accessories. He gave Nobby an acknowledged nod without altering his expression before turning away.

'I know him,' said Nobby. 'That's 'Bulldog' Mason, proper bad lad he is. Him and his brothers did time for smashin' up Jesters nightclub and purrin' four bouncers in hospital. D'yer remember?'

'Yeh, I do,' said Terry. 'Demo men, aren't they?'

'Demo, tarmac, extortion, armed robbery; turn their hands to owt them boys.'

'What are they doin' runnin' a junior football team?' puzzled Terry.

'Search me.'

'And why was he so keen to propose us?'

Blackbank was a smaller but just as notorious a place as the Broughton housing estates, situated on the south-east edge of the city, surrounded by scrap yards, car dismantlers, an abattoir and an old scouring Mill that gave the whole area its permanent, sickly sweet smell of lanolin. Diddicois seemed to gravitate there, one-time caravan dwellers who had graduated up to bricks and mortar, but who still kept a grazing horse in the front garden alongside a battered, old Ford Transit jacked up on house bricks.

Blackbank under fourteens junior football team was run by Bulldog Mason and one of his cohorts, another nasty looking thug who went by the name of Sanchez. Unbeknown to Terry and Nobby, Blackbank were one major misdemeanour away from being *sine die* by the League. They had terrorised and intimidated teams and referees on a regular basis the previous season and had incurred record fines for their misdeeds. Bulldog ran the club as an outlet for his thirteen-year-old son Lee's psychotic behaviour, a junior psychopath in the making.

On hearing a team from West Broughton was seeking entry into the league, Bulldog had relished the prospect of pitting his lads against a side from an estate with a so-called hard reputation and his hand had shot up when Mr. Chairman had asked for a proposer. This had been the very same reason there had been reluctance to second the motion. One bunch of juvenile nutters in the league was quite enough for most of the other clubs, thank you very much. The other fact unbeknown to Terry and Nobby was that the verdict in favour of West Broughton joining was secured by a majority of one. A lot of the other clubs had expressed disquiet at their acceptance, hence the inclusion of the probationary period.

After the meeting had finished the management teams of Blackbank and West Broughton ended up face to face; well, not quite, because Nobby was a good ten inches taller than Bulldog, but they both held their ground, checking out each other's scars, a bit of mutual respect, before Bulldog said in his low growl, 'Fancy a pre-season friendly?'

The boys weighed up the offer for a few seconds.

'Aye, alrate then,' said Nobby, 'yer on.'

Once the date and venue had been settled, the boys from Blackbank took their leave. Sanchez brushed past them with what Terry perceived to be a slight sneer on his face. He had sensed the guy sizing him up and in his mind's eye Terry felt like the head-the-ball had already had him butchered and kneecapped in a remote lock-up somewhere.

After they had left, the guy from Farshaw Juniors pulled the newcomers to one side. 'Did he ask you for a friendly?'

'Yeh, why?'

'I'd think twice about it if I were you.'

'Why's that then?' asked Terry

'It won't exactly be what you'd call a friendly,' warned the guy.

'What, bit rough are they?' asked Nobby.

'Let's put it this way, he's asked every other club here tonight for a game and they've all refused. It's bad enough having to play 'em in the league. It's up to you, but don't say I didn't warn yer,' was the bloke's parting shot.

The old guy with the watery eyes, whose name they learned was Fred, approached them with reams of paper. It turned out they needed to have completed courses and qualified in Emergency First Aid, Junior Team Management and Coaching Courses, and hold a certificate for The Child Protection Register. These would all have to be attended and completed by the start of the second month of the season, and they cost money. Nobby saw it all as a complete waste of time, but Terry saw its importance and was quite impressed with the organisation, especially the child protection bit. *'Pity it wasn't introduced years ago,'* he thought to himself with all the stories he'd heard about pervy scoutmasters, choirmasters and priests, in mind.

Finally, old Fred announced what would be bad news for three of The Albion's players. Mark Ibbotson, Craig Tolley and Jimmy Lunt all had their fourteenth birthdays before the end of August, which meant that they would all be too old to play in an under fourteens side. Fred handed back the registration forms. Terry looked at the grinning, passport sized mug shots of the three lads pinned to them and wondered how he would break the news to them at training on Wednesday.

They took it bad.

'I'll forge me birth certificate,' said Ibbo, desperately. Terry shook his head sadly. 'I will, I've done it loads o' times, honest, you'll never tell.'

Terry looked him in the face and hoped he'd understand there was nothing he could do about it. Ibbo knew he wasn't for moving.

'Aww, Tel, come on man – don't be tight – a bit o' fiddle – they'll never twig.'

'I'm sorry, Ibbo lad. If they ever found out they'd scratch the whole team. I can't tek that chance.'

'Aww, this is fuckin' rip, man,' said Lunty belting a ball away in disgust. Realising that was it, no way out of it, no solutions, the lads became bitter and angry. Terry felt bad. He knew nothing he said or did would make them feel any different. And he knew that even though none of this was his fault, some of their anger would be directed at him, and he accepted it.

'Warra waste o' fuckin' time this has been,' said Tolley, pulling off his boots and slinging them in his bag. Nobby and one or two of the other lads tried to offer words of sympathy as they trudged off the field but they weren't having any of it. A consoling arm around a shoulder was met with an angry brush off. Terry wanted to tell them they were still welcome at training but he knew they would have told him to shove it. All they wanted to do was play football.

The rest of the lads were buzzing knowing they had their first game coming up at the weekend, albeit a friendly, but Terry wasn't in the mood for training any more. Nobby took most of the session.

Terry couldn't help feel that he'd somehow let the three lads down and at the end of training had fallen into one of his depressed moods, taking it out unfairly on Joe who was arseing about with Young Nobby while he had been trying to collect all the balls in.

'You kicked it. You fetch it!' shouted Terry.

'I din't kick it, it wa' Nob-nut,' Joe protested.

'Lyin' dick 'ead,' said Young Nobby, batting Joe on the back of the head.

'Tha's dead, batty boy,' said Joe, going for his mate. They both ended up in a rolling heap on the grass, spitting insults at each other. The two dads exchanged looks as if it was something *they'd* never done in their lives, conveniently forgetting the barbecue incident barely a week ago.

'Hey up! Young un!' Terry shouted over to a kid who was strolling past. 'Kick us that ball will yer?'

The lad trotted over and casually rolled it up the inside of his leg and flicked it into the air with his heel. He juggled it between foot and knee a few times, then balanced it on his foot before flicking it on to the back of his neck. He flipped it back in the air, nodding it up and down then allowing it to settle on the flat of his forehead, steadying it with ease, then back onto his foot, doing a three-sixty, then another, before finally volleying it back to Terry, forty yards, straight to feet. There was a stunned silence from Terry, Nobby and all the lads. Even Joe and Young Nobby had ceased messing about to stand and watch in awe.

'What the... Who the fuck... Hey kid!' shouted Terry eventually. The lad had already continued nonchalantly on his way. Terry made a move to go after him. 'Hey, fella! Wait up!' The lad looked over his shoulder, saw Terry making a move towards him and set off running. 'Hang on kid! I wanna word!' Terry shouted as he disappeared down the snicket and out of sight. He turned back to his lads. 'Did you see that? Did you bloody see that?'

'I saw it,' said Nobby. 'I wonder why he ran off.'

'That's Duane Geddess,' said Joe. 'He goes to our school – at least he's supposed to. He's never there.'

'What, you know him?' asked Terry.

'Yeah, he's a Comanche,' said One Eye. Terry looked at him inquisitively. 'He lives on East Broughton.' Terry nodded. People from East Broughton were called Apache's when he was a kid. Same race, different tribe, but still a slight on the North American Indian whichever way you looked at it.

'Why would he run off?' asked Terry. 'Can we get him to come training?'

'We don't want *him* in our team,' stated Joe.

'Why the hell not - can you do what he just did?'

'Nobody likes him.'

'He's a loner,' added One Eye. 'Won't talk to anybody; keeps himsen to himsen.'

'A weirdo,' contributed Ginner.

'A dirty fuckin' Comanche,' spat Biscuit.

Terry looked at Nobby who raised his eyebrows and shrugged his shoulders.

He wouldn't be letting this one lie. What they'd just witnessed was something special, something extraordinary. He would have to be finding out more about this elusive, enigmatic, yet seemingly despised character, that's for sure.

13

'…Just wait till I get me hands on the dope-dealin' bastard!' Terry fumed, kicking out at the empty plastic bags that littered his garage floor. Little Ginner appeared and stood before him wearing the blue and white striped extra large adult football strip. Terry looked him up and down in utter dismay. The shirt hung six inch below his knees, hiding the shorts that Ginner had pulled all the way up to his chest. He waggled and flapped the nine inches of excess shirt sleeve at Terry in order to show him that his arms were in there, somewhere. Ginner was about the smallest in the squad, so this was as bad as it was likely to get Terry thought to himself until Peycos and Biscuit came into view to be met by raucous laughter from the other lads. They'd both managed to ease themselves into one kit and waddled into the garage looking like a pair of clowns.

'Room for another,' announced Peycos. Even Nobby had to laugh.

'Tek 'em off yer pair o' dipsticks, you'll mek 'em even baggier,' implored Terry.

When all the lads were changed and present, only Young Nobby, Sasquatch, One Eye and Rigger, because of their size, managed not to look stupid, the rest were left fiddling, rolling and tucking excess yardage of the West Brom style replica kit.

'Colours look good,' said Nobby trying to be positive while Terry was imagining all manner of physical torture he would like to inflict on the toothless one for this almighty cock-up. He sighed, produced a team sheet and proceeded to read out the starting line up for The Albion's first ever game.

'In goal: One Eye.' (Pete Lancaster) 'Right back: Peycos.' (Jon Pejkozovic) 'Centre backs: Young Nobby and Sasquatch.' (John Clarke, Ben Neary) 'Left back: Ginner.' (Darren Thompson) 'Right hand side o' midfield: Biscuit.' (Ryan Crawford) 'Centre midfield:

Joe and Rammer.' (Joe Gallagher, Micky Ramskill) 'On the left: Sully.' (Andy Sullivan) 'Up front: Slum and Rigger.' (Steve Lumsden, Danny Mortiss) 'Sub: Basher.' (Billy Ashington) 'No reflection on you Basher, lad, you'll gerron at some point.'

Basher looked disappointed but received a few consoling slaps on the back from those close to him.

The lads were excited and in high spirits as the pickup trundled across the city; too high for Terry's liking. From his wing mirror he could see following motorists and passing pedestrians being showered with twigs and grass cuttings from a garden waste bag that the boys were chucking about on the back of the vehicle.

'Have a word, for God's sake, Nobby, we're gonna get pulled before we even get there.'

The bravado soon subsided as they drove through the streets of Blackbank. The surroundings weren't much different from their own, but it was alien turf, unfamiliar and a bit foreboding.

They rolled round the back of The Quarry Arms into the pub car park where, in the corner, stood a beat up old caravan that served as changing rooms for the Blackbank lads. No sooner had they pulled up than a Pit Bull terrier appeared from nowhere, snarling, baring its teeth and making lunges at the side of the pickup. The lads gravitated to the middle of the vehicle and huddled together in a baggy blue and white mass not daring to move. A group of Blackbank lads appeared at the door of the caravan in their black and white striped Newcastle style kit and began laughing and jeering. A string vest clad Bulldog Mason pushed passed the mocking youngsters and stood there having a chesty chuckle to himself before calling the dog to heel. At his master's command Arnie the Pit Bull ceased its worrying and cowered its way back to his side, but didn't venture too close in case he got a swift boot in the ribs. Mason's dogs always knew who was boss. They say dogs tend to look like their owners and Mason certainly had Bulldog-like features, hence his name, but in this case it wasn't entirely true, the dog was far better looking.

Bulldog was still wheezing a chuckle to himself as the lads gingerly got down from the back of the pickup. 'You should o' said,' he laughed, 'we'd have lent you a kit. Ne'er mind, it's gonna be a warm un, at least you'll get plenty o' ventilation in that strip, eh?'

The lads didn't see the funny side of it. Arnie continued to emit a low menacing growl, and they made sure they gave both dog and owner a wide birth as they went past.

Beyond the pub car park was a dirt track that after fifty yards or so opened up onto the Blackbank pitch. The ground had been formed from grazing land, judging by the three gypsy horses that were tethered nearby. The grass was scorched yellow and the ground baked hard and rutted. The markings were barely visible and the goalposts were bent, leaning and rusty.

The Albion weren't impressed. 'This is shit, innit?' observed Ginner, kicking at a piece of dried horse manure.

'It'll be the same for both sides,' said Nobby. 'Just try and keep the ball on the deck or it'll be bouncing all over t'place.'

The lads had a good warm up although they didn't really need it as it was touching twenty-four degrees. Terry checked his watch; it was already ten past two.

'Where's your ref?' he asked Bulldog.

'He'll be along in a minute; he's just finishin' off his pint.'

Terry slowly began to realise where the Farshaw manager was coming from. After five minutes or so a bloke dressed in a grubby tee-shirt and tracksuit bottoms and clutching a whistle, led a procession of around twenty or so supporters out of the pub and up the track. Loaded from the lunchtime session, they were all in rowdy, riotous form, eager for the Sunday afternoon entertainment to get under way.

Terry and Nobby exchanged looks of apprehension. What the hell had they let themselves in for?

'You run one line, we'll run t'other,' said Bulldog to Terry. 'Forty minutes each way?'

Terry nodded in agreement but wasn't sure who was supposed to keep time as he noticed that the ref, who reeked of booze, wasn't even wearing a watch.

The half-cut official called the two captains together. The lads had unanimously voted Joe skipper for The Albion. Psycho Lee Mason captained Blackbank. The bulldog mini clone swaggered up to the centre circle on short legs that were already starting to bandy. He had a manic looking stare and a fixed smile-cum-grimace; a look, on the whole, that made you step back a few paces when confronted by it; not necessarily through fear but from a reaction that made you think, *Jesus, what the fuck's up with him?* The kid was definitely a card short of a deck.

Joe won the toss and elected to kick off. Footballwise it would be the last thing The Albion would win all afternoon. Joe offered his hand to the Blackbank skipper who snorted at the friendly gesture.

'I'm gonna do you, an' right, pretty boy,' threatened Lee, bringing his face up close to Joe, staring right through him with those manic eyes.

Joe backed off and pulled a face. 'Fuck off, yer fuckin' inbred,' he fired back scornfully. Lee's eyes lit up, he was going to have a fun afternoon.

The whistle blew and Slum touched the ball off to Rigger who laid it back to Joe. Psycho Lee had set off like a steam train at the whistle and was heading for Joe at full tilt. Joe squared the ball to Rammer, a split second later the Blackbank nutter sent his forearm smashing into Joe's face. The force of the assault lifted Joe off his feet and sent him crashing, back first onto the sun baked ground, sending dust into the air and evacuating all breath from his body. He saw the cosmos and little else for a good thirty seconds. Rammer, and those West Broughton lads who had seen what happened, stopped playing. Young Nobby came tearing out of his defence to confront the grinning Lee, but the referee had waved play on and Rammer had the ball whipped off his feet by a Blackbank player who went straight on the attack. Half The Albion didn't know whether to look to Joe, confront the ref or go after the ball. Young Nobby stopped himself in his tracks and tried to backpedal in an effort to stop the wave of black and white shirts that were now surging forward. Sasquatch tried to close down the kid with the ball who slipped it into the almighty gap that had opened up in the Albion's defence.

Any one of three black and white shirted players was on hand to tap the ball in beyond a stranded One Eye who had come off his line to try and narrow the angle.

The ref blew for a goal. Half the lads were still trying to protest, the other half were stood over Joe who was still out for the count.

Lee Mason broke away from the joyous Blackbank players. 'Not so fuckin' chelpy now, are yer, pretty boy?' he sneered as he ran past the concerned Albion lads who were gathered round their floored captain.

Nobby had raced onto the pitch after Joe had failed to get to his feet and was now carefully sitting him up, pouring water down his bloodied face and over the back of his neck.

The referee trotted over and peered down at them. 'I didn't give you permission to come on the pitch,' he said to Nobby.

'He's gorra head injury, yer bloody idiot,' Nobby reacted angrily.

'Well gerrim off t'pitch, I wanna get t'game re-started.'

'Warrabout the foul? He just took him out. He didn't even go for t'fuckin' ball.'

'Din't see owt,' said the ref, trotting back to the centre circle. 'Hurry up and gerrim off t'pitch.'

'You tosser,' Nobby shouted after him while helping a Groggy Joe to his feet. Young Nobby helped his dad walk Joe to the touch-line.

On the other side of the field the spectators were hurling abuse. 'Soft as fuckin' shite, this lot!' – 'One down, ten to go!' Blackbank were having a laugh, psycho Lee lapping up all the sycophantic attention from his teammates.

'You know what it's about now, lads,' Nobby said to the boys as he left the pitch. 'You're playing against twelve men. Try and keep your shape, try and keep your discipline.'

Rigger was The Albion's hard man; he looked it as well, but he wasn't flash with it. He had a quiet but menacing air about him that made you instantly wary. He was one of those kids who had managed to build up a reputation without seemingly trying. He didn't usually go looking for trouble and seeing him in action was rare, but those who had knew what he was about. Subsequently, bullies and a lot of older lads off the estate afforded him a healthy respect. Rigger and Young Nobby, for two, wouldn't be taking any heed of Nobby's last words of advice. The football was secondary now; Lee Mason's card had been marked.

The Blackbank psychopath remained elusive for the next five minutes of the game, but Rigger watched and followed him like a hawk, biding his time.

The referee was ignoring Nobby's shouted requests to allow a patched up Joe back onto the pitch. 'Ho! – Ref! Are yer deaf as well as blind?' He turned exasperated to Terry who was more concerned with Rigger's body language than getting Joe back into the game.

'Keep your eye on Danny,' said Terry after the inebriated official finally relented and waved Joe back on the pitch, 'he's gonna do summat silly.'

Peycos pinged a long ball deep into the Blackbank half. Rigger wasn't even watching. Slum was up front all on his own and the Blackbank defence dealt with the threat easily, virtually unchallenged.

'Danny!' bawled Terry, 'Mind on the game, son.'

Rigger wasn't listening. Blackbank cleared their lines and all of a sudden Lee Mason found the ball at his feet. The Albion's management team instinctively knew what was coming next and together they cringed as their centre forward exacted retribution on behalf of his mate and captain.

Rigger flew at him horizontally and Mason went down as if pole axed. Before he could recover, just for good measure, Rigger stood on his hand and knelt across his throat, crushing his windpipe. Lee Mason's face turned purple and his eyes popped. A posse of Blackbank players immediately surrounded the Albion striker and fists began to fly. Young Nobby was next on the scene, crashing in on the act, scattering black and white shirts in all directions like skittles in a bowling alley. Pretty soon it was a free for all; Arsenal *vs* Man U. didn't even come close, and the Blackbank supporters on the far touchline were going mental, baying for blood. Nobby was going through the motions, ducking and diving, relishing every dig, feeling every sweet connection. *'Oh, to be young again,'* he wished.

Terry was standing with his arms folded, shaking his head. The ref was prancing round the periphery of the mêlée being about as much use as a chocolate fireguard, looking like a – well, a ref.

'Think we should step in?' Nobby turned and asked Terry, as much as he was enjoying it.

'Let's wait and see what them muppets do first,' he said nodding in the direction of the Blackbank crowd who could hardly contain themselves.

It looked like The Albion was gaining the upper hand in the scrapping stakes, much to the annoyance of Mason senior. His lad was in the thick of it, arms flailing aimlessly, face turning an even deeper shade of purple. But he had taken one or two smart direct hits and kept going down in the scrum. There was one Blackbank kid who looked suspiciously older than the rest and was more than holding his own. It had come down to a direct fistfight between him and Rigger and the contest was becoming particularly vicious. It turned out the kid was the son of Sanchez.

Bulldog decided he'd seen enough after his Lee had gone down for about the fourth time. Him and Sanchez came onto the pitch and roughly set about pulling the warring factions apart. Rigger and the Sanchez kid took some separating.

Lee Mason was hyper. He was ranting and raving, slavering and spitting threats at what he was going to do to all and sundry. Most of the Albion laughed and sneered at the demented dwarf, which only served to wind him up further. His dad batted him one round the head in an effort to calm him down, sending him into an instant sulk.

Rigger and Sanchez's lad, eventually parted, were psyching each other out like boxers at a weigh in, trying to exude calm and control, fixed stares; battered, bloodied but unbowed; chests heaving at the effort and the heat, neither daring to gasp air into screaming lungs, not wanting to show weakness, each resisting the urge to wipe away the blood, sweat and snot.

Little did anybody know that the events that took place on that hot August afternoon would start a feud between the pair that would fester and grow each time their paths crossed; two hard kids from hard estates who wouldn't back down, who would take their pride and hatred into their adult lives, a dissension that would turn to vendetta and would end in knives, baseball bats, shooters and murder in years to come.

The game, barely ten minutes old, restarted with a free kick to Blackbank. There wasn't much football to be played from here on in. Battles and altercations were happening all over the pitch and the ref was very selective in what he saw and what he didn't. Every time the ball ended up down the Albion's left side they were being harassed and intimidated by the rabble on the touchline. Ginner and Sully were copping for most of the rough treatment and were having a torrid time, getting things thrown at them, being tripped by spectators encroaching onto the pitch and worst of all being worried by Arnie who was snarling and snapping at their legs on the end of a long choker chain lead as they ran past. Terry eventually told them to tuck in out of the way, a tactic that Blackbank took advantage of by playing the ball down their right at every opportunity.

The Albion was three down by half time, one of the other goals coming from a dubious penalty, and the free kick count going, unsurprisingly, twenty-three to Blackbank – one to West Broughton.

The lads took on gallons of water and tended their knocks as best they could. They didn't even have a first aid kit. There were at least three or four walking wounded who would have come off in normal circumstances but, with only one sub and another forty minutes of open warfare to go, they would have to battle on, not that any of them would have readily volunteered to leave the fray in any case, they were all in this together. They might not win a bent game of soccer but when it came to spirit and fight they were determined to a man that West Broughton Albion would not be found wanting.

Terry said he was sorry to the lads for getting them into a fixture like this, especially as it was their first ever game and would understand if they wanted to sack it and walk away. They were having none of it. They knew they were never going to win this game no matter what happened and the score line would be irrelevant. They were in this now purely for the pride and the passion. They still had forty minutes in which to settle one or two scores and a few of the lads were surprised and hurt at Terry's suggestion. He didn't doubt their commitment to the cause but he'd wanted to see a game of football not a near riot. They could have stayed on the streets of West Broughton and touted for that. The whole point of The Albion was to steer the lads away from shit like this.

From here on in tactics went out the window. Nobby was left to do his rallying and motivating, which leaned more towards how to get a sly dig in without the ref seeing, or where to plant a discreet elbow in order to have maximum effect rather than any positive coaching. 'An eye for an eye, if yer ask me,' he said when Terry gave him a disapproving look.

Terry spent most of the second half watching the sad specimens of humanity across the other side of the field screaming words of wisdom at their offspring: 'Twat the little cunt!' – 'Brek his fuckin' legs!' and that was just from the women.

One positive Terry gleaned from the whole unsavoury encounter was The Albion's fitness levels. The hard training through the summer had paid dividends. The physical confrontations had taken a toll on the Blackbank players and the Albion started to get the upper hand. They had the ball in the net on three occasions but the ref found some excuse to disallow them all.

Joe was still seeing double and Basher came on for him for the last twenty minutes, keen as mustard, ready to be blooded, eager to be as one with the lads.

Blackbank were paggered near the end and the ref decided to blow up five minutes early. The crooked score line read: Blackbank - 4, West Broughton Albion - 0. There were no handshakes, no three cheers, just muttered threats and square-ups. The warm air was volatile as the players milled around. Lee Mason was itching to resume his personal battle with Joe who had just finished throwing up for the third time. (A head scan at the infirmary later would confirm mild concussion.) Young Nobby stepped into his mate's boots. 'You wanna fuckin' start again, yer little shit? Start on me… an' you… an' you…' He moved towards Lee and two of his buddies who were skulking around like a pack of cowardly hyenas waiting to pounce on some injured prey. They reluctantly backed off giving notice of their intent with menaces as to what was going to happen when the league encounter came round.

Eventually, the Blackbank players and their supporters dispersed and Terry wisely kept The Albion back for a warm down, not wanting to promote a pitched battle in the lane or the pub car park.

'See yer back here for t'league game,' said a red faced Bulldog, struggling to rein his choking dog in on its lead.

'Aye, and with a proper ref next time yer cheatin' set o' bastards,' said Nobby.

Bulldog laughed his wheezy laugh, and now not only looked but also sounded like his dog with its lolling tongue and bulging eyes, not having the sense to take the strain off its choker and ease its plight. The hot sun had done its worst to Bulldog's shaved pate; it was beetroot red and looked ready to blister. Sweat stained the front of his mucky vest and Terry caught a revolting mixed whiff of dog slaver, stale ale and B.O.

'Don't matter who refs us,' he said, cockily. 'We've never been beaten on this pitch – come away, yer bastard.' He yanked on the chain hard and Arnie yelped. He left them with that and waddled away, him and his dog, both with their bandy legged gait.

They'd never lost at home because of the fear and intimidation meted out to referees. Any man in the middle caught trying to do his job in an unbiased manner ran the risk of being lynched and a lot of officials refused to go near the place. Blackbank would be under close scrutiny from the league this season. They were on their final warning and were skating on thin ice.

Terry and Nobby assumed that Blackbank hospitality would be in short supply back at The Quarry Arms and decided it best not to linger too long in the car park. Terry wasn't relishing the return visit in the league as they pulled onto the roads of Blackbank, but the lads were. On the back of the pickup they were boisterous and in high spirits again despite the four - nil defeat, showing off war wounds and relating exaggerated tales of battle. They hadn't gone far when they came across two of the Blackbank players, still in their kit, on their way home.

'That's the twat what nutted me,' exclaimed Peycos as the pickup drew nearer. 'Quick, gimme the fuckin' bucket,' he demanded.

As they trundled past, the two unsuspecting kids caught the contents of the trainer's bucket which, until that moment had been full of West Broughton piss, full in the face. It was quickly followed by two overflowing bags of rotting garden waste. The lasting image of the two gobsmacked lads, standing there, soaked from head to toe in human urine and organic crap, promoted bellyaching laughter all round as The Albion headed for home.

14

'If I aren't back in an hour send out a search party,' said Terry, slamming shut the passenger door of the pickup and leaning back in through the open window.

'If you're not back in *half* an hour I'm leavin' yer,' warned Nobby. 'Charity Shield, Sky One, Fusiliers, four o'clock kick off,' he reminded him.

Terry grinned, banged out a *see yer in a bit* on the pickup's roof and walked off into the afternoon drizzle.

Nobby wasn't too happy at having to sit and look after the pickup for any length of time while Terry went about his mission. He was parked slap bang in the middle of Apache territory where your wheels could be whipped away in a breath without you even knowing and be left teetering on a pile of house bricks if you didn't keep your wits about you. He instinctively reached down under the driver's seat to make sure the sledgehammer was in quick and easy reach. He ran his fingers up and down the smooth hickory shaft and felt comforted. He took a few furtive glances around to make sure he wasn't about to be disturbed before settling down with his copy of the Sunday Sport. It took Nobby longer than most to read a newspaper, and even though the seedy tabloid was predominantly full of pictures of female flesh, it would be sure to keep him occupied for a while.

Terry's only starting point was that the lads thought that the elusive Apache lived in one of the flats off De Lacey Avenue and as there were around fifteen blocks of these three and four storey concrete monstrosities, all named after Norman noblemen or major players in the English civil war, it would be like looking for a needle in a haystack. Needles, of the hypodermic variety were strewn around in abundance Terry observed as he wandered through the soulless heart of the estate, the greyness of the day only adding to the flat, two dimensional, monotone feel of the place.

He made his way through concrete lined rat runs and hard, red brick arbours that served no purpose except as a shadowy retreat for users, where muggers could melt away into the darkness. He wondered whether the smashed paving stones that ran between the tower of Gaunt House and Fairfax House that he now paced were once fields in which he had played as a nipper. He didn't doubt they were but the memory was so distant and the present setting too abstract for him to recollect any sense of bearing or location. He stopped at the dank, stinking entrance to one of the tower blocks. A few feet away lay the shattered carcase of a television, its innards – tubes, valves and circuitry – spread around it. Terry looked up into the rain heavy sky. The telly had obviously been dropped from a great height and he didn't suppose whoever had lobbed it had bothered to check or cared if anyone was underneath it. He stood there aimlessly under that fine, feathery rain that seemed to soak you through as much as a torrential downpour, and then peered beyond the wire re-enforced glass doors into the dark, unwelcoming but relatively dry lobby and decided to stay wet.

He moved on and realised he would have to talk to somebody soon, start asking questions. He would just have to be careful who he approached. He came away from the flats and hung around a parade of shops. A woman appeared and scurried on her way before he had a chance to stop her; head down, focus on the pavement, no eye contact, from A to B as quickly as possible, not because it was raining, this was how East Broughton people went about their business, in a climate of fear and perpetual nervousness.

He came across three youths huddled together outside a boarded up bookie's, smoking and chatting. Terry studied them briefly before venturing near. They were charvers, your typical heroes; stripy jumpers and cheap label hoodies pulled over fake Burberry caps, shell suit bottoms with the obligatory stripe down the side, tucked into white socks and nasty looking trainers. One of the youths spat habitually at regular intervals, the pavement around their feet peppered with little flecks of spittle amongst the flattened patches of old, hard chewing gum.

'I'm looking for a kid of about thirteen, call him Duane Geddess. Do any of you happen to know where he lives?' Terry looked at the faces in turn. They all seemed to have translucent skin, anaemic looking with bum fluff growing out of acne chins. None of them spoke. One of them took a drag on his fag and contemptuously flicked the butt sparking at Terry's feet before walking off. The other two followed their mate without saying a word. Terry watched the three skinny charvers walk away. Funny, he thought, how they all acted hard and menacing but looked as though they couldn't knock the skin off a rice pudding. He shrugged and checked his watch. If he didn't get any joy soon he would have to go cold calling, knocking on doors, and he didn't want to resort to that.

Down one street there was a bit more activity. There were noisy youngsters playing out and among them, another gang of five juveniles stood in a group that he decided to make his enquiry to. Two of them looked older than the other three and it was to one of them that he put his question.

'Who wants to know, man? Are you th' D.S., or somink?' demanded the tall Afro Caribbean lad who was dressed in baggier and slightly better designed threads than the heroes he'd approached earlier.

'No,' said Terry. 'He's only thirteen; he's not in any trouble or anything.'

'Hey, you aint no paedy, is yer?' asked another dude suspiciously.

'Yeah, he's a batty-boy, man, innit,' piped up one of the younger kids, a cocky looking little sod who didn't look much older than Joe, 'look at 'im.'

Terry frowned then laughed at the suggestion.

'If yer ain't no bum-bandit what yer want the kid for? You some sorta social worker?' asked the smaller of the older youths, peering from beneath a knitted stripy woollen hat in Jamaican colours.

'Yeah, you could say that,' agreed Terry.

The taller youth didn't seem convinced. 'What yer say 'is name was?'

'Duane Geddess.'

'Nah, bro', never heard of him.'

'You sure? Skinny kid; mixed race.'

His mate got threatening. 'You callin' him a liar, homi?'

'No,' said Terry calmly. 'I just thought that streetwise fella's like you'd know everybody around here.'

'Yeh, well we aint heard o' no Duane Geddess, man – okay?'

Terry looked the two self-styled leaders of the little posse hard in the eyes until he knew he'd made them uncomfortable. 'Okay,' he said finally. 'Cheers, lads.'

He had only walked on a few yards when a scruffy little oik on a BMX rode up to him.

'Who yer lookin' fer, mush?'

Terry stopped in his tracks and looked the kid up and down. He was only about eight or nine. His hair was wild and matted and his hands and face hadn't seen soap in a long time. He was soaked to the skin dressed only in dirty tee shirt with a faded Bart Simpson on the front and a pair of jeans ripped at the knees, but these weren't designer tears. He seemed oblivious to the rain. A solitary toe poked out of a hole in the front of a pair of knackered, canvas plimsolls that he wore without any socks. The BMX he sat astride looked fairly new and had more than likely been purloined from a West Broughton garage over the holiday fortnight. As he looked up at Terry in anticipation of an answer, a fresh river of snot ran from his nose over previous flows, like lava from a volcano that had hardened and turned green at the edges.

'A kid called Duane Geddess,' said Terry, 'd'yer know him?'

The youngster looked beyond Terry to the group of youths who were still looking his way. 'Might do,' he said with all the caginess of an experienced copper's nark. 'What's it werf t'yer?'

Terry laughed at his style, reached into his pocket and flipped a pound coin into the air. The kid watched it spin with unconcealed contempt. Before Terry had caught it the little urchin had already started to wheel away.

'Where you going?' he called after him.

The lad stopped and turned. 'You tekin' the piss or what mush?'

'How much then?'

'Tenner.'

'Fuckin' tenner!' exclaimed Terry.

The kid shrugged a take it or leave it look and left the ball in Terry's court. He weighed up his dilemma. Should he send the cheeky little sod on his way or give in to extortion and get what he came for? What if he coughed up and the spraffer didn't know the Geddess kid, spun him a yarn and pissed off with the tenner? He didn't fancy being skanked by an eight year old.

Time was moving on and he didn't want to have put in all this effort and have a wasted afternoon. He eyed up the scruffy brat warily. It went against all his instincts to trust a son of East Broughton, but he needed to make a decision. The rain had begun to get heavier yet the kid looked like he would be prepared to wait all day if need be.

'You're sure you know him and where he lives?'

The boy nodded slowly.

'Where?'

'Lowry first,' he said, holding out a grubby palm.

Terry laughed. 'Gerraway wi' yer, I'm not that stupid.'

The lad let out a little sigh, like he wasn't in the mood for playing games. 'No dosh – no deal,' stated the cocky young con, safe in the knowledge that he held all the aces.

Terry saw him as an adult, a future tarmac tycoon conning his way across suburbia, relieving scores of vulnerable pensioners of their life savings for new driveways that were guaranteed to lift and crumble within a month of them being laid.

Terry held his gaze and produced a folded ten-pound note. He held it out and the youngster made to grab it. Terry teasingly withdrew his hand.

'If you try and skank me,' he warned, 'I'll come after yer, an' I'll wrap that bike round your scruffy little neck – you understand?'

The kid tutted and pulled a face like he was hurt at the very suggestion. He took the tenner without grace and hurriedly stuffed it in his jeans while nervously glancing a look beyond this easy touch to the gang who were still taking a remote interest in the proceedings. Terry gave him a look of anticipation. The lad raised his eyes and simply nodded at the block of flats that they were standing in front of and that Terry had his back to. He looked over his shoulder. A sign above the entrance to the flats read: **ROM EL OUSE** He quickly deciphered the name of the place from the missing letters.

'Cromwell House,' he said out loud. 'Is this where he lives?' The kid nodded. 'What number?' asked Terry.

The kid shrugged. 'No numbers,' he said. 'Second floor; blue door wi' two big 'oles in it.' And with one final nervous glance at the big lads he was off, pedalling for all he was worth, disappearing into the labyrinths of brick and concrete, no doubt chuffed to bits at such an easy afternoon's work.

Terry felt a little miffed at relinquishing so much money so easily, but if it paid dividends then it would be worth it.

The five youths suspiciously watched the nosey stranger enter the flats. He didn't know if these guys were big hitters on the estate. Well, he knew that three of them weren't, they were only schoolkids, but the other two had a menacing air about them. It was still their turf and he realised that they wouldn't take kindly to anyone they didn't know sniffing around asking questions. He glanced over his shoulder to make sure they weren't following before entering the building.

A stink like a septic tank washed over him as he gingerly made his way up the cold, echoing stairs. Graffiti and daubed slogans adorned the walls and, judging by the smell, the perpetrators' choice of material hadn't always been paint. On the first floor landing, over-flowing black bin-bags of rubbish had been dumped outside a door and soiled disposable nappies lay discarded round about. Behind paper-thin walls he could hear a telly blasting out. Gunfire and overly dramatic background music from the Sunday afternoon matinee western was doing its best to drown out the hungry sounding screams of a baby. He made his way up the next flight and the first floor noises gave way to the sound of a techno rhythm, the urgent, relent-less beat muffled and distant, probably coming from somewhere on the third floor, but still loud enough to drive those closer to it insane.

On the second floor he looked around, checking out all the doors until he saw it, in the corner, a blue door, scratched and battered with two holes kicked through the outer skin just like the kid had said. He knocked and waited. He didn't know what he would say; he hadn't really planned this part. The lad might not even be in and he hadn't thought to bring pen and paper so he could stick a message through the letterbox. He knocked again, a bit louder this time and now he heard a woman's voice.

'If it's Marco, tell him I'll have his money by Thursday.'

Terry heard a key in a lock and bolts being slid back. Looking at the two holes in the door he could well see the need for the extra security. The door eventually opened to the couple of inches the inner chain would allow and the face he remembered from Soldiers field cautiously peered up at him through the gap.

'Hiya, my name's Terry. Duane, isn't it?' he began. The lad looked at him bewildered and a little scared. 'I saw you down at Soldiers field a week or two back,' Terry continued, 'we were having a training sesh. You kicked the ball back to us. D'yer remember?'

'Tell him Thursday,' shouted the woman's voice. 'I'll have it for him by Thursday.'

'It in't Marco, mam,' Duane shouted back into the room.

'Who is it then? If it's a punter, they can fuck off. I aren't entertainin' today.'

'You heard that,' said Duane moving to shut the door, 'she in't entertainin' today.'

'Whoa!' said Terry holding a hand against the door to prevent it from being closed in his face. 'It's you I want to speak to, not your mam. Can I come in and have chat?'

The boy looked agitated. He shook his head. 'Nah.'

'Aren't you even curious as to why I'm here?'

'Who is it?' The woman's voice became irritable.

'Look, I've got to go. Me mam's not well.'

'Listen, Duane, from what I've seen I think you could make a good footballer. I want you to join my team.'

The kid looked up at the strange bloke who had made this extraordinary effort to seek him out. He was nonplussed. 'How d'yer know me name? How did yer know where I live?'

'I'm Joe's dad – Joe Gallagher?'

'Oh, yeah; I don't really know him that well.'

Duane's embarrassment at being an outsider was written all over his face. He bowed his head, his eyes concentrating on his shoes. Terry instantly felt sorry for him.

'Why did you run off like that the other day?' Duane shrugged, kept his head down and muttered something about running errands for his mam and not daring to be late home. 'Look, Duane, this is a new thing for all of us and I'd love you to be a part of it, get to know some of the lads, have a laugh. What d'yer say? Just gimme five minutes to have a chat.'

The kid shook his head sadly. 'Me mam won't wear it. You're wastin' yer time.'

'Let me have a word – you never know,' Terry persisted.

The lad agonised for a while, taking nervous looks over his shoulder. Terry's hand held firm against the door, then, against his better judgement the youngster relented.

'Move yer hand,' he said.

Terry relaxed his grip; Duane closed the door, slid the chain off and let the stranger in.

Terry took in the surroundings while Duane re-bolted and locked. The place was a dump. He placed a fatherly arm around Duane's shoulders while the boy led him into the living room.

'Who the fuck are you?' demanded the prone figure in a slurred, contemptible tone.

Duane's mam lay sprawled across a beat up old sofa that looked as if it could be crawling with infestation. She looked dirty and un-kempt; in fact, she and the sofa looked as one, like they rarely parted company; she was part of it. She was an addict; Terry saw that straight away. She hadn't yet reached that ravaged and wasted Smiffy look, but her skin wasn't in good shape and her eyes had started to recede into their sockets. He could tell she had been a big, healthy girl one time, similar size and shape to Nobby's Kath, but now the weight had started to drop off her bones and skin was starting to hang loose. She was a white lass, and that obviously meant that Duane's dad must be black but there was no sign of a male presence in the place. In fact, Duane had never had a father figure in his life. He'd never even seen his real dad.

Judging by what he'd heard already, Terry also knew that she paid for her smack by selling her body, and he couldn't help but think as he stood before her that there must be some desperate punters about.

Despite having an open mind, he hadn't been quite prepared for this. The place was an absolute shit-hole, and to make matters worse, over in one corner of the room, peering through the bars of an old cot-cum-pen, with big dark eyes, was Duane's younger half-brother, Leo. The toddler had just gone two, but neglect and under-stimulation made him look and act younger. The stronger of the smells in the flat was coming from Little Leo's cot and the dispos-able he was wearing, the sodden weight of which was making it hard for the poor mite to stand at the bars for long periods. His periodic cries for attention and relief from the discomfort would be half-hearted and spasmodic. Over his short life the little guy had learned that nature's mechanism for seeking love and a cuddle didn't always work. He was all cried out.

Duane saw the sense of temporary shock in Terry's face and spoke up for him.

'This is er…' Duane had forgotten Terry's name and looked up at him for guidance. It took a while for Terry to snap out of his barely concealed repulsion.

He cleared his throat. 'Oh… Terry, Terry Gallagher,' he said.

Duane's mam didn't let him get any further. She half sat up and started to rant at him.

'Look, I don't know who's been tellin' tales, burrit's all bollocks, d'yer hear me? There's some bastard gorrit in fer me, an' I'm not havin' it. I'm a good mother, I am. I've been poorly lately, that's all. I told that last bitch that came round; I'm not on t' skag any more, I take me methadone; it's all in me records – he'll tell yer,' she said jabbing a finger in Duane's direction. 'He fetches all me scripts. An' who I have round here's nobody's business but me own. It's hard bein' a single mother round here – It's so fuckin' hard…' She started to shake and tears welled up way back in those sunken eyes. Duane stood there looking at his mam, and Terry felt the awkwardness and the helplessness pouring off the lad. Before Terry could interject she went off on one again. 'Don't lerrem tek me kids off me…' she wailed '…they're all I've got. I'd die if they took 'em away, I swear to God I'd fuckin' kill meself. I do me best wi' 'em, I really do.' Her voice croaked and cracked. She looked appealingly into Terry's face before burying her own in her hands, blubbing uncontrollably.

Something wasn't right and Terry sensed it. She was putting on an act that was pretty convincing, but Terry could tell, an act is what it was and he saw right through it.

Leo had started to whimper at his mother's outpourings, turning eventually into a full-blown cry. He thought the man might be another stranger come to hurt her. She ignored the little fellow as though he wasn't even there. It was left to Duane to go over and comfort his sibling.

Terry had only been in this woman's company for no more than a few minutes but already he felt something close to hate. Her dry, lifeless hair hung down in front of her face and she rocked back and forth in mock anguish. She was pathetic.

'I aren't from Social Services,' Terry said dryly.

The crocodile tears stopped as if they were on tap. She looked up. At least a bit of colour had come into her features, what with all the method acting.

'Yer what?'

'I said I'm not from Social Services.'

'Well where the fuck are yer from then, an' what yer doin' in my house?' she spat at him nastily.

The transformation from distraught mother back to callous smackhead bitch was instantaneous.

'He runs a football team for some o' the lads at school,' explained Duane as he tried to calm down the little one. 'He wants me to play for 'em.'

'Ha!' she laughed scornfully, 'I don't fuckin' think so.'

Duane's face didn't register any disappointment at his mother's dismissal of the notion. He looked at Terry without any change of expression like he knew the reaction long before it came.

'Duane's got bags o' talent, Mrs. Geddess, from what I've seen he'll make a great footballer. You've got to let him have a go.'

She reached for a packet of fags, swept dishevelled hair off her face and lay back in her original prone position. All this thespian bullshit had taken it out of her. She lit the cigarette and pulled smoke in deep, letting the nicotine calm her down while observing the idiot in front of her. This was a new one. Was this guy for real? What was the motive?

'My name's not Geddess,' she said like she'd scored a point. 'His name's Geddess, not mine.'

So what? Terry thought to himself. *I don't give a stuff what your name is, just let the boy play football.*

'Look, all I want you to do is let Duane come training for a couple of hours on a Wednesday and play for us on a Sunday when the season starts.'

'No chance. I need him here to help me look after t'young un an' run chores. I'm not well; I'm findin' it hard to cope at t'moment – for fucks sake Duane! Go an' gerrim a biscuit or summatt – shut the little sod up!'

Duane left the distressed bairn with his pleading arms reaching through the cot bars and went into the kitchen.

It's not a biscuit he wants, you bloody moron, screamed a voice inside Terry's head. She blew smoke at him. His anger bubbled and erupted but he made sure he channelled it.

He leant over and got as close as he dare. 'Listen here, you fucking cow,' he hissed through gritted teeth, 'You give that kid a break or I'm straight down to Social Services first thing in the morning and I'll have 'em both in care in a breath – you understand me?'

She stared at him wide eyed and shocked. He fixed back the stare and she knew he was deadly serious.

'That's fuckin' blackmail,' she said before launching into a coughing fit.

'You'd better believe it,' said Terry menacingly. 'And you can cut out the act 'cos that poorly mother shit don't wash with me.' He backed off as she hawked and spluttered. 'It's about time you got off your lazy fat arse and cleaned this shit tip up a bit, and started to look after that poor little bugger over there instead of leaving it to a thirteen year old.'

The thirteen year old came back from the kitchen clutching a digestive.

'Yeah, go on then, I will have a pot o' tea,' said Terry as though Duane's mam had made the offer. She stopped the coughing and glowered up at him.

'Oh, I've just remembered, we've no milk,' she countered.

'That's no problem. I'm sure Duane'll nip on to the shops and get a pint, won't you fella?'

Duane glanced at his mam and Terry in turn, unsure of what was going down.

'Yeh,' he said eventually. 'Er... I've no money.'

'My treat.' Terry dipped into his pocket and at last found a use for the pound coin his young informant had scornfully rejected earlier. Duane hesitated for a moment, eyes fixed all the while on his mam as if waiting for contrary instructions. They didn't come so he put the biscuit into one of Leo's outstretched hands, took the money and went out onto the streets of East Broughton, in the rain, in search of milk; inside his head a fudge of confused thoughts and emotions.

Philanthropy was something Duane had never had to deal with, especially when it was being directed at him. He couldn't understand why the dad of a kid he hardly knew would go to such extraordinary lengths to get him to play football. He wasn't even sure he wanted to anyway. He knew he wasn't liked at school. He was never there regularly enough to form friendships and was seldom allowed out to play or go places. He'd got used to being a loner, a doormat, a chid carer and general skivvy for his mam. And although he couldn't deny that the benevolent interest this strange guy was showing stirred up something weird inside him, something tingly and warm, the feeling of actually being wanted, he knew that it would only serve to complicate things, add grief and more problems to his already miserable existence.

Why couldn't he have resisted the urge to show off when the ball came rolling tantalisingly towards him that day? What was that feeling; that rush, that sensual thrill, that simple epicurean enjoyment of flicking a ball into the air and performing magic with it that he found too hard to resist? Terry Gallagher knew what it was and he knew that all kids should have the chance to experience it, at every level, no matter what their ability. But he also instinctively knew just from watching Duane for those few short moments that the lad was potentially something special and he so much wanted the chance to nurture that potential, for him to realise and bring out this rare talent.

Duane genuinely didn't know what he had or how he came by it. It was simply a gift he had been born with. In the months to come he would do things with a football that no manual could ever coach and would leave players and managers who witnessed his sublime skills open mouthed and speechless.

As he sprinted zigzagging a shortcut route to the shops through the rain-wet maze of his familiar ghetto, thirteen year old Duane Geddess had never played a competitive game of football in his life and, thinking of the retribution his mam would take out on him because of this interfering bloke from West Broughton, he doubted whether he ever would. 'You've gorra fuckin' cheek, comin' up here pretendin' you're a bleedin' social worker.'

'I never said I was a social worker.'

'You wanna be careful. I know people who could hurt you.'

'Oh aye, who'd that be then? Your pimp? Your dealer? Or are they both the same person?

'I told yer, I don't do drugs any more, an' I ain't gorra pimp yer cheeky bastard,' she said unconvincingly.

Terry picked up a brown stained spoon off a cluttered coffee table that contained loads of evidence contrary to that last statement.

'What d'yer use this for, then?' he said waving it in front of her face, 'stirring your tea? And I understand you're not entertaining today. So what would that be, eh? Singer? Stand up comedienne? C'mon love; do I really look that daft? When I knocked on your door you thought I was your dealer doing a bit o' debt collecting, or a client after a spot o' Sunday afternoon nooky.'

Terry threw the spoon into a cup on the table that had penicillin growing out of it. Duane's mam took a last pull on the tab end of her fag and showed her agitation by grinding it out in the middle of an already full to overflowing glass ashtray like she was trying to bore a hole through it and the table underneath.

'Just what the fuck d'yer want from me?'

'I've told you - cut Duane a bit o' slack, let him play football.'

'Is that it?'

'That's it.'

'No Social Services?'

Terry glanced over at little Leo behind his bars. He was on his knees whimpering among the crumbs of his broken biscuit that had just been added to the mess of rotting food and other filth of his prison floor.

'No Social Services,' he said hesitatingly

'This had berra not cost me,' she warned, 'I've no money.'

'It won't cost you,' Terry reassured. 'We'll sort out any gear he needs.'

'Just Wednesdays an' Sundays yer said?'

Terry nodded in confirmation. Without a cigarette in her hand Duane's mam struggled to appear calm. She continually brushed a hand nervously over her face and through her hair. Her eyes refused to stay on Terry for more than the odd fleeting, edgy glance.

The proposition was simple but it was still a form of blackmail, and being an untrustworthy person, as most addicts are, she automatically felt distrustful of others. The thoughts inside her head were scrambling around looking for an ulterior motive. It was such a bizarre request from a bloke she'd never seen before. If it had involved sex, drugs or money her head would have been able to cope with it better, but this? Just for football? There had to be a catch.

'An' that's all yer want – nowt else?'

Terry started to move away from the spot he'd been standing and almost took the carpet with him, it felt like walking on Velcro. The smell of the place had started to eke its way into his damp clothes and he couldn't wait to get back outside in the rain. 'Just make sure he's at Soldiers field, six o'clock this Wednesday…'

Leo was back on his feet, at his bars, with his arms and those dark imploring eyes pleading up at him. Terry felt a swirling great surge of pity for the little fella and an overwhelming urge to lift him out of the pen and give him a hug and a cuddle, but the overwhelming stink was greater than the urge and he found himself swallowing hard and tearing himself away from the beseeching youngster.

'…And for fucks sake sort the young un out,' he added in frustration at the toddler's plight.

From her prone throne she sat there and considered him, expressionless. 'You sure you're not a social worker?'

Terry didn't wait for Duane to come back with the milk, there was no way he'd have drunk from a cup in that house, it had just been a ruse to get the lad out of the way while he talked terms with his mam.

He shut the battered blue door behind him and the sound reverberated cold and hollow through the second floor lobby. Terry let out an involuntary shiver as he descended flights of concrete stairs. He put it down to his damp clothing but it had probably more to do with what he'd just witnessed. That pair of deep, dark, sorrowful eyes, that had reached down into his soul and ripped out emotions that he tried so hard to keep hidden away, would haunt his every waking hour for the next few weeks. Those pleading little arms reaching out for somebody to love would invade his dreams, and his walking away from those outstretched arms would turn the dreams into nightmares.

As he reached the bottom of the last flight of stairs to the ground floor lobby, a milk bottle exploded a couple of feet away scaring the shit out of him. He looked up in the direction of the resultant echoing laughter and saw three mocking faces peering down at him through the stairwell three storeys up. It was the three younger lads from the posse of five he'd encountered earlier on.

'Yer wanna be careful round 'ere, homi,' a voice shouted a sonorous warning. 'Yer could end up 'avin' an accident, yer naw what I mean?'

Terry exited Cromwell House with the peal of derisory laughter ringing down through the flats after him. The three youths didn't bother him; they were only thinking they were protecting their patch, playing up the gangsta role. He hoped he wouldn't have to be paying too many visits back here in any case; his mission was complete, or so he thought.

It was a moral dilemma that had now taken hold of Terry's conscience. The angel and devil had reappeared on his shoulders, and as he trudged back through the late summer drizzle back to where he'd left Nobby and the pickup, the image of little Leo loomed up in front of him again. He looked to the angel and he saw himself, Monday morning, City Hall, walking through the doors to Social Services, intent on providing information that would carve up what was left of what could arguably be described as a family. Then he saw Duane, he saw magic, he saw cups and glory, he saw a grinning, happy kid, arms outstretched holding out a trophy, then, at once, the outstretched arms became Leo's but Terry only had a dream solution for one kid; Leo shouldn't be there, he wasn't in the script.

Something inside Terry's head began to resent the intrusion and his conscience did its best to erase the haunting image. By the time he reached the pickup it was the devil dancing out a jig on his shoulder.

''Bout time,' complained Nobby. 'They kicked off ten minutes ago.'

'Any score?'

'Nah, Henry's hit the bar an' Scholes's seen a yeller.' Nobby folded his paper, slung it on the dash, gunned the motor into life and turned up the Five Live commentary on the radio. He spun the pickup around while wipers struggled to clear the rain from a greasy, insect spattered windscreen. He looked across at his mate who seemed to be miles away. 'Well, any joy?'

'Yeh, found him.'

'You don't sound too pleased with yerself.'

Terry shrugged. 'Let's see if he turns up Wednesday, eh?'

Nobby knew Terry well enough to suss when he didn't want to discuss things and this was one of those times. They didn't speak again until they got to the Fusiliers, apart from when Nobby started sniffing at the air in the cab and accused Terry of dropping his guts. Terry didn't bother to tell him where the smell really came from.

Nobby pulled up at the T-junction at the end of De Lacy Avenue and York Road. Opposite the junction, on an old limestone wall, the words *I LOVE U PHIL* were scrawled in pink paint. The declaration had been there for years. Terry remembered it being there when he was a kid, when most of East Broughton was still a building site. The hand painted message was well faded now, barely discernible. The pickup's wipers farted and jerked their way across the windscreen and Terry wondered whether whoever it was that had loved Phil still did and if Phil, whoever he was, ever reciprocated the sentiment. Next to the old romantic bulletin, and applied more recently, sprayed in black, was the curious legend *NORRIS IS A DEAD PUFF.* Terry wasn't sure if this was meant to be a statement of fact about a deceased homosexual or a threat with homophobic insult.

The wall was an unofficial boundary between the two estates and York Road was the demarcation zone. On the east side of the road, spread out along its mile and a half mile length, were blocks of purpose-built units, square boxes designed for use as commercial premises, most of which had been vandalised and boarded up – and those that were still in use, the kebab shops and take aways, the greasy spoons and betting shops, were all heavily fortified with metal grilles and roller shutters. Also along the route stood the Duke of York pub, sometime headquarters for the dealing syndicates in between periodic raids by the D.S. and having its licence revoked.

On the west side stood once grand, now grim, but nevertheless still imposing, rows of stone-built Victorian terraces that in more recent times had been converted for commercial use and into which had gravitated the more predatory types of businesses; loan sharks and pawnbrokers; money lenders who these days traded under the more respectable sounding title of debt management consultants; wolves cloaked in smart suits sitting in brightly lit, warm offices, tempting in the stupid, the naïve and vulnerable, the despairing and desperate. These were the people that your mainstream credit companies wouldn't touch with a barge pole, and round here their numbers were legion. Rich pickings. What was left of the giro after the dealer, the publican and the bookies had taken their cut usually went to the parasites on York Road.

'Cheques cashed here' 'Quick loans-no fees' 'Instant cash - no credit check' 'Pay off your debts now!' the dayglo banners of bait flashed by. On the radio, Arsenal had forced their third corner in succession and Alan Parry was getting excited. Terry felt the need for a roll-up and, as Nobby turned right into Sycamore Avenue, the grey clouds parted slightly, revealing a patch of blue sky beyond, from which the sun sent a shaft of light bouncing and glistening off the wet, slate roofs of West Broughton; familiar territory, where Royalist and Parliamentary place names gave way to those of British trees, where Victorian and Edwardian built Yorkshire stone and pre-war red brick buildings replaced Jerry-built prefab concrete and slab.

The social condition of the two estates wasn't all that far apart, West Broughton also had its fair share of squalor and deprivation, but at least its buildings had been made to last. Regardless of what state they were in now, they still projected longevity, evoking a feel for a community and a working-class spirit that was long gone. The place had history; from its few remaining mills that no longer processed wool but stored vast quantities of cheap, imported carpet and laminate flooring, to the pre and post-war urbanisation schemes of the old Urban District Councils that provided affordable rented accommodation for the masses but, more importantly, had had the forethought in planning to create gardens, allotments and parks. And although most of these were neglected, rundown or abandoned now, the fact that they were thought of and applied at the time somehow gave West Broughton a grounding, a living past where generations of families had laid down roots and were once proud to say where they came from.

Having spent little over an hour in the shallow, joyless subtopia that was East Broughton, Terry felt a little better to be back on his own turf, away from a place that felt beyond hope, irredeemable; terminal. Where its inhabitants seemed to have developed a cynical resignation of their lot, while the unscrupulous drifted in and out of the shadows to leech on those still desperate or naïve enough to believe in some magical escape from the drudge.

He tapped his freshly rolled smoke on the lid of his baccy tin and watched the sun begin to stretch its warm reach over the wet streets and houses as they drove along. God was smiling on his home and Alan Parry was going mental. Arsenal had just scored.

15

'…Hundred an' twelve – hundred an' thirteen – hundred an' fourteen…' Joe kept count of the headers, nice and steady, keeping the rhythm going. '…Hundred an' nineteen – hundred an' twenny…'

A hundred and fifty-five was their record and they were getting close, getting giddy, nervous chuckles as one goes astray but recovering well, don't spoil it; keep concentrating. '…Hundred an' twenny-six – hundred an' twenny-seven…'

'…And Lancaster leaps through a foray of players in the eighteen yard box and bravely plucks the ball out of the air…' One Eye snatched the ball mid flight between Joe and Young Nobby and fell theatrically to the ground.

'Bloody 'ell fire, One Eye!' exclaimed Joe.

'You fuckin' one eyed wazzock!' added Young Nobby for good measure.

'Oh, and there seems to be a problem in there,' One Eye continued with his John Motson style commentary while rolling around on the grass still clutching the ball. 'One or two of the Arsenal players don't seem too happy, Mark. Was that a foul?'

Nobby junior started kicking at the ball, not bothering if One Eye's fingers were in the way, mouthing obscenities at him as he did so.

'Well I don't know about a foul, John, but these are dreadful scenes we're seeing now.' One Eye had turned into Mark Lawrenson and was rolling around in the foetal position trying to protect himself and the ball from Young Nobby's probing boot. 'You'd have thought van Nistelrooy and his chums would have learned their lesson by now after those disturbing scenes at Old Trafford. Oww, yer bastard!' he added as Young Nobby landed one right across his knuckles. Joe joined in shoving One Eye's head into the turf and rasping at the hair on his temple with his fist.

'We were goin' for us record then, you arsehole.'

'Well, Mark, I think – oww – the F.A. will throw the book at – arrgh, fuck! – this pair, and rightly so in my opinion – oww stoppit, that hurts yer bastards.'

Joe wrestled the ball away from One Eye's grasp and as he lay there writhing. Young Nobby gave him a final kick up the backside.

They started again. 'One – two – three…'

Sasquatch and Biscuit noticed him first.

'What the fuck does he want?' Sasquatch muttered to his mate.

'Ho, - what the fuck d'you want?' Biscuit demanded out loud.

Duane ignored him, kept his head down and walked the gauntlet of Albion players scattered in small groups around the field, who, one by one stopped their kick-abouts and warm–ups as the skinny kid entered their midst.

'…Seventeen – eighteen - nineteen – wanker!' protested Joe as Young Nobby ignored header number twenty and caught the ball open mouthed. One Eye stopped rubbing his bruised knuckles and looked up until twelve pairs of eyes (well, not quite twelve) were staring at the Comanche from East Broughton.

Terry and Nobby were spacing out the traffic cones the lads had nicked from some roadworks that they used for training and hadn't noticed Duane's arrival. His discomfort was excruciating. He wanted a hole to appear in the ground and swallow him up. He could see Terry about fifty yards away and was willing him to look up and notice him, rescue him, stop the nudging, the sneering and the hateful mutterings. He knew this had been a bad idea. What was he thinking of, pretending he could be pally team mates with a load of West Broughton kids that he knew would hate his guts. The thing that had moved him to turn up at all was the persuasive powers this Terry geezer must posses to have been able to sway his mam like that. It was intrigue more than anything else. If someone he'd never seen before, someone he didn't know from Adam was prepared to go to such extraordinary lengths, to make such an effort for him then he wanted to know why. No one had been so magnanimous to him before and he thought he should at least show his appreciation by showing up like he'd been asked even though it would probably be the one and only time he would. But even that felt like such a bad mistake right now.

'Dad!' shouted Joe. Both Terry and Nobby looked up. It was like a scene straight out of one of those old black and white westerns, the one where Gary Cooper plays the beleaguered sheriff, where he's walking down the street all alone to confront the bad guys and the cowardly locals come together in his wake to watch him go meet his fate.

'Bloody 'ell, he's turned up,' said Nobby.

'Shit,' said Terry, 'I should have told the lads.'

The mood amongst the boys wasn't good as Terry gathered them round and introduced their new teammate.

'I aren't playin' wi' no half-chat Comanche,' Biscuit muttered from the back of the group.

'Me neither,' agreed Peycos.

Duane was squirming with embarrassment and kept his eyes firmly on the ground, biting his lip and shuffling his feet uncomfortably. Nobby felt his unease as Terry lectured the lads, and placed a friendly hand on his shoulder.

'Don't ever forget,' warned Terry staring hard at the grumblers at the back, 'no one individual is bigger than this club. This is a team. We're all in this together, and we make sure we look after one another. Anybody thinks otherwise can sod off and find another club. Is that understood?' No response. 'I said is that understood?' The affirmative came muted and half-hearted. Although Nobby cringed at the clichés, he agreed with Terry's sentiments but thought he still might have a mutiny on his hands.

There existed a lot of bad blood between the two estates and certain families held long running feuds. Ryan Crawford's hatred and intolerance went back to the early eighties when his dad's brother, an uncle he had never known was knifed to death by a member of a notorious East Broughton family. He hadn't even been born but the animosity and prejudice had been instilled from birth. The sectarianism was real, the mistrust mutual and showed no sign of mellowing.

For others it was the constant pillaging and plundering from the east side that had forced certain West Broughton families to take the law into their own hands; retribution at the end of a baseball bat was the only cure for certain insurgent Comanche.

Terry and Nobby well understood the lads' reluctance to accept Duane, Christ knows they had lived through this shit all their lives, but they weren't going to tolerate the persecution of this one individual who had personally done no one any wrong. You shouldn't tar everybody with the same brush but stigma, like tar, tended to stick and was very messy. Gaining their approbation wasn't going to be easy.

Terry watched them jog a few warm up circuits of the rec. In his baggy track bottoms and tee shirt Duane looked rake thin and malnourished, particularly next to Nobby as they ran together at the back of the group; the big fella happily chatting away, trying his best to make the new kid feel at ease. Being able to magically juggle a football was one thing; coping with the physical side of it was another. Would he have the strength and the stamina to play a competitive game, especially against a team like Blackbank? Terry began to wonder if he'd done the right thing.

In the energy stakes Terry needn't have worried. The season for them started a week on Sunday and he had purposely stepped up the training for these last three sessions in order to have the lads sharp for the off. Duane took the shuttles and the bleeps in his stride, barely breaking out into a sweat. He even found the push-ups easy, probably because he had no real body weight to lift. The only task he really struggled with was the piggyback relays. It didn't help that no one wanted to partner him, Rammer drawing the short straw, a reluctant and unenthusiastic horse and jockey.

They always finished the last twenty minutes of each session with a game, and as Terry lined them up to pick sides no one but Rory had spoken a word to Duane. He'd been sent to Coventry good and proper, each and every one of them in a show of unified defiance. For Rory it didn't matter, he only made the numbers up in training; he had no place under threat from a Comanche. Which side of York

Road you came from wasn't an issue with him as a good few of his old acquaintances hailed from East Broughton anyway but he did have to admit to finding the new kid hard work; a conversationalist he certainly wasn't and most of Rory's good humoured banter fell on stony ground. Duane wasn't enjoying being out of his familiar environment. The hostile atmosphere was tangible and Rory's badinage hadn't offered any distraction to the discomfort he felt.

Terry put Duane on the same side of what he perceived to be among the worst of the antagonists. He knew they would do their best to keep the ball away from him but at least it would ensure he wouldn't be on the end of the more vicious challenges, even though the opposing seven were certainly out to give him a rough ride and make their point.

Before he blew his whistle Terry reminded everybody as diplomatically as he could that this was just a knock-about; he didn't want any injuries before the start of the season. He might as well have been talking to a brick wall as Sully was already issuing muttered threats to his opposite number.

'This'll be interesting,' said Nobby as the short-sided game got under way.

'He'll be okay,' Terry said trying to sound reassuring. Nobby looked at his mate knowing there was a hint of misgiving.

'Let's hope so.'

Any doubts Manager and coach had about Duane's ability to cope with the rough stuff would soon be dispelled. With his first touch of the ball he executed a drag back and a deft flick inside to avoid Sully's studs-up sliding tackle, all in one movement, without pause or hesitation, moving forward, stroking the ball past Joe on his outside and gliding past him on his inside like he wasn't even there. As Ginner raced to confront him, Duane slipped a neat pass inside to Rigger and went for the one-two. Ginner clattered into him clumsily and Terry blew for the free kick. It was to be the pattern throughout the game, time and again. Every time Duane was smashed after the ball had gone Terry blew his whistle until finally, after they were six–nil down, the penny dropped and they began to concentrate on playing football.

Nobby was drooling over Duane's silky skills. He was pleased to see that the kid wasn't merely a ball juggler. He reminded him of an adolescent George Best weaving his magic through brutish columns of defenders in those old clips from the sixties. He feigned, swayed and tormented like Eddie Gray at his peak, and ghosted past players with easy acceleration like Thierry Henry with the ball stuck to his feet.

Sasquatch came across to close him down, wary now, no diving in, just jockey. Duane decelerated and stroked the top of the ball with the sole of his boot, teasing, baiting, drawing the defender in, dropping his shoulder pretending to go and then stalling, throwing Sasquatch off balance and then gunning past him making Big-Foot's lunge look hours late.

'Taxi for Sasquatch,' shouted Nobby.

Even when he was two'd up, Duane would conjure up some amazing feat of escapology that would leave Nobby in raptures. Joe and Slum had him cornered in a pincer movement close to the line, no way out. As they moved in for the kill, Duane stabbed the ball arcing with back spin over their advancing heads, spun around Slum's outside and killed the dropping ball with the top of his foot before leaving the floundering pair in his wake.

'Havin' a Cuban, lads?' laughed Nobby. 'Nice try but no cigar.'

One or two in Duane's team had started to communicate; seven - two up and they were enjoying themselves. 'To me, Duane.' 'Inside, Duane.' 'Yes, Duane.' The others felt betrayed and Joe tried to rally his side to avoid humiliation. The last ten minutes of football was frantic, passionate and great to watch. With a few newfound admirers and Nobby's constant cries of adulation, Duane had foolishly turned up the showboating. He'd been giving Sasquatch a torrid time and Terry could see the big lad getting more angry and frustrated. After one trick too many, Sasquatch took Duane from behind long after the ball had gone and made sure that he hurt him. As he lay there with the wind well and truly taken out of his sails, Sasquatch bent over him, offered his hand and a piece of advice. 'Tha's good mate - but don't tek the piss, eh?' Lesson quickly learned, Duane took Bigfoot's hand and got to his feet. Terry had been watching out of a corner of his eye and this time didn't use his whistle. He played an extra five minutes, then, as the light began to fade, reluctantly blew for time.

Nobby and Terry beamed at each other. 'Bloody marvellous, that,' enthused Nobby.

It had been the best session to date and was exactly what Terry had been striving for these last three months or so. It felt like the last piece of the jigsaw had been put in place despite the odd grumbling of discontent that was still present within the ranks.

'Fantastic, lads; great workout, well done,' said Terry. 'Show that sort of spirit and commitment a week on Sunday and we'll do alrate. Did you enjoy that, fella?' He put his arm round Duane and gave him a hug. Duane, still squirming a little with embarrassment nodded in the affirmative while rubbing the bruise on his arse cheek.

Come the end of the Sunday training session, The Albion had split into two camps; those for Duane and those still against. The argument against went along the lines of, '*He might be a shit hot footballer but he's still a Comanche,*' and some still vowed they would never play with a Comanche.

By the end of the Wednesday session, the last one before the start of the season, the majority of The Albion wanted to be on Duane's side for the end of practice game and argued amongst themselves for the privilege. Only Biscuit and Peycos remained doubters and they would have to go with the majority eventually or it would be them who would end up being the outcasts.

As the lads drifted away in small, excited groups at the prospect of their first home game against Farshaw Juniors, Terry called young Duane Geddess back.

'You've forgotten this, son.' Terry held out a plastic carrier bag.

'It's not mine,' said Duane.

Terry still motioned him to take the bag. He did so with a puzzled look on his face. He slowly peered inside, eyes beginning to widen as he made out the giant tick logo and the spanking new leather of the

Nike Air Zoom Total 90's. Duane shook his head and offered back the bag.

'There not...' he began. Terry put a finger to his lips to silence him.

'See you Sunday,' he said with a wink.

16

Ginner felt a sharp sting on the back of his ear and whirled round ready to twat the culprit only to be confronted by Norman, the landlord of the Fusiliers, or to be more accurate, the enormous girth of his beer gut. With no visible means of escape Ginner looked up into the ruddy and none too happy features of the large publican.

'Nah then, what's tha think tha's playin' at?' he boomed.

'Nowt,' protested Ginner rubbing his wounded ear and wondering what the hell it was the fat bastard had used to inflict such pain.

'Nowt? Has thy been messin' abaht wi' them barrels?'

'Have I chuff.'

'What's tha doin' in 'ere then?'

'Nowt – just 'avin' a nosey, that's all.'

'Havin' a nosey?' repeated Norman. 'Have I to tell thee what'd 'appen if tha buggered abaht wi' one o' them valves?'

'No, but tha's gonna,' Ginner muttered under his breath.

'Hundred millibars o' pressure they 'old back,' lectured Norman. 'an' if tha buggers abaht wi' one, that pressure'll tek thee head off thee shoulders…'

The rest of the lads had gathered behind Norman at the doorway of the pump room down in the cellar of the Fusiliers. In various states of undress they were pushing and jostling for position to see Ginner receive his bollocking.

'…Thee brains'll end up splattered all o'er that ceiling – does tha hear me?'

Ginner kept his head low, not wanting to make eye contact with any of the lads who were making faces and gestures behind Norman's back in an effort to make him laugh.

'Does tha hear me, young un?' repeated Norman wanting to make sure he'd got his message across.

'Yeh,' Ginner muttered trying to keep a straight face.

Norman spun around with amazing speed and agility for a man his size. The lads freeze framed. 'An' that goes for t'rest o' yer. D'yer hear warram sayin'? Yer keep out of 'ere, d'yer understand?'

As a favour to Terry and Nobby, Norman had reluctantly agreed to let The Albion use the pub's spacious cellar as their changing rooms but was now having second thoughts. He wasn't keen on kids at the best of times and he didn't relish having to cope with this bunch of cheeky little sods every other Sunday, plus the fact he would now have to go to the bother of putting a lock on the pump room door.

Norman hauled himself back up the cellar steps grumbling and griping while Ginner gave him the V sign. He grumbled and griped at Terry who said he'd have a word, but as he listened to the motors whirring and clicking as they sent beer and lager into the pumps upstairs he understood why the lads would be fascinated at getting a glimpse into this mysterious adult domain; the smell of hops and masculinity, and the reek of stale tobacco and alcohol on your old man after a Saturday night out.

'Still no sign of him,' declared Nobby as he descended the cellar steps. Duane hadn't showed. It was after half-ten and the team sheet still needed filling out. The lads were now sitting around in a bluish-grey mass of nervous anticipation. (Jan had boil-washed the kit in an effort to shrink it, but the dye in the dark blue stripe had leeched out onto the white) 'Shall I have a drive out; see if I can see him?'

Terry had laid down rules about time keeping and the like and didn't want to make Duane an exception. Most of the lads had accepted him now and he didn't want to bring back any resentment. There would be no favouritism.

'No, he knew what time we were meeting. I'll put him down as a sub and see if he turns up.' There was disappointment in Terry's voice.

'Maybe you shouldn't o' let him have them boots before today,' suggested Nobby quietly so the lads wouldn't hear.

'Maybe,' reflected Terry, knowing exactly where Nobby was coming from but not wanting to pre-judge the circumstances for

Duane's non-show. All kinds of permutations were going through his mind and he tried to push away the thought that Duane would let him down on purpose. That bloody so-called mother of his had to be favourite to have put her spoke in. He didn't want to think that she'd renege on their little understanding but he wouldn't have put it past her.

Terry waited as long as he could before he read the team out. Duane's absence had started to sour the good mood amongst the lads. How could their star player let them down like this, especially on the first day of the season? Most of them had accepted him, with great reluctance at first, admittedly, but he'd won them over, they'd made him part of The Albion, he was one of them, or so they thought.

Biscuit and Peycos were still dissenters; they'd never accepted the coffee skinned wizard and the exuberant mood in the changing room soon went from initial disappointment to the old virulence once the pair of them started having a go.

'Well, don't say we din't warn yer – you wouldn't listen to us,' said Peycos.

'You don't ever trust a fuckin' Comanche,' said Biscuit. 'Wait 'till I see the bastard at school.'

'Aye, that's if he ever shows up to school,' added Sully pessimistically.

Nobby skipped down the cellar steps and cut short the growing grumbles of discontent. 'Time to go men, let's be havin' yer – Phwoor! – Who's dropped their guts?' he recoiled in exaggerated horror. Most heads turned towards Ginner who'd let go one of his S.B.D. specials.

'Sorry lads - nerves,' Ginner smiled weakly.

The Albion evacuated their new changing facilities in double quick time and emerged into the fresh air of a bright Sunday early September morning; perfect for a game of footie. A noisy stampede of studs on pavement resounded as they made their way along Guard House Lane, turning left onto the unadopted road of Drill Parade, down the side of the cemetery and into Soldiers Field, barely a two minute jog from the Fusiliers.

Soldiers Field – old West Broughton rec.; the excitement surged as it opened up before them; what a transformation. Hard to believe it was the same toxic wasteland they had first trained on back in June. The hard graft, the long, boring, smelly shifts in Ginner's bedroom, the desperate deterrent; it had all paid off in the long run. They had worked all Saturday afternoon applying the finishing touches; giving the pitch a final cut, stripe and roll, the professional two-tone effect; Nobby mixing lime for the marker, bringing back memories from his council days. They erected the posts early that morning, gleaming with fresh white paint. Nobby had been right, they didn't look bad at all once they'd had a few coats, and Rory's mate's dad had constructed the ex scaffold poles so that the crossbar could be easily dismantled from the uprights after every game for storage back in Ginner's garden.

Kids and balls exploded onto the rich carpet of green in euphoric abandon, and broad grins spread involuntarily across the features of Terry and Nobby at the sight. Farshaw were warming up, resplendent in red and white. There was light dew on the pitch; a shimmering blanket of silver jewels, a faint edge to the early September air, and the smell of freshly cut grass was everywhere. The park echoed to the strains of adolescent voices, and inside two middle-aged stomachs, butterflies started to jiggle and flutter. Terry and Nobby looked at each other, you couldn't buy this feeling. Their old playing days came back to them in a breath and in that instant, both realised how much they'd missed it. It was the start of a new season. Sunday mornings were special again – bring it on.

'Oh, Christ – look who it is,' said Nobby.

Terry's head shot up. For a fleeting moment he thought he meant Duane had turned up, but he was referring to the decrepit looking, grey haired image walking towards them on spindly legs wearing a referee's kit.

'Bloody hell – Spider,' moaned Terry.

'Nah then, Mister Webb, long time, no see.' Nobby greeted the old chap who looked sixty-five if he were a day. 'Still at it then, eh?'

Cyril Webb screwed his eyes up in an effort to make out the face of the person who knew him so readily.

'Fuckin' eyesight ain't improved, has it?' Terry muttered aside. 'Hey up Cyril – how's it goin' me old son?' he offered in an overly loud voice just in case the old git turned out to be as deaf as he was blind.

'Ah - yes...' said Cyril in a tone and manner that was reminiscent of Mr. Barraclough, the softhearted screw from Porridge. He pointed at the pair of them in turn as he recollected voices and faces from the past. '...Yes – now wait a minute, let me see – yes, yes, – I remember...' The lads grinned and nodded in anticipation. '...I remember – Royal Oak, Sunday Alliance. Am I right? Montague Burton,' he pointed triumphantly at Nobby.

Nobby grinned sheepishly, rather embarrassed that the old guy should remember the non-de plume he used to give whenever he was booked or sent off.

'Yes, you had me reaching for the card on many occasion as I remember. You lads must have had plenty of money in those days.'

Cyril 'Spider' Webb had been on the circuit for years. He was Old School, from an era when sportsmen were sportsmen, where it was all about fair play, handshakes and hip-hip-hooray, but he'd always been a crap referee. When Spider reffed you, you could get away with all manner of career threatening tackles, but he'd be straight out with the yellow if you ever used bad language. Nobby saw a lot of yellow, but Spider, bless him, very rarely sent the bookings in to the F.A. Terry's groan at seeing Spider striding across the pitch towards them again was the same groan from all those years ago whenever you got to know he was reffing your game. The senior Sunday leagues were too much for him now. The combination of increasing violence, general nastiness and his failure to control volatile fixtures, along with the growing number of complaints from clubs about his own standards of performance, had left him officiating in the junior leagues where there was always a shortage.

'It's many a year since I refereed on this pitch, and I must say it's looking in fine condition,' said Spider observing the set up with admiration.

'Aye, all our own work, Spi... er, I mean Cyril,' Nobby corrected himself.

'Yes, well – shall we be getting proceedings under way?' he asked, glancing at his watch. 'Would one of you young men be so kind as to run a line for me?' He politely requested, handing over a flag.

'Have a good game Cyril...' shouted Terry as Spider Webb blew his whistle to call the two captains together. '...Please,' he added, more in prayerful hope.

There was a refreshing buzz about the place as the game got under way. Soldiers Field reverberated to the sound of Sunday morning football for the first time in over ten years; the old recreation ground suddenly came alive and it felt right. People passing through stopped and watched. Kids on bikes came and went again to tell their mates '*A game of footie in Soldiers Field; a proper game!*' Folk came out of their houses or watched from bedroom windows. Even Harold Lightowler took time out from tending his pigeons to lean over his garden fence with his slippers, dangly braces, flat cap and eternal tab end to offer shouts of encouragement at the players. On the cemetery side of the pitch stood the Farshaw management and around half a dozen or so keen mums and dads. Disappointingly, the West Broughton support consisted of Rory, Jan and Kath who arrived fifteen minutes into the game. No other parent or guardian of the lads had bothered to come and watch, except, that is, a character dressed in an old grey cagoule and baggy jeans who was wandering up and down the touchline, and who Terry and Nobby failed to recognise straight away as they were too absorbed in the game.

'What's up man, aren't yer speakin'?'

It took a moment or two for Terry to register the unshaven features and the slow, lazy drawl. Nobby beat him to it.

'Jesus H, it's Flash!'

Phil Ashington; old Hacienda stalwart, MDMA pioneer, double good, loved up, twenty four hour party person and sometime dad to Billy cracked a smile at them both, displaying a gold capped incisor that instantly brought the face back to memory.

'Bloody hell, another mush from the past,' said Terry.

Flash was just a couple of years younger than Terry and Nobby; an ex Leeds bad boy who'd done his tour of duty with the pair of them back in those dark days of madness; who'd discovered The Mondays and The Stone Roses back in the late eighties, and had gotten heavily into the rave and acid house scene of the early nineties along with its ecstasy fuelled sub-culture, while Terry and Nobby had turned all responsible, got married and started families. Thing was, Flash did all this, too - all apart from the responsible bit. When Billy was born, Flash was off filling himself up with mitsus, Buddhas and doves. He became a free spirit, caught the wanderlust and was on the scene when Ibiza first started to get going.

Every summer became the summer of love for Flash. He could often be found getting on one at some hedonistic, banging happening alongside the occasional Man U fan, who, ten years earlier he'd have wanted to kill.

Flash had fallen in love with the white island paradise and spent as much time there as he could, acting as a courier for the scouse syndicates, lugging for DJs, working behind bars or handing out flyers in between partying. He came home occasionally, usually when the season ended, to blag some money when he was skint, or pup the missus; and she fell for it every time. He used the old marital home as a part time hotel and doss house and contributed nothing except as a fatherly figure for fleeting moments at a time. Crazy thing was, she was grateful for it, and there were a lot of women around just like her. A part time dad was better than no dad at all, and when he was around she would try and make him do his bit, dragging him out of bed in the middle of the afternoon to go and pick the kids up from school while she got on with the ironing, just to show the other mums that there was still a bloke in her life, albeit pilled up and part time.

He'd come back early this season. He told Terry and Nobby that he was making the effort to settle and do right by the wife and kids. The scene out there had changed these last few years. The place was full of wankers now and he only ever dropped the odd half a pacha whenever the fancy took him these days.

Flash would do his best; he really would, but the reality of a long, cold, dark northern winter looming would test his boredom threshold to the limit and send him into fits of depression that no MDMA induced state could ever lift. Phil Ashington was just another one of life's punters who had come to realise that everlasting nirvana couldn't really be found within a little white chemical pill, and that normality and reality were actually worse than you remember, and fear and paranoia were the real dominating forces in life, stoned or straight.

Flash, at least, had made the effort to come and watch his lad. Unfortunately, Billy was sub again, but despite that he happily offered to relieve Nobby of his linesman duties, a job he would readily accept from here on in, every game, home and away for the rest of the season.

The Albion was two – nil down by half time. The lads had approached the game as if they were playing Blackbank again, and Terry told them so; too much rough stuff; conceding too many free kicks, committing unnecessary fouls in dangerous places. Both Farshaw goals had come from set pieces; they were a good, well-organised side and Terry could tell that the majority of them had been together a long time.

A few of The Albion had become frustrated at how well Farshaw kept possession and Terry singled out Sasquatch and Biscuit, in particular, for diving in. Although the lads were fit, Terry knew it took a lot more to be a half-decent side. Discipline had to be the first and hardest lesson to learn; that would only come through experience and playing together, and he knew that would take time.

To be fair to the lads, they shaped up a bit better in the second half. Basher came on for Sully and they lay siege to the Farshaw goal for long periods, but a well marshalled defence kept The Albion's attacks at bay. A swift counter attack with less than ten minutes to go sealed the points for Farshaw with a three-nil win; well deserved; no complaints. Even Spider managed a five from both managers on the report, despite struggling to keep up with play for most of the game.

Only once did Duane's name get mentioned, Nobby reflecting whether or not his presence would have made a difference. To himself, Terry didn't doubt it would have, but out loud he stated that '*One man didn't make a team,*' and left it at that.

'You had us under the cosh a bit there in the second half,' said Steve the Farshaw manager.

'You're a good side, Steve,' said Terry, offering a congratulatory hand. 'Play some nice football. You've got your lads well organised.'

Steve graciously took the plaudits and told Terry that he'd been at it a long time, that he'd had most of his boys since they were seven. He'd got nearly all of his coaching badges and had played semi-pro in his time. It didn't hinder that Farshaw was also a fairly affluent district; that they probably had decent facilities; that money wasn't a problem and that parents were keen and supportive, judging by the gleaming 4 x 4s and people carriers that transported their team to games.

Terry told the lads to warm down and began to wonder how he would get his lot to away games. He had visions of them on the back of the old pickup in the depths of winter, frozen to the bone; their extremities as blue as their shirts, and knew he would have to be giving some serious thought to the problem.

Ginner sat astride Young Nobby's shoulders, removing the net from a crossbar, when he began to ululate excitedly.

'Fuck's sake, Ginner, you'd berra not have shit again,' said Young Nobby, squirming beneath the little guy's buttocks.

'No - look,' he said pointing urgently in the direction of the old play area at the far end of the rec.

''Kin 'ell, it's him,' breathed Young Nobby.

'It's him!' shouted Ginner, falling to the ground in a heap as the big lad unceremoniously threw him off his shoulders.

All heads turned to the bent-over, forlorn looking figure sat at the bottom of the old metal slide about a hundred yards away.

'It *is* him,' Peycos said to Biscuit.

'The cheeky cunt,' said Biscuit and set off in determined fashion. The others slowly picked up the scent and followed in his wake, jogging at first to catch up, then stepping up the pace until it became a mad dash to be first on the scene; twelve against one; get your hate in first. A three-nil drubbing hurts. Time to crucify the scapegoat.

'You've gorra bleedin' cheek, yer little half-chat,' spat Biscuit, fists clenched, standing menacingly over Duane who hadn't moved, while the others gathered in an intense, breathless, semi-circle.

Luckily, Nobby had seen it all happen and wasn't far behind. Terry had never seen the big fella move so fast. He fought his way through the lynch mob and formed an instant protective barrier.

'Move!' he shouted. 'Away, the fuckin' lot o' yer – now!' They slowly backed off.

Terry arrived soon after and glowered at every one of them and they backed off some more. Nobby dropped to his haunches, put his hands on Duane's quivering shoulders and tried to make eye contact. 'All right, son? What happened?' he asked in a consoling voice. Duane groaned and his slight, hunched frame shuddered and shook but he was reluctant to raise his head. Nobby uttered a few more consoling words, telling him to take his time while the lads stood and stared at a distance.

Eventually, with some gentle coaxing, he slowly lifted his face.

'Fuckin' 'ell,' whispered Rammer, and they all spontaneously moved forward to see the shocking sight. Peycos and Biscuit exchanged glances but said nothing. Nobby, from his crouched position looked up at Terry. Both men were speechless for the moment.

Duane's right cheekbone looked almost welded to his eyebrow; the two were so large and swollen that his eye was no longer visible. Angry shades of red and purple throbbed out at Nobby who stared helplessly at his deformed features and the tramlines of tears and scratches that streaked down the rest of his face.

'Who did this to you, Duane?' Terry spoke calmly.

Duane bowed his head again and distraught sobs welled up from deep inside and shook him like his meagre body would fall apart. He tried to speak but his utterances got lost among surging waves of distress. Terry joined Nobby at the bottom of the old slide and together they tried to calm the boy down.

'They took… they took the boots…' he sniffed and swallowed. '…I'm sorry,' he wailed, breaking down into fits of sobs again.

'Hey, forget about the boots,' said Terry. 'Just tell us who it was did this to you.'

Extracting the information was slow. Duane was reluctant to reveal the identity of his attackers but Terry and Nobby persevered and remained patient with him.

'There were free of 'em,' he finally volunteered.

'Do you know 'em?'

Duane nodded.

'What're their names?'

He took a deep, shaky breath and let out a long sigh. He looked at both Terry and Nobby in turn. The rest of the Albion had crept in closer and were now gathered round hanging on Duane's every word.

'Purcell, Franklin, n' Wishbone,' he whispered in a trembling voice.

'Purcell!' Rigger uttered the name with contempt.

Terry spun round. 'You know him?'

'Know 'em all,' piped up Joe. They all go to our school; year eleven this time round.'

'Bullies, eh?'

The lads laughed.

'Bit more than bullies, dad,' said Joe.

'Dealers, knifers,' said Peycos. 'Think they're gangsta wise; strut around school like they own it.'

'Purcell brought a gun in one time,' recalled Joe. 'Flashin' it around, braggin' he'd used it loads o' times - an' I wun't purrit past him.'

Terry turned back to the lad. 'Why would they do this to you, Duane?' Duane shrugged his shoulders. 'C'mon. They wouldn't beat you up just for the fun of it, would they?'

Duane hesitated again. He swallowed hard, trying not to think of the implications for splitting like this. 'That Sunday you came round,' he began, 'they stopped me on t'stairs on t'way back from t'shops; asked who you were, wanted to know why you were sniffin' around. I wunt tell 'em at first, fought I wa' bein' clever. They fought you was a dealer collectin' lay-ons; hadn't seen you around before, fought you was musclin' in on their patch. They roughed me up a bit - nowt bad - poured t'bottle o' milk down me pants - managed to gerraway...'

'Were there two other older lads with 'em?' Terry interrupted as the penny dropped. 'Black guys?'

Duane shook his head. 'You mean Royston an' Mackie. No, they weren't there; it was just the uvver free. They stopped me again when I came trainin'. I told 'em the truf; said I was goin' to play footie but they din't believe me; fought I was runnin' for you, lickin' shot. They fossick'd me; said they were gonna probe me. They wunt leave me alone, waitin' every time I went trainin'. Then they got mad when they din't find owt; said they were gonna cut me mam an' me bruvver – Took me boots an' did this to me...'

Duane broke down again. Nobby tried to give him a hug but he winced with pain and it soon became apparent that they'd laid into him good and proper. They tried to get him to his feet to take him to the hospital, but he could hardly stand, and closer inspection revealed massive bruising to the outside of his thigh; he'd been kicked to the bone.

'They are fuckin' dead men,' stated Sasquatch as the lads' anger rose above their shame. All of a sudden promises of retribution were being bandied around, only Peycos and Biscuit remained silent.

Having just heard about their reputation, having met these guys first hand and seen what they were capable of, Terry warned the lads off any thoughts of revenge but Rigger wasn't having any of it. As the others postured angrily, he quietly took Terry to one side.

'Don't worry about it,' he said calmly. 'We're back at school to-morrow. It'll be sorted. I'll have the boots back by trainin' on Wednesday.'

'I've told you, Rigger, I don't want you lot to get involved.'

'There'll only be two or three of us at most, no fuss; it'll be sorted - trust me.'

Terry watched him turn and walk away and couldn't believe he'd just taken advice on potential open gang warfare from a thirteen-year-old hard case.

As promised, the boots were paraded triumphantly aloft by Sasquatch and Young Nobby at training the following Wednesday. It had been a clandestine operation between the three of them; no fuss, just like Rigger had said, and he'd sworn his other two accomplices to secrecy as to what transpired; even Joe had been left in the dark. When he'd asked Young Nobby for details, the big fella just nodded in Rigger's direction and said, 'Awesome - proper fuckin' awesome.' As the rest of the lads clamoured for the story that wasn't forthcoming, Rigger stood quietly in the background with a little smile on his face, offering just a nod and a wink when Terry caught his eye. He expounded no further except to say 'Those three won't be botherin' Duane any more.'

Terry couldn't fail to be impressed with the style of his unassuming centre forward and he knew better than to ask too many questions, but he couldn't help wonder what methods three handy thirteen year olds had used to scare three notorious sixteen year olds to such an extent that they'd managed to reclaim the tax as well. Giving up the boots must have been the ultimate humiliation for the East Broughton posse and Terry didn't think they would be letting it lie so readily, despite Rigger's reassurances. He didn't want a war 'cos the only real casualty would be Duane and he felt he'd caused enough grief for the poor kid already.

A lot of awkward questions had been asked at the infirmary, and he sensed that their story had been met with some scepticism by one or two staff. It was the same registrar that had seen Joe after his assault up at Blackbank and he'd raised his eyebrows at seeing them again so soon. Nobby had got angry at the inquisition. He didn't take too kindly to the constant probing and the veiled insinuations. They hadn't exactly come out and accused them of being child beaters, but he knew what they were hinting at. A visit from social services was now on the cards, and Terry despaired at the sorry mess he felt he'd created.

Afterwards, they had dropped him off and watched him limp to his slum. There were no bones broken, just severe bruising. It had been scant consolation to Terry. All this was his fault and nothing Nobby said could assuage his feeling of guilt. Duane had disappeared into the flats and they both wondered if that would be the last they ever saw of him.

They needn't have worried. Duane showed up at the next training session and was treated like a returning hero. Even Biscuit took time out to apologise for doubting him, while Peycos presented him with the retrieved boots.

'I wasn't sure if we'd see you again,' said Terry.

'Why?' Duane asked, surprised.

Terry shrugged. 'Well, I mean after all this nonsense I've put you through, I could well understand you wanting to sack it, a lot of kids would; not really worth the hassle just for a game o' footie, eh?'

Duane looked at Terry and couldn't believe he'd think that he'd give up on him so easily. 'None of it were your fault, Tel. D'yer really fink I'd just walk away after all you've done for me?'

'I know you've got it tough, son, I just didn't want to make things any harder for you.'

Duane shook his head and laughed, then looked Terry in the eye. 'Tough,' he said musing over the word for a moment before shrugging it off. 'What's tough? What's tough when all you've ever known's been the same? Tough don't mean owt to me Tel, I don't know any different. What I do know is you an' Nobby have done all this for me, an' you din't have to. You din't know me, but you made all that effort. You even got me these.' He proudly clutched the pair of retrieved Nike's. 'I've never had a pair o' boots before - never. An' the lads got me 'em back, an' I know they din't like me, an I know why they din't like me, an' now they're me mates, an' I've never had any proper mates - ever.'

Duane paused and looked down at the grass in front of him. That strange emotion brought on by other people's philanthropy gripped him again and he took a moment to compose himself.

'What Purcell an' them did to me, Tel - that's noffing.' He lifted his head and looked resolutely at his benefactor. His facial swelling had eased slightly and, as if in defiance, a bloodshot eye peered through the slit of battered flesh between cheekbone and eyebrow, the bruising having taken on more mature, brown and mustard colours. 'They don't bovver me. I'd tek a fousand mashin's off 'em to play football for you, d'yer naw what I'm sayin'? Tough's tough if that's all you've got like. It don't make no difference, but tough's a piece o' piss if you've got summat to fight for, an' you an' Nobby an' the lads have given me that. I've never felt part of anyfing before, an' now I am, an' that's worth fightin' for – in't it?'

Terry pondered on Duane's desperate philosophy for a second or two until the poignancy of it hit home. 'Aye, you're right, lad,' he said, 'It is that.'

When you're given a lifeline, when you're desperate, you grab it. When you're given a lifeline that is a life in itself, or at least another life, an escape, you grab it and hang on for all you're worth. This is what Duane was doing; repaying a faith and grabbing an opportunity that was unlikely ever to come his way again, and he wasn't about to let the likes of Purcell, Franklin and Wishbone wrest that from his grasp, and in that, and only that, Terry had probably underestimated the magnitude and far reaching consequences of his own benevolent actions.

Only when Terry enquired after his mam and his brother did Duane look totally and utterly defeated. His shoulders slumped, he became morose and it was obvious to Terry that he didn't want to talk about any aspect of his home life. He was becoming two people, and there was one persona, the old one, he would try and shut out until he had to go back to the toils, tasks and misery that lay behind that blue door in Cromwell House.

Terry felt he had to raise the question of social workers.

'They won't send anybody,' Duane said as a matter of fact, 'they never do. They won't come near wivout police protection since one of 'em got stabbed, an' there aren't enough policemen to go around wiv social workers, so they just don't bovver. The one we're supposed to have ain't been near for over twelve monfs, but I'm not bovvered - don't wanna go into care again.'

Terry didn't know about Duane's time spent in care and he didn't want to delve. He sensed a sharp dip in his mood so he quickly changed the subject. 'Any road up; how's the leg?'

'Not too bad - bit sore like, bit stiff.' He looked longingly at the lads sweating away at their shuttles. 'Can't wait to get back to it.'

'You take your time, son,' Terry tried to curb Duane's impatience. 'There's no rush. Bruising to the bone takes some healing'. We don't want you back 'til your hundred percent ready.' He leant across and patted him on the shoulder, and he was more than happy to wait just that bit longer to see the remarkable East Broughton lad with the West Broughton spirit now fully engrained in action.

17

'I aren't gerrin' in that fuckin' thing for a start,' stated Ginner, defiantly.

'Why not?' asked Nobby.

'It's a spacker bus,' said Ginner, full of indignation.

'It's a mobility access vehicle,' explained Terry.

'I don't care what yer call it, you won't catch me ridin' in it.'

'How're yer gerrin' up to Ramsbridge then?' enquired Nobby.

'Dunno; but I'm not gerrin' on that,' muttered Ginner.

'I'll take your name off team sheet then, shall I?' asked Terry.

'Beggars can't be choosers, wee man.' Young Nobby batted him round the back of his head for being stupid and got on the bus.

'You can't mek a silk purse out of a sow's ear,' lectured Rammer, thinking the saying was relevant. And he got on the bus.

'You can't polish a turd,' advised Sully, and he got on the bus to some puzzled looks.

Kath worked for a charity for the disabled that was part council funded, and her boss, an easy going chap, had agreed to let them use the sixteen seater for their away games as long as they topped it up with diesel now and again. Terry and Nobby were chuffed to bits with their new acquisition; the lads, and Ginner in particular, took a bit more persuading.

Nobby stood at the entrance to the vehicle that was in the middle of The Fusiliers car park, beaming from ear to ear, looking like he'd just taken delivery of a brand new Ferrari.

'What the fuck's this?' asked Sasquatch.

'New team bus,' said Nobby proudly. 'D'yer like her?'

Sasquatch gave it the once over and curled his lip.

'Where did yer get this old ram-shack?' laughed Peycos.

'Hey, don't be cheeky else yer can walk. This is your new luxury, air-conditioned team coach.'

'Air-conditioned?' said a doubtful Biscuit.

Sully, exploring the inside, slid open a window and stuck out his mush.

'There yer go, see,' said Nobby pointing up, 'air-con.'

'Who's he then?' asked Peycos pointing to the heart shaped transfer on the side of the bus that let everyone know that it had been kindly donated by the Variety Club of Great Britain and had been presented by some magnanimous but long forgotten celebrity.

'He's a comedian,' said Nobby.

'Never heard of him.'

The lads scrutinised the maroon and cream coloured bus inside and out, and most agreed, although the paint job was a bit shit, it would beat travelling on the back of the old pick-up any day.

Ginner had been horrified, especially when he saw the giant wheelchair access logo at the rear of the bus.

While he argued the toss with Terry and Nobby, the rest of the lads had found their seats and were now, rather cruelly pressing their faces up at the windows making grotesque, lunatic gestures at Ginner.

Nobby finally jumped into the driver's seat and started the engine.

'Orl aboard!' he shouted and impatiently tooted the horn and revved the motor. 'Next stop, Ramsbridge!'

Terry hopped on and Nobby set off. Ginner, having no alternative if he didn't want to be left in the car park looking like a lemon, ran after the bus shouting for it to wait. He scrambled aboard to a volley of derisive shouts and jeers from the lads.

'Fares please,' said Nobby.

Ginner pulled his hoody well over his face and ran the gauntlet of piss takes to skulk at the back of the bus.

The Albion would suffer the pointing and the stares and the sniggers wherever their travels took them that season, but the lads would turn the tables on their detractors by perfecting simpleton faces, slavering speech and silly walks until their persecutors became embarrassingly uncomfortable in their presence. Unsure how to react to the

West Broughton nutters, the lads played up the act all the more until Terry told them to pack it in and have a bit of respect.

'Are you our official linesman now then, Flash?' asked Peycos leaning over the back of his seat.

'I don't know about official, and it's Mr. Ashington to you.'

'You're our official number one supporter, aren't yer, Flash?' said Sully.

'I'm yer one an' *only* supporter, man,' frowned Flash, as he added the finishing touches to a roll-up.

'Is that wacky backy you've got there then?' enquired Sully.

'Old Holborn, man.' Flash produced a petrol lighter with an ornate painted face of a Red Indian chief carved out of ivory on the side, lit his smoke and spat out a loose bit of tobacco.

'Cor, let's have a butcher's at that.'

Flash handed over the lighter.

'Woah, smart,' said Peycos, impressed. 'Where d'yer gerrit?'

'Off an old troglodyte.'

'A what?'

'A troglodyte.'

'What's one o' them?'

'Troglodytes are dudes what live in caves up in the hills in Ibiza, man.'

'Bollocks!' said Peycos.

Flash observed the youngster through the curling smoke of his ciggy for a moment before snatching back the lighter. 'You're a bit too cheeky for my liking,' warned Flash, 'and it's not bollocks, man.'

'That stinks like a Chinese wrestler's jock-strap,' said Sully nodding at the smoke.

'How would you know? Got a bit of a fetish for oriental sportsmen's underwear, have yer? D'yer go around sniffin' 'em or summat?'

'Nooh,' said Sully, squirming at the thought. 'Anyway, can't yer read?' he said pointing to the *'no smoking'* sign at the front of the bus.

'Yeh, man, and you see that one back there?' Flash pointed to the

'*Wheelchair access*' sign at the rear of the bus. 'You'll be needing one o' them if you're not careful.'

'Oh, yeh,' laughed Sully, scornfully. 'I'm cackin' me pants.'

Flash baiting would become a popular pastime as they travelled to away games and he would counter the insolence and the cheek with his own lazy drawled, laconic put-downs until his weary tolerance could take no more. '*Yer twistin' me melon, man,*' would become his warning phrase whenever the lads had gone too far.

Ginner had been laid across one of the back seats, hood up, not daring to show his face at the window, farting away to himself. The obnoxious gases were building up and Young Nobby had issued a final warning. 'If you drop yer guts again, copper-top, yer goin' out this back door, d'yer hear me?'

A moment or two later an F sharp vibrato sound was followed by a muffled, evil chuckle and the lads sprang into action. Basher flung open the rear doors and the roar of the road rushed into the bus. Joe had found the control for the hydraulic wheelchair ramp and Ginner was bundled onto it kicking and screaming. Young Nobby, Sasquatch and Rigger held him down firmly and Joe hit the button. The ramp jerked sharply towards flashing tarmac taking Basher by surprise and almost throwing him off balance and into the road.

'Fuckin' 'ell! Steady, yer doylum,' he said, turning white and stepping back well out of the way. Joe grinned manic and hit the button again. The motor whirred, Ginner screamed louder and this time was in real danger of shitting himself – literally. Terry, from the front of the bus observed the kerfuffle, sighed the Terry sigh and ordered the hapless Ginner be hauled back on board before issuing bollockings to all and sundry. The sated feeling he had earned for his resourcefulness had been short lived, and he was once again left wondering whether it had all been such a good idea. Through his rear view mirror, Nobby chuckled out loud as he watched his mate walk back down the bus chuntering away to himself, his forehead furrowed in that all too familiar careworn frown.

The game against Ramsbridge Colts ended in a one-nil defeat from a dubious penalty after one of their strikers had taken a theatrical dive over One Eye's arms during a one-on-one.

'I got the bloody' ball,' protested One Eye in what was becoming a rather heated inquest on the way home, 'din't I, Nobbs?'

'I dunno,' said Young Nobby. 'I was too busy coverin' for Ginner after he'd gone walk-about.'

'I definitely gorra hand to it,' he insisted.

'Pity yer din't gerra hand to t'penalty instead o' divin' t'other way,' said Slum.

'Oh aye, an' how many goals have you scored so far then, Alan fuckin' Shearer? Mebee I'll start stoppin' 'em when ye lot start scorin' 'em.'

'Can't score goals if you're not gerrin' t'service,' stated Rigger.

'Don't blame midfield,' piped up Joe. 'We hardly gorra kick today, It wa' like watchin' sky tennis wi' ye lot hoofin' it over us heads...'

And so it went on, all the way back to West Broughton; accusations, claims, counter claims and condemnation. Terry listened quietly to the lively debate with a smile on his face. *At least it shows they've got a bit of passion,* he thought to himself. *That'll do for now.'*

Come the following Wednesday Duane declared himself fit, eager and ready to train but Terry, being cautious, restricted him to just a few steady circuits and a stretching programme in order to loosen him up.

At the end of the session Terry gathered the lads round and in a calmer setting got them to air their grievances and opine as to what had gone wrong on Sunday. He latched onto any valid points raised and turned criticisms into constructive solutions. He explained to the lads how most of what was going wrong on the pitch was of their own making, and how nearly all of it was down simply to lack of communication. Lack of positive instructions from team mates that in turn led to panic football; hoofing the ball instead of playing it out of danger. Having confidence to switch play and open up the game, pass and move, support and protect. They had to get over a psychological barrier, play to their own strengths not their opponents and learn to apply in a game what they did in training.

'All the great sides have an almost telepathic understanding,' explained Terry. 'It comes from playing together as a team and not just a bunch of individuals; knowing instinctively when and what your team mates are going to do; it all takes time, but when you've got that, the football becomes easy and playing the game is what it should be - fun. Remember, communication creates confidence and that's what we need to start doing.'

'Very impressive,' said Nobby as they gathered in the cones. 'You talk a good game; I'll give yer that. D'yer think they'll tek any notice?'

Terry shrugged. 'If they only take a bit of it on board, I suppose it's a start. They can only get better, can't they?'

'What about Duane, are yer gonna give him a go on Sunday?'

'I might give him t'second half. I wanna make sure he's fully recovered.'

'He seemed okay tonight - keen as mustard.'

'Aye, he's certainly raring to go,' agreed Terry.

Midges performed a crazy dance above their heads as they left the field laden with balls and cones. Terry mused on no points from two games, no goals for, and four against, but what was really in his thoughts was the fact that the nights were drawing in; summer was at an end and that autumnal feel was in the air. There wouldn't be too many more light nights left like this. The clocks were going back next month and soon it would be too dark to train, and with not enough funds to hire a gym for the winter months another headache he could have done without was fast looming.

18

Malcolm Littlefare popped an extra Tamazipan and cleverly turned his stripy jumper inside out so that the hole that he thought was directly in line with his heart wouldn't show. It was where he'd been shot, he liked to tell people, but they all laughed at him. Silly bastards, didn't they know that his body had special healing powers? No bullet could ever kill him, not even from an Uzi nine millimetre. Him and The Terminator, they were the same. Even so, it wasn't nice being laughed at; most people were stupid and he couldn't be doing with them much of the time; best to hide the hole, he had a mission to complete.

Malcolm shut the front door behind him and swished the chrome car aerial through the air so it extended itself along its telescopic length. He carried it everywhere with him, nobody knew why; perhaps it wasn't just a car aerial to him but a cosmic wand with special powers; whatever, it seemed to offer some sort of protective comfort and he wouldn't be seen stepping out of the house without it. His medication was kicking in and he set off on his mission to nowhere with a bold sense of purpose and determination.

The Littlefares were your original Adams family; a bunch of odd looking, strange acting head-the-balls, most of whom were on or had been on various forms of treatments and therapies, whose case notes were full of diagnosis ending in the word path: psychopath, sociopath, neuropath; a challenge for even the most dedicated psychoanalyst. Thankfully, only a couple of the Littlefares were what you would call out and out dangerous, and they'd been safely tucked away in some soft cell yonks ago, the rest of them were just a harmless bunch of nutters who either had the piss taken out of them or were simply given a wide berth. 'Inbreeding' was the general diagnostic conclusion from your average man in the street.

Malcolm was probably in his late-twenties, a lolloping, Lurchlike character who could regularly be seen pacing the streets of West Broughton with his steady but determined march. He walked on the balls of his feet, heels never touching the ground which made him look as though he was bouncing along, propelled by springs tucked under his half-mast strides; swishing away with his aerial at some unseen adversary while singing a popular tune of the day at the top of his voice.

He bounced past Razi's where Betty Lightowler, just leaving the shop, stopped in her tracks before making sure she gave him a wide berth. He swooshed by her, oblivious, never even saw her; on past the club where a group of kids showered him with abuse and threw stones. Those who were on bikes followed, circling and taunting, just keeping out of the way of his aerial as he whipped and flashed it through the air in an increasingly agitated manner. He turned into the snicket where he finally escaped his now bored tormentors before striding out into the open space of Soldiers Field.

Slum stopped himself in his tracks, as did the startled Huckfield left back who had been homing in for the tackle. Malcolm swished his way between the gob-struck pair clearing a passage with his chrome stick. The tune of the day was Kylie Minogue's '*I Just Can't Get You Out Of My Head*,' and Malcolm was giving it his best rendition as the cocktail of pharmaceutics he had swallowed earlier got to work on the receptors in his brain.

'Oh, bloody hell, Mad Mally,' groaned Nobby from the touchline.

The twenty-two players stopped playing and stared nonplussed, hands on hips, thankful of a breather as Mally sang, whooshed and swiped his way across the pitch while the referee blew his whistle and waved his arms at the intruder.

Rigger, who was closest to the official, warned him off. 'Don't do that, ref; you might upset him. He's only passin' through.'

The bemused man in black heeded Rigger's advice and stood and stared with the rest of them.

'Oh, that's my favourite,' said Jan, latching on to Mally's song, and her and Kath joined in with some harmonies.

'Fer Christ's sake, don't encourage him,' said Terry.

219

Mally happily lolloped his way across the pitch oblivious to everything around him, taking the route of the old path that wasn't there any more; in his own Ptolemaic world, where he was the centre of the universe, where, to him, the only thing that was bizarre was the fuzzy maelstrom of noise and colour that revolved around the blurred edges of his cosmos.

Mally regularly walked his route but with no obvious pattern as to a schedule or time of day, and the lads had always allowed him access across the pitch even in the early days when the new grass was just beginning to take. Ginner would scan him with his telescopic sight, the cross hairs lined up alongside his temple. 'Mally, you fuckin' divot. Shall I purra slug in yer head? Put yer out o' your misery?'

'Leave the poor bugger alone,' said Joe.

'What's with the bleedin' car aerial, anyway?'

'It's his light sabre, innit?'

'Yeh, well I'm Darth Vader, an' I've gorra death ray pointed at that empty fuckin' head – choom! – Another Jedi bites the dust.'

'You're as crackers as he is,' said Joe shaking his head.

'Where d'yer think he's off to?'

'Nowhere,' said Joe.

Just like he was doing now, Mally had taken his regular route up Drill Parade and out of sight.

'There's some right loonies round here, in't there?' said the nearest Huckfield player to Sully as they watched Mally continue on his road to nowhere.

Sully looked at his opposite number. 'Yeah, there is,' he said deadpan and started grunting like a pig in his face. The Huckfield lad, not sure how to react, said nothing but took a few, safe steps back and kept well out of Sully's way for the rest of the half, and was mightily relieved when the puddled left winger was replaced by the skinny black kid at half time.

Terry recognised them straight away, the baseball caps, the puffer jackets, the gleaming trainers and the bling. Royston and Mackie were sitting on the bashed-in roof of one of the old burnt-out cars that now lay at the edge of the rec. near to the cemetery path.

'Take over for a bit,' he said to Nobby.

'Why, what's up?'

'Don't know – might be trouble.' He nodded in the direction of the two black lads and set off to confront.

'If you've come looking for bother, you've got me to reckon with. 'Terry stood in front of the rusting wreck and glared up at the pair. The two black lads seemed engrossed in the game and chose to ignore Terry's opening gambit.

'Which is the kid they call Riggs?' asked the bigger of the two, eventually. Terry had identified him as Royston, the self-styled leader of the posse who had done most of the talking on that first encounter.

'Never mind him,' warned Terry. 'You got issues, you sort 'em out with me.'

'This Riggs got a bit of a reputation. Scare th' shit outta ma boys. I fought I betta come n' see yer legend wiv ma own eyes, yer know what I mean?'

'Like I say, none o' my lads need concern you. Sort yer gripe out with me, else piss off.' Despite being on his own turf, the two dudes seemed unconcerned with Terry's threat.

'So, you's a football manager then?' said Royston, ignoring Terry's ultimatum. 'I knew you weren't no social worker soon as I saw ya. Same as I knew you weren't no dealer, man. An' if you was D.S. – Well, bwoy, you had to be the dumbest mother fucker I ever saw on East Broughton.'

'So, why all the shit with Duane?'

'Hey, sorry 'bout th' likkle guy, man.' Royston held his hands up. 'T'weren't noffink t'do wiv us man, yer unerstan'?' He shook his head in regret. 'That Purcell - him an' his boys they is idiots, man, yer knaw what I mean? I tried to tell 'em but they wun't listen. What yer need t'unerstan' see is them boys get paranoid easy. If they see a new face on th' scene nosin' aroun' they get nervous, man, they gonna loose out if somebody else starts takin' a piece o' they action. Is bad enough wiv th' eastern fugees on th' streets now innit...?'

At that moment a roar went up. Mackie leapt off the roof of the

221

car and started jumping around cracking his wrist in the air. Duane had just curled a shot into the roof of the Huckfield net with the outside of his left boot, on the angle, twenty-five yards out. Terry had just missed The Albion's first ever, competitive goal.

'Maaan! D'yer see that?' exclaimed a wide-eyed Mackie. 'Th' Duane kid, man, he a fuckin' genius!'

'I saw it, man, I saw it,' said Royston, almost as equally impressed.

On the pitch Duane disappeared under a celebratory mob and Terry was in a state of frustration and confusion, not knowing which way to turn. After the celebrations had died down he turned back to Royston. He had to get things straight.

'So what do you want with Rigger?'

'Noffink, man. Just curious t' see th' dude who put th' frighteners on Purcell an' his crew, is all, an' to see if you all really was a football team like th' likkle guy said.'

'And what about repercussions?'

Royston laughed. 'Repercussions? Man, after what your Riggs an' his boys did - you kiddin'?' Purcell's layin' low man, he ain't been seen on th' streets these past two weeks. You ain't noffink t' fear from him.'

'So where do you fit in? I thought this Purcell character was one o' your boys.'

'Listen man, them guys is bottom o' th' league, yer unerstan'? We use 'em as runners, lerrem have a small piece o' th' action in return. They is lickin' shot small time. If they t'ink they is big time, they is deluded man, I warned 'em to lay off; if they can't take th' good advice... ' Royston clicked his tongue, '...they takes th' consequences. Purcell, n' Franklin, n' Wishbone got what they deserved man. I takes ma hat off t' your boys.'

Terry took a deep breath, he couldn't believe he was standing there talking parley with a pair of small time gangstas while, at his back, his team were going through their finest hour to date and he was missing it. If this Royston dude was being honest, then fine, because he really didn't need this nonsense, but he didn't trust them

222

entirely, and he still felt slightly uneasy at them hanging around. Terry was about to take his leave of them and get back to the game when Royston's mobile rang. The tone was P.I.M.P. by Fifty Cent and just before he answered it a high pitched *weeeooh – weeeooh* sound started to escape from somewhere in the region of Mackie's trackie bottoms. Terry stood bemused while Royston spoke into his phone, no doubt wrapping up a deal, speaking in a curious street style patois in which could be heard his ancestral Kingston roots, his hometown broad Tyke, American gangsta rap and Ali G. Terry understood little of it. Meanwhile, Mackie was jigging about in an agitated fashion, kicking at his left ankle with his right boot while cursing profusely as the annoying sound, a bit like a car alarm going off on a Sunday morning, showed no sign of letting up.

When Royston finished his conversation, Mackie tore into him. 'You fuckin' done it again man!' he screamed at his mate.

'Hey, I din't do noffink, man.' Royston held out his hands, one of which was still clutching his mobile, pleading innocence.

'Change th' tone man,' Mackie pleaded. 'It's th' tone what's doin' it. Change it back to Snoop Dog or sommink.'

Mackie was serving a two-year suspended for possession with intent to supply. He'd been lucky to get away with community service and a tagging order that imposed a seven p.m. to seven a.m. curfew but on East Broughton the villains were usually able to stay one step ahead. Mackie and his mates had devised a way of removing the tags, and they had quickly turned this flaw in the crime deterrent to their financial advantage. Tagging was commonplace on the estate and there was no shortage of takers for the ingenious scam.

Granny Mackie was a big bosomed, God fearing Baptist; a first generation Afro-Caribbean refugee who had come to England on the Windrush back in the fifties. In her seventies now, she was still a formidable woman who liked to think she afforded a healthy respect from her numerous grandchildren who always paid her regular visits now she was on her own in her little ground floor flat. They were good kids, she said, especially the boys, and she would die a happy woman if they all turned out like her eldest nephew Uziah, a.k.a.

Spangla who had done so well for himself over the years; such a smart, polite, well turned out boy who proudly drove around in brand new cars, showing all what could be achieved through hard work and endeavour. She held him up as an example and role model and told the others to follow his lead and they wouldn't go far wrong.

Mackie and his brothers would give each other knowing looks as granny Mackie lectured away at them. Oh, they would aspire to cousin Uziah's achievements, make no bones about that seeing as he held sway to seventy-five percent of the narcotics coming in and out of East Broughton and as rumour had it was well connected with the yardies.

Granny Mackie led an insular life, revolving around her church and her bingo, letting all other aspects of the modern day sail past her in blissful ignorance, just like she had sailed into that Southampton port fifty years ago, blissfully ignorant of what her new life in the mother country would hold for her. She had let her faith consume her since her Alvin had passed away; long time ago now, thirty-three years almost. He had been a good, strong man and she had sheltered behind him, maybe relied on him too much in those early days when there was still lots of stigma around and coloured people were still classed by many as second class citizens. Now all she had was her God, and her daughters' children of course, her doting grandchildren who cynically used their visits to granny as a cover, using the tiny flat as a stash house and a base for their scams.

It had been good business at twenty-five quid a week per tag and granny Mackie had happily and innocently worn them about her person as if they were some new, fashionable ankle adornment. God only knows what story her eldest grandchild had spun her about the strange looking contraptions but it had worked, and she had heeded his instructions not to leave the house after seven o'clock under any circumstances. She never ventured out at night anyhow, she had her soaps to watch on telly and her gospel CDs to listen to, the lads could safely go about their nightly affairs without fear of harassment from the authorities.

Trouble was, granny Mackie's memory wasn't so good these

days; she hadn't been to bingo in ages and one Thursday night she decided she was feeling lucky, so she donned her coat and petunia hat and caught the number thirty-six bus into town.

It was the National that night, the jackpot was ninety grand, and granny Mackie was three numbers off a full house when the sixteen strong, tooled up tag-team burst into the giant Mecca ballroom. It took five burley officers to manhandle her kicking and screaming from her seat while the rest of the team did their best to keep her fellow bingo players, in the shape of an increasingly angry, baying mob of mainly middle aged women and pensioners at a distance as they came to granny Mackie's aid using their dabbers as weapons.

It took them a full twenty minutes to isolate and subdue her in the confines of the manager's office where one brave officer made the mistake of trying to lift her skirts and promptly received a Kingston kiss smack under the jaw from the toe end of her patent leather shoe. She had five tags in place around one ankle and four round the other.

The guys up in the control room had thought they had a major technical malfunction on their hands as the screen flashed up nine simultaneous curfew violations. It was either that or an organised revolt they had speculated while tracking the signals heading towards the city en masse. They were taking no chances and an armed S.W.A.T squad were put on standby as backup for the tag team who were being scrambled while granny Mackie had stepped off the bus humming *The Old Rugged Cross* to herself. In a little over half an hour she would discover that her impressions of her favourite grandson had been way off the mark, as had her declaration of: '*Lord, do I feel lucky tonight.*'

Mackie and the other eight tag absconders had their suspended sentences and the community services increased and the tags had been re-vamped and modified to incorporate an audible alarm if the curfew times were breached again, but the micro chip was proving a tad too sensitive and a certain pitch in Mr. Fifty Cent's polyphonic ring tone that Royston had on his phone was triggering the alarm at regular and annoying intervals and not even during curfew hours.

Mackie was going mad.

'Change th' tone man or I swear t' God I'll shove that t'ing so far up yo black nigga ass you be shittin' text fo' a year - you hear me?'

'Chill, bro', I'll change th' tone - I'll change th' tone, okay?'

'Just do it man - do it now, okay?'

Terry decided to slope off and leave the wrangling pair to it. He wondered how much more bizarre this Sunday morning could get what with Mad Malcolm's pitch invasion and now this pair of jokers chelping away at each other above the din of the faulty tag.

He couldn't help but laugh; it was that strange, hybrid language that these youngsters used that made him have a chuckle to himself; so many influences, it was neither one thing nor the other. He could understand the Jamaican connection, that was part of their history, engrained culture, and Terry loved the way the Rastas spoke; he was a big reggae fan, inspired by their Mick's unsurpassed knowledge of the genre and his rare collections of sounds from 'Sir Coxsone' Dodd's Studio One label and Lee 'Scratch' Perry's Black Ark stable. Terry knew his stuff thanks to their kid and he had gotten heavily into the dub scene, taken to new levels of innovation by the likes of King Tubby, Prince Jammy and Scientist back in the early eighties. But the emergence of hip-hop and the gangsta rappers preaching hate, homophobia and violence hadn't endeared him to the new, urban phenomenon. But there was nothing new under the sun; all this stuff had its roots in those primitive, pioneering sound systems that had evolved around Brentford Road and Cardiff Crescent, Kingston, Jamaica, where emcees used to be called toasters, and Terry knew that the old stuff was infinitely better, but he would say that wouldn't he? And of course he couldn't be doing with the baggy, shimmering polyester, the in-yer-face attitude and the bling. But what didn't work at all for him was the language these kids had adopted. He knew for a fact they didn't talk like that ten years ago when they occasionally sat behind a desk at East Broughton Primary. New York gangsta style speak just didn't sound right in a Yorkshire – Caribbean accent, and even as the world shrank and old dialects died out, he would never be able to listen to these guys converse without smiling to himself.

The Huckfield right back had decided he would rather be facing the crazy pig impersonater than this kid, as Duane tormented and tied him in knots for the umpteenth time. The Huckfield management were pulling players out of position in an attempt to stifle the super sub, but they soon lost their shape and were in total dissaray while The Albion mounted attack after attack.

Duane collected the ball off Ginner deep in his own half and once again set off on a raid. He played a neat one-two with Joe on the half-way line and dazzled past three or four despairing Huckfield players before ghosting around the now utterly demoralised full back, quickly looking up and delivering an inch perfect cross into Rigger's path who met the ball full on with a bullet of a diving header which flew past the flapping goalie and into the back of the net. Sweet. This was the kind of football Terry had wanted to see, and he kept a Jose Mourinho kind of aloofness as the lads celebrated the second goal, but deep inside he was leaping around ecstatic. He just gave a satisfied nod and a discreet thumbs-up when the lads looked for the reaction from the touchline. At his side, Nobby was bouncing up and down, whooping and punching the air in delight, as were Royston and Mackie atop the old burnt out car in the distance.

The lads, no longer under pressure, began to play football. At last they started to ooze confidence and they stroked the ball around, keeping possession, short, neat little moves making the already knackered Huckfield players work and chase. The anger and the frustration and the in-fighting of the previous games was gone, they were playing with smiles on their faces, playing for each other, and Terry had been right; the football, all of a sudden, became easy and a joy to play. Terry still believed that one man didn't make a team, but he knew that young Duane Geddess made one hell of a difference. Huckfield were no mugs, they had won their last two games, but Duane had torn them apart time after time in this second half and had made them look poor. What would he be like when he was fully fit? The thought was frightening.

Despite The Albions' total domination of the second half, they failed to increase the scoreline and the game ended two-nil, but it was the manner of their first victory of the season, even though he had missed some of it, which pleased Terry so much.

The scene at the final whistle was as if they had won a cup final, such was their relief at breaking the duck. And among the throng of high-fiving, hugging players were Royston and Mackie seeking out their likkle superstar to pay homage and offer laudation. Nobby raced on to the pitch to intervene but Terry called him back.

'It's okay, there's no bovver.'

'What they want with Duane then?' Nobby frowned.

Terry shrugged his shoulders. 'Looks like he's just found another couple o' fans.'

Nobby didn't appear over friendly at the introduction; he just glowered as Royston offered his hand. Duane's bruises were still visible albeit fading and he wasn't totally convinced that this pair had nothing to do with it despite their assurances.

'Big fella don't smile much, do he?' observed Royston.

'Oh, he'll be smiling plenty in t' pub tonight, don't you worry,' said Terry. 'How's the leg?' he asked Mackie, noticing that the annoying sound had finally ceased.

'S'alright, fanks,' snapped Mackie, obviously not wanting to talk about it.

'So, where th' boys playin' next week?' asked Royston

'Why?'

''Cos we wanna come watch. If you's all don't mind, that is,' he added

'Why?' Terry asked again, suspiciously.

'Why you fink, man?' said an incredulous Royston. 'Yer got yerself a megastar here, in case you's all hadn't noticed.'

Nobby had cottoned on to the conversation from a few feet away and gave Terry a look that he hoped he would reply in the negative. He didn't trust these guys and feared an ulterior motive. Royston felt Terry's reluctance to accept them and got a bit angry at the prejudgement.

'Oh, I see. We is th' bad boys, innit? Don't matter we had noffink t' do wiv Duane's mashin'. We is still scum in you an' th' big fella's eyes. We is trouble wiv the big T, innit? What yer fink we gonna do man, break out th' crack pipes? Spread a few rocks round yer precious boys?' Royston clicked his tongue, annoyed and disgusted at the familiar stereotyping. 'You fink we hang around th' school gates? You fink we is pushin' th' shit on th' kids like th' fugees? Let me tell you, homi, I ain't never pushed anyfink on anyone in me life, seen? What we provide is a service, yeh? It called supply 'n' demand. Them punters, they seek me out, I give 'em th' shit they want, yer unerstan'? Hey, do I take a moral stand?' he slapped a hand on his chest. 'Look it me man. I is black. Is th' man gonna look out fer me? I don't fink so. You know where I come from, homi, what chances was I ever gonna get? Zilch, fuckin' zippo, man. I look after number one, just me an' me brodders. Yer don't like th' way I talk, yer dis me style, yer dis me freds, I don' give no shit, man. I do what it takes to survive yer unerstan'? But I ain't no pusher, man. I ruin no one's life, they ruin they own, seen? I offer you's th' hand o' friendship, yer turn me down is fine, but don't yer ever judge me bro' 'cos you's don't know me, okay?' He gave Mackie the nod and they turned to walk away, then Royston decided he hadn't finished and turned back to Terry. 'I fought you was okay - I still fink you is okay. What you has done fer Duane, man, seekin' him out like yer did; he is one lucky likkle fella. Pity there ain't more dude's like you aroun' fer some o' th' boys in th' hood. We only come down 'cos we was curious, t'see why you'd do somink like this. Now we know. You is doin' somink werfwhile an' I teks me hat off to yer. We only wanna watch th' kid. You don't wanna make no peace wiv us is fine, we'll keep us distance, but you's can't stop us watchin' Duane an' th' boys. Th' aint no apartheid in th' parks, man.' He turned to go once again. This time Terry called him back and half reluctantly gave him the details for next week's game up at Blackbank.

Royston gave him a level look and nodded.

Terry had mixed feelings again. While the East Broughton massive ingratiated themselves with Duane and the rest of the Albion, Nobby fixed them with a beady stare. He could well understand Nobby's stance; the image of the state of Duane's face that Sunday would stay with them both for a while, and his mate would think him crazy for allowing them to be associated with a pair of East Broughton bad boys, dealers at that, but Terry had taken on board what Royston had to say, he knew where he was coming from and had a certain amount of sympathy with his lot. The choices for guys like him were stark and simple, survival any which way and how. Selling drugs was probably the only way if you lived in Dodge City, where the potential to make big money was massive, as were the chances of being shot or stabbed, but these were chances guys like Royston and Mackie were willing to take, especially when you saw the likes of cousin Spangla riding around giving it large.

Terry didn't want to act the hypocrite; who was he to judge these lads when he was quite happy to allow Flash, the M.D.M.A. king to be part of the setup. Nobby would argue that this was different; Flash was an old mate, an ex comrade in arms; a devil you knew was better than two you didn't. But as Royston had pointed out, you couldn't physically stop them from turning up and watching.

It took a lot of reassuring from Duane that Royston and Mackie had nothing to do with the assault before Nobby took the scowl off his face. The big man had taken a protective, almost fatherly concern in Duane's wellbeing since that incident; thank God he hadn't seen the flat and the mother, Terry thought to himself.

19

Terry padded into the bedroom from the bathroom leaving a trail of wet footprints in his wake. He let his bath towel fall to the floor and observed his physique in the bedroom mirror from various angles. He gave his stomach a satisfied pat.

'I wish you'd dry yourself properly in the bathroom,' said Jan as she applied mascara. 'Look at the state o' the carpet.'

Terry watched his wife get ready with a smile on his face. She was looking unbelievably desirable in just her bra and knickers, which was becoming patently obvious as she observed her naked husband through the reflection in the mirror. He was in a good mood, a brilliant mood and they were getting ready to celebrate The Albion's first win with a few sherbets in The Fusiliers. She could bollock him all she wanted; right now it was like water off a duck's back.

'And you can keep that thing away from me,' she warned. 'I don't want my mascara smudging.'

'Can't we just have a quickie before we go out?'

'No.'

'Not even a little mess about?' Terry pleaded.

'No, I know your mess abouts. You won't be able to control yourself. Any road we haven't got time, we're supposed to be meetin' Kath and Nobby at eight.'

'After t'pub then?' Terry lived in hope.

'Depends - maybe - if you're not too pissed.' Jan looked from Terry's forlorn features to his throbbing manhood and tutted. 'Fer God's sake, get some boxers on.'

Jan gave Rory his orders and instructions for the night in front of Tracy the baby sitter which made him feel like a right dick-head, but the lass with parrot perches for earings wasn't listening, she was settling down for a double dose of soap with her giant bag of mega-munch crisps and her bottle that said 'Irn-Brew' on the label but really had cider in it. She let Rory do what he wanted as long as he didn't disturb her while she watched Emmerdale and Corrie and he was back home before the pubs shut.

'What're you lookin' so bloody cheerful about?' asked Norman as he topped up the pint of Guinness.

'Well it in't the taste o' your ale for a start,' said Terry taking the top off his pint, while flashing a wink at old Arthur seated on his stool at the end of the bar.

'There's nowt wrong wi' my ale, yer cheeky sod,' said the sour faced landlord. 'You don't see Archie here complainin'.' He placed the fresh pint Terry had just ordered for him in front of the old salt-dog. Arthur grinned, gave Terry the thumbs up, docked his tab, tipped back his head and emptied two thirds of what was his twelfth pint of the day down his throat in one go as if it were a sluice, then went back to his musings, steaming across the Sargasso Sea, dreaming of Cuban rum and the finest Havana cigars.

'We won today,' said Terry, beaming.

'Aye, I heard. What did tha do, gi' t'ref a back-hander?' said Norman unimpressed.

Terry tutted and pretended to look hurt at the disparaging comment. 'You won't be saying that when we start filling that empty cabinet over there with trophies.'

Norman let out a chesty, sardonic laugh. 'If ye lot ever win a trophy I'll bare me arse. Any road, that cabinet's reserved for t' darts an' doms.'

'Darts an' doms?' Terry scoffed with equal sardonism. 'When was the last time that lot won owt?'

'Nineteen seventy-seven,' intervened Arthur, 'Queen's jubilee.'

'Who the hell asked you, Statto?' Norman turned on the ancient ever-present punter.

'I know 'cos it was me what lifted t'trophy. One defeat all season. Good side we had back then. Never been t'same since I retired.'

Norman shook his head and unceremoniously plonked down a glass of gin and tonic in front of Terry, looking at him expectantly.

Terry was unimpressed. 'Where's the lemon?'

'You're the bleedin' lemon. Where d'yer think y'are, Holiday Inn or summat? Think theeself lucky tha's got ice.'

Terry handed over a load of old iron, guaranteed to wind up the fat, miserable old get, knowing his mince pies were bad and he would struggle counting it into the till. He deliberately left it five pence short in order to confuse him even more.

'Keep the change,' Terry shouted, leaving the bar with his round of drinks.

No sooner had he got back to the table when his mobile rang. Jan glanced up at him with that familiar look of trepidation. She hoped to God it wasn't Tracy the babysitter ready to impart some Rory inspired catastrophe. There was an audible sigh of relief when it turned out to be Steve, the Farshaw manager. He had some interesting news to impart and was surprised that Terry hadn't already heard. It transpired that Blackbank had been involved in a pitched battle up at Tan Edge United that morning; players, parents, and eventually the police; all fighting in lumps and apparently plenty of blood was spilled and quite a few arrests made. It would be the final nail in Blackbank's coffin according to the league secretary, who would make it official at next week's league meeting. Blackbank would be well and truly *sine die*, thrown out of the league in disgrace.

'Bloody hell,' said Terry. 'We were supposed to be playing 'em up at theirs next week.'

'Well, you won't be now,' said Steve. 'They're history, mate; finished. You won't be sorry, I don't suppose.'

It was true; Terry hadn't exactly been relishing the visit. The lads had played some delightful football today and he didn't want them slipping back into their old ways, as would have inevitably happened, but most of them would be disappointed. They had been looking forward to renewing acquaintances and settling a few scores, especially Rigger. Bulldog Mason would have to be looking elsewhere to slake his offspring's thirst for violence and confrontation.

Back at the Gallagher household Rory was having his own telephone conversation.

'What colour are yer knickers?' – *Silence* – 'How big are yer tits?' 'D'yer smoke the pole?' – *Pause, silence* – 'I said, Do-you-smoke-the-pole?' he spelled it out slowly. Any casual observer might deduce that Rory had called up a sex chat line, but he was actually talking to Christine from Mumbai. The Indian call centre operative didn't have a clue what the funny sounding English guy was on about, but she still tried to sell him some double-glazing anyway. Not really knowing what response he should be getting from his smutty suggestions he put the receiver down. Bored and puzzled as to why Joe and his mates always seemed to get such a laugh out of it, he snuck out of the house and onto the estate in search of any kind of excitement.

Terry and his mate spent the rest of the night in a world of their own, jabbering away like a couple of old women, all self congratulatory, back-slapping stuff; master tacticians all of a sudden, like they'd been in the football management game for years. And as the beer flowed, so did the verbal vainglory and jactation; they could certainly show some of these so-called football league managers a thing or two. Jan had to remind them that they'd still only won one game, and they looked at her in that typical '*Stick to your cooking and your cleaning*' way that most blokes do when football's the subject, and went back to wallowing in their semi-sozzled magniloquence.

'I don't know why they bothered to ask us out,' sighed Jan.

'I know,' said Kath, who seemed to be miles away.

Jan looked at her mate, who had been unusually quiet all evening. She sensed that something was bothering her, but she wasn't opening up. They were best friends; they told each other everything, even intimate stuff. They were more like joined twins than girlfriends, they even knew one another's period patterns, so for Kath to be like this was odd, way out of character. Jan had never seen her like this and wasn't sure how to broach it.

'You okay, Kath? You've hardly touched your drink.' Jan placed a hand over hers that were playing with her ringed fingers in an almost agitated fashion.

'What? Yeah, I'm fine,' she said, trying to act breezily, but she quickly removed her fidgeting hands from under Jan's concerned touch and took a pretend sip of her gin and tonic. Jan left it, and they engaged in small talk for the rest of the evening, but she was worried for her friend, having dismissed all possible notions as to the reasons for her acting like this, knowing full well she'd have confided and shared any problems with her. Nobby was being his usual daft self so there were no clues there. The Clarkes simply didn't do crisis and they parted company at the end of the night with Jan feeling a bit awkward and more than a little puzzled.

'Did you notice anything different about Kath tonight?' Jan asked her man as they strolled arm in arm down Guard House Lane.

'Yeah, she's had her hair cut ain't she?'

'No, I don't mean that. She was acting a bit…well, sorta weird.'

They turned into Drill Parade and were immediately illuminated by the flames of a burning car, freshly stolen, dumped and set alight on the cemetery lane near to the entrance to Soldiers Field.

'How d'yer mean, weird?'

'I don't know… kinda distant… very quiet - not like her at all.'

Terry shrugged. 'Can't say I noticed.'

'No, you wouldn't.' Jan said no more on it, but deep down she sensed all was not well with her chum, and usually her instincts were never wide of the mark.

They sauntered past the blazing wreck and felt the heat of the inferno against the chill of the autumn evening. A gang of youths had been drawn like moths to the flames and were flitting about in silhouette performing urban tribal ceremony, hurling rocks and planks of wood as if in some sacrificial offering to the God of anti materialism. Ginner, Sully and Peycos were on the scene, lurking somewhere among the shadows, not necessarily to cause mischief but to make sure nothing and nobody got near what was now their hallowed turf.

In the distance a pair of sirens called and answered, getting louder as they drew nearer. Fire tender and meat wagon attending call outs in pairs; tender to tend the fire, and meat wagon to protect the fire crew from the inevitable ambush from missile throwing youths as they tried to do their job. This was sink estate entertainment; fun and games for the "socially deprived" courtesy of every council tax contributor.

Terry barely looked up as they strolled on through the rec., into the night, past the pitch where he could still smell battered grass and mud and hear the echoed shouts of jubilation in victory from earlier that day.

Tracy, Joe and Rory were watching some spoof scary movie when they got in.

'Has he behaved for you, Tracy love?' asked Jan. Joe smirked and Rory tutted. *Why the fuck did she always have to embarrass him like that?*

'Yeh, no problem,' drawled the teenager without a clue whether or not her charge had behaved as he'd only walked through the door fifteen minutes ago. He'd been watching the pyrotechnics up by Soldiers field, purely as an observer, mind. Gone were the days when he used to ride shotgun alongside Asbo and his crew in hot-wired motors or act as the Molotov MC, getting his kicks hurling petrol soaked rags stuffed into bottles through the windows of joy ridden wrecks. He'd stayed on the scene just long enough to watch the tank go up, always his favourite bit, from a safe distance so that his mam, who had a sense of smell keener than a sniffer dog, wouldn't detect the smoke and the fumes on his clothes and go up the wall.

Terry glanced at his watch. It was ten past midnight. Everybody was still up, bright eyed and bushy tailed. Jan made herself a coffee and settled down to watch the rest of the film with the kids. Terry went a bit sulky and took himself off to bed disappointed that such a great day wasn't going to end with a bit of nooky like he had planned.

20

Young Nobby had been an enormous baby, ten pounds ten ounces when he was born and it had been a difficult time for Kath; almost eighteen hours in labour and to make it worse he'd been breech. Too far down the uterus and considered too dangerous by the doctors and midwife to deliver by caesarean, Kath had screamed her way to motherhood. Young Nobby had ripped her to bits internally; she suffered a lot of haemorrhaging and had to have transfusions, which had resulted in her having to undergo an emergency hysterectomy.

The Clarkes were naturally disappointed they couldn't have any more kids; Kath, because she came from a big family; three sisters and three brothers. Nobby, because he knew what it was like to be an only child. They had never dwelt on it; they had accepted it and moved on like they did with everything in life. Now, all of a sudden, at the age of thirty-eight, something inside Kath Clarke had come to the surface. It wasn't exactly a longing. There was no anguished yearning for more babies she knew she would never physically have. It was more of an emptiness inside her, a sort of unfulfilled feeling that she had simply woken to one day, like there was something or someone missing. She would look around and expect to see other kids - her kids; children she knew she should have but didn't. She was puzzled. What did these feelings mean, and why were they getting stronger? And above all, why now when her biological clock was ticking away towards menopause, why would she be feeling like this? She had wanted to tell Jan, she really had but she didn't know what to say without feeling stupid. She wouldn't have known how to explain it anyway. She felt exasperated, both at the way she felt, and her inability to talk about it; not to Jan and not even to her Nobby who she shared everything with, and even he had begun to notice that something wasn't right. She would try, but something just made her clam up inside. He'd never seen her like this before and she could see in his face the hurt she was causing him as he tried to understand what was going on with her. He thought it was something to do with him, and he would get frustrated when she assured him it wasn't, but was unable to offer him any other explanation for her vacant moods.

It had all started when that nice young lad Duane had begun to stay for his tea after school before training on a Wednesday. At first it had felt good, her and three males sat round the table, talking, laughing. She had enjoyed fussing round them and just having that one extra person around felt right, sort of fulfilling, like a missing piece of jigsaw had been found and clicked into place, although before that she hadn't even been aware there was a piece missing. She had thought of Jan and Terry and Joe and Rory and realised that what she was feeling her best mate must be feeling all the time. If Jan had known she was thinking like this she'd have put her straight right away and told her to remove the rose tinted spectacles. Having *three* smelly guys around the place certainly wasn't the blissful ideal Kath perceived it to be, and that's probably why Kath felt unable to explain herself to her friend. She didn't want the illusion shattered, and now she had begun to realise that an illusion is all it ever was and ever likely to be and that realisation had left this indescribable feeling, a hollow emptiness, an unsatisfied void, irritable and frustrating like an itch that couldn't be reached.

* * *

The Tan Edge United representatives were at the centre of attention this evening. Those eager to get the lowdown on last Sunday's bloody encounter with Blackbank were jostling for position around the tables at which they were ensconced. The old ballroom at the Victoria Hotel was buzzing with first, second and third hand tales surrounding the scenes of violence and mayhem. Afforded near celebrity status were those bearing eyewitness accounts, especially the ones who had injuries and battle scars to show. The Tan Edge Chairman and club Secretary were looking a little jittery and nervous. Although they were being lauded as heroes by all the other clubs present for making a stand against the league's bully boys, they realised that the committee would have to be seen to be making an example against such disgraceful behaviour and were expecting to receive heavy fines and disciplinary measures from both the league and the County F.A., and could well have done without all this unwanted attention right now.

As the league meeting got under way Terry took his seat next to an unusually quiet Nobby and glanced over at the glum looking Tan Edge table and thought, there but for the grace of God and the hand of fate that dealt out the fixtures.

Tan Edge: another small enclave on the periphery of the city, full of strangely proud working class people who would claim autonomy from the rest of the metropolis if ever they were given the chance; where you were still considered a stranger, an outsider, unless you'd lived there for at least thirty years; where an odd hubristic, prickling sensibility seemed to be engrained in its community, probably stemming back to when past generations had toiled twice as hard for less pay than their counterparts in other quarters of the city in the now defunct scouring mills and tanning sheds that used to dominate the area.

Tan Edge players and parents had been intimidated and humiliated on previous encounters with Blackbank, as had all the other teams in the league, but last Sunday they had been ready for them. They had turned out in force; dads, uncles, parents from the other Tan Edge sides, the under twelves and under thirteens, all present and prepared for any nonsense from the Blackbank psychos, and they didn't have to wait long for them to oblige. The atmosphere had been ugly and tense before kick off and with the game barely ten minutes old, Lee Mason had singled out and stalked his first victim ending with the kind of assault his old man was used to dishing out on any Saturday night. He had taught his lad well, such a proud parent.

It had been the cue they had been waiting for and during the inevitable pitch invasion that followed it was the referee who became the first major casualty, going down in the middle of the ensuing melee with a broken jaw from a single punch as he held the red card

239

aloft at no one in particular.

The rest of that morning's events were recorded in the statements from parents, bystanders, police and the hapless, jaw-wired ref, which were now in the form of a lengthy report on a desk at the County F.A.'s headquarters. Inevitably, Blackbank had been given a lifetime ban from the league. They were decreed *sine die* in their absence, officially booted out owing hundreds in fees and fines that the league didn't stand a cat in hell's chance of recovering. Tan Edge were fined two hundred quid for their part in the fracas but escaped any suspension and deduction of points due to the unanimous vote in their favour from the the rest of the clubs, and in a private get together after the meeting, all the other teams present agreed to contribute an amount towards the fine as a gesture of thanks for making a stand and doing everybody a favour.

At the under fourteens level the reigning league champions were automatically entered into the prestigious County Cup; a tough, Countywide competition, as the name suggests, where the champions from all the other junior leagues were pitted against one another. West Broughton Albion had taken the place of last season's league winners, St. Botolphs, who had quit for a different conference in order to avoid having to play Blackbank again. Farshaw and Blackbank had finished joint runners up. Steve from Farshaw knew how hard a competition it was; the standards were high and no team from their league had won it in decades so he had declined the invitation to his side in order to concentrate on the league, and now with Blackbank blackballed so to speak, an anomaly had arisen; who would represent the district? Rather than nominating the fourth placed club, the committee decided to make a draw from the remaining teams interested.

Terry might have expected a bit more than the half-muted response from Nobby when Mr. Chairman dipped into the baize bag and announced West Broughton Albion as this year's cup representative. '*Miserable get*' he thought, suspecting his mate was sulking 'cos it was his turn to drive, nursing his orange juice while he was getting stuck into the Guinness. There were sharp intakes of breath and knowing looks from most of the other managers. *The newcomers in the County Cup? They wouldn't get beyond the first round.*

Nobby's mood didn't alter much in the ensuing weeks, and Terry found himself making all sorts of excuses for his mate, putting a lot of it down to the hectic schedule of courses they were having to sit through after work; Junior management course, first aid course, preliminary coaching badge. A lot of it meant sitting behind a desk writing stuff down and being lectured at and Terry knew that Nobby's attention span would be tested to the limit, bringing back bad memories from his school days, what with his dyslexia and all. But his mood didn't seem to lift much even when they got down to the practical side of the coaching sessions and it wouldn't be until some weeks later that Terry would become aware of the full extent and cause of Nobby's uncharacteristic depression.

* * *

Colin the Boxer dog had the yellow coloured police cone firmly in its jaws and was giving it a good savaging. Terry sighed. It was the third one Colin had ripped to bits and setting things up for this morning's training session was taking forever.

'Give over, yer bloody daft mutt,' he said trying to prise the battered and chewed lump of misshapen plastic from the dog's vice-like grip. Terry made a grab round his head and felt rock solid neck muscles rive and shake, power personified. Colin uttered a low warning growl as Terry's hands slipped over slimy, slaver covered plastic. He knew Colin was only playing and growled back at him. A tug of war ensued, and man and dog snarled at one another, Terry marvelling at the awesome strength, and shuddering at the thought of the damage this fine beast could inflict if it really wanted to. The human tired first and the dog ripped the cone from his grasp opening up the skin on the palm of his hand on a jagged piece of plastic.

'Bastard!' he flinched as the red oozed into view.

The victorious Colin took his plastic prey a few feet away and settled down on the grass to chew and misshape it some more.

Great, he was getting nowhere fast here and no bugger else

seemed to be helping. He tied his hankie round his hand and looked over to where Nobby and some of the lads were having the craic. At least the big fella was looking a bit happier than of late, but he always was when he was around the lads. They should have been playing Blackbank today so instead of wasting the free Sunday, Terry had decided to fit in extra training instead.

They weren't up for it, he could tell. He glanced down at his makeshift bandage that was slowly turning ruby and thought, '*Right yer buggers, I'll teach you to go all complacent on me.*' If they thought they were out for a Sunday doss and a Cuban they were in for a shock. He finished spacing out the rest of the cones while fiendishly dreaming up all manner of lung bursting stamina tests.

Unaware of what was in store for them, the lads were gathered round Peycos who was holding their attention with a tale about Ibbo and Tolley, two of the kids whose birthdays had come too soon for them to be part of the Albion. Without the football to keep them out of mischief, the pair of them had drifted back into their old ways.

As Peycos told it, they'd heard of someone on the estate who was after a pet bird, and, as luck would have it, they knew where there was one to be had. Trouble was, this particular bird, an African Grey parrot, wasn't exactly for sale and was most reluctant to leave its corner by the telly in the living room of the semi with its two juvenile abductors, and let them know it with a violent display of flapping feathers, loud squawks and bad language. In panic mode they had scrambled back through the kitchen window that they had forced in order to gain entry and sped off down the road on Tolley's moped. Dawn was breaking and, in the twenty odd years he'd been a milkman, Alan Briggs had seen most things on this estate and nothing much fazed him these days, but the sight of a madly determined Tolley screaming down Oak Avenue towards him at full throttle with a shit-scared Ibbo clutching a wire cage with a demented parrot inside it, all white knuckled and clinging on for dear life at five in the morning really took the biscuit. It was hard to tell who or what was making the most noise as they sailed past the totally bemused Mr. Briggs in a flurry of blue smoke and feathers; the knackered old moped, a hysterical Ibbo or the now completely mental African Grey.

'Did they manage to flog it then?' asked One Eye as the laughter died down.

'Yeh, got hundred an' fifty quid fer it.'

'Hundred an' fifty quid for a parrot?' said Sasquatch.

''Ere, them Afican Greys cost five hundred nicker to buy,' said Nobby like he was an authority.

'Yeh, but listen to this, right,' Peycos continued. 'The geezer hands over his dosh, all chuffed to bits an' that. Two days later, right he's got Tolley by the throat, proper mad, demandin' his money back.'

'Why, did it fall of its perch or summatt?' Nobby chuckled. 'Was it pining for the fjords?' He put on his best John Cleese voice. 'Was it a deceased parrot?' He felt a bit stupid when nobody else laughed with him and gave him funny looks. It was a faux pas both him and Terry often found themselves making when trying to be witty in front of the boys, totally forgetting about the generation chasm. What the fuck was Monty Python?

'No,' said Peycos, pulling a face and getting back to the story.

It turned out that as well as a full vocabulary of the most offensive swear words, the bird had started to recite its name and address at regular intervals. Realising he had bought a parrot that really belonged to somebody only a few streets away, the irate punter had sought out Tolley and Ibbo, demanding they took the foul-beaked bird away and give him a full refund of his hundred and fifty quid.

Having spent a whole day hawking the now dishevelled looking parrot around the precincts, the parades and the pubs and clubs, trying unsuccessfully to find a buyer in a desperate attempt to recoup some of the hundred and fifty quid they had already spent, the hapless pair were left with unwanted goods on their hands and decided that the only alternative was to burgle their way back into the house and return the bird to its rightful owners.

They were mightily relieved when the officer told the man in the dressing gown he could put the baseball bat down now, but they knew they'd landed themselves in it good and proper as the policeman made notes, trying to make sense out of the spontaneous but odd statements they were both coming out with. It didn't help that Alfred the parrot, as they had learned was the bird's name, was calling them both a pair of fucking cunts and making derisive squawks at their comeuppance.

'Why didn't they just knock on t'door an' say "*'ere, we've found yer parrot, mister?*"' reasoned Slum.

'We're talkin' about Ibbo an' Tolley 'ere don't forget,' Joe reminded him.

Slum nodded his head like he should have known better than to ask that sort of question. 'Good point, well put,' he said.

'Are you gonna do summat about this 'ere dog o' yours?' Terry shouted over to One Eye, effectively breaking up the impromptu gathering. 'We're not gonna have any bloody cones left at this rate.'

One Eye tried to coax his dog away with the old, punctured football that he normally liked to savage, but Colin wasn't having it, he merely glanced disinterestedly at the deflated ball that his master was kicking at his face. Obviously the chemicals in the moulded resin tasted better than those in the white, synthetic leather.

'Why d'yer call him Colin?' ventured Terry, a question he'd been meaning to ask One Eye for ages.

''Cos we din't really like Raymond,' replied One Eye without a hint of facetiousness.

Terry looked into his face searching for a sign that said he was taking the piss, but it was always hard to tell with Pete Lancaster when his good eye was looking right back at you but the other was staring out across in the direction of West Broughton cemetery. Terry wasn't about to get a straight answer to his question because at that moment Duane arrived breathless beside them.

'Sorry I'm late. Tel, had to go somewhere for me mam.'

'That's okay, son, we haven't started yet - and I don't think we ever will by t'looks on it,' he said, watching Colin pounce on a fresh cone.

Just then, Terry had an awful thought; a flash that went through his head in the instant that Duane mentioned running an errand for his mam. It was that image of him racing through the East Broughton streets, with Royston and Mackie and his hooded posse loitering on a street corner – *Royston and Mackie* – 'Shit!'

Duane and One Eye looked at him inquisitively as the realisation hit him.

'Royston and Mackie,' he turned to Duane in a bit of a panic, 'd'yer know where they live?'

Duane nodded.

'C'mon, let's go.' Terry caught hold of the youngster's arm and set off across Soldiers Field at a pace. He glanced at his watch as they ran. It wasn't too late, there was still time.

Duane wondered where the hell they were going in such a hurry; he'd only just got here.

'Have you seen 'em at all this week?' asked Terry firing up the old Trani.

'Who?'

'Royston and Mackie. Did you tell 'em that the game with Blackbank was off?'

'No, I ain't seen 'em,' said the lad looking out the passenger window watching his mates disappear from view.

'Where they off to?' asked Nobby.

'Search me,' said One Eye. 'He said summat about findin' Royston an' Mackie.'

Nobby shook his head and tutted. *What the hell was he bothering with them for?*

'What we doin' in training then, Nobby?' enquired Ginner.

Nobby watched Colin start to devour his fifth cone and said, 'Ah, bollocks to training, we'll just have a kick about.'

The resulting cheers echoed around the rec. and resounded back at them off the surrounding houses.

Terry wouldn't normally have gone to these lengths, but he had visions of the pair of them turning up at The Quarry Arms expecting to watch a game of footie and being confronted by a bunch of pissed up head-the-ball racists wondering what the hell two East Broughton niggas were doing wandering around their car park on a Sunday afternoon. The scenario was too horrific to contemplate. Terry could see the look on Royston's face, and the words, '*Stitch up*' and '*Revenge*' were most prominent in his head as they drove into East Broughton desperately searching the streets, hoping to God the pair of them hadn't yet set off up to Blackbank.

As they motored down Charles Street, Duane spotted Mackie's old, black Golf about three hundred yards away, Royston emerging from Ladbrokes clutching a betting slip, climbing into the passenger side.

'There they are!'

Terry floored the accelerator and frantically flashed his lights. The old pickup gathered speed in its own worn out time. 'Move, yer bloody thing, move!' he urged and flashed some more.

Two hundred yards away the old black Golf took off with a screeching wheel spin and a cloud of smoke. Terry leant on the horn and flashed for all he was worth. The VW sped away into the distance and at the end of Charles Street performed a handbrake turn and disappeared round a corner.

There was no sign of them by the time Terry had slewed the old bus into the Avenue. He banged the steering wheel in frustration and slowed down to a crawl. They trundled along slowly while Terry pondered his next move. He was about to abandon the search, leave them to their fate and plead forgetfulness for not warning them that the game was off, which was the truth in any case, whether they believed him or not was another matter, when Duane spotted them again as they passed a narrow side street.

'There!'

Terry pulled up sharp and Duane was out of the pickup in a flash. The car had been backed into the tight cul-de-sac and two crouched figures were shielding themselves behind the doors that had been flung open. In between the crook of the drivers door pillar the barrel of a gun was pointed straight at the fast approaching youngster.

'Fuck! Duane, man!' Royston appeared from behind the blacked out window on the passenger side. Terry was close behind and just in time to see Mackie rise from his cover and tuck the Berreta hastily into his pants.

'Who the fuck d'yer think you two are, Starsky an' Hutch?' said Terry. The relief on their faces was immense and Terry could tell they'd been shitting it.

Royston was not best pleased. 'No! Who the fuck d'yer t'ink *you* are, man?' he raged. 'What you t'ink you doin' flashin' lights all aroun' th' place – you on a deaf wish or sommink?'

Terry looked nonplussed. The two guys were really rattled. In hindsight he slowly realised that flashing his lights at cars around the streets of East Broughton was probably not the brightest of things to do, but Jesus, shooters? In his mind's eye he could see Nobby shaking his head in his *'told you so, but yer never listen to me,'* fashion. For all their bonhomie he began to wonder what league this pair were really in for them to be so shook up when somebody flashed at them, but then again, he was mightily relieved he had caught up with them when he thought about the possible carnage that could have unfolded up at Blackbank when guns were brought into the equation.

Terry explained himself as best he could, and the mention of Bulldog Mason and his henchman Sanchez hardly raised an eyebrow; sure they'd heard of them and their reputations and Terry felt a bit silly when Royston thanked him for his concern and all that but they were big boys now and were quite capable of looking after themselves thank you very much. Terry could well see that; it probably made it easier not to be scared with a pistol tucked down your pants, but did they have the bottle to use it? Had they used it? He looked into Mackie's sweat soaked face as he removed his baseball cap, revealing a neat, tramlined head of plaits. Mackie hadn't even turned twenty-one and, Terry wondered, what were the odds of the guy ever reaching thirty? What an existence; barely four years out of school and living your life forever looking over your shoulder in perpetual fear. Shootings were commonplace on East Broughton, so much so that they barely created news any more. Scores of woundings and the dozen or so annual fatalities no longer attracted interest or caused outrage, and the police only made the occassional token purge, in what was essentially a no-go area for them.

Terry, once again found himself wondering how he managed to get into these situations. How did looking after a bunch of kids come to this? He glanced down at the urchin from East Broughton, his face still full of naive innocence, despite all he'd been and was going through, and tried to picture him in another six years, without a job, without hope, stepping into a dead man's shoes on a street corner, face hooded, with a gun in his pocket, and these images always served to remind him that this was why he was doing it, this was why he put himself through all the shit. And somehow, and he didn't have a clue why, he found himself actually liking these two guys despite them being potential bad news, and the feeling was mutual. The twenty-two year old Royston had just given the middle-aged bloke a bollocking for not being street wise when he should have been, but the respect both him and Mackie had for the forty year old was growing deeper by the hour. He didn't have to do what he just did, he didn't really know them; didn't owe them any favours, but he'd made the effort, an almighty effort in their eyes, and all to stop them running into any grief up at Blackbank. It was a gesture of unnecessary probity that they both appreciated and would remember for a long time.

They all managed a laugh and a joke once the adrenaline and the lactic acid had dispersed, and before they parted company Royston and his mate felt they knew a bit more of what Terry Gallagher was all about and they wanted to be part of it, not least for Duane, who, for them had become a symbol, a focus of hope, of a dream that could still be fulfilled. And from here on in, Royston and Mackie would be accepted into the club, who, along with Phil Ashington would complete the most unlikely bunch of crusaders to the cause of West Broughton Albion Junior Football Club.

''Ere, I got sommink fer youse, ma man.' Mackie reached behind his head and removed a slender gold chain from the rest of the bling hanging there and clasped it around Duane's neck. A small, tooth shaped pendant made of amber hung from it, and the wide-eyed youngster looked from it to Mackie speechless. Mackie nodded at the kid, pleased with himself. 'Now, you wear that, you look after it, yeah? It ma good luck charm, innit. It gohn bring you good luck too, seen? We 'as all got high hopes fer you kid.'

'Well, what d'yer fink, Duane?' asked Royston.

'Aww, it's proper smart, Mackie. Fanks man - fanks a lot.'

'Is ma pleasure, innitt. But don't go showin' it to that bitch of a muvva,' he added as a warning. 'Don't want her sellin' it an' spendin' th' money on smack, okay?'

'Don't worry, I won't,' Duane assured him, feeling as chuffed and as proud as he did the time Terry gave him his boots.

While Royston chatted away to Duane, Terry pulled Mackie away to one side. 'Nice gesture.'

Mackie shrugged. 'Is noffink, man.'

'Why the gun?'

Mackie looked Terry in the eye with a steel cold stare. 'Protection, innit.'

21

The one thing Terry Gallagher had begun to pride himself on was his resourcefulness and his uncanny ability to come up with solutions to any problems that came his way. Thus, one Saturday afternoon in October, he found himself at the back of the Alladin's cave that was Rigger's garage in the company of Rigger's old man, Bob.

Bob Mortiss epitomised what Terry would have classed as a real hard man; an ex para, some even say he was S.A.S. Bob, like his son, was unassuming but his reputation preceded him and the mere mention of his name afforded a certain amount of fear in those who crossed him and a great deal of respect from all others. He wasn't a villain; had never been in any serious trouble with the law, and would always use reason to settle any differences before resorting to his fists. He detested knifers and the cowards who carried guns. He'd seen enough slaughter and genocide on his travels to sicken the coldest of men; the aftermath of massacre in African villages, women raped and tortured, babies with their throats slit. The so-called hard cases around here were nothing but punks to him. They knew nothing about real fear. One or two he'd crossed paths with had taken a pot shot at him in the past, but when you were used to being pinned down between incessant cross-fire from AK47s and grenade launchers for days on end on the edge of the jungle in Sierra Leone, he saw these would-be gangsters as no more than a nuisance, and whenever he caught up with them they were taught a lesson they would never forget and the only weapon he ever used, apart from a psychological one, was his fists.

He'd also worked on the oilrigs out in the North Sea, helped to put the fires out and cap the wells over in Kuwait after the first Gulf War, and now did stints away from home working for a security firm acting as a part time bodyguard to the stars.

In between all this he'd worked as a contractor, dismantling and removing the heavy plant and machinery from the pits after Thatcher had systematically closed down the coalfields back in the eighties, and Rigger had told Terry he thought his old man still kept some lights that he'd acquired from one of the collieries somewhere at the back of the garage.

The heavily tattooed, strong-armed Bob slung an old trolley jack to one side like it was a piece of Meccano and they fought their way to the back of the garage past block and tackle, chains with links an inch thick and other pieces of industrial scale junk that he'd collected on his travels. Terry smelled the oil and grease and took in the sights of what appeared to him to be half of England's engineering legacy while Bob clanked, clattered and rummaged about. An old phosphur bronze gear wheel came rolling past and Terry had to be sharp on his feet as it just missed his toes.

'Keep meanin' to weigh that bugger in,' said Bob. 'Still fetches a good price does gun metal.'

The heavy, toothed wheel wobbled its way to the front of the garage before deciding which way to fall, crashing onto the concrete floor with a dull, metal ring that reverberated through the outbuilding.

'Here they are,' said Bob finally. 'I knew I hadn't chucked 'em out.' He yanked into view four massive, dust covered ark lights with the halogens still intact. 'Got these when they shut T'Prince O' Wales pit down,' he said, giving them a once over with an oily rag, 'knew they'd come in handy fer summat.'

'How much d'yer want for 'em,' asked Terry.

'Nah, don't want owt for 'em. You can have 'em if yer can purrem to good use.'

Terry wasn't sure that he could, but he took them anyway. Bob carried three and swung them onto the back of the pickup with ease, while Terry huffed and puffed and struggled with just the one.

Terry knew that Flash had served his apprenticeship as an electrician before being seduced by the Madchester scene and all things smiley, but the worn out hedonist nearly choked on his roll-up when Terry produced the mega lights.

251

'What the fuck d'yer expect me to do wi' them, man?'

Terry shrugged. 'You're a sparky aren't yer?'

'*They* won't run off two-forty,' Flash said aghast. 'You can't just plug them fuckers in next to t'telly.'

'Just have a deck at 'em, see what you can do,' said Terry, undeterred.

With a frown on his face, Flash scrutinised the old pit equipment like he was Arthur Negus casting an expert eye over some priceless antique, and lo and behold, on the Wednesday before the clocks went back, three giant arc lights had been bolted to the top of Ginner's garage and one nearer to ground level on his fence. A trail of heavy duty cable snaked from Ginner's garden, along the foot of the fences of the remaining houses, into the snicket and up to the street light that had had its metal plate front smashed off. Here Flash was standing, illuminated by the torchlight being directed from some of the lads who were gathered around like mini Igors to Flash's eerily lit Boris Karloff-like features. In his hands were two cables with their bare copper ends exposed.

'Ready?' came a shout from somewhere in the dark of Soldiers Field.

Flash nodded his head, slowly and deliberately.

'Ready!' Young Nobby shouted back in reply.

'Would you care to hold my hand, young Fellow?' said Flash in a Vincent Price voice and a manic look in his eye.

'Not fuckin' likely,' said Rammer, backing away with his torch.

Flash let out a spine chilling evil laugh in the best Hammer horror tradition and brought together the two wires.

Across West Broughton, lights dimmed and tellies flickered, but Soldiers Field became bathed in a radiance sharper than sunlight. The old pit lights that had once guided England's main source of energy up to the surface and into waiting wagons, shone in all their glory once again. Whoops and hollers echoed across the rec. and the lads pinged balls about in childish delight, casting their long, sinister shadows over the dayglow green field and into the cemetery.

Betty Lightowler and a few of the neighbours came out to express their annoyance at their evening being turned back into day, but Terry was used to receiving rollockings from the nagging old fishwives by now. He didn't give a stuff. He met their collective wrath with a broad, indifferent smile that only served to wind them up even more.

Flash returned from his control centre at the end of the snicket grinning from ear to ear, and a mightily pleased Terry gave him a well-earned slap on the back.

'Fuckin' well nish, man,' he observed, satisfied with his efforts.

Terry smiled and nodded in agreement, happy that yet another problem had been solved satisfactorily, and all courtesy of the National Grid.

* * *

The sound of air bombs; loud reports preceded by banshee screeches resounded over West Broughton rooftops in the lead-up to Bonfire Night. Cold, damp evenings and the smell of spent fireworks hung in the air heralding the end of autumn and onset of winter.

The lads were busy chumping for firewood for what would be the biggest stack in the area, the only difference this year was that they'd built the fire at the far end of the rec. and not in the middle of what now was the pitch as in previous years.

Terry saw Bonfire night as an opportunity to make a bit of money, boost the dwindling funds by making it an organised event; pie and peas, parkin pigs, toffee and all that. For the lads it was a time of warfare and covert operations between other gangs on the estate; raids and counter raids, repelling the would-be pyromaniacs, defending your territory with home-made projectiles made from old bits of lead pipe that fired bangers at any insurgents bent on incendiary mischief.

For young Rory Gallagher this was the best time of year. He was in his element, and he'd saved a tidy stash of money from working with his dad in the summer to spend on things that made the loudest possible noises. And Razi Ahmed, despite his protestations about the undesirable, hooligan elements in his midst, had no qualms about breaking the law and selling fireworks to under aged kids, after all, he was a businessman and this was always a good time of year to maximise profits, but he still didn't like it when the squibs he'd flogged came back to him through his letterbox, lit.

Plot night had been a great success, Jan and Kath worked their socks off with the food, and they managed to make just over a hundred quid for the club's coffers. Everybody had a good night except Betty Lightowler who came out to complain that the noise was terrifying her cat. She needn't have worried as two weeks later Colin the Boxer had it by the throat and shook it to death. One Eye had to carefully persuade his dog to loosen its grip before taking a furtive look around and discreetly dropping the ragged feline carcase over the cemetery wall. Colin, not knowing he'd done wrong, looked up at his master with big, doleful eyes and a mouthful of black fur, saddened at having his new plaything taken away.

Work, for Terry and Nobby had begun to ease off; tree pruning, leaf clearing and general maintenance kept them going through the shorter days. They were down to two days a month at Garden Springs now and Terry's visits to old Herbert became less frequent. Only a few hardy souls were allowed out onto the patio at lunchtime, usually for no longer than fifteen minutes at a time and the weather had to be unusually mild, which was rare. Sheila, the care nurse who had gotten used to Terry's social calls, said he was welcome to sit with Herbert indoors, but he graciously declined. He was always in his work gear, usually shitted up to the eyeballs, but he was also reluctant to sit amongst scores of confused geriatrics stinking of stale piss and the heating turned up full.

* * *

Nobby had been counting down the days to his 40th birthday and the bash Terry and the lads had organised for him. Now he was using all manner of persuasion and coersion in an effort to get Kath to leave the house, but she wasn't having any of it. She was having a panic attack brought on by the plethora of pills she was taking for what her doctor had diagnosed as depression.

Terry received the distress call from Nobby on his mobile while he was helping Jan prepare the spread down at the club. Jan immediately called a taxi, threw her coat on and left her unwilling spouse in charge of proceedings while she made her mercy mission dash up to the Clarkes'.

'How is she?' she asked when Nobby opened the front door, but the look on his face already told her it wasn't good. He led her into the living room where Kath was curled up in the corner of the sofa, staring into space, barely acknowledging her friend's presence. Jan looked into her mate's eyes and saw genuine fear, but what she was scared of, Kath couldn't tell them, she didn't know. Jan held her trembling hand and tried to be subtle and understanding in the way she put her questions, trying not to appear too probing. She was no psychologist but she knew Kath like nobody else, and to her, the diagnosis of depression had been the easy, stock answer.

Nobby showed Jan the array of pills she'd been prescribed and he concurred. The short-term improvement in his wife had been overshadowed by the onset of more worrying symptoms that she hadn't suffered from before she started popping this junk; panic attacks being one of them.

When it came to health issues, Jan Gallagher was as passionate and as scathing as her husband was about most things, and she had good cause to be. Her gran had only gone into hospital for observation after a fall at home. She contracted MRSA within days of her admission and was dead within a month. There was no avenue of recourse. The shutters came firmly down in Jan's face when she started asking questions in what she thought were the right departments and that had served to compound her bitterness. Her gran had had a good quality of life before her fall, before her nightmare started. She'd been as bright as a button and sharp as a razor with maybe another five, who knows, even ten more years ahead of her.

She'd gotten closer to Terry's way of thinking after her gran died. Her man wasn't an activist or anything like that. He didn't go on marches or throw missiles at riot police. He was just an ordinary working class bloke who seemed to have an insight on how things were and how the system worked, or rather deliberately didn't work. Terry's take on the world could be articulated sometimes with jaw dropping philosophical poignancy and at others with the angry, vulgar rhetoric of the gutter, as when supporting his wife's attack on the National Health Service, when his words of wisdom were: *"We're paying for too many pillocks in suits, sat at desks juggling figures in a desperate attempt to retain Trust status and keep t'gravy train flowing instead o' spending t'money on disinfectant and looking after folk."*

Jan knew that spouting politics from an armchair would never change anything but she was determined that no quack sawbones of a GP was going to ruin her friend's life by doling out certain pharmaceutical products that guaranteed them junkets and freebies from the drug companies. From here on in she was on a mission; first to slowly wean Kath off the valium, and second to somehow get to the bottom of it all.

It was clearly apparent to Jan and Nobby that she wasn't for budging this evening. Kath begged her fella to go on with her mate and enjoy himself, but he was adamant he wasn't going anywhere without her. Kath's chin quivered and soon the tears started to spill down her face. His birthday was ruined and it was all her stupid fault. The big guy looked awkward trying to console her as best he could. He stroked her arm hoping that would stop the sobs, looking up at Jan helplessly, hoping she was going to offer some solution; she was a woman, she knew how to deal with these things. But all Jan could offer right now was her sympathy and a heartfelt hug for them both.

Outside, the taxi sounded its horn and Jan reluctantly took leave of her friends promising she'd be round the next day. She slammed the cab door, took a quick last glance and a wave at Nobby, framed and silhouetted in the doorway. The poor bloke looked so helpless and vulnerable, like a big lost kid, uncomprehending and confused, eyes pleading for her to do something, to take the pain away. Jan knew he'd have desperately wanted to be with his best mate and all the lads tonight but she also knew that his first and only thoughts would have been for his Kath and that heavy horses wouldn't have dragged him away from her under any circumstances.

Terry's spirits sank when he saw his wife on her own. He was doubly shocked to see red around her eyes; she'd had a little weep to herself in the cab and he began to realise that this crisis with Kath must be more serious than he had appreciated. But this was the Clarkes; even the second coming wouldn't have shifted them off their domestic axis of bliss, and Nobby not showing for his Fortieth – what was going on?

Jan kept an eye on Young Nobby for the rest of the evening in between her and Terry moping over their drinks, just to see if any of this was affecting him. But it wasn't. He was your typical thick-skinned fourteen-year old adolescent, oblivious to the tribulations and upheavals of the adult world, even when they were affecting his own family. He was as loud and as boisterous as the rest of them throughout the evening and did himself more than justice at the buffet, as was his wont.

Terry took to the microphone and compered a sports quiz he'd compiled, but his heart wasn't in it. He skipped over the jokes and the quips and went through the motions. It just wasn't the same not having the big fella up there with him, ad libbing, fending off the hecklers, taking the piss. It felt like his right arm was missing, and although it was usually the other way round, Terry began to realise just how much he missed his mate and how much, subconsciously, he must have relied on the big, permanent fixture; unappreciated and taken for granted. Terry actually felt lonely up on that stage and he took time out in-between questions to observe the lads, split into teams of two or three; how they paired up, who gravitated to whom. He studied his Joe and Young Nobby, argumentative, annoying, insulting, sadistic, execrable, like they hated each other's guts, but inseparable; now locking heads in an effort of sheer concentration.

'*Apart from Newcastle, which other football league club plays at St. James Park?*'

And the one-time outsider, young Duane Geddess sat with his new mates; accepted, now part of the gang. But he would never be like Joe and Young Nobby, how could he? He could never take the piss out of the big lad like Joe did. He could never trade insults with such vitriol and nastiness like they did. He could never swap digs and punches like they did, which were meant to hurt and cause pain, and ever get away with it. He realised what those two had was something special. Although it seemed to be borne out of violence and confrontation it was something unique and he would remain jealous of it for the rest of his life. But he was drawn to it, fascinated at how such a relationship worked. And whenever he was in their presence he would sit and observe, soaking up the banter and the verbals like a sponge, trying to fathom what it was that made those two tick. Of course, Duane got the mickey taken out of him, none of the lads escaped that, but with Duane it was always watered down, good-humoured stuff. No one said anything that could have been considered offensive or have started a fight. He was sensitive to the fact that he was being treat with kid gloves, but he wasn't sure how he'd react if he were treated the same as the rest of them treated each other. He was never sure when there was a genuine feud going down or if everyone was just having a laugh. It was that knife-edge social skill type situation that he hadn't got round to mastering yet and for now, at least, he would be quite content to remain on the periphery as an observer, learning, taking it all in.

Sasquatch sat with a self-satisfied grin on his face, safe in the knowledge that he had The Albion's mastermind as his teammate and partner. In every group or gathering there was always one know-all; one anorak whose knowledge of all things trivia surpassed all others, and One Eye was the man. The fact that Sasquatch hadn't yet answered one of the questions himself didn't matter as he preened and postured, cockily looking down on all those who were struggling, laughing away at the collective brain hurt. With eighteen out of the twenty questions correct and the nearest contenders getting a mere eleven right, 'Team Sasquatch' breezed the quiz and flaunted their free pints of coke and HMV gift tokens at the losers.

Nobby kissed his now sleeping wife gently on the forehead and tucked her arm under the duvet. He sat and watched her for a few minutes then picked up the bottle of pills from the bedside table. He studied the label for a while without taking in what he was reading. He put them back and stared up at the high bedroom ceiling, the same ceiling Nobby's old man must have spent hours looking at while coughing up shredded bits of lung and tissue almost thirty years before. The sadness from those times had crept back into the room, but Nobby didn't need or want to dip back into long forgotton childhood memories. Now was all that mattered to him, but even he needed an escape, a numb zone where the tumult of emotions couldn't get to him. He sighed a big, heavy sigh and fumbled around in the depths of his bedside drawers until he came across the remnants of the summer skunk, the crumpled plastic bag of dried-up but, judging by the smell, still potent weed. He dipped his nose in and allowed himself a little smile as the musky aroma brought happy holiday memories flooding back: him and Kath going at it hammer and tongs, like a couple of eighteen year olds, off their heads. Pissing himself, literally, with hysterics as Tel went off on one when his barbie failed. A brilliant holiday, but it all seemed to be a distant memory now.

Downstairs, Nobby rolled a big fat three skinner and lined up the tinnies. By the time the opening bars to Match Of The Day hit his ears he was well on his way to the blocked out oblivion he was hoping to achieve. He pulled the ring on his fourth can and held it up to Gary Lineker. 'Cheers,' he said, 'an' 'appy birthday to me.

Back at the club the D.J was packing his gear away. Jan was wrapping the remnants of the buffet into little parcels and was distributing to those who wanted it. She made sure Duane went away loaded with as much as he could carry. Streamers and decorations were torn down; balloons were burst. The '*Happy 40th, Nobby*' banner was folded away. Gordon the steward dodged kids as they wore holes in their party duds, pulling knee-skids across the polished floor, while he tried to stack chairs on tables ready for the cleaners in the morning.

On a table near the stage, on its own, stood a small, gift-wrapped parcel. Inside it was an inscribed silver tankard that read: '*To Nobby - On The Occasion of your 40th Birthday - Love from the Lads*' they had all chipped in to a man, even Duane.

Terry picked up the forlorn looking gift and took it with him. '*Happy Birthday big man.*' He mouthed the words quietly to himself as Gordon killed the rest of the lights, leaving the room in darkness.

* * *

Christmas, like Nobby's Fortieth, went pretty much uncelebrated at the Clarke and Gallagher households, among the adults at least. The lads were all aware of Kath's illness, but to be fair it wasn't part of their domain and they carried on as normal.

Kath's condition remained as concerning but as baffling as ever, Jan making no headway at all as to what was going on in her mate's head. Terry felt awkward and a little useless whenever he and Jan called round, and he inevitably ended up dragging Nobby off to the pub for a couple of hours respite while the women sat and talked. But even Nobby was becoming hard work, Terry finding it difficult to hold his attention for any length of time before he went off in his own silent little world.

'Maybe she needs to see a therapist,' suggested Jan later, rather desperately in Terry's opinion, 'get some counciling.'

'What, you mean see a trick-cyclist?' said Terry aghast.

'A psychoanalyst, yeah, what's wrong with that?'

'Jan, love, these quacks deal with puddled celebrities who have fat egos and equally fat wallets - total waste o' money. And where would Nobby n' Kath find the dosh to pay for a shrink?'

'You can see specialists on the NHS.'

Terry laughed sarcastically. 'Oh, aye and how many years d'yer have to be on that particular waiting list then? Anyway I can't believe you, of all people, would put your faith back in the NHS after what your gran went through.'

'I know,' Jan sighed. 'I'm just starting to get desperate for her, that's all.'

'You're doing your best, love; as long as you're there for her, that's as much as you can do.' He understood her frustration and was reluctant to offer his own theory on Kath's condition because it was the typical trite male prognosis when it came to female mystery ailments. He thought it must have something to do with her going through '*the change*'. Hormonal: the onset of menopause. But he wasn't stupid enough to say it out loud. Women were always touchy on that subject. It was tricky terrain for a bloke; a no-go area, really, and he didn't fancy having his head levied by his missus, so he resisted the urge to proffer what he knew could be diagnostic dynamite and bit his tongue.

22

'Hands off cocks – on socks. Game's on!' shouted Terry, nicking a line from his favourite film. He thumped on Joe's closed bedroom door and got a few muffled groans in response.

It was a cold, crisp January morning and Terry had just taken a call from Steve up at Farshaw to say the pitch was playable. It was the first return game of the season, Farshaw. Terry was looking forward to this one, especially as they hadn't played for almost a month, what with the Christmas break and the odd postponed game which you were always likely to get at this time of year.

Joe had taken some prising from his pit this morning and he now sat at the breakfast table with his chin in one hand staring vacantly into his porridge, idly stirring it with his spoon. His dad stood over him with a frown on his face.

''Sup wi'yer?'

'Nowt,' replied Joe without lifting his head.

'What's wrong wi' yer porridge?'

'Nowt.'

'Well eat it then.'

'Not hungry.'

'Do you want some beans on toast instead?'

'I said I'm not hungry,' Joe snapped.

'What d'yer mean you're not hungry? You can't play a game o' football without owt inside yer, you divot. You need the carbohydrate - energy levels.'

Joe kept his head down and offered no response, tracing patterns in his breakfast with the tip of his spoon. Terry shook his head and went off into the kitchen in order to avoid the inevitable showdown.

'What's wrong with him, then?' he asked Jan hoping she could shed some light.

'I don't know. What *is* wrong with him?' she threw the question back.

'Won't eat his porridge, says he's not hungry.'

'He might be coming down with something,' Jan shrugged placing four rashers of bacon onto a slab of bread and smothering them with brown sauce. 'There's a nasty Flu virus going around. Brenda at work had it all over Christmas.' She plonked another slab of bread onto the sauce-smothered bacon and offered the doorstep to Terry.

'Didn't say owt about being poorly, just said he wasn't hungry.' Terry bit into his sandwich and the sauce oozed out and over his fingers. Jan went to see if she could shed some light.

'Are you not feeling well, love?'

'I'm not hungry, alright?' Joe snapped again. He slammed his spoon down and stormed off upstairs muttering. 'How many times do I have to say it? What the 'ell's wrong with everybody?'

Jan went back into the kitchen and pulled a face. 'Well I've never seen him like that before,' she said, a little shocked at her boy's reaction.

'Chuffin' great,' said Terry with a mouthful of bacon sarnie. 'Hardest game of the season and he decides to throw a wobbler. Well he'd better perform, breakfast or no breakfast. If he starts playing like a tart, he's coming off, no messing.'

Jan looked at him and thought: '*well, talk about bloody typical. Your son's obviously got a beef about something and all you're bothered about is if he's gonna perform for your precious bloody team.*' She shook her head and went back to the cooker.

Young Joe Gallagher didn't have the flu, but he had discovered girls, and one in particular. Lisa Boocock, Tracy the babysitter's younger sister, had started to arouse his latent testosterone and throw his young hormones into disarray. Natural curiosity, probably perpetuated by visits to Ginner's porn sites on those hot, boring summer days, had pushed his inquisitiveness towards the real thing, see what all the fuss was about, and in Lisa he had a fanciable and more than willing collaborator with whom to explore and experiment. He'd had stirrings and feelings that took the blinkers off. She had laughed at his innocence and he had blushed at his own naivety; embarrassed at his nervous, shaky fumblings while she had appeared calm and cool and, dare he say it - experienced. But Christ she was sexy and she did things to him that made him shudder with pleasure and any boyish guilt he might have had for wanting to be with her more than his mates was soon overridden by the forbidden sensations he was feeling. He was changing, no doubt about that; things were sprouting and other things were dropping, including his voice. He was fourteen now and even on the bus going to games sometimes he thought some of the stuff the lads got up to was pathetic and childish. Arseing about like they did sometimes put him right off and he wished he could distance himself from it. But the other thing crucifying him was he'd sworn Lisa to secrecy. He couldn't risk having all the lads take the piss out of him. The pressure to end it would be too much and he didn't want to end it, no way. It was killing him. Fucking dilemma, or what? He wanted to tell the world. He didn't know if this was love or whatever, but bloody hell it felt good, but it felt shit as well. It was like an aching hurt that made him not have any appetite, and his mam and dad - Jesus how would they ever understand?

He threw his washed and pressed kit into his bag on top of his boots; his dirty boots that he hadn't been bothered to clean since the last game. His old man wouldn't be too pleased about that once he spotted them, but sod it; right now he didn't give a stuff. He made a mental note to take down all his Leeds United posters when he next had a minute and replace them with something a bit raunchier. He double-checked his sheets for stains, perfected his scowl in the mirror and trudged off down the stairs as noisily as he could, hoping it would be enough to wake up his sleeping brother.

Young Nobby rose into the air at the far post like a migrating salmon and planted a sweet header from Sully's corner into the back of the Farshaw net. Luckily the ref hadn't spotted him using the Farshaw left back as a human ladder in order to gain the height and the Farshaw protests went unheeded. One – nil to the Albion five minutes before the break; great time to score and well against the odds seeing as Duane had failed to show again.

Royston and Mackie always picked him up and gave him a lift to the Fusiliers every Sunday without fail. They'd waited twenty minutes after the appointed time before deciding they'd better call on him. They'd laid siege to the door, adding to the existing holes and dents in the process. They got no response. They got no response from the neighbouring flats they tried, either. People were too scared to answer their doors.

It wasn't the return to the fray Terry had been hoping for; star man gone missing again and the team Captain going all morose and sulky, so the half-time scoreline came as a bit of a shock and an unexpected bonus, especially as it had come against the run of play.

Terry tried to prime the lads for the inevitable onslaught that would be coming their way in the second half. He knew they would be under the cosh and he deliberately aimed most of his motivational words at Joe who, although not having a bad game, in Terry's eyes wasn't fulfilling the inspirational role he felt his Captain should.

'Where's this whiz-kid winger I've been hearing so much about, then?' asked Steve on his way back out for the second half.

'Poorly,' lied Terry.

'Pity, I've been hearing lots of good things about him. I was looking forward to watching him play.'

'It's the one game I really wanted him to play in,' admitted Terry. 'These things can't be helped,' he said, wondering at the same time what the hell had really happened to him.

As the ref blew his whistle to get the second half started Duane was in fact making his way across town from the infirmary to what he now regarded as his second home, number twenty-seven Ash Terrace, West Broughton: The Clarke's. He didn't know why he was heading there, it just seemed to him the most natural thing to do. He didn't have enough money for the bus fare so he'd decided to walk. He'd never even thought about sharing the taxi with his mam. He didn't want to go back home and he needed to tell someone, explain why he hadn't shown for the game. He knew everybody would be up at Farshaw, but he headed for the Clarke's just the same. He hadn't eaten since the previous day; he felt shaky and weak, and the cold was beginning to bite through the thin cotton WBA training top he was wearing. He felt numb, not just with the cold but with the events of the last six hours or so.

He didn't know exactly what it was that had woken him from his sleep in the early hours, but something had drawn him out of his bed and over to the cot in which his little brother lay. He had instinctively reached in and felt Leo's face. It was cold. He turned on the light and looked back into the cot. His skin was blue. Duane called for his mam. He ran into her room but she wasn't there. He found her slumped and comatose on the sofa where she spent most of her life. She wasn't for waking. He fumbled around the clutter and junk on the coffee table until he came across her mobile. He punched in three nines and the phone emitted a series of beeps warning that the battery was about to die. A woman's voice came on the line and calmly asked which service he required. The phone beeped some more as he hurriedly gave her the necessary information. He wasn't sure how long he'd been talking to himself before he realised there was no one on the other end of the line. Had they gotten his details? He began to panic and ran back into his room, lifting the limp body of his brother onto his own bed where he shook and rubbed and cajoled. He crudely wrapped him in his own thin duvet and tried to breathe some life into his lungs. He did this for God knows how long, five, ten minutes? He ran back and shouted at the dishevelled lump on the sofa and got nothing more than a semi-conscious grunt in reply.

Duane felt his heart thumping, racing through his skinny chest. He unbolted the door and slapped and slammed his way down flights of concrete, out into the freezing January air. It was just after six in the morning and sparkling jewels of frost glinted up at him from cracked pavements. He drew needle sharp air into his heaving lungs and his anxious breaths turned to crystals as he desperately scoured the silent avenues for signs of a flashing blue light or the sound of a siren.

It took thirty-five minutes for the ambulance to arrive. Duane had almost given up hope, thinking they either hadn't got his details down or had put his call down to a hoax. The services didn't relish call outs to East Broughton, especially the paramedics who never knew what risky situations they were about to land themselves in while trying to save lives, more often than not without police protection.

After a lot of desperate shouting and shaking, Duane managed to wake his mam from her stupor while the guys in green got to work on little Leo. While her two colleagues were busy finding a pulse, administering oxygen and hooking the poor mite up to a drip, the other paramedic tried to glean details from Duane's mam but experience quickly told her she wouldn't be getting far with this one and directed most of her questions to the frightened youngster.

In the back of the ambulance the paramedic tried to fill her report out. It was like extracting teeth. *Linda Marie Caldwell – age thirty-three* took about five minutes to establish in between being told for the third time that no, she couldn't light a fag. Caldwell did her distraught-face-buried-in-hands routine and it was left to Duane to fill in the blanks when his mam became incoherent.

The early Sunday morning roads were empty as the ambulance made its dash across the City and Leo's deliverance from his living purgatory to intensive care was mercifully swift. For Caldwell, the six or so hours she had to spend hanging around hospital corridors and waiting rooms interspersed with giving statements and answering question after bloody question were a drag.

'What d'yer fink's wrong wiv him?' Duane had asked his mam.

'How the fuck should I know?' came the terse reply. Duane didn't bother to talk after that. After what seemed like an eternity a doctor came and took him into a room where he was given a thorough examination. He gave blood and urine and was asked lots of questions. Finally he plucked up courage to ask some of his own.

'What's wrong wiv me bruvva?'

'Do you know what malnutrition is?' asked the man in the white coat. Duane had heard of it but couldn't explain it. He shook his head.

'Your brother hasn't been getting enough food inside him,' explained the man. 'And when you don't eat enough, especially the right type of food you become ill and that can mean that your body isn't strong enough to fight off other illnesses and so you can become even more poorly. And that's what's happened to Leo. Have you heard of pneumonia?' Duane nodded. 'Well that's also something we think he may have and sometimes it can be quite serious.'

'Is he gonna be alright?'

The man brought himself down to Duane's level and smiled reassuringly. 'We think so, but he's going to have to stay with us for a while until he gets better and that may take some time.'

Duane gave a resigned nod and the consultant continued to look into the boy's face, examining his features, puzzled. There was something odd about all this: one parent family, junkie mum who didn't give a shit about herself or her kids. The statements and reports were forming an all too familiar picture; he'd seen it a hundred times before, but what was baffling was the anomaly that was appearing: one kid neglected to the brink of starvation, while his sibling, albeit slightly underweight for his size was seemingly as fit as a butcher's dog. The only theory that came near to satisfying him was that this young chap must have developed his survival skills from an early age and that seeking out sustenance – whether begged, earned or stolen had become a priority instinct.

No doubt what had helped set Duane apart was his twice weekly visits to the Clarkes', instigated by Nobby who'd decided from the onset that what this spraffer needed was a few of Kath's Yorkshire puddings down him. And so, from the start of the season, Duane had sat down to Sunday roast at the end of every game, home and away and a Mount Everest of a dinner at the end of Wednesday training; full mashings, the works; a culinary challenge that his diminutive stomach had only just managed to conquer, finally leaving a clean plate after many valiant attempts, much to the delight of mister and missus C and the chagrin of Young Nobby who usually mopped up when Duane declared himself stuffed.

Kath and Nobby Clarke were like a mam and dad he'd never known; so warm, so friendly. He wanted to tell Young Nobby just how lucky he was. His life was carefree, utopian and he just didn't appreciate it. He often felt like screaming at his new mate when his mam asked him what he fancied for his tea, just the way she asked it; casual, caring, loving.

'*I don't know – owt – whatever.*' Dismissive, like her asking was an irritant: '*Don't care; just cook woman and stop bothering me.*'

'*You don't deserve her, yer spawny bastard,*' thought Duane.

That's why he paced on, through the streets, in the cold; drawn like a magnet to the warmth and welcome he knew would be waiting, and the first thing she'd ask: '*What're yer havin' to eat, love? Gerrin front o' that fire, you look absolutely perished.*' And as he strode up Hill Top Lane, the Arctic wind cutting through him, doubling him over, he dreamed of the Full Monty English breakfast she would conjure: bacon, double fried eggs, beans, tomatoes, mushrooms, fried bread, steaming mug o' tea, four sugars – not far to go now.

Someone in Social Services would be getting their arse kicked. Leo was down as middle to high risk. Someone had been falsifying visiting records. No one had been near in nearly eighteen months. East Brougton visits were the short straw. Only the brave and most dedicated ventured near.

Caldwell was told, pending further investigation, Leo was likely to be taken into care. There was a strong case for wilful neglect. This time there were no histrionics, no mock anguish, wringing of hands and tearing at hair; just a divest resignation and a demand to be taken home. The only time she showed any emotion was when her request was refused and she screamed for someone to order her a fucking taxi.

Linda Marie Caldwell had been at the hospital for six hours. Not once had she asked anyone about the welfare of her youngest son.

Terry parked the team bus back in its bay at the disabled centre and walked over to where he'd left the pickup, musing over the Albion's two-one defeat and rueing the chances and near misses that would have given them their first victory over Farshaw. Steve's team were good, but Terry could see the vast improvement in his own side since their first encounter back at the start of the season and this game could have gone either way. He relived Rigger's header that had slammed against the bar, over and over; only, in his mind, the ball ricocheted into the back of the net instead of over and out for a goal kick. And the other twenty yarder that had hit the post and come out to Joe whose outstretched leg deflected the ball into the goal, instead of bouncing off his knee like it had and flying off on a tangent.

The conditions hadn't been good today, the ground was still frozen under the couple of inches that the sun had melted, and the wind hadn't helped but he wasn't looking for excuses; it was just frustrating knowing that the lads hadn't been second best in this game, they'd given their all and had come away with nothing to show for it. Terry tried not to think about the difference Duane might have made because he couldn't fault the boys this morning. He just hoped Farshaw wouldn't end up being their bogey team, the side that held the Indian sign over them.

He waited for what seemed like an age for the core-plug to go out. There was ice on the inside of the windscreen and the diesel engine in the old Trani coughed, spluttered and protested until finally and reluctantly it kicked itself into life. He turned the heater, which worked when it felt like it, on full in a vain attempt to clear the windscreen. A blast of icy air shot through the vents and made him shiver. He thought his hands might stick to the steering wheel and his arse develop piles if he sat there much longer, so he decided to go back to the relative warmth of the bus, and the lingering presence of a dozen steaming, defeated bodies, while the green beast warmed up.

'Where are yer?' Nobby's abrupt baritone demanded at the other end of Terry's mobile.

'Just parking the bus.'

'You'd best get over to ours and bring your lass with yer.'

'Why, what's up?'

Terry heard a big sigh, 'Oh it'll wait 'till you get here, just don't be too long about it.'

Nobby hung up leaving Terry a little puzzled, but intrigued. He climbed into the pickup that was just as bloody cold as when he had left it. He turned the wipers on in an effort to help the temperamental heater clear the remaining ice from the windscreen and guessed that whatever was going down at the Clarkes' probably had something to do with Kath. And it did, but it also had plenty to do with Duane Geddess and his sibling, Leo.

A hundred questions, and as yet, no answers. Glances of anticipation and the silence excruciating. Duane sat there in front of a clean plate, staring awkwardly into his mug of tea like he was studying the leaves, not really wanting to make eye contact. Jan, Nobby, and Terry followed Kath's every move as she tidied up around them with her coat on. She wrang out the dishcloth and dried her hands on a towel. 'We've got a little bit o' bad news...' she said eventually, her voice quiet and calm.

Duane had sat in front of the warm gas fire and bared his soul; poured his heart out; unloaded years of bottled up grief, pent up emotions, shite and misery to this woman who he'd grown to love over these last few months; a love he had tried, but hadn't come close to feeling, for his own mam and he didn't feel guilty for that. The relief he felt was immense. Kath had knelt beside him in front of the fire and held him to her as his heart-wrenching story had unfolded and this had prompted a tidal wave of outpourings. He told her everything, dragging stuff up from deep inside him, things that he'd repressed and stored away in a dark place, spewing forth, purging himself until his emotional well had run dry, and he had knelt there with his head nestled against her breasts, totally spent. She had rocked him back and forth like the child he had never had the chance to be, the tears drying on his cheeks and his eyes stinging.

Kath had shed some tears of her own alongside him while she listened to the distressing stories and incidents that had blighted his fourteen years. She heard how he'd been taken into care as a five year old, not to see his mother again for another three years. He told her how he'd been forced to stand and watch as she was systematically raped by three men; acquaintances, punters - he couldn't remember. How he had also been abused by some creep his mam had been seeing over a two and a half year period. And about the endless stream of junkies, wasters and down and outs that had passed through his life; real scum of the earth; filthy parasites who made his flesh crawl; some who he had to pretend to be nice to. if he didn't want to end up covered in knocks and bruises; others best staying out the way of, for the very same reason.

Duane had had to get used to the beatings; drink and drug fuelled back-handers, slaps, kicks; the cigarette burns on his arms and legs. That's why the pounding he had received from Purcell and his droogs hadn't bothered him unduly. Being used as a punch bag had battle-hardened him over the years, but the wall he'd built up around himself had come tumbling down this Sunday morning. His emotions were now exposed raw and the vulnerability this created was tempered by the care and concern of this woman, somebody else's mam. God, how he wished he belonged to her.

Kath had listened to the events that had led up to Duane knocking on her door, frozen to the bone, when he should have been weaving his magic with the lads up at Farshaw.

Caldwell had traded their electric tokens for fixes and they'd gone all over Christmas without heating in the flat. Duane had learned to cope, he didn't have any other choice, but the cold and the damp and the neglect had been just too much for little Leo to suffer and his poor undernourished body had finally succumbed to the conditions he had been forced to endure. His last source of any real sustenance had come in the parcel of chicken drumsticks, ham and cheese sandwiches that Jan had sent Duane off with after Nobby's birthday do. His brother had shared out the food under meagre candlelight while the mother slunk into her familiar stupor and the proceeds from what should have been keeping them both warm coursed through her veins.

Kath knew Duane had a brother; he'd confirmed this when she'd taken an interest after he'd first started to call round. She'd asked a hundred questions, just being friendly; chatty as was her nature but Duane had been reticent to talk too much about himself and his family and she had put it down to his natural shyness. Now she knew everything and the shock at learning the extent of his deprivation seemed to trigger something inside her. Something had fired her up, and although she didn't know it yet, she was about to embark on a mission that would provide therapy for her condition that no over-qualified shrink could ever come up with.

Learning about little Leo's plight had touched Kath so much that she now felt duty bound to respond and do something. She didn't know yet what that would be, but all of a sudden she felt she had a purpose, a goal. And when her two other fellas had got back from football, moody and noisy, young Nobby banging about in the hall, slamming his gear down and storming off straight upstairs and banging his bedroom door shut, his dad shouting some obscenity after him, Kath had dragged her husband into the kitchen ignoring his crabbiness and had launched herself into a précised tale of the morning's events. She'd been like a whirlwind, jabbering away while multitasking all over the place, making endless pots of tea while explaining that Sunday dinner would be late today and she was rustling up bacon sarnies just to put them on, then resuming her story, picking up her thread where she had left it, full flow.

Nobby had looked absolutely shell-shocked, as much to do with the sudden transformation of his missus as the shocking revelations he was hearing.

When she had briefly left the room to shout her son down for his sandwich, there had been the inevitable awkward silence in the kitchen. Nobby had slumped onto a chair opposite Duane, not knowing what to say to the lad.

'Did we win, Nobby?' Duane eventually ventured in a half-whisper.

'What...? Er... no - lost two-one.' Nobby was miles away.

Young Nobby had come thundering down the stairs demanding to know why they were only having bacon sarnies on a Sunday after-noon. He had blustered into the kitchen where the sight of Duane stopped him dead in his tracks.

'Oh, nice to see yer, Duane,' he boomed sarcastically. 'Where the fuck were you – *again*?' he added for emphasis. At that moment Kath Clarke did something she had never done in her life. She raised her hand to her son and it was a resounding full-bodied crack to the back of the head, something Young Nobby was quite fond of doing to oth-ers and rarely had it done back to him. He didn't like it. The shock on his face was reflected on the others present, including his mam who couldn't believe what she'd just done.

'Christ, mam, what were that for?' he wailed.

'I… I'm sorry,' she stuttered, thrusting his sandwich at him and flushing up at the same time.

'Jesus,' he exclaimed while rubbing the back of his smarting bar-net with his spare hand.

It was at this point that Nobby had decided to get on the blower to Terry.

Terry stood uncomfortably in the Clarkes' kitchen, listening to the story Kath was repeating for them. He felt a right dick. He didn't know much of Duane's saga, the kid had never opened up to him, and he'd never pushed him on anything he didn't want to talk about. But he'd seen what he'd seen in that half hour visit back in the sum-mer and that had been enough. He knew about Duane's mam and he knew about Duane's brother Leo and he'd kept quiet; hadn't told anyone about what he'd witnessed, not even Jan. Now, hearing that the little guy was hooked up in intensive care down the infirmary made him feel sick. His guts churned and he decided he needed to sit down. He sipped at some tea but it didn't make him feel any better. A massive feeling of guilt overwhelmed him and added to the sick feel-ing. He was catching Kath's words in snatches, not really listening; not really wanting to listen. He formed an image of Leo, first in his filthy cot, arms outstretched, pleading, then of him lying in hospital full of tubes and wires. Stomach acid surged and he swallowed it back down sending him into a coughing fit.

'You all right, Terry, love?' Kath broke off.

'Y… yeh,' he rasped and spluttered. 'Tea's gone down t'wrong hole.'

Kath resumed to an appalled but fascinated Jan while Terry asked Nobby to find him some Rennies.

Kath tried as best she could to involve Duane in the re-telling of his story. It wasn't easy for him sitting there, having his life regurgitated in front of other people, even though they were the only people he was ever likely to trust. He reverted to shyness and nodded or shook his head when Kath needed to confirm certain details of what he'd told her. Jan engaged him in friendly chat and sent him heartfelt looks of sympathy when Kath got to the more harrowing accounts of his life at home while Terry sucked on an antacid and kept quiet.

Jan was as much intrigued by her mate's sudden change of demeanour as by Duane and Leo's plight. Kath cleared away cups and plates like a woman possessed; washed and dried breakfast pans with super quick efficiency, and while she finished preparing Sunday dinner with her back to them, Jan managed to give Nobby an inquisitive look as if to say, '*what's going on?*' but all she got was a puzzled, '*don't ask me,*' look in return.

They watched her slide a joint of meat into the oven and set the timer.

'There,'she said, wiping her hands on a tea towel, 'all done.'

'Kath love,' said Jan. 'Why've you got your coat on...?'

Kath had hardly been out of the house in weeks. She hadn't been to work since before Christmas. Now here she was, sitting in the back of her little blue Micra, Duane squashed in between her and Jan, Nobby at the wheel, Terry sitting beside him, unusually silent and pale, insisting she be driven up to the infirmary.

She'd dismissed their protests, their cautionary warnings about interfering. She'd ignored her son's whingeing about Sunday dinner being late. She wouldn't be taking no for an answer. She was determined, single minded and on a mission.

Duane took them up to the ward and Kath used her charm and brazenly lied about being a relative in order to allow her access to intensive care.

Little Leo was just as Duane had left him earlier in the day; mildly sedated with an array of tubes and wires inserted into tiny orifices. Kath's heart turned to mush as soon as she saw him. She dropped to the side of the bed and gently lifted a minute, coffee coloured hand and stroked it with her own. She gazed into his unconscious features and almost at once silent tears began to stream down her cheeks. He was more gorgeous than the picture her minds eye had painted. He had a pure, almost angelic face and he looked so peaceful as he slept, oblivious that for the first time in his short life someone cared; someone loved him instantly, unconditionally.

Kath stroked the small, tight black ringlets on his head and gazed at the longest, curling dark lashes on the end of closed lids that hid those piercing, hazel, bottomless pools that were his eyes. He remained so still and lifeless that Kath wasn't sure he was still breathing and she had to constantly check the banks of screens and monitors at the side of the bed that were oscillating and beeping, confirming his vital systems were still functioning.

Jan held Duane's hand and they both stood back and watched in silence as Kath attached herself both emotionally and physically to the sick child.

Outside the room Terry and Nobby watched the scene through the glass part of the door. Terry's heart was thumping so loud he was certain his mate would hear it.

'You knew, didn't yer?' Nobby said eventually without taking his eyes away.

'Knew what?'

'You must have known all about Duane and the young un after that day we went looking for him.'

'I saw his mam and I saw the kid. I saw how they lived. I saw his mam was a junkie. That's all.' Terry had a defensive tone in his voice.

'Why didn't you say owt?'

Terry sighed. 'I dunno,' he said after a long pause. 'I tried to get Duane to open up a bit when he first came training, but whenever I brought his homelife into the conversation he'd just clam up. He obviously didn't want to talk about it so I didn't push it.'

'Well he's certainly opened up now.'

'He certainly has,' mused Terry.

They both pondered through the glass some more, but Terry needed to get something off his chest. 'Listen,' he said eventually. 'That day, that day I found Duane – I did a deal with his mam.'

Nobby looked sideways at his mate. 'How d'yer mean?'

Terry stared straight ahead. 'The place was an absolute shithole, Nobby. You've never seen owt like it, man. And the poor kid was just sat there, sat in his own shit, and that bitch just didn't give a fuck. I was ready to turn her in, there and then, I swear to God I was. And she wasn't for letting Duane play for us, no way. So, I blackmailed her – I don't know why I did it, I just did. Don't even ask me why.' He bowed his head. 'I threatened to go to Social Services if she didn't let Duane play for us... so... we did the deal.'

Nobby raised his eyebrows unsure whether or not he needed to form a moral stance on this little revelation. Terry looked up in anticipation of a response. He could almost hear the cogs whirring.

'Well say summat for Christ's sake!'

'Well, how do you feel about it?' Nobby asked calmly.

Terry let his head drop again. 'How d'yer think I feel? The poor little bugger's in there wired up to all that shit, and I could've prevented it. I could've done something about it but I didn't – I feel fuckin' awful. He wanted me to pick him up, held his arms out to me, looked at me with them eyes...' He swallowed hard. '...I walked away. Walked away just so Duane could play football for us...' Terry's voice petered out and he shook his head in shame.

'Look,' said Nobby, desperately searching for the right words. 'Okay, you screwed up. You did it. You feel crap about it, and rightly so, but it's no use beating yourself up over it. What's done's done.

The kid's gonna be alrate. He isn't gonna die – get over it, mate.'

'I didn't tell Jan,' Terry admitted.

'She need never know.'

'Duane don't know either.'

'It'll be our little secret.'

Terry heaved his shoulders and let out an almighty sigh. Nobby's take on things allowed him just a tiny crumb of comfort.

'I won't go to heaven, will I?'

Nobby laughed. 'Absolutely no fuckin' chance.'

23

The higher the bus climbed deep into the Pennines the bleaker the weather became. They'd set off in cold winter rain that had slowly turned to driving sleet and ultimately banks of snow flurries that had started to settle on the adjacent hills.

Nobody much was looking forward to this one. Flash was cocooned in his cagoule and beanie hat dreaming of Ibiza. Royston and Mackie, now bonafide West Broughton Albion supporters, who travelled to all the games without fail, resplendent in dayglo puffer jackets clashing alarmingly with bobble hats in Jamaican colours, gazed miserably out of the window behind their mirrored shades.

During their travels, a culture clash had developed between Flash and the East Broughton massive that Terry found highly amusing. They thought Flash was a smelly old hippy, and what Flash thought of them he never said, but they always found time to pass disparaging remarks at each other and generally take the piss. And the contentious subjects were usually to do with clothes, appearance and music. They would sit on opposite sides of the bus trying to outdo one another with the volume on their personal stereos; Flash, with his battered, old Walkman and his Ibiza sounds and his ancient Stereo M.C's tape that he played to death; Royston and Mackie with their state of the art iPods, listening to Dizzee Rascal, Wiley and Roll Deep. Today, though, everyone was quiet, even the lads were unusually subdued, most of the noise on this February morning coming from the drone of the bus's engine as Nobby dropped her through the gears in anticipation of yet another incline. Only Terry appeared upbeat and that was mainly because his boys had already proved the doubters wrong. They were on their way to play Goit Stock Juniors in the fourth round of the County Cup, just one game away from the quarterfinals, when nobody had given them a cat in hell's chance of progressing beyond the first round. It had been a good run and the lads had played exceptionally well in all the previous rounds, but the competition was getting stiffer and they'd only won the last game after extra time. But Terry had gee'd them up, they'd performed superbly, beyond everyone's expectations, done themselves proud already and there was nothing to stop them going further. They had nothing to lose. The league was beyond them now, but he told them that this cup was the one, the Holy Grail, the equivalent of a Premiership side winning The Champions League Cup, and he expected them to give it their all and go for it.

'Where the 'ell d'yer find a piece o' grass flat enough for a pitch round 'ere then?' commented Nobby as they rounded the umpteenth bend to be confronted with yet another rise.

'I'm buggered if I know,' said Terry. 'Lads'll be needing oxygen if we go much higher.' He peered out of the windscreen at the grey-white flakes that were driving horizontally at them. 'Hope they don't call it off after we've come all this way.'

Being in the County Cup was all well and good if you were drawn at home, but The Albion had been away in all the previous rounds as well as this one, and having to travel the distances sometimes was a bind.

Goit Stock was one of those small market towns perched high amongst the peaks close to the Yorkshire-Lancashire border where the obligatory mode of transport was Land Rover or tractor, where the highlight of the week was the Tuesday cattle auction, where everybody spoke in a peculiar dialect that was neither Tyke or Manc, and everyone wore green wellies, brown corduroys, quilted body warmers and starched check shirts, and everywhere stank of sheep and cow shit slurry.

The Variety Club Sunshine coach looked oddly out of place as it trundled through the slushy deserted main street, past the only two pubs and the tiny cenotaph in the square on the right where the directions Terry was clutching told them to take the next turning, down the lane, through the five bar gate, over the pack horse bridge, past the silos, (watch out for any stray sheep) hang a left, over the cattle grid, another two hundred yards and you should see the clubhouse and pitches in front of you.

'At least the directions were good,' remarked Terry screwing up the piece of paper as the clubhouse came into view.

'Maan – lookit der size o' that,' exclaimed Mackie as they rolled past the higgledy-piggledy cricket pitch with its drystone wall boundary. 'Bwoyy, I be hittin' sixes n' fours all day long on that t'ing man.'

The Goit Stock management and players converged at the clubhouse door and watched The Albion tumble out of the bus with a mixture of bemused wonderment and intrigue on their faces. They were farmer's boys, big, healthy looking lads with ruddy complexions and wild, sticky-out hair. They pointed and whispered comments to each other like they were watching aliens alight from a spaceship, like contact with the outside world was a rare and fascinating occurrence. A delinquents' outing would have been a more apt description as the rag-bag army filed past, none too happy at the over-the-top attention they were receiving, making them feel like freaks in a sideshow.

'What you fuckin' gawpin' at, yer woolly back?' snarled Peycos at one lad who was staring a bit too much.

'We weren't too sure if you'd be calling this one off,' said Terry exchanging pleasantries with the Goit Stock manager while eyeing up the badly undulating pitch that had collected pools of water in numerous places under the blanket of slush that now covered any grass.

'Ahh, we'll play it alright,' said the man with the leathery weather-beaten face, 'got to – fixture congestion.'

'Fixture congestion?'

'Aye, don't get too many games played up 'ere December, January an' February, what with the weather. Tend to get a backlog o' games come March, April. Got to get this one out the way, it bein' cup an' all. Ref sez he's prepared to gi' it a go. That'll do for me. An' anyway, my boys like it like this,' he said with a smile and a wink.

As the two teams prepared for kick off, waves of winter weather were being driven down the valley on arctic-like gusts that whipped and cut horizontally into anything that got in its way. Sheets of hailstone battered and stung exposed legs and faces that had already turned to raw shades of red and purple. The Albion collectively looked like a pack of cowering, shiteing dogs, pulling their already saturated, oversized strip around exposed parts in a futile defence. The Goit Stock lads didn't seem half as bothered, the onslaught of hail merely adding that extra glow to their already florid features.

The Goit Stock centre forward, a giant of a lad whose ample, pink belly was showing between his shirt and shorts because his kit was a bit on the tight side, launched the ball deep into The Albion's half with a crude toe-ender. It was the cue for a cavalry charge as all ten Goit Stock outfield players surged into Albion territory. The ball landed without bouncing but with a dull splat on the edge of West Broughton's eighteen-yard box smack in front of Sasquatch who tried to play it out wide to Ginner but it fell a good yard short in the mud and the Goit Stock right winger was straight onto it letting fly first time with what seemed like another toe-ender. It cleared The Albion's bar by inches.

It didn't take five minutes for Terry and Nobby to suss the tactics here, if tactics was the right word. This was going to be blood and thunder stuff, an all out frontal assault with no inclination to play what could be described as football, but on this pitch and in these conditions that was going to be difficult anyway. With the ground soon looking like Glastonbury after a wet festival weekend and the elements acting as Goit Stock's twelfth man, The Albion found it hard to get out of their own half and soon succumbed to the tractor boys' pressure. A scuffed half clearance led to another speculative twenty-yard toe-ender that this time ended up sailing over a stranded One Eye, whose feet seemed glued to the spot, and landed with a plop in the back of the net. Five minutes later, on a rare excursion into their opponents half, West Broughton forced a corner and with the help from a sudden gust from down the valley, Biscuit's set piece curled straight into the far top corner of the Goit Stock net.

This was set to be the pattern for the day, an abundance of freaky goals played out in a lottery where no one could have predicted the outcome. At half time and at three - one down, Royston and Mackie could hack no more. They begged Nobby for the keys to the bus. Thoroughly pissed off and frozen to the bone they teetered away with white plastic bags tied to their feet protecting the precious G-Units from the ankle deep mud, slush and sheep shit. Flash took great delight in taking the piss, rattling off a volley of verbal abuse from behind the narrow slit in his cagoule, from which only his eyes were visible; pointing his flag at them with unconcealed scorn as they waddled away like a pair of multi coloured penguins, the like of which had never been seen and would never be seen again around these parts. Mackie turned his head briefly to face his tormentor and the biting, sleet filled gale. If he wasn't so cold and stiff he swore he'd go back and shove that flag right up Flash's arse.

Terry put Sully on for Duane at half time; he was never going to shine in those conditions. The youngster slipped into the recently vacated sub-suit with Sully's body warmth still evident but he still needed to go and sit with Royston and Mackie on the bus in order to thaw out properly. Basher came on for Slum who had spent most of the first half cowering behind one of the big Goit Stock centre backs whose ample frame provided good shelter from the elements. It was a gamble for Terry, using his only two subs in one go like that, Sully and Basher were by no means classy footballers but they both had the passion and the desire, and despite the atrocious conditions he knew they would give their all. And they were both chomping at the bit as the sound of the referee's whistle was whipped away into the ether by a sudden vicious gust, as though Indra and Aeolus were both a bit pissed off at the audacity of these kids daring to turn out for another forty minutes after what the two Gods had thrown at them in the first half.

Sully slid into the first tackle with his usual tenacity, studs showing as by way of introduction to his opposite number and eager to get his clean kit as quickly caked as the rest of the lads.

Terry realised that trying to play constructive football was never going to win this one. They were going to have to be as gritty and determined as their hosts. He made each and every one of them roll

283

their sleeves up. He made Joe, Ginner and Rammer take off the gloves they'd been wearing. He told them that the cold and the wind and the wet were just an illusion. He made them picture the quarter-finals in spring weather, on their own midden for a change, and playing the type of football they were meant to play. He'd dangled the carrot, created the vision; they just had to go out there and do it, and Sully's sliding tackle set a benchmark. It wouldn't be pretty, but it would have the desired effect.

Nobby shook his head under his L.U.F.C. bobble hat. Many a time he'd laugh to himself at Terry's odd methods of motivation, but once again he found himself taking off his sodden item of headwear to his mate at the end of the game when the Albion came out five-four winners in the most bizarre game they would play all season.

The lads got back onto the bus in dribs and drabs; some with smiles on their faces, happy at getting that one out of the way, and even happier in the knowledge that they were in the draw for the quarter finals, but one or two were not so happy as the warmth slowly returned to their extremities creating painful hot-aches and chilblains.

'Awwoohh! Me toes have got fuckin' frost bite,' wailed Ginner, hobbling to the back of the bus

'I can't even feel *my* fuckers,' said Rammer. 'I think they must've dropped off.'

'Should never o' been played man,' complained Mackie. 'That ref should be reported to der F.A. Child cruelty innit.'

Flash tutted in disgust. 'Shurrup moanin', yer set o' wussies; we won din't we?'

'Yeh, by a freaky own goal in der last minute. That game wus a joke, man; could've ended up twenny-six - firteen. Yer couldn't call that football.'

'I thought Rigger put it in,' said Nobby.

'I fought it wa' Basher got t'last touch,' said Biscuit wringing out his sodden socks, then slapping his raw-looking feet in an effort to bring them back to life.

'No way,' insisted Mackie. 'It wus der big fat kid, man, I swear I saw 'im slice it into der net.'

'Yeah, well, you must be right,' said Flash sarcastically, 'sat here, grandstand view, all nice an' cosy an' warm. You'd have a berra view than anybody, wouldn't yer?'

'Who arksed you, hippy-trip?' snarled Mackie.

'Supporters? I've shit 'em,' sneered Flash.

'Now, now, girls,' interjected Nobby. 'Calm down. No fightin' on the bus.'

'Tell der soap dodger, man, he start it.'

'*He start it*,' mocked Flash. 'Fuckin' fearweather fans.'

The pair growled and spat at each other some more until Royston made his mate go sit by the window out of harm's way. Mackie simmered and seethed, sucking at his teeth, reverting to Kingston cuss, where he could be heard uttering the occasional '*Raass*,' '*Blood*,' and '*Claatt*,' in-between casting hateful sideways glances at Flash who wound him up some more by smiling and blowing kisses.

Back in the cosy warmth of the Clarke household, Kath and Jan were wading through reams of paperwork on fostering and adoption. Kath had spent every available lunchtime sitting at the computer since she had gone back to work; looking up agencies, reading and printing off case studies, checking out local authority policy. In the weeks it had taken for little Leo to come out of intensive care, Kath had honed her knowledge on the subject to such a degree that she could quote whole sections of legislation like The Human Rights Act 1988 (article 8) or The Childrens Act 1989(7)(b) and L.A.C. 98/20. She had armed herself with as much ammunition as she could for her crusade, insuring herself against any possible failure. And failure wasn't an option. Failure was unthinkable. Failure meant plumbing the depths of depression and despair. She'd been there and she didn't want to go back. She would remain positive and utterly focused, but she already knew from some of the things she'd read that it wasn't going to be easy.

Kath Clarke had things clear in her mind now. She knew what it was she wanted and that was to adopt a child. The trouble was she just didn't want any child. She knew the child she would like but she also knew that the adoption process simply didn't work like that. You couldn't merely go along and cherry-pick the kid you desired. There wasn't a conveyer belt of youngsters, looking for a home and some-one to love, that you could pass on and reject until the one you wanted came along. That's why she was doing her homework. That's why she was being thorough before she registered with any particular agency. It didn't harm that she worked for a disabled charity that was part funded by the council. She had one or two contacts at Social Services that could maybe offer her sound advice and steer her in the right direction. And, of course, she had Jan who had promised to help and give her all the support she needed, and more importantly to keep her grounded when her expectations might want to race ahead of her.

Jan had no inclination. Probably never in a million years would she have guessed that Kath's problem was to do with child longing. Like both their spouses they had known each other since primary school. All their problems were shared problems, and Jan had helped her through the postnatal trauma she'd suffered after Young Nobby was born, but she'd gotten over that and the subsequent hysterectomy without too much anguish, her and Nobby quickly coming to terms with the reality that this would be their one and only child; disap-pointed, naturally, but resigned, they got on with their lives.

Fourteen years later, a shy, skinny half-caste lad came into her life and unlocked something that had been shut away deep inside her for all that time. And the feeling and emotions were so complex and interwoven that when they surfaced she didn't know how to deal with them, in fact she wasn't entirely sure what they were; she couldn't put any of it into words, couldn't talk to anyone about it and that was when she started to go in on herself. A complacent G.P. and a mixture of valium and librium based drugs merely compounded her problem and sent her spinning deeper into a black hole where she became more and more detached from reality, her family and her friends.

Irony could be a weird and wonderful concept sometimes, thought Jan when she ran the sequence of events by in her head: a pair of siblings, one of whom innocently becomes the symptom, the other, via tragic circumstances turns out to be the cure.

For Jan, the penny finally dropped on that cold January afternoon up at the infirmary, watching her mate emerge like a butterfly from a chrysalis; the transformation instantaneous, jaw dropping; the urge to care, the need to nurture, the answer so simple, so natural; the question so complex, unfathomable, unaskable.

Kath knew that most local authorities and adoption agencies now favoured keeping siblings together wherever possible. It was a commonsense policy that had seemingly taken the powers that be ages to realise, that keeping what was left of a family together retained some form of stability in their topsy-turvy lives instead of having any last contact with real kin torn apart at a time when they were likely to be at their most vulnerable, and in some cases where a brother or sister were unlikely to see each other ever again. She also knew that a good percentage of prospective adopters only wanted, or were able, to adopt the one child. Kath placed no such restrictions on herself and her husband. Nobby was more than willing to accede to her wishes, and what she wished for was two kids and she knew the two she wanted. From her point of view, her case couldn't be more straightforward and simple. Except, of course, that Duane wasn't yet in care and even if he were, it would be down to Social Services to decide whether or not it would be on a temporary or permanent basis.

In Kath's mind, from the stories she'd heard, there was no question that this woman, this so-called mother, was incapable of looking after her kids, but for now all this was hypothetical. She would have a word with Duane; tell him of her plans, her neat, well thought-out solutions to all their problems. Her newfound positiveness making for a perfect happy ending, where Jan's cautionary warnings of the potential pitfalls were tidily cropped, edited and stored away in the back of her mind.

Kath should have heeded her mates' warning about planning so far ahead because when she did get to speak to Duane, after her men had landed from the frozen wastes of Goit Stock, she would find that he hadn't read her script, and she wasn't at all prepared for the determined and defiant reaction from the youngster when she posed the possibility of him being taken into care. She'd never seen him react like this, and it soon became obvious that his earlier experiences were still with him and had left a scar.

He made it plain to her, there wasn't a cat in hell's chance he was going back into a home, no matter what, and she knew from the upset in his face, the rigid fear; the look of agitation at the mere suggestion, that he meant it.

Duane had painted a picture of his life that was painfully true. There had been no exaggeration; in fact, his words alone could never convey the torment and the suffering. But his cry for help hadn't been for him; it had been for his little brother. Yes, he enjoyed the sanctuary and the escapism the Clarke household afforded him. Yes, he wallowed in the love, care and generosity these wonderful people showed him. Yes, he longed for the carefree life that Young Nobby had where you took everything around you for granted. Yes, he wanted all that. But his mam, for whatever else she was, was still his mam. She needed him, couldn't live without him, maybe for all the wrong reasons, but she relied on him. Here, the boot was on the other foot. She took *him* for granted and something within him felt duty bound to be there for her, regardless.

The way Duane looked at it, he didn't have a choice. There was no agonising. To him, it could never be. Why? He didn't know. It wasn't up for analysis. Maybe it had to do with some deep-seated inkling of a time long ago when maybe his mam had loved him; a time before her 'Illness' when she might have cared? Surely all mothers had some love for their kids, whatever circumstances they found themselves in. While ever she was alive he would subconsciously cling on to this notion without ever really thinking about it.

Duane had contingency plans of his own. He knew how to pull the wool with the social worker. He would scrub the flat spotless. Tidy away all his mam's junk. Insist she stay straight until after the visit. It would be hard but she would have to do it because she knew she needed Duane as much as he didn't want to go into care. They would paint a picture of coping, getting by; making an effort, and that would pacify them for another twelve months. It had worked before. They hadn't been bothered by social services for well over a year now, and it would work again. Duane couldn't, wouldn't ever abandon his mam.

Kath reacted to Duane's stance, at first with shock, then hurt, and finally with the realisation that, despite all, this young kid still loved his mother without conditions and with a dogged loyalty that amazed her and brought tears to her eyes again.

24

Terry hated the arse end of winter with its grey, nondescript days that despite their shortness seemed to drag and linger. He longed for old-fashioned spring weather that you just didn't seem to get up North anymore. He harked back to bright, fresh March days when fields were full of crocuses and borders were resplendent with primulas and primroses; a vibrant show of colour heralding a definite change of season; when, as a kid, the Easter holidays somehow never failed to be sunny. In the old days you could confidently have your bedding plants in by the end of April. Now, you daren't take the risk until mid June. If this was global warming he wasn't impressed. The southern counties might be benefitting, but up here all you got were gales, late frosts, or torrential rain for weeks on end.

Today was one of those days. Low scurrying cloud being blown along, above which loomed lumbering cumulus; rain-heavy, teasing and tormenting but not quite yet ready to drop their load.

The grounds of the Garden Springs nursing home mirrored the weather; bleak in the absence of any colour, the wind whistling with a melancholic air through the leafless beech and poplar trees. A bunch of crows cawed loudly in protest as a pair of magpies flew into their territory, settling on the roof of the home with a cocky defiance.

Terry planted his fork and turned the damp, cloying soil in the bed with as much enthusiasm as he could muster for a Monday morning, which wasn't much. He paused to watch as a small squadron of crows scrambled themselves to dive bomb and harry the black and white intruders in a noisy and frenzied display.

Sheila, the care nurse caught his eye. She was striding out towards him, her long coat wrapped tightly around her uniform with her arms crossed in front of her to keep out the cold.

Outnumbered, the magpies beat a reluctant retreat, clicking and cackling as they went.

Terry watched her approach, puzzled as to what she could want at ten in the morning. He knew there would be no patio outing today, far too cold for that. He hadn't seen Herbert for a while but she knew he was loath to come indoors for a visit while in working mode.

'Alrate, Sheila love,' he greeted her cheerfully, which belied his real mood, but she was always bubbly and smiling so it would appear rude not to reciprocate. But today she wasn't bubbly or smiling; in fact, she didn't lift her head to exchange his greeting. She stood in front of him with her arms still folded, shifting her feet uncomfortably.

'What's up, love?' he asked, sensing something wasn't right. Eventually she lifted her head and looked at him. She searched his face with a pained expression before she finally spoke. 'Herbert passed away at the weekend,' she said softly.

Terry tightened his grip on the fork handle and she continued to look at him.

The next few moments were the awkward ones. Her not knowing what to say, Terry trying his best to avert his eyes while doing all he could to cope with the empty, sinking feeling he was experiencing. A weight had just dropped from his chest through his stomach, taking everything inside him with it, and he didn't know what to do. Two people, barely acquaintances, unsure what to say to each other or how to react. Should she remain professional, detached? Should he show his emotion to someone he hardly knew? Did he know what his emotions were at this moment?

'I'm sorry,' she said. Then, the nurse, the carer, slowly unfolded her arms and offered them to him. He released his grip on the fork and gently fell into her embrace. He suddenly became aware of his grubby, soiled hands, maladroit as he made an effort to keep them away from her coat. Now he looked as awkward as he felt.

At a distance, Nobby had stopped what he was doing and was taking the opportunity to build a roll-up as the scene unfolded before him. Quite a lot went through his half perverted mind as to what he thought might be going on with the nurse and the gardener. The thought that two people, who, in their own special ways cared for another were coming together briefly to share that bond and acknowledge their loss never entered his head.

'When?' asked Terry.

'Saturday night, in his sleep. Just drifted away nice and peaceful,' she said reassuringly.

Terry nodded his appreciation. 'Is he…?'

'He's in the mortuary now, love.'

He nodded again.

'Listen …' he said, '…I… er, just wanted to say thanks for looking after him. I er…'

'I was only doing me job,' she said trying to bring an air of professionalism back into her voice, knowing it was hard for him to get the words out right now. 'And it wasn't just me, there's a whole team of us in there you know.'

'I know,' he said. 'But you really did care, didn't you…?' Terry took her hands in his, not worrying too much about the dirt now. He looked her in the eye. '…I could tell.'

Now it was her turn to feel awkward. She pulled her hands away from his and turned away. 'Just doing me job,' she muttered with a hint of emotion in her voice. She folded her arms across herself again and walked quickly back indoors to get on with her work. He watched her go, back to the sluice room and the constant line of bedpans. Back to the stink of piss and shit; the loneliness, the confusion and the dementia. Terry shook his head in pure admiration. He wondered how on earth the lass coped. How did she deal with the daily suffering and the inevitable demise? Would poor old Herbert become just another statistic? Would she remember him in six months time? Some poor old bugger she only ever had a one-way conversation with. Shaved his chin, wiped his arse. Did she blank it and get on with it? She would have to, he thought. You'd go bloody mental otherwise. Time to get real. He didn't doubt that some other terminal candidate for the knacker's yard was already occupying Herbert's bed before the mattress had gone cold. Roll up, roll out. They were queuing up for places at the likes of Garden Springs and good old Nigel didn't rest on his laurels, he knew the game, and nurse Sheila would be going through the motions, flipping over helpless dead-weights almost twice her size with an expert hand, relieving the bed sores, chatting away to her new charge; inane conversation in that loud condescending way, like talking to a retarded child. But everybody did it, didn't they?

The sound of his mate approaching brought Terry back from some distant place.

'Nah then, yer bugger, what the 'ell's…'

Terry stopped Nobby mid flow. 'Herbert's dead,' he said.

* * *

The two women and one man strode purposefully down the hospital corridor. The man held a briefcase in his hand, full of papers that needed to be signed and countersigned. One of the women carried a bag full of children's clothes, a mishmash of stuff that didn't really match but that would approximately fit a three year old. They stopped outside an office before knocking and entering.

Terry removed his suit from the wardrobe. It hadn't seen the light of day for years. It was his wedding suit and, remarkably, it still just about fit him.

Nobby didn't possess a suit; he would be wearing his battered crombie, which was even older than Terry's whistle, and didn't fit him nearly as well. Both Jan and Kath were slightly embarrassed at their husbands' sartorial lacking. Neither of them had any formal attire. They never went anywhere posh or smart enough to warrant it. It wasn't everyday you went to a wedding or a funeral. But today was one such day. It was Herbert's funeral and they'd all taken the day off to pay their respects.

Terry stood in Nobby's kitchen and looked at his mate. His mate looked back at him. Both were resisting hard the urge to take the piss out of one another because they knew just how ridiculous they must appear. Their efforts at making themselves presentable and smart hadn't worked. They weren't used to dressing up and it showed. Casual, fine; no problem, but you didn't do funerals casual, so they both stood and eyed each other up as to who looked naffest while the women got themselves ready. They felt even worse when the girls came down stairs because they *did* look smart. But it was easy for them; they both worked in offices, and had a hundred combinations of black to choose from.

'Why're they buryin' him up at Highmoor?' Nobby asked while struggling with the confines of his shirt collar.

'Dunno. That's what it said in the obituary. Seems strange dunnit? I allus thought he was a West Broughton lad born and bred.'

'I wonder who'll have put the notice in the paper,' mused Jan. 'I thought he didn't have any relatives living.'

'I think he has a daughter in Australia,' said Terry. 'He showed me a photo of her once in t'club. She married a doctor over there. Proud as chuff he was.'

'Poor old lad,' said Kath sadly. 'I hope there's gonna be someone there to see him off.'

'There'll be us,' said Nobby getting more and more frustrated with his shirt collar.

'Yeah, I know,' said Kath. 'But it's not the same as family is it? I din't even know the guy.'

'I only knew him to say hello to,' said Jan, 'can't say I ever had a long conversation with him.'

'That don't matter,' Terry said with conviction. 'What's important is that we're there for him today. I'm sure he'd have appreciated it.'

They all nodded in solemn agreement and slowly filed out of the house and into Kath's Micra for the drive up to Highmoor. Once behind the wheel, Nobby flicked open the top button of his shirt and ran his fingers between neck and collar, breathing a sigh of relief, unworried that he now appeared more dishevelled than ever.

Kath had been forced to come clean about her pretence as Leo's aunt when staff had started asking too many questions on her visits to the hospital. They had thought it odd that a woman who they now knew wasn't a relative like she had claimed would visit regularly maybe two or three times a week when the mother had never come near.

The doctor had questioned her at length about her interest in the child, and she had told him the truth, spoke from the heart, and he had listened and understood her plight and had been sympathetic, but the situation had left him with a professional dilemma. Dr. Mitchell was an excellent paediatrician, and he had soon observed how this woman's visits had hastened the child's recovery; what a tonic her presence and love was proving to be. But he also saw the growing attachment between the two and this wasn't going to be good for when the youngster would finally have to leave and be taken under the wing of social services, as inevitably he would.

The day the care order would come into place was fast looming and the doctor advised Kath, as diplomatically as he could, that her visits should now be less frequent. Leo was over his bout of pneumonia, was gaining weight on a daily basis and beginning to look like a healthy three-year-old toddler should. Kath had outlived her usefulness as far as he was concerned and he thought that detachment at this juncture would be best for both of them. He regretted that in his capacity he couldn't get involved with the adoption procedure on a personal level but wished her luck in her efforts. He deliberately kept the handover date to himself.

Little Leo Caldwell didn't know these blank, emotionless faces. His large, dark eyes darted about the room nervously as the nurse fitted him into strange clothes, a stripy tee shirt that was slightly too big despite him having managed to put on almost eight pounds in the seven weeks he'd been there. The nurse talked to him in soft, comforting tones, reassuring him everything was all right, while the man and the two women looked on impassively.

The friendly nurse squeezed a pair of diddy trainers onto his feet, tied the laces into big bows, patted the soles when she'd done and gave the little chap a big smile. He looked down at the trainers in bewilderment; he'd never had what could be called real shoes before, and he looked from them, to the smiling nurse and to the three strange faces in turn.

'There now, don't you look a smart young man?' said the nurse, stepping back to admire him.

Leo wasn't sure. He somehow knew something was going down and he began to feel slightly scared and vulnerable as the four adults continued to scrutinise him.

'Mam,' he said, holding his arms out for the nurse to come back close to him. He called all friendly females mam, most of the nurses and those lovely ladies who came to see him with Dede. Dede was how he managed to pronounce Duane, and he wished that they were here now.

'Mam – Dede,' he appealed to the nurse who came back to his side to give him a reassuring cuddle. She sensed he was on the verge of getting upset while the three officials from social services were becoming increasingly impatient. The man sighed and looked at his watch. A few moments later a suited Dr. Mitchell breezed into the room and apologised for keeping them all waiting.

They talked for a while in hushed tones, going over various bits of paper with the occasional nod or shake of the head, while the nurse patiently did her best to keep Leo calm by talking to him in mock excitement about his new clothes. Then, on a signal that Leo neither saw nor heard, or would have understood, the nurse melted away into the background and one of the strange women took her place. She held out her hand to him, but from a distance, and not warm. He instinctively drew back, and she closed in with her out-stretched hand, trying to coax him off the bed. He heard words of reassurance but not like the nurse's, and he became scared. He knew scared well, but this was a different scared. He sensed something was about to change and he didn't want it to. He seemed to know his sanctuary of love was about to disappear and he began to whimper. He tried desperately to look around the woman for the nurse but he couldn't see her.

'Mam! – Mam! – Dede!' he cried out. The doctor now joined the woman. He spoke soothing words. Leo knew the doctor, the nice man, and he momentarily calmed down. The doctor spoke some words to the woman, and then he lifted Leo off the bed and gently but quickly handed him to her. Leo tried to be a limpet but the doctor had done this many times before; a moment of professional detachment executed with all emotion put to one side. The party quickly left the room and headed at pace down the corridor, but little Leo didn't scream and create like a lot of kids being taken into care did. He merely whimpered; scared to death of the unknown, catching the eye of the doctor before he was whisked out of the room with a look that would haunt the paediatrician for a long time, a look that noted his betrayal, one of shattered trust, a shaming look.

Leo's near silent departure served to disturb the doctor some more until he realised that it was because there was nobody there for him to scream and cry for. No parent and child being torn apart. No distraught mother fighting social services in a kiddie tug-of-war.

Caldwell had been informed of Leo's impending care order by letter, but it lay unopened under a mountain of shit and junk; her only concern being the loss of child benefit that would affect her purchasing power. Sixty quid a month didn't buy nearly enough heroin to fulfil her needs, but she would miss it all the same.

Kath had reluctantly agreed to the doctor's request and had limited her visits to once a week, but the stay away days had been killing her and she often whiled away the time at work daydreaming of the moment she would see him again, when his eyes would light up and sparkle at the sight of her and Dede and he could practice the smile he had so recently learned.

She had tried to teach him her name, but he was so far behind in his speech, 'mam' and 'Dede' were the only real decipherable words he could manage amongst the gobbledygook he uttered. Kath didn't mind; she secretly loved it when he opened his arms to her and called her 'mam'. And it was with this image in her head that she smiled to herself while sitting in the back of her car alongside Jan as they drove up to Highmoor. Only a few more hours until the image became reality. The thought pacified her, and she could get up to the hospital a bit earlier than usual, seeing as she'd taken the day off for Herbert's funeral.

As she allowed herself to close her eyes and relax back she was totally unaware that the focus of her thoughts was now sitting, fearful and apprehensive, between two strange women in the back of a dark blue people carrier waiting to turn out of a junction that they had just passed a few yards away and less than a moment ago.

Saint Cuthbert's chapel was a quaint eighteenth century stone building that used to be the parish church of Highmoor in days gone by. It was the only place of worship left in the metropolitan area that still had its own attached cemetery; a sizeable acreage of sloping moorland that offered panoramic views across certain sections of the city where dark, weathered, lichen-covered gravestones and tombs of the eighteenth and nineteenth centuries marked a clearly discernable line between the old parish boundary and the more recently reclaimed land with its neat, well kept rows of memorials of all shapes and sizes, in the most imaginative polished materials.

An empty hearse and a solitary black limousine were the only other vehicles in the small, gravelled car park. The strains of a requiem being played on the chapel organ could just be heared above the noise of footsteps on shale. Kath had chosen to wear a discreet black hat that she was struggling to hang on to as they approached the entrance to the little church. It was a bitterly cold and windy day again.

Inside the chapel, all was calm and serene. A verger solemnly nodded a greeting to them all individually while handing out hymnbooks and prayer sheets. All the pews were empty save for a couple seated at the front; a smart looking woman, probably in her late fifties, and a tall, distinguished gentleman of a similar age with coiffured grey hair and a remarkably healthy looking complexion.

Herbert's coffin lay at the altar flanked by two large, lit candles. Terry stared hard at it for a moment, then, bizarrely and without warning, an image of Herbert raced through his mind; that of him storming a path through the jungle with his machine gun blazing away, only the image wasn't of him as a young man but of how Terry last remembered him, except that the old man had come very much to life and wasn't in a wheelchair anymore. Then, all of a sudden, Herbert becomes Captain Hurricane, snapping trees like they were matchwood, scattering Japs in all directions, the end of his Bren gun glowing white-hot. Terry involuntarily gritted and ground his teeth, mimicking the picture that he saw inside his head until Jan snapped him out of it and ushered him into a pew halfway down the aisle. He blew air out of his cheeks and idly let his gaze search the interior of the old chapel: stone buttresses, sweeping oak roof beams, the tiny stained glass windows. He allowed his eyes to fall anywhere except Herbert's coffin in an effort to stop his crazy imagination running away with him

The woman at the front turned to the four of them, smiled and nodded in acknowledgement of their presence. Terry could tell that she was Herbert's daughter.

Nobby's off key baritone was killing the twenty-third psalm until Kath gave him a dig in the ribs and shook her head at him disapprovingly. He sheepishly mouthed the words to the rest of the hymn.

The vicar spoke of the man he had never met, in glowing terms. This made Terry smile to himself. The accolades were spot on, as it happened, but he wasn't to know that. The person in the box might have been a right bastard for all he knew. The giveaway being the occasional glances he made down to his sheet during the prayer for the departed just to keep checking who the departed was, inserting his name at the appropriate moments.

While the minister quoted from St. John, Nobby started to doze and Terry's mind went off on one again, from steaming Burmese jungle to rare, balmy summer afternoons up at Garden Springs, to a blood-spattered, ransacked semi in a West Broughton street. All that he knew of his old friend was being bandied around in his head; pictures of violence and despair that he tried to alter, changing the outcome; little scenes where he became Stephen Spielberg, shouting '*cut*' at the things he didn't like and making new endings.

Someone entered the chapel and the wind caught the old oak door, slamming it shut against its frame. The noise echoed through the stone building, interrupting the reverend while in full flow, rousing Nobby from his slumbers and bringing Terry back from his fantasy film-set at the same time. Six heads turned simultaneously and the minister paused patiently while the person took a pew at the back. Terry and Nobby recognised him straightaway. It was Stan Willis, Herbert's old mucker from the working men's club. The old boy looked a bit frail as well as totally dishevelled and windswept. He wore a dark beret on his head that was slightly skewiff, and an old grey mac buttoned all the way up to the neck to which he'd pinned a line of medals that seemed to sit at the same obtuse angle as his beret. Terry was warmed to see that one of Herbert's old pals had made the effort to come and see him off. He gave him the thumbs up but the old chap wasn't looking. He'd already pulled the beret from his head revealing long but sparse whisps of grey over his otherwise bald pate. He bowed it reverently and knelt stiffly in silent prayer to a lost comrade.

Terry tried his best to resist but yet again found himself surrendering to his mind visions as the rector read out the Nunc Dimitis: *'Lord, now lettest thy servant depart in peace; according to thy word...'*

Stan Willis, like a lot of the old guys who had fought in the war had his own story to tell but rarely did.

'...For mine eyes have seen thy salvation...'

Among other places, he'd been at Monte Casino, another theatre of untold horrors and futile conquest. And what scars, emotional and physical, he'd carried for all of his life since, God only knew.

'...Which Thou hast prepared, before the face of all people...'

He looked all of seven stone, wet through, in his old age, and Terry couldn't ever imagine him lifting a rifle, let alone humping a full marching pack across Sicily and through Italy – but he had.

Stan had also been the victim of muggers; once, in broad daylight as he left the post office with his pension and twice on his way home from the club after a couple of gills when he'd only had a few bob in his pocket.

'...To be a light to lighten the Gentiles, and to be the glory of thy people Israel...'

For King and country – for King and fucking country. Terry thought of Stan and Herbert as lads, as the fresh young fighting men they were, and he put them in a scenario face to face with those cowardly wankers, those tossers who had done what they did to Herbert without conscience or mercy. Herbert and Stan's assailants were faceless in Terry's imagination but he knew their type and it was easy to paint a picture, and in his make believe movie Terry had given himself co-star billing alongside the two of them and he made sure he knocked the fuck out of those cunts. And he didn't limit their numbers, he brought them all on, the scum of East Broughton and beyond, and the four of them stood shoulder to shoulder, (he'd decided to bring Nobby along in a supporting role) showing the same compassion as they had been shown - fucking none.

'...Glory be to the Father, and the son, and to the Holy Ghost...'

Jan gave Terry a nudge. 'Are you alright?' she hissed with a frown on her face. Terry nodded, annoyed at having his revenge imagery interrupted. 'Well stop grinding your teeth then,' she added while continuing to give him a funny look.

'...As it was in the beginning, is now, and ever shall be, world without end. Amen.'

The four pallbearers lifted the coffin from the bier and manoeuvered it into place over the grave. It was an old family plot bought by Herbert's wife's parents many years ago and Herbert's burial would complete the sepulchre. Herbert's wife had been a Highmoor girl, which explained why the funeral was so far away from West Broughton.

Nobby hated this bit. He'd witnessed his dad's funeral as an eleven year old, and, when he had joined the council straight from school, had spent his first six months as a gravedigger before being transferred to parks and pitches to be with his mate. He hated family plots, especially if they were old, and stone dividers hadn't been placed over preceeding coffins. He'd lost count of how many times his boot had gone through a rotten coffin lid and into the decomposing mush of a corpse. And the resulting rising stink would make him scramble up the hole in terror, wretching his guts up as he desperately clawed his way out. Unfortunately, his screams of panic would often alert nearby workmates, the older guys who had worked the cemeteries for years, and they would cruelly surround the hole, blocking his exit, taunting and jeering: '*Hey up, young un, this bugger's still alive - quick, it's comin' after thee!*' And the petrified sixteen year old would find superhuman strength, the adrenalin soaring through his veins, and tear himself out of the grave sending his tormentors flying, and they would end up rolling around pissing themselves. But Nobby was becoming a big lad. He was starting to fill out, and towards the end of his short tenure as a gravedigger the wiser of the older blokes left him alone having witnessed his brute strength at first hand.

Any colour had drained from Nobby's features as the unwelcome memories came flooding back. He wanted this bit over as quickly as possible and wished to fuck that the reverend would get on with it.

'*...Seeing now that our brother, Herbert, has been set free from the physical body to enter into a new life with a spiritual body stronger and better than the flesh, we commit his spirit into God's hands...*'

Not looking to fare much better was old Stan. The wind was gusting at his back and he wilted and wavered a few times and any minute now Terry thought he might end up joining his old pal six foot down. He looked to be crying but it was just the effects of the late March weather making his sad bloodhound eyes fill up with water.

'*...And it came to pass, as they were much perplexed, behold, two men stood by them in shining garments; and said unto them: Why seek ye the living among the dead? He is not here, but risen...*'

Stan fumbled around in his mac pocket and eventually produced a white handkerchief and was about to wipe his runny nose when the wind took the piss again and whipped it from his hand. All assembled pretended not to notice or watch it skeet and flutter away catching on one or two headstones as it went, before coming to a rest in a rather macabre fashion, wrapping itself around the flower urn that belonged to a fairly new grave.

'...*Unto God's gracious mercy and protection we commit you; the Lord bless you, and keep you, and give you his peace, now and for evermore. Amen.*'

Stan cuffed his runny nose on his mac sleeve and Nobby hurried away to throw up.

There was an abrupt and frustrating end to the burial service, not anti-climactic as such, more of a hollow reluctance to accept it was all over, like Terry was expecting the minister to perform a resurrection of the sort that he had kept going on about during the service. He watched the man of the cloth walk slowly away, his cassock billowing behind him, stark white against the cold grey of the day and he felt like shouting after him: '*Hey! Is that it then pal?*'

'You must be Terry, I've been hearing a lot about you.' The woman offered her black leather gloved hand. 'I'm Caroline Goulding and this is my husband Michael.' The tall, distinguished looking man stepped forward, greeted Terry in a distinct Australian accent and shook him warmly and firmly by the hand. 'I'm Herbert's daughter,' she continued.

Terry said he was very pleased to meet her but wished it had been under different circumstances. He made all the other introductions except for Nobby who was still barfing up behind a nearby tree.

Caroline Goulding thanked everyone individually for coming and paying their last respects to her father. 'I placed the obituary via e-mail,' she explained. 'I wasn't sure if anyone would show, but I'm glad you all did. I know he would have appreciated it.'

Some of the staff at the nursing home had told her all about Terry the gardener, who would come and spend his lunch hours in the old man's company, his only visitor, and she had been keen to find out more about their unique relationship. But Terry, rather embarrassingly, couldn't tell her any more than him being a neighbour and aquaintance who had felt culpable as to what had happened; guilty that no one had been there for him, guilty on behalf of the police whose investigations up to nearly eighteen months later had produced nothing, guilty that he'd been forgotten about and left to stew in a nursing home, guilty on behalf of a society that didn't appear to give a fuck. Only he didn't tell it like that, he just said he'd felt duty bound and it was the least he could have done. He chose not to mention the one way conversations, nor the strange, almost spiritual, bond that had developed on their regular summer get togethers; the purging of his own demons, the way he had learned to put a new perspective on things, the new inner calm he had felt after their meetings; better than any anger management class. He would miss all that and as the finality of it all came home to him at last, he started to fill up and, as if in a last defiant show of his old self, he stoically choked back the emotion instead of letting it all out and embarrassing himself.

Herbert's daughter studied Terry's face like she knew his thoughts, like she knew there must have been something special between this man and her late father. She smiled a warm smile, embraced him and kissed him on the cheek, leaving a faint pink smudge. 'Thank you so much,' she whispered to him.

Terry shrugged. 'For what?' he asked in that bashful diffidence that he hated himself for. Why did he always feel uncomfortable when praise or thanks were being dished out?

'For being there for him. For showing that you cared - for everything.'

'He got well looked after in the home, you know,' he said trying to deflect the gratitude.

'I know he did, and I've already thanked them. But they also got very well paid for it. You didn't have to do what you did, but you did it anyway...' She paused for a moment and seemed to look deep inside him. '...So now I'm thanking you.'

Terry modestly nodded his appreciation. 'Look,' he said diverting the attention away from himself. 'We're having a few drinks back at the club. You and Michael are quite welcome to join us if...'

'Thanks,' she said, cutting him short. 'We really appreciate the invitation but we have a plane to catch. My husband is a very busy man. His services are in great demand back home.'

Jan politely enquired as to the nature of his work and learned that Michael Goulding was a highly respected neuro-surgeon back in his hometown of Adelaide.

Terry was relieved to have the focus of attention off him for once as the soigné and incredibly talented Aussie, feeling as Terry had a few moments ago, fielded questions from two fawning and mightily impressed Yorkshire lasses.

Ten minutes later. and sensing her husband's discomfort at the scrutiny and the unfamiliar cold weather, Mrs. Goulding thanked them all once again and said her goodbyes, wishing a green faced Nobby, who had gingerly returned to the fold, a speedy recovery from whatever it was that was ailing him.

As he watched them return to the black limo, Terry couldn't help but sense that this had been a long awaited closure for Caroline Goulding, nee Johnson. Her sharp declination to take a few drinks with them, an hour or so out of their premium rate time affirming to him a need for her to draw a line under a tragic part of her life. He couldn't blame her. Why would she want to sit in a dingy Northern working men's club on a cold, March afternoon with a handful of misfit strangers in an area where her dad had been savagely beaten within an inch of his life and been left a total vegetable; an area where she'd grown up as a kid that was probably now so alien to her it might as well be a different planet.

Terry could see that this moment must have come as a big relief to her. He knew how massive her feeling of guilt and helplessness must have been over these last ten months and being so many thousands of miles away, wishing that her dad's end would come swiftly and mercifully pain-free.

Thankfully, it did and she was now free to get on with her own life, with her too-good-to-be-true super spouse, in a land where you didn't have to wrap up from the cold and the wind and the rain, where the sky didn't feel on top of you, where the days weren't bathed in a gloomy half-light for six months of the year, where the people didn't carry around the misery of their social deprivation, hunched shoulders, stooped over, eyes fixed to the litter strewn pavements. No, he didn't blame her for wanting to get out of here as quickly as she could. In her shoes he would have done exactly the same. But what of the memories? In a bright, sunny, opportunistic land on the other side of the world, no doubt, given time, it would be easy to forget that a place like the Broughton estates ever existed. Of course memories of mum and dad would stay with her forever, and maybe, from time to time, she would think of a certain philanthropic landscape gardener called Terry Gallagher.

'Stan, love, you look absolutely perished,' said Jan in a concerned voice, handing him a bunch of tissues and urging him to sort out his snotty nose. 'Have you eaten today?'

'Eh?'

'I said have you eaten at all today?' she said louder.

'Aye - I think so,' he said in his quavering voice but with doubt creeping in when he thought about it some more. 'I had to get three buses in order to get up here you know,' he said going off on a tangent.

'What time did you set off?'

'Eh?'

'I said what time did you set off to get here?'

'Ten o'clock'

'Ten o'clock?' repeated Jan, appalled.

'Aye.'

'You're telling me you've been out of the house since ten this morning?'

'Aye – why, what time is it now?'

'It's just after half-two.'

'Ooh, is it…? Half-two…? I'd best be off fer that bus. You can't rely on 'em you know.'

'You're going for no bus, Stan Willis. You're coming back to the club with us. You need a couple of stiff brandies and a pie down yer.'

'Oh - are yer sure?' he said unsurely.

'Yes,' said Jan.

'Eh?'

'Yes, I'm sure,' she said remembering to speak louder.

'Are yer sure you've room?'

'I've no doubt we've room for a little un like you, Stan,' she laughed.

'I… I lost me hankie you know.'

'I know, love. We all saw it fly away.'

'It was clean this morning was that,' he lamented.

'Ne'er mind love, here have some more tissues.'

While Jan was sorting the old chap out, Kath was dealing with a sick husband.

'It must be summat you've eaten,' she said looking up at his drained features.

'It in't owt I've eaten,' insisted Nobby.

'How d'you know?'

''Cos I know,' he said getting irritated at her probing.

'Well what is it then?'

'It's to do with bad memories,' he said gingerly holding his stomach.

'Bad memories?'

'I'll tell you all about it when we get to t'club. Now can we please gerraway from here?'

Terry was scrutinising Stan's row of medals with interest, but the old guy was having difficulty remembering the campaigns and confusing his D.S.O. with his George Cross. It was a sad state of affairs and Terry wondered how much longer Stan would be able to adequately look after himself. How long would it be before he was forced into a home, not one like Garden Springs, you needed money to get into a place like that. Or, who would call round regularly to make sure he was all right, hadn't taken a fall and been left lying in the cold for hours or even days. Who was there close by who cared, who would have the vigilance to keep an eye on him? Was there anybody?

Terry fingered the medals and sadly mused on the futility of it all. He looked up into Stan's features. He saw the beginnings of confusion, perhaps the onset of Alzheimer's. It must have taken a gargantuan effort for him to make his way up to Highmoor; trying to make sense of timetables, waiting for a bus in the cold that he thought might never come, fumbling for his pass in his mac pocket with bony hands that had turned blue, unsure which stop to get off at, trying to remember which bus was the right connection; was it the sixty four or the forty six?

Stan Willis had been part of the British Eighth Army serving under Montgomery and General Alexander. He had helped secure the beachhead at Salerno, punched vital holes in the Gustav Line, fought hand to hand at Anzio and played his part at Monte Casino. Terry wondered if any of that long and drawn out campaign had taken as much out of him, shortened his life, as much as had his day trip up to Highmoor. He watched him shakily down his second double brandy, wiping the back of his hand across his mouth with a satisfied sigh but still failing to remove the smear of mustard, a legacy from his recently devoured beef sandwich, which remained on his chin.

'Herbert won the V.C. yer know,' Stan said to Terry who seemed momentarily lost in thought, gazing at the old man's gongs.

'Yeah, I know, Stan,' he said slowly looking up. 'He showed it to us one time.'

'Aye, Victoria Cross. Not many lads won them yer know...' He paused with sadness in his voice. '...No, not many won them.'

'This little lot are just as impressive, Stan,' said Terry carefully handing back the row of medals. 'You make sure you look after 'em, d'you hear?'

'Aye, I keep 'em in a tin under t'bed yer know. It's not often they see t'light o' day now.'

'Do you have anybody come round to see you these days, Stan?' enquired Jan. 'Family or neighbours?'

Stan pondered the question for a few moments. 'Audrey comes and sees me,' he managed to remember.

308

'Who's Audrey?'

'Eh?'

'I say, who's Audrey?'

'Oh, just a lady friend, you know,' he said with what looked like a sparkle in his bloodhound eyes. 'She comes and does a bit for me, and meks a bit o' dinner now and then, sees that I'm alrate,' he added with a slight nod and a wink.

Jan and Terry exchanged knowing looks and smiled. Maybe they'd underestimated him. It looked like that fragile and forgetful demeanour belied a reserve of vitality and stamina when he needed it. Life in the old dog yet.

Nobby came back from the bar with his third pint, his third pasty and another brandy for Stan. He was feeling better.

'Well you've made a quick recovery,' commented Kath as half the pasty disappeared in a flurry of flaky pastry. 'What was all that about?'

Nobby swilled down his snack with a good measure of lager before telling everybody about his graveyard phobia.

'You weren't like that at your mam's funeral,' said Terry.

'That was different; me mam was cremated. I've no problem with cremations. It's that graveside thing what does me. That hole, and the smell; it just gets me going.' He shuddered at the memory. 'There's no stink in the world worse than rotting flesh, believe me.' They did and he continued to regale them with morbid tales of his six-month stint as a gravedigger, like when they knew there was a cortege due in and all the lads would don grotesque rubber masks and line up either side of the cemetery gates leaning on their spades, just for a laugh, but those of the bereaved who weren't too caught up in grief to notice filed complaints at the disrespect, once they'd got over the shock. Funny thing was, said Nobby, half the buggers he worked with didn't need masks, they were the oddest assortment of weird looking fuckers you would ever have the misfortune to meet, and one of them in particular, Bill was his name, had the capacity to scare the shit out of an impressionable sixteen year old whose imagination was apt to run away with him.

Bill was just a funny looking misshapen old guy who suffered with curvature of the spine. He didn't say much, and when he did he'd only speak to one or two of the older men. He had a perpetual dewdrop hanging from the end of his hook nose, not just when he was digging but when he was eating his sandwiches as well, which put Nobby off as much as anything. He reminded him of Boris Karloff's assistant, Igor, from the old Hammer horror films.

Nobby especially hated lunchtimes. The makeshift canteen was a dingy stone outbuilding full of old monuments and broken headstones. If the weather was fine he would eat outside in the fresh air, but on cold or rainy days there was no alternative, and Nobby, who for the only time in his life failed to have an appetite, would sit and gingerly nibble at his sarnies and involuntarily listen to the animal-like noises these freaks would make while eating; low growls and grunts; noisy gulosity and gourmandising. And over in the corner, in the darkest recess of the building, perched on an ancient stone plinth, would sit Bill, hunched over his dinner like some grotesque gargoyle, picking at his food with hands that looked like they had never seen soap and water. Nobby half suspected that Bill lived in the cemetery, like he'd been there all his life. The place fitted him so well. He looked like death was his friend. He belonged there. The picture of him going home to a house, a wife maybe, even kids, just didn't work. Neither did him walking the streets or going to a pub. That was nearly twenty-five years ago. Strange guy. Strange time. They used machines to dig the graves nowadays, and he didn't suppose old Bill was still around, except maybe in spirit, lurking in the shadows amongst the broken epitaphs.

Nobby felt a shiver go through him and asked if they minded changing the subject now please, and the girls were more than happy to do so, but at least his stories had given Terry, for one, a bit of a laugh on an otherwise sad day for him, appealing as they did to his sense of humour that was as black as his pint of Guinness.

While Gordon filled his order, Terry turned from the bar and looked back at his little party. Nobby and the girls sat round the table chatting away; and, on the maroon, velour fixed seating, next to Stan, where he always sat, was Herbert, glass of pale ale in his hand talking to his mate about the good old days. Terry couldn't quite make out what they were saying but it was good to hear his voice again after all this time. He stood and watched them for a while with a big smile on his face.

'Eight-twenty, please, Tel,' said Gordon. Terry turned to the steward and with the smile still on his face, handed over a tenner. When he returned to the table with the round of drinks, Herbert had gone and he kind of knew that would be the last he saw of him. No more crazy imaginings, no more wild scenarios. The anomalous but unique relationship had at last come to an end, served its purpose, whatever that was. And Terry felt okay about it. No more anger, no more angst. That searing feeling of injustice had taken a back seat, at least for now, and that was cool.

Terry distributed the drinks: pint of lager for Nobby, half for Jan. Brandy for Stan, Guinness for himself and an orange juice for Kath. She'd already had a gin and tonic and that would be enough for her as she was driving and had to drop everybody off, and anyway, she didn't want to turn up at the hospital smelling of booze. She would insist they make this their last round; she had a visit to make and she couldn't wait.

25

Little Ginner was being his annoying self again, holding his boots up by the laces and swinging them into Sully's back just for the hell of it.

'If you don't pack it in you little ginger twat I'm gonna fuckin' drop yer,' Sully turned and warned his tormentor for the last time. Ginner grinned at provoking a reaction and casually moved on to Joe where he proceeded to do the same. Joe whizzed round in a flash, snatched the boots from Ginners grasp and raced off into the toilet where he unceremoniously dumped them down the bowl and flushed.

'Me boots! Yer fuckin' bastard,' Ginner screamed, tearing after him. A noisy scuffle ensued and it wasn't long before Sully and Young Nobby joined them and the noises and the cursing got louder. 'Gerroff me, yer bunch o' tossers!'

'You're gerrin' what's comin' to yer, you annoyin' little get.'

After a few more minutes of what sounded like an enormous struggle, the toilet flushed again followed by a gurgling scream. Joe, Sully and Young Nobby emerged soon after looking a little wet and ragged but with big grins on their faces, followed at last by an annoyed and totally drenched Ginner clutching a pair of dripping wet boots, his face almost as red as his hair. The rest of the lads in the changing room fell into fits of laughter at the sight, and Ginner fell into an immediate sulk.

'There were no need fer that,' he moaned. 'Look at me soddin' boots. I can't wear them, they're piss-wet through.'

'Serves yer right,' said Rammer.

Young Nobby took his top off to reveal a chunk of flesh missing out of an upper arm. 'Look at that,' he said in alarm. 'Did you bite me, yer girl?' He poked at the bloody wound. 'Oww! That chuffin' hurts.'

'Good. I'm glad,' Ginner muttered, glowering up at the big lad.

Terry came down the cellar steps. 'Alright, what transpires?' he asked casting suspicious glances around the room.

Everybody stayed quiet and looked dumb, and then he saw Ginner sitting in his own little pool of water and raised his eyes up to the heavens. He knew better than to ask for an explanation. 'Right,' he said, 'I don't know, and I don't really give a stuff what's going on, but Norman's on the warpath again. He says it sounds like World War Three down here. This is us last warning, so get yer arses into gear and gerron that pitch – now.'

The Albion had won its last three league games in fine style and they'd started to play some of their best football of the season. There was a cocky air of confidence in the dressing room that was reflected by the relaxed and totally chilled demeanour in some of the lads, and the hyper annoying antics of others. It made for a fine blend of assuredness and aggression on the pitch but a volatile clash of psyches off it. Terry and Nobby saw no harm in it. Okay, the shenanigans might get out of hand now and again but there was never any real animosity attached. It was what this lot would call team spirit and they were allowed to get on with it despite the scrapes and bruises and the occasional head being flushed down the lav. Trouble was, Norman, the landlord of The Fusiliers didn't look on their capers as mere team building. He hated the cheeky little sods, especially the Duracell kid, and wished he'd never agreed to let Terry and Nobby use the pub's cellar as their base. The grumpy old bastard was fast coming to the conclusion that the extra revenue he earned from their patronage after games every other Sunday afternoon wasn't worth the hassle and the noise.

'Ah, bollocks to the miserable old get,' said Nobby when Terry told him he'd been moaning again. 'We can allus ask Gordon if we can use t'club.'

Terry agreed; he felt that they didn't need to beg or go cap in hand to anyone now. The only reason they'd selected The Fusiliers as their base in the first place was because of the convenience. It was only a spit away from Soldiers Field whereas the club was almost a mile away.

The Albion had become a strong unit, united throughout, from top to bottom; players, management and supporters, and all that mattered to them today was that they were playing in the quarter final of The County Cup, and if Norman and The Fusiliers didn't want them, sod 'em, they would go elsewhere.

Terry's team talks were getting shorter. He'd spent all season drilling them; driving home his philosophies, reiterating his theories on how they should be playing the game, and Nobby, for one, had got sick of hearing it, but it had worked. They had started to listen and had slowly but surely fashioned themselves into a tight little outfit, and now, just as Terry had predicted, were really beginning to enjoy their football. Confidence was sky high and for each and every one of them the games couldn't come quickly enough.

Terry's words were cautionary: overconfidence breeds complacency. Don't get sloppy. Stay disciplined. Keep it tight. Don't underestimate the opposition. Teams who get to the quarterfinals of The County Cup are no mugs and Buckley Rangers had a reputation for being hard but quality opponents.

There was an extra air of anticipation around Soldiers Field that morning. Buckley Rangers had come well supported, noisy and cocksure. The atmosphere was charged and both teams looked well up for it as they waited eagerly for the referee's whistle. That is until One Eye started waving his arms about and gesticulating towards the touchline.

'What's he going on about?' said Terry, straining to hear his goalie's desperate shouts.

'Summat about not having a left fullback,' said Nobby.

They both scanned the pitch for evidence of a red head but found none.

'Where the fuck is Ginner?' shouted Terry at anyone who might shed some light.

'He went off to dry his boots wiv his mam's hairdryer,' offered Biscuit who was the nearest to them.

'Fer Christ's sake,' Terry muttered disbelievingly under his breath.

The referee, whistle already to his lips, looked over to see what the problem was.

'Only ten men on t'pitch,' shouted Nobby.

The ref started to do a head count, like he should have already done anyway, just to confirm it.

'He's here,' shouted Joe as Ginner hastily emerged from his back garden.

Derisive jeers and ironic cheers went up from the Buckley crowd.

'Come on yer useless ginger pillock,' shouted Slum at the embarrassment his teammate was causing.

Ginner ran a diagonal gauntlet of name-calling and general slagging off from the rest of the lads much to the amusement of the Buckley players.

'I'm gonna fuckin' do you at half time,' threatened Young Nobby as Ginner took up his position.

A flustered Ginner pulled a face. 'Fuck off,' he snarled back out of the side of his mouth like getting grief from the big fella was the last thing he needed seeing as he had been instrumental in causing all of this.

The play didn't always come through Duane like it had in the early days. It didn't need to. Everyone was assured of their own capabilities and of those around them. Defence, midfield, attack; all had developed an understanding, not quite telepathic as Terry had tried to elucidate, but they all, to a man, now knew where the gaffer had been coming from. In fact Duane hardly touched the ball at all during the first ten minutes, just a short touch back to Ginner while he gauged his marker, being aware of how quickly he was being closed down; a sharp glance over his shoulder, how much space was he being allowed; doing his homework, thinking all the time. Ginner inside to Young Nobby - all feuding and altercations forgotten now. Young Nobby over to Peycos at right back, switching play, opening up the game, no more hoofing the ball in panic mode; keeping possession, making Buckley work, letting the opposition do all the chasing just as Farshaw had done to them at the beginning of the season.

Almost twenty minutes into the game and it was tight, neither side managing to carve out any clear-cut opportunities. Buckley, as reports had suggested, were a hard, niggling side that had one or two players who liked to leave a foot in; a snapping midfield that liked to harry and nudge, who weren't averse to applying a sharp elbow here and there, but who could also play a bit when in possession. They were a team who would have wound The Albion up in the early days. The lads would have quickly lost all discipline, football out the window in order to match the physical challenge. Now it was different. They took the rough stuff with smiles on their faces. And most, but not all, had learned to jump straight back up when on the end of a crude and nasty challenge without a hint of retaliation. That part had been the hardest lesson for any of them, but they had found, just like Terry had said, that it served to wind their opponents up even more. A psychological battle was always more worth winning than a physical one. Now, whenever Buckley had possession, The Albion shut them down quickly, not allowing them to move the ball around, hunting in packs where necessary. They weren't used to it. Frustration was setting in and one or two had started to argue amongst themselves.

The Albion's left-winger had been unusually quiet up to then, until One Eye casually rolled the ball out to Ginner who stroked it up to Duane with a shout of '*Time.*' It was the one thing he didn't need, and as his marker came to close him down he executed a break that was like a bullet out of a gun. He left his man for dead and was eating up the yards into Buckley territory. The move had created that open-mouthed effect, especially from the Buckley players and supporters. It was something that you would have to study time and time again in slow motion to get some idea as to what he actually did and even then wonder if it was at all physically possible.

The Buckley right back approached, crouched stance, ready to backpedal, ready to jockey, eyes on the ball. Duane decelerated ready to joust; parrying and feigning, caressing the ball, stroking it with the sole of his boot, drawing the fullback in, tempting him, inviting the tackle, biding his time, waiting for the moment and only the rest of The Albion knew what would happen when that moment came. It came. The Buckley defender was on his arse and Duane was long gone. He had what seemed like an age to look up before picking out Rigger's run to the far post with a peach of a cross. Rigger rose above a defender who had restricted his goalie's path to the ball. He flapped at it and Rigger planted his header into the back of the net.

The Buckley players looked stunned as The Albion celebrated. They were still stunned as the ref blew his whistle for the restart because they were dispossessed almost straight away. Rammer won the ball and laid it inside to Joe who went on a mazy run, beating three shell-shocked players. Rigger had made another diagonal run and Joe had only to thread the ball between two stretched defenders to put the striker in on goal again but he elected to take it on himself and struck a right foot shot that fizzed inches over the bar.

Royston, Mackie and Flash were all bobbing around excitedly on the touchline. The game had suddenly come alive and The Albion's midfield slowly started to take control and dominate for the rest of the half.

Buckley desperately harried and hassled while The Albion kept it simple; pass and move, pass and move. Where there was no way through they simply played it back and started again, inviting the Rangers onto them, waiting for the gaps to appear, Young Nobby looking like Beckenbaur with every touch, poking and probing away, switching play, spreading it wide, trying to find Biscuit in space, hoping to get Duane off on another run. It was good to watch and the Buckley followers had gone strangely silent.

Terry and Nobby exchanged glances almost in disbelief at how the lads had suddenly clicked over these past few games, and on this evidence they were only getting better.

Duane inside to Rammer - one-two back to Duane. Duane with a three-yard burst shaking off a challenge lays it up to Rigger. Duane comes inside. Rigger holds off the centre half and lays it back into Duane's path. Duane shapes to shoot, sees the challenge, flicks it square to the advancing Joe just as the sliding tackle comes in. Joe, on the run, up to Slum - screams for the return - crunch! Slum is chewing turf; scythed down from behind before he can tee his captain up for the shot. Free kick: edge of the eighteen-yard box.

There was jostling and pushing as Rigger and Young Nobby mixed it up amongst the Buckley wall. The ref blew his whistle and Duane shaped up to shoot but instead flicked it sideways to Joe who curled a right footer. Young Nobby leaned into the wall and the ball sailed through the gap. The keeper was rooted to the spot and the ball hit the back of the net with a satisfying thwack. Two-nil to The Albion.

Royston and Mackie went ape. Flash threw his linesman flag in the air and Joe did an over-the-top celebration for the West Broughton fans, crowning it all with a canter down the touchline, hand outstretched inviting high-five slaps from the posse as he went.

It wasn't like Joe to act so flash and demonstrative, even though it was a pearler of a free kick, and Jan, being the intuitive mother she was, thought she knew why he was showing off.

Terry had of course been observing the game as a whole, but Jan, as all mothers do, had been concentrating solely on her eldest lad and had noticed that his attentions hadn't always been on the pitch during these past forty minutes. He'd been casting occasional glances towards the touchline and it hadn't always been to receive instructions from his dad.

Lisa Boocock and her mate Cheryl were among the West Broughton contingent that morning; all pointing, giggling whispers and chewing gum. Tight threequarter jeans with big turn-ups. Short bomber jacket with fake fur collar, hair swept back tight off her umpa-lumpa made-up face. Giant brass parrot perches for earrings, and the most inappropriate footwear in which to watch a game of football.

Jan had observed the interaction, and it had confirmed to her that something was obviously going on with her son and the younger sister of their baby sitter. Lisa was a very pretty girl, despite the semi-chav style, and certainly looked a lot older than her fifteen years.

Jan smiled to herself as certain reservations went through her head. She would have to fight hard to keep those overprotective motherly feelings in check. It was inevitable that Joe would discover girls at some point, but it was still a bit of a shock now that he had, and Lisa Boocock of all people. She would have to be having a word with Terry about having a word with Joe about certain things, but then she saw the frown on her husband's face as he monitored his son's movements back into position for the restart. The OTT celebration hadn't pleased him. Best not say anything for a while.

At half-time Terry had the lads sitting in a semi-circle, warning that the next forty minutes were likely to be the hardest they'd faced up to now. Nobby was going round eulogising it here, lauding it there: 'Great football, lads. Tremendous stuff. Best I've seen all season. Semi-finals, fellas, semi-finals. Come on!' he urged with clenched fists.

'Where's the council pop, Tel?' asked a parched Sasquatch.

Terry looked around. Rory was the water boy and he was nowhere to be seen. 'Where the hell's Noriega?' he asked annoyed. (Terry was reading about C.I.A involvement in South American drug cartels and their links with the Panamanian dictatorship during the eighties and nineties.)

Nobby offered to to run back to the Fusiliers to get the water.

Joe had been getting on Rory's tits these past few weeks. He'd been a proper bastard to him for no reason and he was pig sick of it. They'd had one or two epic battles, full-on encounters; no quarter asked for, and none given, and he had plenty of bruises to show for it, but he had given as good as he got. His pillock of a brother hadn't come away unscathed and no way could he claim any outright victory. There would come a day when he would be able to match him physically, and he vowed to do him good and proper when that time came. Until then, Rory had unearthed something that would act perfectly as divine retribution.

Rory had been rooting around in Joe's room for his Tony Hawk's Underground disc for the Playstation that the wanker had borrowed without asking, when he came across something very interesting tucked away in a corner of his bedside drawers. A set of passport size photos of Joe and Lisa Boocock in compromising poses. Nothing too raunchy, but intimate enough for him to have a field day with. Rory's eyes had lit up at the discovery. '*Revenge is mine,*' he said, while tucking the pictures into the back pocket of his jeans.

Nobby met Rory as he was coming out of The Fusiliers swinging his water bottle carrier. 'Come on 'ere, yer wastrel, lads are dyin' o' thirst.'

'I forgot to bring it out, din't I?' Rory lied. They both hurried back to the pitch, Rory with a self-satisfied smirk on his face, not daring to believe getting his own back would have turned out to be so easy.

'...Let's keep it simple, lads, and if somebody makes a run for you, if a man finds space, use him, play him in; work the options...' Terry stopped talking and looked at Joe. He was miles away, well, a few yards away at least. '...Are you listening?' Joe looked up slowly, unaware that his dad was talking directly to him. 'Yeah, you. What did I just say?'

Joe didn't have a clue. He looked around at his smirking team-mates who weren't about to dig him out of the shit. He shrugged his shoulders.

'Play the options, Tel,' offered Sasquatch.

'Play the options,' repeated Terry and immediately rounded on his son. 'Something you didn't do at all in the first half,' he said jabbing an accusing finger in Joe's direction. 'If you wanna play on your own, here's a ball, sod off and do it somewhere else.' Terry kicked it at him, smacking against his legs. 'This is a team, and I know you're all sick of hearing me say it, but it's playing as a team that's gotten us this far. No one individual is bigger than the team, and when I talk I expect everybody to listen, and that goes especially for you – got that?' He stared hard at Joe, who slowly, and in his sulky way, nodded his head. 'Everybody got that?'

'Yes, Tel!' the rest of them shouted as one.

'Right then, let's go book us a place in the semi-final.'

With the exception of Joe, the rest of The Albion took up their positions with eager and determined cries of battle. Joe took to the field with a body language that was the opposite of when he'd left it at the end of the first half. His shoulders were slumped and his head was down. He was seething. His dad was a bastard. Where was the praise for his free kick? *Nice goal, Joe. Well played, son.* Fucking liberty singling him out like that. In his own mind Joe had thought that his was one of the better performances of the first half. He'd also noticed that Steve, the Farshaw manager, was watching from the touchline. Maybe he'd show him just what he could do; really turn it on, impress the guy then hand in his transfer request. That'd bloody show 'em, him playing in Farshaw colours, Champions elect; stuff yer County Cup. His anger quickly began to override his sulk. There wasn't only Duane who could turn a trick or two. He'd make his old man eat his words, whatever they were. He'd bloody well show him an' right.

'Gimme the fuckin' ball,' Joe dropped into space and screamed at Sasquatch. Sasquatch obliged and Joe set off in single-minded fashion, head down, hackles raised. He body swerved the first tackle but in doing so lost full control of the ball. He slid into the second challenge that had become a fifty-fifty. His tenacity won him that encounter and he emerged with the ball at his feet again. Prompted by great shouts of encouragement from Royston and co, while Terry remained stony faced and tight lipped, Joe strode forward ignoring the numerous calls for a pass. He was condensing play and as the Buckley defence squeezed up Slum and Rigger had nowhere to go and were in danger of being caught offside. There was no chance of that in Joe's mind as he was determined to go it alone anyway. The challenge from the centre half threw him off balance. He spun off his shoulder but somehow managed to stay on his feet and the ball fortuitously popped out in front of him again. As the full back came across to cover, Joe managed a shot on goal but he'd already run out of steam; he was stretching and the goalie easily smothered the strike. The West Broughton massive roared approvingly. Terry had his arms folded across his chest and the furrow on his forehead had grown deeper.

Now, every time Joe got the ball he'd solo it, mustering every turn and trick he'd ever learned. When they came off he looked pretty good, but Buckley were getting wise to him and pretty soon he started to run down blind alleys and into brick walls.

'Who's he think he is, Ronaldo?' Young Nobby quipped to Sasquatch as they watched Joe execute a brace of neat step-overs from their vantage point on the edge of their own eighteen-yard box. Now he was being quickly closed down from all sides. Duane was in acres of space over on the left, arms raised, screaming for the pass. Joe tried a Cruyff turn to get him out of trouble but he was over-whelmed by Buckley shirts and had the ball taken from him.

The lads were beginning to get annoyed with their captain, and what was pissing them off even more was the fact that he wasn't making any attempt to win the ball back after being dispossessed. He was fast expending all his energy playing the Prima Donna, and the rest of them had to work harder because of it. The smooth, flowing football of the first half had gone out the window. They were begin-ning to lose their shape and Buckley was starting to take advantage and hit them on the counter.

'Pass the fuckin' thing, yer greedy bastard,' Biscuit shouted on his way back to defend after committing himself forward on the last attack. Gaps had opened up between The Albion's midfield and the defence and Buckley were seizing the opportunities to get themselves back in the game.

A fierce, angled shot from one of the Buckley strikers produced a fine one-handed save from One Eye, tipping the ball, which was des-tined for the top corner, over the bar.

The *ooohhs!* echoed around the park followed by a newfound burst of encouragement from the travelling Buckley contingent. Hav-ing scrambled to his feet, One Eye screamed at his teammates to rally. Most were looking daggers at Joe whose head was on the floor as they breathlessly prepared to defend the corner.

You could have planted spuds in the furrows on Terry's forehead now. He told Sully to warm up. One Eye plucked the ball out of the air from the resulting set piece but as he came to ground the ball popped out of his grasp. As he scrambled to recover it a Buckley player steamed in and almost took the ball and One Eye's head with it. With tempers already starting to fray the West Broughton goalie jumped to his feet and locked foreheads, stag-like, with the Buckley kid. The ref had already blown his whistle for the free kick but One Eye didn't take kindly to the challenge and retaliated like he would have done six months ago. It can't have been a pleasant experience being eyeballed by The Albion's goalie close up like that and it didn't help when Young Nobby and Sasquatch stormed in to push, jostle and verbalise the Rangers player. Inevitably his teammates came to his aid and a goalmouth melee ensued. It was the last thing Terry had wanted to see. He couldn't believe this was happening especially after witnessing the near total football of the first half. He shook his head at the scene and watched on helplessly as the ref tried to restore some order. He saw all discipline evaporate with that familiar juvenile show of partisan unity. He couldn't allow them to cave in now, not after they'd come this far. They were still two up with twenty minutes to go, so he decided to remove what he perceived to be the cause of all this. He hauled off his captain, his lad for Sully.

Joe looked stunned. He stood in the middle of the pitch not wanting to believe that Nobby was waving him over. When it sank in, his head and shoulders hit the floor again and he trudged off the field totally dejected. He didn't even offer Sully his hand, making sure he came off a good few yards away from where his dad and Nobby were standing. Sully didn't care; he just wanted to enter the fray as quick as he could. He was relishing this rare chance to play in the middle of the park where he could get stuck in, and he eagerly took to the field shouting words of encouragement to his mates, clenching his fists, urging them to get their heads up.

Joe, sitting with his forearms on his knees, socks rolled down exposing his shin-pads, stared trance-like at the blades of grass between his legs. He tried to keep his emotions in check but it was hard. Every time he felt himself well up he breathed hard to stifle it, but then that hurt feeling, that surge of self-pity kept filling him up inside and he choked again. He felt his eyes moisten but he was damned if he was going to blub, especially when Lisa was in the vicinity. But he couldn't prevent that potent mix of anger and humiliation washing over him again so he tried to relive his moment of glory. In his head he saw the ball curl around the Buckley wall and ripple the back of the net but it didn't help, it only made him feel worse. He was so devastated, and the resentment and frustration he felt made him want to see his team lose right now.

The referee had been sensible after the goalmouth kerfuffle; he'd issued stern warnings to the players but hadn't booked anyone. Unfortunately the yellow card was straight out of his pocket after Sully's first challenge had served warning to the ever-growing cockiness of the Rangers midfield as to the nature of his intent. Terry cringed and wondered if he'd done the right thing, but he needn't have worried. Sully's introduction managed to underline The Albion's steely resolve not to be worn down and pretty soon he and Rammer reinstated their dominance in the middle of the park; battling away, winning possession, retaining possession, keeping it simple, playing the options. All of a sudden they looked like a team again.

Nobby strolled over to Joe and threw him his training top. Joe looked up briefly before lowering his head again.

'Best purrit on, Joe lad, keep yerself warm.' Joe slowly wrapped his top around his shoulders and continued to sulk in silence. 'Superb free kick by the way.'

Joe looked up with a scowl. 'Huh,' he muttered scornfully and turned his head away again.

'S'up, are you pissed off 'cos your dad subbed yer?'

'Wun't you be?'

Nobby shrugged, 'Dunno – depends.'

'Why me?' Joe asked looking up so Nobby could see the genuine hurt in his face.

'Why not you?'

'I run me bollocks off; I score a goal. It's not as if I were t'worst player on t'pitch.'

'Depends on how you look at it,' said Nobby. 'We don't have best or worst players. Your dad's got you all playing as a team, working together as a unit. It only takes one player to stop working in that unit and you *all* start to look like bad players. He brought you off 'cos you started playing for yourself. You forgot about your teammates and we started to lose us shape.' Nobby let Joe stew on that for a second or two. 'Your mam seems to think that your mind might have been on summat else,' he added.

Joe looked up sharply. 'How d'yer mean?'

'She seems to think you were too busy playing up to t'bit o' skirt; doing a bit o' showboating for t'woman like.' Nobby nodded in Lisa's direction with a knowing smirk and a wink. Joe looked over at his now not-so-secret girlfriend who was still all whispering, chewing gum giggly with her mate. He said nothing and bowed his head again as he started to colour up. 'It's different when Duane does his stuff, innit?' he eventually countered defensively. 'You all start bleedin' droolin' whenever he's on t'ball.'

Nobby sighed. 'Here, let me show you summat.' He squatted down next to Joe and produced a small black book. In it were the complete statistics from The Albion's first season: team selections, results, goals, assists, scorers, the lot.

'Joe Gallagher,' said Nobby running his finger along a column. 'Goals: five, plus today's, of course, that's six. Assists: seven. Substituted: until now, none. Duane Geddess,' he paused until he found the appropriate line. 'Goals: eleven. Assists: sixteen.' Nobby paused again and looked at Joe to see if he was getting his point across. He continued. 'Substituted: three.' He closed the book. 'We all know what Duane can do, but at the end of the day he still delivers, he still works for the team. D'you hear what I'm saying?' Joe slowly nodded his head. 'You don't have to perform all that shit to prove what a good player you are. Play to your strengths, Joe lad, 'cos you've got plenty. Maybe you had too many distractions today, eh?' Joe looked up at him and Nobby raised his eyebrows.

Joe heaved a heavy sigh and let his head fall again. Nobby ruffled his hair and left him to ponder.

Deep down Joe knew Nobby was right. He had acted like a bit of a prick, and he probably had been showing off in front of Lisa, and no, he hadn't been listening to his dad. He'd heard it all before and thought he knew better. But he still felt disconsolate. It was nice getting the accolades from Nobby. He seemed to appreciate it when you did something good in a game and he always let you know, but it would feel even better coming from your dad, but it very rarely, if ever, did.

For some reason, maybe for a couple of reasons, Joe felt he had to be the star attraction today, and it had backfired on him. He had simply wanted to impress a few people and he now realised he had spectacularly gone about it the wrong way. But his dad – fuck's sake, why did he always end up hating his old man? And what about his mother – Jesus, no hiding owt from her, is there? At least Lisa had the good sense not to come over to him after he'd been brought off. Anyway, if his mother started asking too many awkward questions he would simply deny it and say she was talking daft, although she could always tell when he was lying, he'd go bright red just like he did just then in front of Nobby.

Why was his life starting to become so complicated and messy? It never used to be like this before females came on the scene. He consoled himself to the fact that at least he'd managed to keep the lads in the dark over his new muse.

Peycos's twenty-yard drive was desperately cleared off the line by a Buckley defender. They scrambled to clear their lines but The Albion's attacking pressure had now built to such an extent that even the defenders were pushing up and taking pot shots, but never was it reckless. Terry had always encouraged his fullbacks to overlap and attack, but not without ensuring they had the necessary cover first.

Young Nobby had found his voice and was directing operations expertly from almost the halfway line; telling players when to go, pulling players into covering positions, soaking up any attempts at a Rangers breakout and setting up wave after attacking wave. He was doing a fine job as stand-in captain, and later Joe would graciously hand over his armband, insisting that he did the honours for the rest of the season.

Duane set off on another raid down the left flank. The massed ranks of Buckley defenders, which now included both their strikers, gravitated towards him. He feigned another dart down the line but at the last second dropped his shoulder and executed a lightning quick flick of the ball that sent him inside, throwing at least three Rangers players off balance and causing two of them to run smack into each other. Duane danced across the pitch looking for an opening, searching for the slightest chink. He elegantly rode a couple of desperate lunges and as another Buckley player committed himself he saw the opportunity he'd been waiting for. Sully arrived in space, Duane laid the ball square to him then darted off at a right angle into the hole left by the floundering opposition. He called for the through ball but Sully had read it instantly and a slide rule pass was already on its way. Duane megged the statuesque centre-half and found himself with only the goalie to beat. As the keeper bore down on him, he calmly side-footed the ball into Basher's path and he finished it with a simple tap-in.

It was Basher's first touch of the ball, having come on for Slum with ten minutes to go. It was also his first ever goal for the Albion, and the rest of the lads celebrated with him accordingly, safe in the knowledge that there were only five minutes left and they had just booked themselves a place in the semi-finals of the County Cup.

'Good win,' said Steve shaking Terry's hand. 'Your lads have come on leaps and bounds. Pity we're not gonna meet again this campaign.'

'Cheers,' said Terry, 'yeah, it is.'

'So, semi-finals, County Cup, eh? That's some achievement in your first season.'

'Aye, I suppose it is. And it's been nice proving a few people wrong along the way. So, what brings you down here then, Steve?'

'Well, seeing as we'd no game this weekend I thought I'd take this opportunity to come and have a look at your superstar I've been hearing so much about, being that he's allus injured or poorly whenever we play each other.'

'There are no superstars in my team,' insisted Terry.

'You've got to admit, the kid's a bit special.'

'Duane's a good player,' Terry said cautiously.

Steve laughed with incredulity at Terry's understatement. 'Good player?' He raised his eyebrows. 'Good player?' he repeated. 'Terry, have you the remotest idea as to what it is you've got here?'

Terry didn't like the way Duane was being referred to as 'it', as if he were a commodity already. He said nothing.

'Who've you got watching him?'

'How d'yer mean?'

'Which clubs?'

Terry shook his head. 'I haven't got any clubs watching him.'

The Farshaw manager raised his eyebrows again. 'You're kidding me. Why on earth not?'

Terry didn't know what to say. He'd never thought about it before. Duane was an Albion player, why would he want to alert other clubs. Steve meant professional clubs, he realised that now, but he genuinely hadn't considered the possibility of a pro outfit wanting one of his lads.

Steve gave him a look like he should have known better. 'Come on, Tel,' he reasoned. 'You didn't think you were gonna keep a player like that a secret forever, did you? Pot-hunting for The Albion year after year? I don't think so. Time to get real, me old son; you've got a diamond in your midst, and you know it. The kid's one-in-a-million. I've spent years trying to unearth a lad with that much talent and you've gone and done it in one season, you lucky bugger.'

'It's a long, hard road before you get to become a pro,' said Terry, like his cautiousness had been well thought out. 'A lot of it's luck. There's been hundreds o' kids who were world beaters when they were fourteen, and ninety-nine point nine percent of 'em end up on t'scrap heap.'

Steve shook his head. 'Not this one, Terry. This one's special, believe me. I've been in the game long enough to know by now. I've only watched him for eighty minutes and that's been long enough.' He started to walk away. 'You're gonna have to relinquish him soon, Terry, you mark my words. Get on that blower sharpish or somebody else will. After all, this is why we do it, isn't it? Hiya Joe, how's it goin'?' said Steve ruffling the downbeat youngster's hair as he walked past. 'Nice free kick, fella.'

Joe looked after him and was in two minds to say something, but then thought better of it and went back to his reflections on the day's events.

'*No, it bloody well isn't why we do it,*' Terry thought to himself as he watched the Farshaw man walk away. He felt like shouting Steve back and telling him exactly why *he* was doing it. But now that he did come to think about it he wasn't at all sure. He didn't know how he'd explain his motives for creating this kids' football team without sounding naïve and a little disingenuous and having the Farshaw manager laugh at him again.

His reasons had been so clear cut and transparent ten months ago when the notion of The Albion had formed in his head on Mrs. Gladstone's back lawn. Now, here he was, him and his lads in the semi-final of the most prestigious cup competition, and all of a sudden those reasons seemed a bit fuzzy and unclear – *Pot-hunter?* – Jesus, is that how the guy saw him?

Maybe it was time to take stock; look outside of himself and do some serious analysis. Had he really lost sight of his vision for these young lads? Had this cup run gone to his head? Had it become a blinkered quest for glory, an unswerving, selfish act on his part? He supposed his demeanour might have taken on a rather grim, Jose Mourinho kind of dourness of late, but surely his guiding principles remained the same.

Terry tried to think at what point it had all stopped being mere fun and escapism and morphed into death or glory at all costs. He looked around Soldiers Field and saw his lads' faces: ecstatic, delirious with their achievement and yes, he realised that it did become a different ball game when things were at stake. It all took on a different dimension, but that was bound to happen. So, his fundamental rationale for doing all this might have become a bit blurred around the edges recently, but he was sure it was there lurking in the background somewhere. Maybe if they failed to get beyond the semis it would come back to him with a little more clarity.

As for the Duane thing, well, Steve's comments and observations had certainly thrown him. He genuinely hadn't thought beyond dragging the kid out of his miserable milieu and giving him an opportunity to play. Having him feted by football league clubs was taking it all into yet another dimension and Terry had never contemplated that far ahead until now.

Steve had taken Terry's reticence as a selfish desire to hang on to his star player while in the pursuit of silverware, which wasn't the case, but it had woken him up to the fact that there would soon be a lot of outside interest in his boy wonder and he would have to accept that. His worry wasn't for the eventual loss of his remarkable discovery, nor did he doubt Duane's ability to one day hack it in the professional ranks. It was more for the youngster's vulnerability given his situation.

Terry could well imagine the scene: youth development officers from all the top clubs queuing at the battered, blue door that had been kicked to bits, all clamouring for the wonder-kid's signature, and inside, sitting on her filthy throne surrounded by bloody hypodermics, Caldwell, holding sway over the proceedings like some junkie auctioneer, negotiating her cut before allowing her eldest son to go to the highest bidder. And what if, say, a London club came in for him, how would she cope on her own with mother's little helper two hundred miles away?

Dream opportunities never before envisaged; an extraordinarily talented skinny urchin suddenly with the world at his feet; a once in a lifetime chance to escape the incubus only to be shattered by a mother's cynical embargo.

Terry could see it all ending in tears.

The noise in The Albion changing room grew to a tumultuous level as it filled up with players; a raucous clamour of near hysteria that had nothing to do with them winning the game.

Joe, in his current sombre frame of mind was one of the last down the cellar steps. What he encountered when he got to the bottom shook him in his boots. The realisation that he was the cause of all the commotion hit him in a tsunami-like wave of ridicule and derision.

Pasted around the walls of the dressing room were at least half a dozen A3 sized computer printed blow-ups of him and Lisa Boocock enjoying a tongue sandwich.

He stood transfixed as the cacophony of caustic quips assaulted him from all directions. He wanted to turn and race back up the steps but that would be a girl thing to do, so he remained, nakedly shamed-faced scarlet and took it, like a lamb to slaughter.

Ginner was standing on a bench with his face pressed up against one of the images, his tongue going ten to the dozen in crude mimicry of the enlarged photo. Spontaneously filthy jokes and witticisms peppered Joe's ears. Everyone was a comedian and, boy, was this funny.

'Fuckin' 'ell, Joe – Lisa fuckin' Boocock?'

'Dip yer bread, Joe lad!'

'Gallagher, yer shady stud muffin!'

'Where's she got her hand then, Joe?'

'Where's he gorris cock, yer mean.'

''Ere, have yer done this yet, Joe?' Peycos had pulled one of the posters from the wall and was simulating oral sex with his penis and Lisa's image.

'She'd use that specimen as a tooth pick,' quipped One Eye.

'At least I'm not deformed,' countered Peycos. 'That thing o' yours goes round fuckin' corners.'

''Ere, she could gerrus *all* in her gob in one go, could Lisa,' added Ginner.

'Aye, 'cept she wunt go near anybody wi' ginger pubes,' said Young Nobby.

'He an't got any pubes,' said Slum flicking his towel at Ginner's nether regions

'Bollocks,' sneered Ginner, doing his best to avoid the wet flashes of snapping cotton. 'Anyroad, I've had her.'

'In yer dreams, wee man.'

'Anyroad, she's had more prick than a second hand dartboard has that one.'

'How would you know, yer little ginger ferret? Nearest you've ever come to doin' it is wiv a computer screen an' t'four fingered widow.'

'It's common Knowledge,' he sniffed.

Young Nobby continued to bait him. 'I've heard that you can't even fetch yet, yer little spunk bubble.'

'Who's told yer that?' demanded Ginner offended.

'Common knowledge,' mimicked Young Nobby.

''Course I can fetch, yer big idiot.'

'Aye, but there's no tadpoles in it,' quipped Biscuit. 'It's just tatty watter.'

'Fuck you, dog breaf.'

Young Nobby had managed to deflect the attention away from his mate, and Joe had done well not to rise to any of the bait. He'd kept silent with as much dignity as his situation would allow him to muster. Young Nobby had laughed along with the rest of them, but he hadn't resorted to some of the more stinging jibes dished out by Joe's persecutors, and he was ready to come to his mate's defence by putting down any of the muppets, especially Ginner, whom he thought might have gone too far. And now the rest of the lads had started to round on Ginner 'cos he was easy to wind up, and they had collectively begun to taunt him on his perceived lack of pubescent progress.

After the ten minutes or so it had taken the lads to exhaust their wit, after the jokes had lost their impact, when the innuendoes had become tiresome, Joe wearily removed his shirt and got to his feet to go for a pee. He glanced up, and there at the top of the cellar steps was his younger brother with a manic look in his eyes; a steely look of victory, of sweet vengeance, and he was ready for the inevitable payback, coiled like a spring waiting to be chased all over the streets of West Broughton.

Joe looked up at him without emotion, all fight and fire gone, extinguished with a hose full of humiliation; drenched in self-pity, no spirit left for confrontation. He gave Rory a tired nod of the head, like he was acknowledging his ingenuity and reluctantly accepting defeat this time.

Rory relaxed for the moment, a little disappointed and a bit puzzled. Victory was his but Joe's reaction had disarmed him; best not get too complacent. No doubt he'd have something up his sleeve. He'd have to be on his guard all the more for what he anticipated would be the mother of all counter retribution coming his way.

Thoughts of revenge were the last thing on Joe's mind at that moment in time. He pondered on his cursed relationship with Lisa as he emptied his bladder and, although all that he'd gone through that day was none of her making, he was beginning to feel that women were more trouble than they were worth.

26

On the evening of Herbert's funeral Kath had walked through her front door after visiting the hospital and had stood in front of her husband with that vacant expression on her face and his heart had sunk. He'd seen that look before and he knew what it meant.

'Kath?' he had jumped up, worried. 'Kath, what's up love?'

'He's gone,' she'd said staring blankly.

'Who's gone?'

'Leo,' she'd whispered. 'He's gone. They've taken him.'

She had fallen into his arms and her body shook as she cried out her emotions. He had held her there for what seemed like an age as he tried to figure out how best to comfort her.

She relived that moment when she walked onto the ward and saw the shape of another sickly looking child asleep in Leo's bed. Her slight shock had turned into a bit of a panic when she looked quickly around the other beds and couldn't see him. She'd run out into the corridor frantically searching for a nurse who could tell her of the whereabouts of Leo from ward seven. Another eternity seemed to pass until someone confirmed to her that the child had been taken into care. She vaguely remembered demanding to see the youngster's consultant, Doctor Mitchell, but Doctor Mitchell wasn't there, and she'd wandered back out into the corridor in a daze, clutching a bag of Milky Bar buttons.

The rest of the evening had been a blur. She couldn't remember driving home. There was just this abiding image inside her head of a bewildered and frightened kid in the hands of strangers, and then she was breaking down in her husband's arms.

It was at moments like these that Nobby felt totally useless, in-adequate, and he'd wished Jan had been there to take over and say the right things. It had been time for him to man up. There was no way he was having his Kath return to the state she'd gotten herself in over those past winter months. He'd felt guilty, thinking in hindsight that maybe both he and his lad hadn't done enough while she was ill. Maybe they both could have helped a bit more with the household chores, the washing up, a bit of cleaning and hoovering; alien activities to both of them. And she just got on with it and they shamefully let her; getting through the routines of the day in a pill-induced fug, doing what she had to do for her fellas, feeling guilty herself for having to send her man down to the supermarket with a list 'cos she wasn't up to venturing outdoors. She could tell he hated it and invariably he brought back the wrong stuff. On the domestic front Nobby was worse than useless and he was the first to admit it, and the only way he knew how to make it up to her was to let her pursue her quest with his full blessing and to help her fulfil that quest in any way he could. Now that he knew what they were up against, what they were fighting for, they would do it together. Her crusade was his crusade. He'd be her rock he'd make sure of that, no need for prozac or tamazipan. He would be her inspiration and, he hoped, that would keep her from tipping over the edge. He'd held her close to him, feeling the cold of the night still on her coat and in his mind he began to plan his assault on the two attic rooms at the top of the house.

A lot of the stuff up there had belonged to his mam and dad and had lain undisturbed after his mam had passed away, twenty years ago. It would be hard for him to sift through and dispose of a lot of the things, but twenty years was a long time, and Nobby wasn't the type to dwell on the past, sentimental as a lot of it was. He would keep the photographs and some of the more personal items, like his dad's fob and watch that didn't work anymore and bits of his mam's jewelry; cheap and sparse but part of his childhood memories. It was time to turn Kath's dreams into reality.

* * *

Nobby stood back to admire his handywork; that was the painting finished. The new Velux windows were in, just the carpets to go down then they could think about beds and furniture. It was all coming together nicely and looking good. Terry had helped him rip out the old skylights and together they had transformed the two dusty old attic junk rooms into cosy little bedrooms.

Kath came up the stairs with a mug of tea for her man. She smiled up at him, grateful for his efforts at creating her vision. He took his tea and gave her a hug.

'What d'yer think then, love?'

Kath rested her head on his shoulder. 'It looks great,' she said.

'It'll look even better when t'carpet goes down.'

They stood in silence with their arms around each other for a moment. Nobby sipped at his tea in quiet contemplation of a job well done. Kath, in her wistful frame of mind set to wondering if her dreams would ever be complete. Against her better judgement she allowed herself to imagine the room with a child in it, with all the accompanying sights, sounds and smells; unmade beds, toys, posters; tidy, untidy; she didn't care. What she did fret about was the increasing possibility of none of it happening, of having her Nobby go to so much trouble and effort for nothing. She saw the room with blank walls, empty drawers and a bed that no one ever slept in. She began to sob silently.

'Hey, what's all that about?' Nobby soothed and hugged her closer to him.

'Nowt, it's just me being silly.' Kath produced a tissue and sniffed away the tears.

'Everything's gonna be alright, love, you wait and see.' Nobby manoeuvred her head onto his chest and stroked her hair. He gazed over at the freshly painted blue wall and hoped to God that it was.

Nobby knew how fragile his wife's state of mind was. Keeping her thinking positively at all costs was the task he'd set himself, but it was a fine balancing act and he realised that any small setback, any negative thought, could send her spiralling back into depression, and he feared that this time there would be nothing to bring her out of it. He had to be her link of hope, her focus against failure, but remaining upbeat and positive was proving such a hard task for Kath, especially when she was being stonewalled at every turn.

"I'm sorry Mrs. Clarke, I'm afraid we are not at liberty to divulge that information." She was sick of hearing it. From the people at the hospital through to every department at City Hall, no one was willing or able to tell her the whereabouts of Leo Caldwell. The hospital had confirmed that the child had been placed in the care of social services and would more than likely be fostered out at some stage but that was as much as they could tell her.

She put the phone down at the end of another fruitless enquiry like she'd done endlessly on her lunch break for the past couple of weeks. She picked listlessly at the food in her tupperware sandwich box and gazed thoughtfully at the little bag of MilkyBar buttons that lay on her desk, the very ones that she had taken into the hospital as a treat for Leo that night. They were his favourites and she had been looking forward to see his little face light up when she waved them in front of him.

She fingered the bag of chocolate and wondered where the little fellow was and what he was doing right now. She missed him so much.

Despite losing contact with Leo, Nobby had persuaded Kath to press ahead with her plans to get on the adoption register, his reason being that you never knew if and when the little guy's name might pop up. Kath had done so reluctantly. Reluctant because she didn't want to have contact with and fall in love with another child, maybe a little girl who would prove too hard to resist. She didn't want to run the risk of having her heart torn apart some more. But she'd gone ahead and done it anyway and their first home assessment was coming up soon. She hoped Nobby would have the carpets down and the beds and furniture in by then.

Up at Cromwell House, Duane and his mam were having their own assessment. A social worker was giving the flat a good going over and was asking plenty of questions.

Duane had been well primed and prepared for her visit. He'd kept a keen eye on what came through the cloth-covered hole in the battered blue door that had served as a letterbox for the last couple of months. His mam very rarely took interest in the mail except when it

337

was giro day, so Duane had made sure he opened and read anything that came in a brown metropolitan council type envelope, and he'd promised Kath that he'd inform her if he saw any correspondence that might shed any light on the whereabouts of his brother.

The letter notifying them of the social worker's visit duly came through and he'd done his best to make the flat look presentable on the day.

The scabby piece of furniture that served as a coffee table had been cleared of all trace of narcotics, penicillin type growths and other toxic waste. In the absence of a vacuum cleaner Duane had worked minor miracles on the sticky carpet and torn vinyl flooring. Leo's prison pen remained in the corner of the room, minus its sodden urine soaked mattress, and he'd insisted that his mam relinquish the grubby quilt that she wrapped around herself, and basically lived in, to undergo a few boil wash cycles down at the laundrette.

Caldwell had sat and watched the youngster graft away with a big cynical sneer on her face, barely lifting a hand to help, while casually dropping her fag ash over the areas he'd just cleaned. The fact that he was doing all this for her benefit didn't seem to register or matter.

'I've noticed that there isn't much food in your cupboards or fridge, Mrs. Caldwell,' stated the woman from the Social, making notes on her return from the kitchen.

'You try fillin' a fridge on t'fuckin' pittance that I get,' said Caldwell. Duane gave his mam a sly look as if warning her against upsetting this woman. 'Anyway, I 'avent sent him down to t'shops yet. I thought you'd want him 'ere to ask him some questions.'

'You send Duane to do your shopping?'

'Aye, well he helps me out when I'm not feelin' too good. You people should know I'm not well. You ought to dry draggin' heavy bags up them fuckin' stairs – be the death o' me they will.' She started into a pseudo bout of coughing as if to emphasize her point and the ash from her fag fell down her front.

'What exactly is your illness, Mrs. Caldwell?'

'It's that there M.E., innitt.'

The woman with the clipboard file raised her eyebrows. 'And has this condition been diagnosed by your G.P.?'

'Nyahh - can't be doin' wi' quacks an' saw-bones.'

Social Services stared at her levelly whilst continuing to write. 'I see,' she muttered. 'You are a registered addict?' It was a question but she posed it as a statement of fact. She peered over her glasses and in turn over her clipboard, waiting for a response. Caldwell nodded. 'And I understand you are undertaking a methadone programme?' Caldwell nodded again, vaguely. 'And how would you evaluate it at this moment in time?'

'Come again.'

'How are you finding the progamme, is it helping you to stay off the heroin?'

Caldwell nodded again. 'Yeh... s'pose it is... yeh,' she lied. She quickly became bored with the constant probing questions and showed her agitation like she always did, nervously raking fingers through her bedraggled hair and lighting one fag after another.

The woman wrote a lot; too bloody much for Caldwell's liking. Why couldn't she just hurry up and piss off and leave them alone?

The woman asked Duane to show her his room, and she completed her report by quizzing the boy at length, out of the way of his mother's continuous foul-mouthed interruptions. She noticed Duane's boots and footie kit folded neatly at the bottom of his bed.

'You like to play football, Duane?'

'Yeh.'

'They're a nice pair of clean boots. Did your mum buy you them?'

'Nah, Terry... er... Mr. Gallagher, me manager got me 'em.'

'Oh, did he?' she said with a spark of interest. 'So, you play for a team then? Tell me about it.'

Duane gave her the low-down on The Albion and the more he told her, the more intrigued she seemed to become, her pen never leaving her pad as she latched onto a subject Duane was more than happy to talk about.

At the end of the visit Duane had warmed to the woman who had appeared a bit starchy and aloof at the beginning. She had shown a genuine interest in his football and he hoped that might have deflected her attentions away from the other stuff. He thought the assessment had gone better than he could have hoped for.

'Have you any questions you would like to ask, Mrs. Caldwell?'

Caldwell stared at her with barely concealed contempt and blew smoke in her direction before dismissively shaking her head.

'Can I ask a question - please?' said Duane while nervously casting a glance over at his mam whose her eyes bore into him disapprovingly.

'Why, yes of course you can, Duane.'

'D'yer know where me bruvver is?'

The question seemed to take the social worker by surprise. 'Erm… I'm sorry, love, I don't at this moment in time,' she stuttered her reply, 'but you've no need to worry because I'm sure he's being well looked after.'

'Can yer find out, an' can I go an' see him?'

Duane's request had her totally flummoxed and she stuttered some more. 'Errm… I'm not sure that's possible at the moment, dear. Maybe when all the reports are drawn up and all the assessments are made. Once the situation has been reviewed, maybe we'll be able to sort something out…' she tailed off and nodded in a vaguely encouraging manner. Duane looked disappointed at her answer, and Caldwell aimed her best look of scorn at the woman whose feeling of awkwardness at being put on the spot was plainly obvious. '…Well,' she said finally, 'thank you both for your cooperation, and oh…er, good luck with your semi-final, Duane. We shall be in touch.'

'Thank fuck fer that. I thought she'd never go,' said Caldwell on hearing the door shut behind the departing social worker. 'What've yer done wi' t'phone, Duane?'

'What d'yer want t'phone for, mam?' he asked, although he knew full well why.

'Never you mind, just gimmee the fuckin' phone – an' don't you dare look at me like that,' she added viciously.

The look Duane was giving her was one of resigned disappointment. His shoulders slumped and he sloped off, reluctant but obedient to get it. He tossed the mobile into her lap and watched her fever-ishly tap in the all-important number. She looked daggers at him as she waited for the pick-up.

'Marco? It's me…' she said, and Duane turned sadly away at hearing the name of her dealer and shut himself away in his room. '…Yeh, yeh. How long? Yeh? Good, I'm fuckin' desperate…'

27

Terry was having a restless night. It was the eve before the day of the semi-final, but his tossing and turning in bed had nothing to do with pre-match nerves. He was having a dream, only it wasn't just a single dream but one of those multi layered metaphysical affairs, full of surreal and abstract links that seem to take you across fractured dimensions and leave you feeling exhausted once awake; where memories of the night's subconscious adventures become instantly patchy and ultimately fade away silently into the ether by the time you've taken your first yawn and stretch of the day. The odd thing about this particular dream was that it was a partial regression, a recurrence of something or at least somewhere he'd dreamt of before, and although he wouldn't remember the details, there would be something tapping away in the recesses of his mind over breakfast, something that would make him edgy, like an uneasy intellection of something pending, and that something wouldn't feel good.

Jan tutted as Terry's flailing arm caught her across the back of her head. He grunted, shuffled and turned over, falling restlessly into another diorama of his surreal slumber.

'God, you were fidgety last night,' said Jan, plonking another round of toast on the table. 'And you sweated like a pig,' she added. 'I've had to strip the bed this morning.'

'Probably down to that lump o' cheese I had before I hit the sack,' said Terry lowering his newspaper and taking a fresh piece of toast.

'Daad…'

Terry lowered his paper again. 'Yes, General Noriega.'

'You know when we've won the cup?'

'*When* we've won the cup – *when* we've won the cup – now that's the sort of positive attitude I *do* like to hear.'

'*If* we win the cup,' Rory corrected himself, 'what happens then?'

'We go into Europe,' said his dad taking a bite of toast

'Don't talk daft.'

'We go to t'pub and get hammered. What d'yer mean, what happens then?'

'Well, d'yer go into an higher league or owt?'

'Nope; it just means that we'll be the best team in the county at that age group.'

'But we're not even top of our league, are we?'

'Nope.'

'Can we still be top?'

'Nope. Looks like Farshaw'll be champions. We've an outside chance o' finishing third if we win us last two games.'

'But how can we be t'best team in t'county if we're not even top of our league?'

''Cos it's a cup competition,' explained Terry. 'It's like the FA Cup when sometimes you get non-league teams getting as far as t'fourth and t'fifth rounds by beating Premiership teams. It's called giant killing.'

'Yer mean like when Sunderland beat Leeds in seventy-three?'

Terry stopped chewing his toast. He didn't need reminding of that even though it was over thirty years ago, and despite him being only nine at the time. 'Er… yeah - sort of.'

Rory dipped a soldier into his egg and frowned, he began to look more like his dad every day whenever he did that; it was all these confusing little anomalies in life that did his head in, and he couldn't understand why people laughed at him whenever he asked these questions; like in cricket, why did they have to play all these test matches? When did they ever get down to the real thing? And how the hell do you raise a building to the ground? Same as the odd word he still couldn't pronounce, like umbrella. What was so funny? Underbrella sounded much better and at least described what you did with it.

'Da-ad.'

Terry lowered his paper some more and gave Rory a level look in anticipation of another unwelcome question.

'Who's this 'ere Noriega?'

Terry smiled. 'Noriega? He was a geezer from a place called Panama in South America, who had a face like a sieve and who turned out to be a bit of a bugger...'

'Is everybody on board?' Nobby shouted from the front of the bus.

'No, the Comanches aren't here yet,' came the reply from the back.

'They're here now,' said Peycos as Mackie's old black Golf came screeching round the corner into The Fusiliers car park.

'Where's Duane?' asked Terry when only two of them jumped out of the car.

'We woz gonna arks you ver same fing, man,' said Royston, worried. 'Ain't he here?' Terry shook his head. Royston turned to Mackie. 'He ain't here, innit.'

'Fuck's sake, Tee man, we waited ages for 'im on ver corner, din't we, bro?'

'Yeh, man, when he never showed after ten I went an' call on 'im. Finish up kickin' shit out ver door - raise noffin' but ver dead man.'

'We fought he must o' walked on early like, yer know whatta mean?'

'Shit, that's odd,' said Terry.

'Yeah, s'what we fought, innit,' said Royston. 'That bitch muvva never usually leave th' 'ouse, know warram sayin'?'

Terrry at once got an uneasy feeling and he pondered his options for a moment.

''Sup?' asked Nobby, joining the group.

'Duane's gone awol again,' said Terry. Royston and Mackie shrugged and nodded in confirmation.

'Marvellous,' stated Nobby. 'What we gonna do?'

'Give Kath a ring; see if he's turned up at yours.'

Nobby ran back to the bus for his mobile.

344

'What if he's not there, Tee?' asked Royston.

'Christ knows,' said Terry anxiously glancing at his watch.

Nobby came back a few moments later shaking his head. 'No, he's not there. Our lass sez she'll leave it as long as she can before her and Jan set off, just in case he shows.'

'Look, you lot get off or else you're gonna be late,' said Terry, finally making a decision.

'What you gonna do?' Nobby asked.

'I'll have a drive round in t'pickup; see if I can spot him.'

'We'll come wiv yer,' volunteered Royston.

'No, you two go on t'bus with Nobby, give him hand. Assistant managers 'til I get there, yeh?'

Their eyes lit up, chests swelling in honour. 'Sure fing, Tee, s'gonna be cool man, right?' assured Royston, offering Terry a consolidatory fist.

'Let's hope so,' said Terry feeling slightly stupid at having to clash knuckles. He gave Nobby the team sheet. 'If we're not back before you have to hand it in, put Duane down as a sub.'

Nobby took a glance at the sheet and noticed that Terry had left Joe out of the starting line-up. He very rarely, if ever, defied his mate, but he thought this particular decision was unfair. For whatever mistakes Joe had made in the past couple of games, he didn't deserve to be left out of the semi-final.

'*Sod it,*' Nobby thought to himself as he made his way back to the bus where the rest of The Albion were clamouring to know what was going on, '*I'm in charge now, so I make the decisions.*' Joe would be starting and he would face the consequences later.

'Mek sure you bring ver likkle fella back wiv yer, man,' shouted Mackie as he got on the bus.

Terry gave him a wave and the thumbs up, but he let out a deep and worried sigh as he did so. Duane had failed to show for various reasons in the past, but this time Terry felt it was different. Something wasn't right; he could sense it and he climbed into the pickup with a feeling of trepidation, clueless as to where he should begin his search.

'*This is stupid,*' Terry said to himself after a fruitless fifteen minutes of trawling the dingy avenues and back streets. He was wasting time. The County F.A's ground and headquarters, where the semi was due to be played, were almost an hour's drive away. If he was ever going to get to this game he would have to find Duane fast.

Terry parked the Trani and decided to head for the flat. Maybe Caldwell was playing silly buggers. Perhaps she might have sent Duane down to the shops when Royston called, deliberately making him late if she was that way out. Knowing her, she was unlikely to answer the door to anyone early on a Sunday morning.

Random thoughts were rattling around inside his head as he jogged along quiet, empty streets and across littered wasteland, past the spot where he first encountered Royston and Mackie and his crew, not least the fact that he was going to look a right pillock after taking Steve's advice and alerting half-a-dozen clubs to the promising youngster called Duane Geddess who would be playing for West Broughton Albion in the semi-final of the under fourteen's County Cup competition this Sunday.

He manoeuvred his way past a gruesomely stained old mattress and a discarded, bent wreck of a pushchair that were hampering his access through the doors of Cromwell House. The unwelcome but familiar stench of stale piss assaulted his nostrils again. He glanced up through the dank, murky hollow of the stairwell, maybe just to check there weren't about to be any missiles lobbed down at him, before reluctantly climbing the stairs.

All was quiet on the second floor landing until he broke the silence with a few hard wraps on the beleaguered blue door. He paused and listened while his knocks echoed away dying into the grim concrete walls - nothing. His second round of hammering was louder and made with his fists before trying to poke at the piece of cloth that hung at the back of the hole that served as a letterbox. He shouted through the aperture and thought he heard whimpering but he wasn't sure because his own shouts were bouncing back at him from all corners of the landing. He listened some more but it had all gone quiet again. Terry sensed that someone was in there and his senses were also combining to tell him that all was not well. Something wasn't right and he instinctively got to his feet and aimed a kick at the door.

'Duane! Are you there? Can you hear me?' Terry's echoed shout shocked him as it came back at him because it sounded desperate. He was. He aimed another kick at the already battered door that shook itself inside its jamb but nevertheless remained locked shut.

'I can fuckin' hear yer,' shouted an angry voice from somewhere up on the third floor. 'Give it a fuckin' rest or I'll come down there an' mek some fuckin' noise o' me own.'

One or two neighbouring doors opened slightly and frightened but inquisitive faces peered out through the gaps, only to quickly shut them back inside once they'd caught his eye. They were used to this sort of thing, especially on a Friday or Saturday night, but first thing on a Sunday morning was a bit much.

Undeterred, Terry launched himself shoulder first at the resilient piece of timber. It hurt but he thought he heard a slight splintering of wood. He launched himself again and he heard metal crashing across lino as the Yale gave out, but the door still stood firm. He gave his now bruised shoulder a rest and aimed another kick. This time his boot went through the outer skin, adding another hole to the otherwise tough old fire door. Working up a sweat, he now fired a volley of kicks that finally smashed away the sliding bolt and the door parted a few inches, only to be halted by the security chain that still stubbornly denied him entry. Terry backed off exhausted and slithered down the facing wall for a breather.

'Ho – Fuck-pig!' came the voice from upstairs. 'Have you gorra fuckin' deathwish or what pal?' Pack it in or you'll be eatin' 'ospital dinners for a fuckin' month. D'yer hear? Noisy cunt!' added the voice for good measure.

Terry leaned his head back against cold concrete and silently listened to the guy rant as trickles of perspiration ran down his face. He sat quiet for a while and heard nothing except for his heart pumping, the blood roaring and pulsing through his ears. Eventually, in the distance, somewhere on the third floor, a door slammed shut, a trigger for one last effort. Terry heaved himself up and threw himself at the stubborn barrier. The chain separated itself from its fixing, tearing away shards of wood from the disintegrating doorframe. He crashed through the threshold and the door swung wildly on its straining hinges.

He took a moment to gather himself, rubbing his sore shoulder that felt as if it might be bruised to the bone. The smell of the place brought back unwelcome memories and he immediately thought about Leo. He appeased himself with the knowledge that at least the kid had to be in better surroundings than this now. He wouldn't have to endure the beseeching eyes and the pleading, outstretched hands soiled with his own filth this time round.

'Duane?' he called tentatively. 'Duane?' he called out again, a little louder, hardly daring to move from the bare, damp hall. He accidentally kicked the busted Yale lock that went scurrying across the floor before smacking itself to a halt up against the skirting. He thought he heard the whimper again and he slowly edged his way towards the sound, into the room that still had the meagre curtains pulled across the window where a small shaft of light penetrated the gloom through a gap at the top where they didn't quite meet.

Then he saw her.

He froze stock still in shock. He'd been half expecting to come across something terrible, but the sight that confronted him still managed to stop him in his tracks. He tried to swallow but his saliva glands had stopped working and his sweat had started to dry cold on him. He peered into the half-light and held on to his breath. She was dead; he could see that. He inched his way into the room on feet that were reluctant to move until he could see her face, tipped back at a grotesque angle. One eye had settled up inside her head while the other, from behind a half-closed lid, stared out beyond him. Her head wasn't the right shape; it was puffed and swollen. Curiously, just one side of her face, the one that was turned away against shoulder and settee, had become a ghastly, grey-blue colour; heavy and deformed, like all fluid had drained and settled there from other parts that were now colourless, waxy. There was vomit from her mouth, dried and congealed in a reservoir between her neck and shoulder.

Terry held his sleeve up to his face and tried to breathe sparingly. At some point she had let go of all her bodily functions and the smell was unbearable. He recoiled and tried to stop himself gipping; in the process he knocked something off the coffee table. He stepped back and stooped to pick it up then stopped himself. In the gloom he could see it was a used hypodermic, the brown dregs of its deadly contents still visible inside the plastic cylinder. He edged away even more cautiously than he had entered the room, like he was stepping through a minefield.

A noise, a stifled sob told him he wasn't alone in the room and he turned to see Duane curled up against the wall at the back of the door, head tucked into his knees, rocking back and forth.

'Duane?' Terry uttered the name in a whisper that came out of his mouth half choked. He squatted down in front of the boy and was about to say, '*Are you okay?*' but he managed to stop himself. Idiot. Of course he wasn't okay. He held his shoulders and tried to lift his head to look into his face, but his body seemed locked into the rocking motion, his head remained down. Terry wasn't about to force him.

All the words that came into Terry's head, any utterances of comfort and sympathy seemed pointless, futile. Words were useless at this moment in time.

The kid hadn't acknowledged his presence. Discovering his mother like that had obviously sent him into deep shock. He rocked; slowly, rhythmically silently, save for the odd whimper, the occasional shuddering sob and he'd been like this now for the past two hours.

Terry eased himself alongside the youngster and carefully, ever so gently placed an arm around his slight shoulders. There they both sat, mute and motionless save for the cold comfort afforded by a soft embrace and the lamentable manifestation of the trauma brought on by shock - back and forth, back and forth.

Duane had risen that morning and performed his ablutions like he did every Sunday; a quick wash in cold water, climbed into his trackie bottoms and his Albion training top, into the kitchen, found a dish and a spoon that hadn't been left caked in shit for days, poured himself some rice krispies, a quick sniff of the milk, lucky there was still some left to be had, and he hadn't even cast a glance at the putrefying lump on the couch. His mother didn't usually come out of her catatonic state until after lunchtime anyhow, and never took kindly to having the moth-eaten curtains drawn back, where the reaction would be more alarming than that of any self respecting vampire.

It wasn't until he was getting ready to leave the house that he went to rouse her, just to see if she wanted a drink making before he left, and found her cold and lifeless.

He'd gone to bed early the previous night, not because he had an important game the next day, it was just to stay clear of his mother's dealer and part time pimp.

Marco had brought a punter round with him, a shady looking guy with piercing eyes and a predatory, hungry look about him, off his face on something or other. Duane had shut himself in his room out of the way and had wedged a chair up against the door just for good measure.

Marco and Caldwell had an arrangement. Whenever she was desperate for drug but couldn't afford it, he had a regular queue of customers lining up to slake their perverted lust on her wasted body. They would pay him, and the money, in turn, would pay for her fix.

Duane hadn't gone to sleep, he'd lain awake for hours, not thinking about the pending game and its outcome like most of the lads were probably doing; he'd thought about *them* and what *they* were doing: Peycos, Biscuit, Sully and Basher, no doubt still out on the streets, up to no good, bragging as to how they were going to annihilate the semi final opposition the next day, a team from the other side of Wakefield who went by the name of Panthers. '*Panthers?*' He could hear them taking the piss. '*What sort of a fuckin' name was that for a football team?*'

Ginner and Sasquatch, sat up well into the night, caning the old broadband, trawling the worldwide web for the most weird and bizarre sites they could find, and telling everybody on the bus in the morning of the strange, impious things that went on in the world. And what about Joe; would he be getting it on with Lisa down some darkened back alley, or would she have smuggled him in on some baby-sitting job, doing the business in front of the telly on somebody else's shag pile? Or would he be up at Young Nobby's fighting in lumps, knocking seven bells out of each other over something petty and trivial while Resident Evil played on the X-box?

Duane had an open invitation to stay over at the Clarkes' on a Saturday night. He'd only ever done it the once, when, ironically his mam had chosen to have a bad night and had been in a helpless, distraught state when he had come home after footie the next day and had implored, no, demanded that he never do it again. Saturday evenings were now spent at home, alone in his room.

He thought about his half-brother. He thought about him a lot. He hoped he was with a nice family and not in a home like he'd been one time. He dismissed his own bad memories and tried to picture Leo in a clean, warm house, surrounded by toys and people who took time to play with him, to give him a cuddle. Invariably, the picture that formed was always that of the Clarkes' terraced home and the people looking after Leo always turned out to be Kath and Nobby.

His thoughts had helped him while away the lonely hours, and before he settled down to go to sleep, he reached under the bed for one of the old footie mags Young Nobby had let him have, immersing himself in a Wayne Rooney profile in an effort to drown out the noise and the painful image of his mother being fucked by a stranger in the other room.

Terry stared blankly at the corpse opposite him on the settee. He'd been doing this for over ten minutes now, trying to put into motion some sort of thought process that just wasn't happening. It was all too surreal. Not a word had passed between Duane and himself, just the occasional sob or whimper, calmed by a reassuring hug.

Slowly, Terry's numbed emotions began to form. He hated that woman. Even in death he fucking hated her. How could she do this? Dying on the kid was bad enough, but why did she have to do it like this? Why did she have to find the most sordid and grotesque manner to exit her fucking worthless existence? Selfish, inconsiderate, callous bitch.

Out of the dingy shadows he could have sworn she was laughing at him, taking the piss - *pick the bits out of this mess you fuckers* - determined to leave behind her a lasting stain, an indelible mark of misery for those who had cared, for those who had depended and ultimately for those who had to pick up the pieces.

'I'm not going anywhere, son,' Terry said softly, 'I just need to make a phone call.' He eased himself up and away from the wall, leaving Duane in the same foetal position, rocking away without any reaction. He walked past the stinking body and silently wished it a rotting eternity in hell. He pulled out his mobile and went into the kitchen where there was more light and punched in three nines.

It took another phone call and thirty-five minutes for the emergency services to respond and the operator caught a volley of verbal the second time round; not because it was an emergency, it obviously wasn't any more, but it was typical; once he'd given them the location; East Broughton, Sunday morning, no rush, probably a hoax, get there when we can attitude. It all served to stoke up his mounting anger. He'd already written off the semi. The game would be half-over now anyway. That wasn't the reason, he told himself, and of course it wasn't entirely, but not being able to lead out and watch his lads was nagging at him and wasn't helping his mood.

The paramedics were first on the scene closely followed by the police, who, after seeing the circumstances brought in more police, then forensics arrived, and after about an hour the place was crawling.

Some geezer was dusting the area around the body while a photographer, who looked as if he was trying to impersonate David Bailey, clicked and flashed away from all angles with speedy efficiency; Terry half expected Caldwell to suddenly spring awake and strike a pose for the guy. Uniforms were flitting around clutching rolls of stripy barrier tape which they used to seal off the landing in order to keep out the inquisitive neighbours who, all of a sudden, had dared to venture from their holes to have a good old nosey. A uniformed policewoman led Duane's sorry figure temporarily out of the way into his bedroom, and Terry sat and watched it all with mounting impatience because over half an hour had passed since an officer had told him to sit there and someone would come and take a statement in a few minutes, and when finally someone did come to talk to him, a stroppy D.S. who had been looking forward to a steady Sunday morning shift and who obviously resented being there, he was full of the usual silly set of questions.

'…And were you known to the deceased, Terry?'

'No… Well, yes. I'd met her once before.'

'And was that in her, shall we say, her professional capacity?'

'What? No.' Terry looked incredulous. 'I've told you, I'm her son's football manager.'

'And the damage to the door,' said the officer scribbling away in his pad. 'You did it, you say?'

'Yes,' replied Terry, wearily.

'Why did you have to force entry if you were known to this woman?'

'Well she could hardly answer the fuckin' door herself, could she?'

D.S. stopped writing and glared up at Terry. 'There is no need to resort to bad language. I'm only trying to establish the facts and sequence of events,' he said in an annoyingly calm voice. He cocked his head to one side, poised his pen and raised his eyebrows in anticipation of further enlightenment from his witness.

'I couldn't get any response and I thought I could hear something inside.'

'And what was that exactly?'

'Like somebody crying. I just sensed that something wasn't right.'

'You sensed something,' he repeated and wrote without looking up.

'Yeah,' said Terry, 'so I forced the door.'

'So, you forced the door, and this is how you found Mrs... Mrs. Caldwell?' he said, checking his notes for the name.

'Yes.'

'Are you a drug user, Terry?'

Terry sighed. 'No, I'm not a drug user. Look, is any of this relevant? The woman was a junkie, she took too many drugs; she overdosed. She died.'

'And how do you know that's the case? Forensic expert are we?'

'It's not exactly rocket science, is it?' said Terry nodding in reference to all the evidence that was still lying around.

'No, but it is *a* science, and we have people who are experts in that field, so I think we'll leave that particular diagnosis to them, shall we? Speaking of which, is the doctor here yet, Millsy?' he called to a passing officer.

'Not yet, Sarge.'

D.S. turned back to Terry. 'Sunday morning,' he said screwing his face up. 'Not a good time is it?'

Another constable in an ill-fitting uniform, and who looked barely old enough to shave, approached. 'Bit more info, Sarge,' he said looking at his notes. 'Appears that another male, five-ten to six foot, Afro-Caribbean appearance, wearing multi-coloured knitted headwear tried to gain entry to the premises earlier in the day, approximately between nine-thirty and ten a.m.'

'That'll have been Royston or Mackie,' interrupted Terry.

D.S. looked up straight away. 'Royston Morrison and Jerome Mackie - you're acquaintances of these two?' he asked surprised.

'Yeah, well, I just know 'em, as Royston an' Mackie,' said Terry. 'They pick Duane up on Sundays and give him a lift to games.'

'Games?'

'Football games,' said Terry exasperated. 'I told you. I manage a football team. The youngster plays for my team, West Broughton Albion. He should've been playing in a semi-final this morning. He didn't show, so the guys call for him, get no answer, we wonder why, we get worried, I come looking for him, sense something isn't right, break down the door; mother dead, kid in bits, I phone you guys, you show up when you feel like it.' Terry looked at his watch. 'An hour and a half later I'm still here, and then you start asking all these daft questions.' Terry folded his arms and sat back on the uncomfortable and not so sturdy kitchen chair. D.S. observed Terry with the degree of contempt his official position allowed him.

'Your attitude really isn't helping matters, Terry. Like I've said, I'm only trying to establish the facts. I don't want to be here any longer than you do, but if you don't cooperate, then that process is likely to take all day and I'm quite prepared to wait that long, or however long it takes, until I'm satisfied that I've got all the facts in a manner and an order that I'm happy with. Is that clear?'

Terry raised his eyes to the ceiling. 'What else would you like to know, Sergeant?'

'Let's start with your relationship with our friends Mr. Morrison and Mr. Mackie, shall we…?'

Terry told the officer all he knew about Royston and Mackie which really wasn't much; just a couple of guys who followed his team around and enjoyed watching the skills of young Duane Geddess. He wasn't even going to begin to try and explain to the copper why they did that, and he hadn't even been able to confirm their full names because he didn't know them, so the policeman said he'd enlighten him on the illegal activities of The Albion's most celebrated supporters, just so that he knew the type of company he was mixing with. When he'd finished reeling off a list of past misdeeds and assorted felonies, Terry was neither shocked nor impressed. He didn't care what it was they did to keep their heads above water, or what they'd been convicted of, as long as it didn't involve selling drugs to kids; which he knew they didn't, and as long as what they did didn't affect The Albion, he wasn't bothered. And as for supplying shit to Duane's mam, well if that's what the D.S. was suggesting then he was way off the mark and Terry told him so.

The Sergeant had that unconvinced look about him all through the rest of the interview, like he thought that his interviewee knew more than he was letting on and it was beginning to really annoy an already pissed off Terry. The guy was a fucking idiot, acting all Miss Marple when he should be out on the streets sorting out the shot lickers. People like Caldwell were beyond redemption. She never wanted a cure. In Terry's opinion she got what was coming to her anyway. It was only a matter of time. She'd spun the chamber and pulled the trigger - unlucky this time; sorry love, no second chances. She knew the odds and didn't give a fuck about the consequences. Doctor Terry's verdict: assisted or self-inflicted overdose. Case open, case closed. But for whatever reason Perry Mason felt different; or maybe he was just trying to pan his shift out, work up a nice lump of overtime for himself and the boys, making sure that being dragged out of the station on a Sunday was going to be made worth his while.

Duane was finally led away to a waiting panda car, past pockets of rubber-necking flat dwellers pointing and tutting and swapping theories, creating Chinese whispers until versions of the morning's events had been embellished beyond reason.

A doctor eventually put in an appearance, another inconvenienced soul, annoyed at being dragged off the golf course even though he was supposed to be on call. He breezed in, pronounced Caldwell dead, had a quick chat with D.S. and breezed out again, come and gone inside ten minutes.

It took a small army of police and paramedics to stretcher the body awkwardly down the two flights of stairs and into a waiting ambulance, and pretty soon the flat was quiet and empty again save for the baby-faced constable, the Sergeant and Terry, doing his best to remain cool while, inside, he silently seethed as he watched the bloody-minded copper write seemingly endless notes. He was sure the bastard was doing it on purpose, keeping him hanging around as long as he could, making his point - sanctimonious fucker. That's what you get for telling it like it is. They were all the same. There's no getting the better of these boys. Terry's eyes bore into him and at last he deemed to raise his head from his scribbling as if he knew he'd tested this bloke's patience to the limit, sensing the pressure cooker atmosphere that was likely to explode any second.

He looked up nonchalantly and pretended to look all surprised that Terry was still there.

'Right then,' he said dismissively and as casual as you like, 'off you go.'

At that moment Terry was dangerously close to committing assault. 'Is that it?'

'Yes - that is unless you've anything to add to what you've already told us.' Terry got to his feet and headed for the door. 'Er, we may need you to come down to the station in the next few days, just to dot a few Is, cross a few Ts, sign a statement, that sort of thing – oh, and if you see Mr. Morrison and Mr. Mackie before we do, let them know we'll be getting in touch.'

Terry laughed scornfully at the copper's cheek and got out of the place as quick as he could. He passed the joiner on the stairs, on his way to board up the door and secure the flat. He felt like telling him not to bother, he was wasting his time. As soon as the fly-be-nights got wind there was an empty flat they would be in like a shot to make doubly sure that it was. But they'd be left disappointed; there was nothing worth nicking in there. The tradesman whistled a happy tune in time to the beat his footsteps were sounding out up the steps. '*Cheery fucker.*' thought Terry, and why not: emergency call out, Sunday afternoon, double time. Nice work if you can get it. It seemed like anyone could create a nice little earner from a tragedy.

Terry ducked under a line of barrier tape that had been left strung across the entrance to Cromwell House. Small pockets of hard-line gossipers were still hanging around and heads turned and stared and gossiped some more as they watched him walk away. He took a deep breath but the air wasn't any fresher than it had been inside. It was another grey, typically damp East Broughton day and he wondered if the sun had ever shone on this place. His shoulder was killing him. He performed a few neck-rolls and stretches as he walked to try and alleviate the stiffness of having sat around for two hours.

'Who yer lookin' fer this time, mush?'

Terry looked down to see the snot-nosed little scruff who had blagged the tenner off him all those months ago. He was sitting astride his bike that he'd managed to turn into a chainless, battered

357

wreck and he propelled it with the same knackered old plimsolls that he'd been wearing on their first encounter. He wobbled alongside, looking up enquiringly, displaying his perpetual septum caked, semi-molten Vesuvius flow of snot.

'I'll tell yer where they live for a tenner.'

'Not this time, fella.'

'Tell yer what,' the kid persisted, 'call it a fiver seein' as you're an old customer.'

Terry would normally have chuckled at the youngster's sass but now was not a good time. He ignored him and carried on walking.

'Fiver's a good deal, innitt, chor? Wassa marra wi' yer?'

'I aren't looking for anybody.'

This didn't deter the youngster, and he stubbornly push-pedalled along in Terry's wake.

'Gi' us a fiver anyway. I found yer that other kid, din't I? Go on mush, gi' us a fiver. Go on, don't be tight; a fiver's not much is it? – Orr, go on, gi' us…'

'Fuck off!!'

Terry had continued on his way before the shell-shocked spraffer had recovered from the verbal blast that had stopped him in his tracks and almost knocked him off his bike.

'Miserable cunt!' the lad shouted after him as a parting shot. Not such an easy touch this time, but always worth a try. He gave a little shrug, turned his bike around and ran with it to gain some momentum before jumping on and freewheeling down a slope.

Nine-year-old extortionists - stupid, bloody-minded coppers – users – dealers - human fucking baggage. Terry tried to hawk up a spit-ball and and fleg out the poison he felt was washing around inside him but his mouth was dry and only the tiniest pellet of spittle hit the pavement. The poison stayed put. All thinking and reasoning was banished. It was the only way to keep the anger in check, keep the rising emotions at bay. He had to block out the scenarios that were straining to take stage in his head; the little plays that wanted to enact things as they should have been and not how they were. He battled with the M.C. in his brain, outwardly manifested by the grinding of his teeth. His exiled thoughts were hammering on a locked door that was struggling to remain shut. He walked.

In his self-imposed fatuous state he was oblivious to the four figures that watched him from across the street. Capped and hooded, they shadowed him, silently, furtively, checking him out like they were stalking prey. Not much stood them apart from your local bunch of charvers except that they were maybe slightly scruffier, if that were at all possible, and they had darker, dirty looking skin.

'Hey!' one of them shouted. He got no response. 'Hey!' he shouted again removing himself from the pack and slowly wandering across the road. 'Hey, don't ignore me, my friend.'

The voice wasn't English and although the tone wasn't aggressive it had an undertone of menace about it.

'Hey, maybe you wanna do business, yeah?'

The guy stepped in front of Terry and back-pedalled as he spoke. He looked Eastern European, probably Albanian or from somewhere around that neck of the woods. There were a lot of them on the streets of East Broughton these days. He was of a similar height and build to Terry and had dark, close-set eyes that sat beneath brows that were thick and almost met. He was probably in his mid to late twenties but the permanent five o'clock shadow made him look older and added to the Machiavellian demeanour. Terry hadn't noticed any of this, or if he had he ignored it. He walked on vacantly as if the bloke wasn't there.

'What's your choice, my friend? Whatever you want, I got. You like Charly? I got rocks, Asda price for you – no? I got some brown, Afghani special, nice an' pure, not cut with shit, I guarantee. Hey, hey, stop one moment, I show you...' he put his arm out to try and halt Terry's progress while he fiddled inside his jacket. Terry brushed him aside without breaking stride. 'Ohh! Ohh! Wassa marra wi' you, silent man? You been on the marchin' powder I think, no?'

Terry saw sanctuary. The pickup came into his view on the other side of the road but was quickly obscured by the fool who was dancing around in front of him trying to bar his way.

'Wos your problem, mister – you can't speak or something? You dumb mother fuckin' bitch.' The guy's failure to communicate was making him agitated and he started to gesticulate and wave his arms about in front of Terry's face. 'Hey, we got a *shurdhmemec* here,' he shouted to his three mates who laughed and shouted something funny back in *Gheg*. They closed in, intrigued by a *budalla* who wouldn't even open his mouth to say no thanks, go away, or fuck off. Maybe they could have some fun here. If he wasn't a punter looking to score, perhaps they could relieve him of some *leke* he was carrying anyway.

'Hey *zoti* - heloo,' he taunted like he was talking to a simpleton. 'You been sucking too many cocks, mister? Somebody take your tongue?' He stuck out his own and drew an imaginary knife across it. 'Hey, we got a cock sucker here.' He grabbed his crotch and pulled a face like a mad Mauri performing the Hakka. His mates gruff-gurgled with amusement. Terry walked. The guy got nasty. 'Wassa marra, dumb fuck? You don't like a joke, eh?' He tried to halt Terry with a push in the chest. 'Mebee you find it funny if an I cut off your prick as well an' shove it up your arse, eh?' He produced a small lock-back knife and bared the blade. His eyes flashed and he grinned, certain of provoking a reaction now. He got none. 'You don't talk still? Mebbee I make you squeal instead.' He moved forward menacingly.

Inside Terry's head electrons had started to collide. That little old devil was dancing a jig, ripping out nerve endings and slamming them together creating cerebral fission. The grin had been the trigger. That sickly stomach turning grin of pure evil, and it was about to detonate a reservoir of suppressed anger that would meet his persecutor, this purveyor of misery, this peddler of death with a force that would be both relentless and remorseless, a rage without pity or mercy. The locked door was about to yield. Wood splintered, metal bent and a million issues roared through his senses. Hate riding triumphant on the crest of a wave and the devil chortled insane as the sparks ignited and blew the little demon into oblivion.

The force of the blow was super-human but the accompanying guttural snarl was pure animal. The guy with the blade knew very little as he stepped onto the punch that simultaneously broke his jaw and lifted him off his feet. His head hit the road with a sickening crack and the knife flew out of his grasp. He wasn't ever going to get up from that, and Terry made sure he wouldn't. He was on to him in a millisecond, straddled his chest, raised the bastard's head by the scruff and slammed it back into the tarmac - and again - and again - and again, until he went all limp and rag-like and his eyes rolled up into the back of his head, but Terry wasn't about to relent. He set about pummelling the now lifeless features with his fists in a sustained frenzy. Flecks of spit formed in the corners of his mouth and his eyes blazed wild.

'Laugh – now – cunt! – Not – fuckin' – grinnin' – now – bastard...!'

The first kick sent a searing pain through his body but the adrenalin ignored it and he maintained his assault. The second boot landed in the same area and he felt his ribs go. The third boot came from the other side, caught him in the side of the head and knocked him clear of his victim. His skull chimed, and with every short, sharp gulp of air, stabbing pains shot across his chest. The force of the connection sent him reeling but his reactions were still quick enough to prevent another swinging kick from smashing into his face. His left forearrn deflected the shot and with his right hand he caught hold of the back of the heel and gave it a sharp twist with all that he had left in him. His attacker let out a piercing scream as the cruciate and surrounding ligaments snapped, and he fell to the floor writhing in agony, cursing in his mother tongue. Terry took another hit to the kidneys and it was like somebody had applied the brakes. He fell into treacle and did his best to counter the flurry of kicks and blows that now rained down on him from the two adversaries still left standing. He felt himself start to go under as his resistance weakened. Everything went distant and slo-mo. He still heard voices, raised and angry but they seemed way off, miles away now. His vision was a kaleidoscope of blurring flashes and when he closed his eyes he felt himself falling, like the cold, damp tarmac had opened up and swallowed him, and he fell into darkness, down, down, and he smelled ether, like the laughing-gas dentist had just placed the hazy yellow rubber mask over his face, and everything began to swirl, round and round and the voices got caught up in the swirl and they came and went in waves and surges like he'd entered bedlam on bad acid. Then he landed on a bed of cotton wool, and somewhere inside his ringing head his senses picked up on a distant memory. The smell of ether gave way to one of frying onions and greasy hamburgers. He heard police horse hoofs on hard, beleaguered roads, batons being swung and heads being cracked and the Zulu-like tribal chant of Leeds! – Leeds! – Leeds!. He opened his eyes and the leering face of a number two cropped East-End docker flicked a calling card in his face. *'Congratulations you norvern cant – You just fackin' met Millwall.'* He saw the flash of a cherry-red, but felt nothing. The Bushwacker disappeared and was immediately replaced by a shaven headed monstrosity. Face and head beetroot red and raw, skin peeling in large flaky layers, veins and arteries pulsing purple, fit to burst behind an armoury of bling that hung heavy from a neck as thick as an elephant's leg. The stink of onions gave way to a gut wrenching smell of back axles and B.O. Bulldog Mason's yellowing string vest overflowed with festering body secretions and rank sweat dripped through the holes into his face. His laughter rang hoarse and loud as he bayed into the sky like the dog he was. Nicotine chipolata fingers formed a steam hammer fist, and in the background, the snide psychotic Sanchez urged on his Fuhrer. *'Do him! – Do him! – Shoot him! – Fuckin' shoot him!'* He felt nothing; not even the cold barrel of steel that was being held to his head, but he saw the Japanese soldier who was now holding the other end of the rifle and whose savage screaming had a moment ago been the sound of Bulldog Mason's manic laughter. *'Hoorudoappu! Hoorudoappu!'* the little yellow man in jungle fatigues barked frantically, jabbing the barrel at his temple. *'Hoorudoappu! Hoorudoappu!'* he screamed and slid the bolt back and a bullet click-snapped into the breach. Terry looked up from his bed of cotton. The little guy was urging him to do something but he didn't know what. He didn't speak Japanese. He didn't have any hand grenades. He didn't have a kukri he could flash and fling into the chest of his would be executioner. There was no Herbert Johnson he could call on to come and rescue him in his hour of need; he was dead. Stan Willis was at Monte Casino and Captain Hurricane was just a fictional character from a kid's comic. He laughed softly to himself and allowed his head to rest against cold steel. If death was to come, he wanted it to come now. He was tired, so tired. He looked up into the soldier's face to urge him to pull the trigger, he just wanted to sleep, but the Jap had gone and in his place, now holding a pistol to his head and shaking with fury was a crazy looking Albanian drug dealer.

'Mirupafshim debil' he hissed.

Terry squeezed his eyes shut and waited for the end...

'Drop der fuckin' gun, mo-fo!'

The guy holding the pistol to Terry's head now had a Berretta held to his. Mackie's voice went up an octave. 'I said drop der mother fuckin' gun, bitch, unless youse wants yo brains spread across der street!' Not daring to move his head, the guy's eyes flicked around in their sockets glancing over to his mate, uncertain of what to do. Mackie got fidgety. 'Ya feel lucky, bitch? – Do ya? – Fuckin' try me, bro. Drop der fuckin' gun!'

Royston was positioned close to the other guy ready to pounce on any sudden movement. The bloke looked jittery and kept the lock-back that he'd picked off the road well hidden up his sleeve. Stand-off. Royston's eyes flitted sharply back and forth. His mate had slipped comfortably into his South-Bronx gangsta mode, and he watched his performance with nervous admiration, but he was sure he'd heard those lines before somewhere, and he'd have probably taken the piss if all this didn't look so serious.

The Albanian slowly eased the gun away from Terry's semi-conscious figure and dropped it to the ground. Mackie kicked the pistol, skidding away across the road, like he'd seen in the movies a hundred times. He'd always wanted to do that and it felt great. 'Okay, now back off.' Mackie motioned with his .38 and the guy carefully did as he was told. Totally in charge now and wallowing in the power and subservience a piece could command he started to strut his stuff. He stepped around the geezer with the shattered leg who was whimpering and squirming about on the floor. There would be no bother from him. Seeing Terry was in a bad way, he motioned over to Nobby who'd been standing back, bewildered at the unfolding scene 'Get him outta here, bro.'

Nobby moved in to assist his mate and couldn't help but stare at the prone figure of the guy who was laid out on his back staring at the sky, and at the dark patch of red that was soaking into his hood and the surrounding piece of road.

Terry came to and saw two big, strong muscular arms fit under his own. He winced with pain as they locked together against his chest. '*Fuckin' hell,*' he thought, '*It's Captain Hurricane; he does exist after all.*' Then he saw the blue and old gold crest with the legend: '*L.U.F.C League Div.1 Champions. 1990-91*' tattooed on a forearm. He just about managed a smile before he passed out again.

Nobby lugged his buddy over to the pickup and laid him out across the passenger seats. Mackie told him to get out of it sharpish. He and Royston would deal with this shit. He had everything under control. He told one of the Albanians to keep the beefing cripple quiet and ordered the other to hand over his mobile. He complied only after Mackie told him he was losing his patience and levelled the shooter at him again. He held the phone in the sleeve of his hoody and started to tap in three nines with the tip of the gun, but before he made the connection, a siren sounded in the distance. Mackie smashed the phone to the floor where it disintegrated. He took the heel of his boot to the bits that remained intact. Someone had already called the law.

'This dude don't look too good,' said Royston crouching over Terry's first victim. Mackie went over and peered down at the guy who stared motionless right back at him. He got a bit closer and waved the gun in front of his face.

'That because he brown bread, man,' stated Mackie like he came across dead people every day of the week.

'Jeesus, holy mother fuckin' shit,' said Royston.

'Watch out fer der red stuff, man,' Mackie warned Royston clear of the ever-widening pool of blood at his feet.

They both stepped away from the body and Mackie turned to call one of the Albanians over, but they'd heard the siren and were already legging it down the street, hampered by their injured brother who was haplessly hopping along using his mates as crutches.

'Hey!' shouted Mackie, raising his gun at the fleeing trio.

'Leddem go, man,' hissed Royston forcing Mackie's arm down, 'we need to get outta here quick-style, bro.'

Mackie watched the Albanians disappear round a corner and then he scoured the scene to make sure there was no evidence of them or Terry having been there. He left the pistol where he'd kicked it lying in a gutter a few yards away.

People had witnessed the fracas and some still watched from street corners or from the balustrades of nearby flats. To these observers Mackie pointed with great deliberation, then put two fingers up to his eyes and held the gun in the air. He was saying that he'd seen each and every one of them and he knew who they were. Royston and Mackie were faces around there. They were Spangla's lieutenants and that would be enough to buy the required silence.

'C'mon, man, let's go fer fuck's sake,' screamed Royston from the open doors of the Golf. He revved the engine impatiently as the sound of the siren got closer. Mackie tucked the piece into his belt and ran to the waiting car.

Spectators slowly melted away, and by the time the panda arrived at the scene, the street was deserted save for the body of a dead immigrant lying in the middle of the road with the back of his head stoved in.

28

"Chronic remorse, as all the moralists are agreed, is a most undesirable sentiment. If you have behaved badly, repent; make what amends you can and address yourself to the task of behaving better next time. On no account brood over your wrongdoing. Rolling in the muck is not the best way of getting clean."

Terry concurred, at least with the first and last part of Aldous Huxley's statement. What he thought about the repenting bit, he wasn't sure. Most of his feelings and emotions lay dead or dormant inside him. Numb. The psychological anaesthetist had been to work on him and he felt nothing, not even about the probable and serious consequences of his actions, which, for the most part, were still a blur. He got flashbacks, like little pieces of x-rated jigsaw puzzle, but none of them fit. He wasn't able to sequence the events after he'd left Cromwell House, hadn't been able to tell Jan or Nobby or any of the others exactly what had gone down, but they all knew that someone had died and Terry, although he couldn't remember everything, knew he was responsible. The weird thing was he didn't give a shit, and he wasn't worried that he didn't give a shit. The only thing that had bothered him over these past three days was the pain and discomfort from his injuries, and of course the concern for Duane; at least that part of last Sunday remained crystal clear in his mind.

He gingerly reached across the bed and read to himself the report from Monday night's paper for around the tenth time. The incident hadn't even made the front page. Although murder wasn't a daily occurrence in East Broughton, gangland and drug related executions weren't uncommon and rarely commanded banner headlines these days. They were treating it as unlawful killing but, reading it again, still failed to stir any feelings of fear, guilt, or remorse. Nothing.

He also knew nothing of the frantic discussions that had taken place at the foot of his bed and in his front room, lasting well into the previous Sunday evening.

He'd looked in a bad way and Jan and Kath had wanted to get him straight to the hospital. Royston and Mackie had been adamant. It wasn't a good idea. If they didn't want him implicated in all this, best wait until the heat had died down. Nobby could see how frantic Jan was at the sight and state of her fella, but he knew that Terry's saviours were right. Terrified of the consequences, Jan reluctantly agreed to wait until the middle of Monday before they took him to casualty. They concocted a story about him falling from a tree he was pruning while at work and in doing so, hoped no one would make the connection to Sunday's incident. That night Jan pumped him full of as many painkillers as she dared and stayed up by his side keeping a close and fearful watch over him until morning came.

Apart from a mass of cuts and bruises, a lot of which, once he'd been cleaned up, didn't look half as bad as they had when Jan first clapped eyes on him, amazingly, scans and x-rays revealed just two broken ribs, mild concussion, a fractured thumb and a battered kidney that was still causing him to piss blood. Nobody at the hospital questioned the story. Again, the only thing that was of concern to Terry was that he was told to stay off work for at least four weeks. He'd never been on the sick in his life, and the thought of having to mooch around the house for a month really pissed him off. The other thought of probably having to spend a lot more time than that in a prison cell never really entered his head.

Terry threw the newspaper to one side, opened *Brave New World* at chapter one and began to read. He'd barely got beyond the first page when Jan came racing up the stairs and burst into the room in a mad panic.

'There's a really scruffy bloke at the door asking for you.' She'd gone drip white and was shaking like a leaf.

'Well who is it?' asked Terry as calm as you like.

'Says his name's Smiffy and he really needs to see you urgent.'

Terry tutted, raised his eyes to the ceiling and wearily put his book down. 'Well, I suppose you'd best show him up then.'

Jan looked at her husband as if he were still badly concussed.

'Oh, Terry, are you sure? I don't like the look of him one bit.'

'Not many people do,' he said dryly. 'It's okay, love, I know him; you can send him up.'

'God, you know some odd people. You make me wonder sometimes.' She went back downstairs shaking her head and reluctantly let him in. Smiffy thanked her with a '*Ta, love,*' and treated her to the infamous cavernous grin. It scared her to death, and as she nervously watched him amble up the stairs, she wondered just what the hell it was her husband had got himself caught up in.

'Tel, me old cocker, long time no see. How's ya diddlin?' Smiffy-No-Teef plonked himself down on the edge of the bed without waiting for the invitation. He offered his hand, then withdrew it again when he saw Terry's heavily strapped thumb.

'I've been better, Smiffy. To what do I owe this unexpected pleasure?'

'Brought yer vees, charver, fought vey might cheer yer up a bit.' He reached into his shell suit and threw a bag of weed and a porno mag onto the bed.

Terry took a despairing look at the copy of *Mature Cum-loving Sluts* and groaned. 'For fucks sake, Smiffy, you shouldn't have done.'

Smiffy shrugged modestly. 'Least I could o' done, chor.'

'No, I mean it, yer daft pillock. You shouldn't have done. What's the wife gonna say if she sees this lying around?'

'Dunno. Don't she like a bit o' porno?'

Terry looked at him askance before giving up and shaking his head. 'What're you really here for, Smiffy, and how did you know I was confined to me bed?'

'Vere's not a lot vat goes on round 'ere vat gets past me, Tel, yer should know vat... It's like vis va sees...' Smiffy was keen to get quickly down to business and he went straight into his hushed, conspiratorial mode; looking around the bedroom as if there might be certain people he didn't want listening in, lurking in the wardrobe. '...I've had a visit...' Terry raised his eyebrows, that is, he managed to raise one of them, as the other was a mangled lump of flesh with four stitches in it. He urged Smiffy to continue '…I've had a visit from Mister Spangla's Yardie boys,' he hissed.

'Who?' Terry asked innocently.

Smiffy fired off a look that reminded Terry of James Findlayson, that browbeaten little actor in the old black and white Hal Roach movies.

'Nah don't fuck abaht wi' me, Tel boy – you know who I mean.'

Terry shook his head. Smiffy sighed. 'Fing is, chor, his goons have been round an' started leanin' heavy like. Freatened to fire me plants, said vey were gonna torch ver buildin' an' it's all to do wiv some shit what went down last Sunday.'

'So what's it to do with you?'

'Noffin' man, but vey seemed pretty desperate to keep it quiet. Vey know I'm ver eyes an' ears around here. Wanted to find out how much I knew.'

'And?'

'All as I know is a fugee gorris head smashed in; don't know why, an' I'll swear blind I don't know who by.' He paused and gave Terry a funny little look. 'It's not just me, Tel, all ver uvver boys on ver estate have had visits, an' when mister Spangla starts frowin' his weight around you'd berrer comply wiv whatever it is he's askin', believe me. Ver man wants total hush on vis one.'

'Sorry to keep sounding so thick, Smiffy, but what's all this got to do with me?'

Smiffy leant back and puffed out his hollowed cheeks. He looked Terry straight in the eye. 'How d'yer come by vem injuries, charver?'

Terry sent the look straight back. 'Fell out of a tree.'

'Yeh, an' I just fell of a fuckin' log…'

At that moment, Jan poked her head round the door and stopped the conversation dead. 'Er… would anyone like a cup o' tea?'

Terry shook his head.

'Aye, I'll have a brew, love,' grinned Smiffy horribly. 'Plenty o' milk an' just four sugars, I'm tryin' to cut down, yer know.' He brazenly looked her up and down making her flesh crawl and then leeringly watched her leave the room. 'Nice woman, your missus,' he said turning back to Terry, 'very nice. Now, where was we…?'

They both participated in a bout of verbal sparring for the next twenty minutes with Smiffy firing off innuendos without actually making any clear accusation, Terry deflecting and feigning ignorance and admitting to nothing. Smiffy told him how hard it was being banged up for long periods. Terry told him he could imagine, but, '*If yer does the crime, yer does the time.*' he countered with a smile.

Smiffy was puzzled by this one. He couldn't get his head round why somebody like Terry Gallagher would be mixed up with immigrant shot lickers and powerful West Indian syndicates, but he knew that somehow he was, and that he wasn't about to about to give anything away, not a sausage.

'Look, let's cut yer bullshit,' said Smiffy eventually. 'I know you had summat to do wi' vis.'

'Prove it,' said Terry totally non-fazed.

'Don't get me wrong Tel; I'm not out to prove owt. Between you an' me, ver less vere are o' vees buggers on t'streets ver better it'll be fer all of us.'

'So, what is it yer want from me?'

'Your trust.'

'How's that?'

'If ver law ever does come knockin' on yer door, I want yer to know it won't have come from me, but more important is I need yer to let Spangla an' his crew know vat. I'm mekin' a nice livin' for meself now, chor, I don't want to see me dreams go up in smoke…' He paused, realising what he'd just said. '…Well, I do, but not like vat if yer know what I mean. I just need yer to tell 'em to lay off. I know you've got ver clout.'

Terry thought for a while. He didn't have a clue where Smiffy had got this perceived notion about him having gangland connections, but he decided to go along with it.

'If I do this for you,' he said eventually, 'I want you to try and do summat for me.'

'I'll do me best, yer know vat.'

'What do you know about wartime memorabilia?'

'What, yer mean guns an' swords, fings like that?'

'Medals.'

Smiffy rubbed his chin. 'Somefing in particular?'

'A Victoria Cross, but not just any VC. The one I'm looking for has a certain inscription on the back.' Terry reached for pen and paper off the bedside table and wrote something down. 'It's got something like that on it,' he said handing over the scrap of paper. 'I need to know if it's still in the area.'

'None o' vis has owt to do wi' Spangla, has it?' Smiffy asked worried.

'No, I swear.'

'Why do yer...' began Smiffy. Terry cut him short.

'No questions. I need you to be discreet.'

Smiffy took the note and stuffed it in his shell suit. 'I'll see what I can do, chor.' He took a noisy slurp of tea. 'Ahh, just what ver doctor ordered,' he said with his big toothless grin.

'Who the hell was that?' asked Jan as she emptied almost half a can of air freshener into the room after Smiffy's departure.

'He's the geezer that flogged us the footie kit. He came to ask us a favour.'

Terry left it at that; he didn't want Jan getting embroiled and any more upset than she already was. She had it in her head that Terry must have been attacked and that he'd acted in self-defence, and that this person's death was nothing more than a tragic accident, and that if he'd only go to the police she was sure it could all be sorted out. What she didn't know was that Terry's amnesia was selective, and although he genuinely couldn't remember details, he knew that he'd killed a man in an unbridled rage. Maybe he could provide a strong case for diminished responsibility, but the regrets simply weren't there, and under the same set of circumstances he might - no, he was certain that he'd do exactly the same again.

'And what sort of favours does he think you can dish out in your state?' she scoffed while opening a window to let some fresh air in.

'You'd be surprised,' he said cryptically.

Jan turned from the window and looked at her husband wistfully. Fate. It had only needed Nobby and the others to turn up a few minutes later and she might now be gazing at an empty bed. She shivered at the thought, and her mind wandered back to three days ago when Nobby had dragged him seemingly half dead to her door. At first she thought he'd been in a road accident, and the sight of him had almost made her pass out. They'd laid him out on the settee and Nobby was only able to tell Jan as much as he'd witnessed. Terry, in his semiconscious state kept mumbling *'She's dead'* and *'They've taken Duane away'* and when Royston and Mackie had shown up they kept jabbering on about dead Albanian fugees and shooters and the need to lay low. Her head had been fit to explode with the nightmarish confusion of it all, and she was sure she would have had a bout of hysterics had it not been for Kath showing up and calming her down. Her only consolation that afternoon had been managing to get him upstairs to bed, out of the way before the lads had come home. She didn't want them seeing their dad like that and she would work out a story later.

As Terry's head had hit the pillow, his swollen eyes had opened and focused hazily on his mate.

'Did we win?' he managed to croak.

'Two - one. Penalty, dying minutes – Joe scored it.'

Terry allowed himself a hint of a smile before he closed his eyes and went comatose again.

Typical, she remembered thinking at the time, people are dead or lucky to be alive and all he can think about is who won a bloody football match.

Jan now watched her man propped up against his pillows looking a bit battered, but amazingly perky considering all. She offered up a silent prayer of thanks for his deliverance, scarcely believing how calm and seemingly unaffected he was by all this. And he had to admit to himself that inside he felt buoyed by the fact that someone, somewhere behind the scenes, was pulling strokes for him. The only thing that was worrying him now was how he was going to get rid of an obscene publication and a bag of smelly skunk that were at that moment stuffed out of sight under Jan's pillow.

29

'Personally, I prefer 'em mature,' said Nobby leafing the pages of Smiffy's get well present and cocking his head to one side to get a better perspective of the more bizarre sexual positions that were on show. 'Yer can't beat a bit of experience. Ooof! Look at that. Every orifice. Go on girl.'

'D'yer mind,' said Terry, 'I've just had me dinner,'

'You know what your trouble is don't yer? You're a prude,' said Nobby without waiting for an answer.

'Aye, and I'll be a prude without a pair o' bollocks if our lass catches me with that. Just make sure you get it out the house without her seeing it.'

'Warrabout the dope?'

'Yeah, that as well. It bloody stinks.'

Nobby put the offending items into the carrier bag that contained his lunchbox and looked for somewhere to sit that wouldn't get soiled by his work pants and have Jan after him. He had splashes of what looked suspiciously like blue paint all over him, on his clothes, his hands, and even in his hair. Terry looked his mate up and down and wondered what on earth he'd been up to but couldn't be arsed to ask.

'Mrs. Sanderson was askin' after yer; sez she hopes you feel better soon.'

'Very kind of her,' said Terry.

'So, how are you feelin', yer bad lad?'

'Alrate. Ribs are still a bit sore, and there's still spots o' blood in me piss, but apart from that I feel fine.'

'Good. So what did Smiffy want? Can't have been a social call.'

Terry told Nobby about the persuasive and advisory council that had been offered to all the rogue elements on and around the Broughton estates.

374

'He was shittin' it. Kept going on about yardies and a character called Spangla. I'm sure he must have summat to do with Royston and Mackie.'

Nobby nodded his head. 'Mackie and Spangla are cousins.'

Terry looked surprised. 'How d'yer know that?'

''Cos I met the geezer last night in t'Duke.' He allowed Terry a further look of surprise before continuing. 'I got a call from Mackie saying Cousin Spangla wanted to see me. I told him there was no way I'd be steppin' into t'Duke O' York. He said it wouldn't be such a good idea to refuse. He told me eight o'clock sharp and advised me not to be late.' Nobby laughed. 'Cheeky pillock, I almost told Mackie he could tell cousin Spangles to go fuck himself, but he said it'd be for your benefit, so I went along…'

Nobby had parked Kath's Micra near a street light that was still working, not that it would have mattered to any prospective joyriders. He'd paused outside the dimly lit Duke of York and through his jacket touched the long kitchen knife that he'd slipped into his pocket before he'd left home – just in case. It was a pub he'd never been in before, not even in his fearlessly reckless youth, and there weren't many drinking establishments around that he could say that about.

The place had been empty save for one old boy ensconced in a corner and a group of youths playing pool in another room. A couple of bandits flashed away to themselves against a wall, and the strains of an old dub tune sounded out from some hidden speakers. He'd stood at the empty bar and looked around. It was an old building, Edwardian. High ceilings and dingy, nicotine yellow anaglypta walls. The place stank of foist.

A po-faced landlord appeared and jerked his head at him in lieu of asking him what he'd like to drink. The bloke looked thoroughly fed up with life, and who could blame him, having to run a place like this. He pulled his pint, took his money, slung it in the till, slammed the till shut and disappeared into the back, all without a single word. 'Nice fella,' muttered Nobby taking a sip. At least the lager was cold and sharp.

A black guy with dreads appeared as if from nowhere and tapped him on the shoulder. He said nothing but motioned him to follow. No one had spoken a word to him yet and he'd wondered if everybody around here communicated with jerks of the head. The rasta led him to a corner of the pub where an imposing figure dressed all in black with shades to suit stood guard over the entrance to what appeared to be the snug. The guy with the dreads seemed to vanish as mysteriously as he had showed, and the giant doorman, again, without saying a word, signalled to Nobby that he should raise his arms ready to be searched. The bloke felt steel behind cloth as he frisked, and raised his eyebrows before bringing Kath's best carver into view with a *tut-tut* and a shake of the head.

'Now what on earth were we planning to do with this?' the big guy said with a rather well educated sort of a voice that belied his appearance.

'Oh, it talks,' said Nobby sarcastically. 'I was begining to think I'd gone deaf.'

'Excuse me?'

'Fergerrit,' said Nobby.

The strapping fellow looked rather hurt and disappointed at the find and held the knife between his thumb and forefinger at arms length like he was holding a pair of soiled underpants. 'You can collect this on your way out. This way please.' He pushed the door open with his free hand and showed Nobby into the room.

Uziah Browne, a.k.a. Spangla, gangland heavyweight, second cousin to Jerome Mackie, and granny Mackie's favourite nephew was sitting alone at a table that was empty apart from a couple of scabby beer mats and a large glass of mango juice. He was speaking into a state-of-the-art ultra-slim mobile phone, and Nobby allowed himself a quick look around the small, foisty smelling snug while his summoner was preoccupied. The dirty, threadbare fixed seating hadn't been changed in decades and in places the ancient foam innards had sprouted through the surface like synthetic mushroom spores. The walls were bare save for a remarkably intact sixties era poster for Mackeson which archaically declared that it *looks good, tastes good and by golly it does you good.* It was a pokey, nondescript little hole and if this was what the self-styled Godfather of East Broughton used as his headquarters, then Nobby wasn't impressed. Snug it certainly wasn't. There was no one else in the room.

It was hard to tell from where Nobby stood, but if he got to his feet he imagined Spangla would stand well over six feet tall. He was fairly well built, of similar shape and physique to himself. He wore a black cashmere turtleneck sweater under an expensive looking black leather jacket, a Rolex on one wrist and a heavy link twenty-two carat gold bracelet on the other. A pair of Ray Banns shaded his eyes and his head was shaved close to the bone. The look made it difficult to pin an age on him but Nobby guessed mid thirties. He spoke in a rich, thick voice that somehow still managed to sound soft with the qualities of velvet and black coffee. Barry White and Issac Hayes came to mind. Spangla ended the call and placed the phone with measured precision neatly beside his mango drink. He leaned back and gestured his guest be seated. '*Here we go again,*' Nobby thought to himself as he took up the silent offer, hoping they wouldn't be communicating by sign all evening. His host made a spanned pyramid with his fingers and observed Nobby with what looked like a certain amount of intrigue, but it was hard to tell while he had his sunglasses on. Nobby didn't like the fact he couldn't see the geezer's eyes. Shades, indoors, at night. What was all that about? He took a good measure of his lager, let out a belch and nonchalantly looked around the room again, before casually returning his gaze to see if the overlord was ready to say what he had to say. He was, but there were no formalities, no introductions.

'How is yer man?'

'Who, Terry? Bearing up,' Nobby shrugged. 'Could be a lot worse, I suppose.'

Spangla nodded. 'He's causing me a few problems this week.'

'Oh aye, an' how d'yer work that out?'

'He killed a man.'

'He gorrin to a scrape, a bloke died,' Nobby shrugged again.

'How d'yer know it was Terry that did it?'

Spangla laughed softly. 'People don't take a shit on this estate without me knowin'. I have at least half a dozen eyewitness accounts as to what happen before you an' me boys show up. Your man Terry did it alright.'

'So, how's it causing you problems?'

'You know who I am?'

'Yeah, you're a drug dealer.'

Spangla chuckled to himself. 'A drug dealer.' He repeated the words and mused over them like he'd never heard the phrase before, decided they left a nasty taste in his mouth and took a sip of his mango.

'No my friend, you got it wrong. I ain't no drug dealer. Them boy's yer man Terry have a ruck with, the boy what get his head mashed up, they is drug dealers. I trade in commodities.'

'What's the difference?'

'I tell you the difference, Nobby, my friend,' said Spangla leaning forward. 'Them fugees on the street, them boys lickin' shot outside the school gates; yer family doctor an' his masters, the pharmaceutical giants, know what I'm sayin'? They is what *I* call drug dealers, cause n' they is preyin' on kids n' people who is curious, naïve, or ignorant, or scared, or vulnerable or desperate, or stupid or hypochondriac or any combination o' those you like to choose. Whereas, on the other hand, among other things, I supply a product for a specific market, specialist yer might say. My client base is professional, an' it goes as high as you can get. My customers include lawyers, barristers, celebrities, sportsmen, politicians, an' police chiefs; the so-called pillars of society, the very backbone of our great nation. These are educated people. They ain't supposed to be stupid. They all know what they want, an' what they want is the best, an' they're willin' to pay top dollar for it, an' in return I guarantee total anonymity an' discretion. I ain't exploitin' anyone. I fulfil a demand like any good businessman.'

'It's still illegal,' said Nobby.

'So is murder, my friend, but people don't always go to jail for it.'

378

Spangla sat back to gauge Nobby's reaction but he got none. He sighed. 'Yer know somethin', Nobby? I grew up takin' shit from people. When I was a kid I was bullied almost every day on these streets by white kids who didn't like the colour of my skin, or because of who I was - even though I was born here. When I was ten, my mam an' dad split up. They gave me a choice. I could stay here with my mam an' my sisters, or I could go back to Jamaica with my father; a hell of a choice for a ten year old to make. Well, I decided to go with dad. I'd heard my family talkin' tales of the Caribbean, the beaches, the weather, yer know, all the usual shit. I'd be getting away from the beatin's an' the name-callin'. What did I have to lose? The travel, the adventure; boy was I exited …' Spangla paused as though he was about to wallow in a bout of nostalgia, then he clicked his tongue and behind the shades his eyes became steel hard. '…We lived on the outskirts of Kingston. Ghetto. My father found it hard to get work. He drifted from one dead end job to another. He'd come home in fits of depression after another wasted day poundin' the streets seekin' employment. Then he fell in with a bad crowd; rude boys, yer naw? Became a small time gangsta. Started carryin' blades n' guns. But now he got a few dollars in his pocket. He can put food in his boy's belly an' clothes on his back. But he also get a taste for the rum; he get careless an' star' shootin' his mouth off. One day it get him into big trouble. He get a bad mashin' an' a cut that severed an artery. I get the call from a neighbour an' I rush to his side. He died in my arms in a pool of his own blood. I was fifteen. Word didn't get back to Englan' 'bout my daddy or my predicament for another two years. By then I had grown up, seen? I had to; I had no choice. An' bwoy when you on your own, when there's no one else, let me tell you, in Kingston, you grow up fast. By the time I was nineteen, I save up enough money to buy me a gun, a Glock seventeen, nine millimetre. For four years I been keepin' my eyes open an' my ear to th' ground. I done my homework. I seek out my father's killer; find out where he takes a drink and a smoke. I watch his movements for three days. Then, one night, I follow the motherfucker. I pick my moment an' I call his name. I let him turn an' see

379

his executioner. I tell him who I am an' why I'm here. I take my time, watch him fear up; see him loose his bowels. Then I pull the trigger; a single shot straight between th' eyes. I stand over him an' I know he's dead, but I pump another three slugs into his chest, an' it's the' best fuckin' feelin' in th' world. The last four years o' my life melt away an' I feel like I'm reborn. From that moment on I know that my purpose in life is to make sure that me and my own are never shit on by anyone ever again, an' I mek damn sure that those who try will live to regret it.'

Nobby found it hard to believe that even as a child the person sitting in front of him would ever be a victim of bullying. He was going to ask him which junior school he had attended but thought better of it, just in case recollections of thirty or more years ago came seeping out from their respective memories and made a connection. Spangla didn't look too much younger than him and he couldn't ever recall bullying any black kid, but his memory wasn't so sharp these days, he found it hard to recollect things that happened a week ago, so he thought it best to keep quiet on that one.

'It's a tragic tale,' conceded Nobby, 'but livin' out your life with a massive chip on your shoulder don't sound like fun to me.'

Spangla allowed himself a wry smile. 'Of course you are right my friend. For a few years after, I did walk around with a giant chip on my shoulder. I was an angry young man, more so after I dumped the gun an' caught the next plane back to Englan'. I was gonna make a fresh start, seen; put my past behind me, get meself a job, get my head down, work hard an' mek my family proud o' me. Tshh, out th' fryin' pan into th' fire. T'ings here were no better than in Kingston. Was th' time o' th' Iron Lady; bwoy, rough. Al th' brothers I ain't seen fer years, all them kids I sat nex' to in class, walkin' th' streets, hangin' roun' th' parade. Findin' work was hard even fer th' white kids, so what chance a black boy have? Only so many vacancies at Burger king or yer Pizza Hut. An' yer know what hit me th' most? It was th' looks in these kids' eyes, like they was dead, like they'd just given up, know what I'm sayin'? Like their souls had been ripped out. So what you expect when most of 'em take to dealin' an' usin'?

Weren't no different fer them as try to stay on the straight n' narrer, try n' do things th' right way; play th' game, strive fo' an education to better themselves. You seen my man George on th' way in? George, he come from a good, law abidin', God fearin' family. He try an' stay on th' right side o' th' tracks. Can't find hiself a job since he leave school, so he decides to go back to th' classroom. Spends four years at night school, studies hard, comes out with a degree in English, with honours. A year an' half later th' employers is still shuttin' th' door in his face. Then, one night he's walkin' home an' he gets jumped by three guys. He puts two of 'em in hospital; hurts one of 'em pretty bad, bit like yer man Terry, an' th' other one runs off. Different story in court: his word against theirs. George does eleven months in Armley for GBH. British justice in action. Chip on ma shoulder? What do you think? Y'see Nobby, back then I knew it was simply a matter of choices: remain a victim; stay persecuted, or stand up an' fight. I chose to fight. I already knew how easy it was to kill a man if n' you had so much hate in you. An' I knew I could do it again if I had to, but I soon came to realise that the threat of death was enough. Fear is the best weapon, it open doors an' get you places you wouldn't dream of. But then, I see fellers gettin' mashed up, gettin' killt, getting' banged up fer twenny years, an' I get to thinkin', creatin' fear alone, it *aint* enough. Brute force n' stupidity ain't gonna get you very far, 'cept a visit t' th' undertakers or a long spell at Her Majesty's, seen?' Spangla tapped his temple. 'You gotta use yer brain. Think an' act like a business man not a criminal. After five years, I figure the heat die down an' it safe enough to go back to Jamaica. I renew old aquaitances, meet some new contacts, an' pretty soon I find meself part of a thrivin' import-export operation yer might say, an' all of a sudden, Nobby, my eyes are wide open. I go from Conference league to Premiership like that.' Spangla snapped his fingers. 'I learn pretty quick, an' my most important lesson is, the higher you go, the higher the stakes; the higher the stakes, the bigger the fall, so you better mek sure you act pretty smart all o' the time, know what I'm sayin'?' He paused, and although Nobby was listening patiently to his tale, he could see from the look on his face that he was wondering if there was going to be a point to all this.

'What I'm tryin' to mek yer understand here is, the people an' organisations I deal with are all legit on the surface, but underneath they're all rotten to the core; corrupt as fuck, man, an' you wouldn't believe how far up th' shit goes. I'm talkin' high office an' even government departments here, an' it's international. Those who have th' power an' the money didn't come by it by bein' honest an' doin' things legal. They use lawyers who are as bent as they are to mek their dealins' appear legal. Bein' a criminal is so much easier when you're at or near the top. Sure, what I do is illegal, but I'm in some very good company, my friend, and you can be certain it's as a friend you want me - not an enemy.'

'So, why's a place like East Broughton so important to a guy like you if you're not dealing on the streets?'

'Because it's still home to my family. As crazy as it seems, I know that they're safe here. Here's where I first earn respect; down on th' streets, th' hard way. Now, around here my word is law.'

'So how come you let the Albanians and the rest do what they want?'

'I don't exactly let 'em do what they want, but everybody gotta mek a livin', seen, even th' undesirables. You gotta let everybody have a piece o' th' action, as long as there's enough to go round. It's called maintaining th' status quo. That way you keep a peace o' sorts; an uneasy peace mebee, but it's better than havin' war on th' streets. That's why I have people like Royston an' Jerome. Them boys are my generals in th' field, my eyes n' ears. Anything bad goin' down, it's their job to know, an' we nip any shit in th' bud, so to speak.'

'You mean they do all your dirty work.'

'Sure, sometimes it's dirty, but bein' down on th' front line is th' only way to learn. They're still apprentices getting' to know th' ropes, an' yer can't get a better groundin' than on the streets of East Broughton. You see, Nobby, when you're young, an' you been there, you'll bear me out on this I'm sure, you tend to be a bit headstrong; headstrong an' naïve. Yer get a bit o' power an' it goes to your head. You think you can tek on th' world; you're king o' the block, that is 'til yer meets yer match, or you do somink stupid as you're bound to do. Well, o' course, Cousin Jerome, he have to find out th' hard way. I used to watch him swankin' aroun', struttin' his stuff down th' street thinkin' he was th' dogs bollocks 'cos he have a connection. It was only goin' to be a matter of time, an' now he's walkin' round with a ball n'chain roun' his ankle. But he's learnin' fast. I heard what he did on Sunday. His quick thinkin' prob'ly save yer man Terry from gettin' a bullet through his head. It's nice to see him usin' his brain fer once. Mebbe once he gets th' ankle bling removed I might think about givin' him a promotion; mebbe get him a passport, let him broaden his horizons so to speak, give him a line o' work that's mebbe a little less dirty.'

Nobby tried hard to think what line of work less dirty the guy had in mind and all he could imagine was Mackie sitting uncomfortably in club class on his way from some exotic location with half a dozen cocaine filled condoms stuffed up his arse. He finished his pint and set the empty glass down on the table. 'Why'm I here?' he asked, wanting to move the proceedings on.

'You're here so I can offer you a piece of friendly advice, and to mek sure you pass that advice on to yer man.'

'Which is?'

'Like I said before, I could've done without last Sunday's little incident. I've had to spend a lot of time and manpower making sure yer man Terry's performance doesn't come to th' attention of th' police. Even though this place is perceived as a no go area, which it is when I want it to be, there are still plenty of informers an' narks out there who get it made well worth their while to chuck up, know what I'm sayin'? I've pulled the zip up an' thrown a blanket over this one. Now you probably won't appreciate the effort all that takes, an' normally I wouldn't go to such lengths, but I've done it 'cos th' boys've been tellin' me 'bout what you guys've done for th' little brother - Duane? Let me tell yer, Nobby, Royston an' Jerome speak very highly of you an' Terry; you've made a big impression, an' if two white guys can earn respect from somebody like those two, well, you gotta be doin' somethin' good n' right, an' any endorsement from them is good enough fer me. So this is th' advice I'm offering: talk about what happened to no one; friends, family, no one, yer understand? Not even among yerselves. Mek out like last Sunday never happened apart from somethin' yer might've read about in yesterday's news, yeah? After tonight, you an' Terry mek sure you stay outa East Broughton for a while, keep a low profile. Burn all th' gear you were wearin' including yer shoes.' Nobby raised his eyebrows. 'Forensics is very high tech these days my friend, better to be safe than sorry...'

At that moment there was a brief knock on the snug door, and big George entered with a fresh pint of lager that looked like a mere half in scale to his giant hand. He set it down in front of Nobby and nodded towards his boss's half-empty glass of mango. Spangla shook his head and waved him away without a word. Nobby watched the doorman amble away back to his duties and wondered how the hell he knew that he'd finished his pint and was even in need of another for that matter. His puzzled frown made Spangla smile. 'Carlsberg Export - right?' he said knowingly. Nobby took the top of the pint and nodded in agreement. Spangla chuckled softly and Nobby's frown disappeared.

'What's that then?' said Nobby looking at Spangla's thick yellow drink. 'Egg nog or summat?'

Spangla shook his head and took a small sip. 'Pure, fresh mango juice,' he said. 'Ma boys mek sure it's available for me whenever I'm in th' area.'

'I tek it you don't drink then?'

Spangla shook his head again. 'Don't touch alcohol, don't smoke, don't do drugs of any kind, an' I expect those who work fer me to follow my example, while they is on duty that is. What they do in their own time is their business, but I won't tolerate anyone who has a habit, yer understand? People who have their judgement clouded with shit ain't of any use to me, yer know what I'm sayin'? Sure I used to like a toke on th' herb in ma younger days; relieve th' stress after a hard day, but I grew out of it. Besides th' stuff that on the street now, all this skunk shit, it ain't no good fer th' kids, it's too strong, man, wipes yer out, destroys too many brain cells. They've bred th' fuck out of good old, natural sinsemilia an' left us with Frankenstein ganja.' Spangla shook his head and pulled a face. 'You ever do drugs, Nobby?'

'Not really; bit like yerself. Did a bit o' dope in me youth, don't bother these days,' he lied. 'Never touched chemicals in me life. Like a drop o' the old amber nectar now and again,' he said raising his glass and not realising what he'd just said was a contradiction in terms.

Spangla nodded and leaned forward. 'Them boys o' yours, you mek sure they keep kickin' a ball. You an' Terry point 'em in th' right direction. You do yer best to keep 'em on th' level, yer hear?'

Nobby couldn't help but laugh. What kind of moral preaching was this he was hearing? Double standards or what?

'I know what you're thinking,' said Spangla, picking up on Nobby's incredulity. 'You're thinking this guy's nothing but a fucking hypocrite, but think on this, Nobby, my friend: is the head of Allied Breweries an alcoholic? Does the chairman of Imperial Tobacco smoke? Like I've said, th' only place my poison goes is to those who are rich enough an' who should be wise enough to know better. If they're stupid enough to melt rocks an' shovel piles o' showbiz sherbert up their snobby noses, that's their problem, who am I to stop 'em? Besides, narcotics ain't th' only commodity I move around th' place, but you don't want to hear about that, I'm sure. So, you happy with what I arks yer to do?' he asked leaning back onto the old fixed seating like it was some swanky leather number at the head of a boardroom table.

'What about the Albanians?

'What about 'em?'

'What if they go to the police?'

'Don't worry about them,' reassured Spangla, 'they're long gone. Them particular fugees were illegal; part of an ATM gang controlled by th' Kosovans an' the Russians.'

'ATM gang?'

'Yeah, th' old cash machine scam. Credit card fraud. Fitting false fronts onto cash machines an' stealin' pin numbers. Supplemented their income with a bit o' dealin'. We knew what they were doin'. They miles away now. Last thing they'll do is go to th' police.'

'I still don't understand why you let these East Europeans operate on your turf,' said Nobby.

Spangla chuckled velvet again. 'Because they create a diversion. Pig feed, seen. When Babylon come sniffin' we mek sure any trails lead to them boys first, an' when th' law is busy chasin' th' fugees, they is leavin' us alone.' Spangla tapped his temple like before. 'Krypton factor, Nobby, my friend. We know their every movement. We use their presence to our advantage. They work for us and they don't even know it.'

'But these 'ere Kosovans, the guy's bosses, won't they come looking for revenge?'

Spangla smiled. 'Highly unlikely. People like yer dead fella, they is just cannon fodder. Same as yer slave girl prossies; they is all here illegal, don't matter to those guys pullin' th' strings. Life is cheap where they come from. Thousands more waitin' in th' wings ready to take th' place o' him who got his head bashed in. This is yer real European Community in action, Nobby. Th' black market economy here is massive, staggeringly so, and a good percentage of it is human trade. Slavery is alive and well in th' twenty-first century, believe me.'

Nobby took a long drink. He had to admit, Mister Spangla appeared to be quite an astute character; more so than the dickhead politicians who appeared on his telly every night and who obviously didn't have a clue as to what was going on around them. He spoke in an almost sterile accent, no doubt honed over the years from dealing with the so-called elite, only occasionally slipping into passages of Jamaican patois and homespun East Broughton. Nobby was beginning to warm to the guy and felt a bit of a twat for calling him a drug dealer earlier, even though, at the end of the day, that's still what he was. And he kind of understood and accepted the perverse morality the bloke attached to what he did. Who was he to judge? The man was under no obligation to justify himself to the likes of him, and after all, he was using his power and influence to keep his mate out of the shit. He was beginning to appear to Nobby as a thoroughly nice chap and not as some ruthless hood who earned his bones as a raw nineteen year old. But there was still an air of mystery about him, aloof and untouchable, and the Ray Banns were doing a fine job in promoting that persona. They say the eyes can tell you a lot about a person, a gateway to the soul and all that, and Nobby tried his best to get a good look at the man behind the sunglasses but all he saw was his own reflection. Uziah Browne was staying anonymous.

'The police are already talking to Terry,' said Nobby.

'How so?'

'The business with Duane's mam; the reason he got into this mess in the first place.'

'Ahh, yes I heard about that,' said Spangla. 'Overdose I do believe.' He tutted. 'Sad state of affairs.'

'She was a smackhead.'

'Mmm,' mused Spangla. 'I understand she was a seasoned junkie, been using for a good number o' years. Unusual for someone like that to O.D.'

'What're you saying?' Nobby asked, intrigued.

'Oh, I aren't speculating anything, it's just that there's a lot o' nasty stuff doin' th' rounds at th' moment; shit you wouldn't sell to your worst enemy,'

'Well, whatever; it seems it's all still under investigation, and it looks like they haven't finished with Terry yet.'

Spangla shrugged. 'Apart from yer man bein' involved, the two incidents aren't related. Just keep shtum. Stick to what I've told you an' things should be okay.'

Nobby wasn't so sure. 'Two suspicious deaths in one morning within half a mile. How can you be certain they're not gonna start asking awkward questions?'

Spangla sighed. 'Look, my friend, I ain't offerin' you guarantees, just some honest advice. Last Sunday afternoon God opened up th' heavens. Th' rain washed away most of what could have been used in forensics. So far, yer man Terry been one hell of a lucky mother. I

387

done all I can fer him, all you can do now is do like I say, an' we all hope his luck hold out. Remember, Terry was only present at one incident. After he gave his statement he went straight home; saw nothin', spoke to no one, yer understand?'

'Thanks,' said Nobby. 'I appreciate what you've done. Anything else?'

'Just one more thing: change th' colour o' your pickup.'

'Change the colour?'

'Paint it,' said Spangla. 'And do it sooner rather than later.' He bowed his head and made an open palmed gesture telling Nobby the meeting was over and that he was free to leave. Nobby necked the rest of his lager and stood up to go.

'Just as a matter of interest,' said Nobby before he turned to depart, 'do you still kill people personally, or do you have somebody to do that for you now?'

As the words left Nobby's mouth, Spangla's mobile began to ring. Spangla ignored it and gave him what Nobby thought would have been the coldest look if only he could have seen his eyes.

'I would have thought you to have known better than to ask a question like that,' said Spangla softly, but with menace. 'I only told you my story to illustrate a point within a very private conversation.' He paused to allow the atmosphere to freeze a little. 'Now if you will excuse me, I need to take this call.'

Nobby slowly backed away followed by the rigid Ray Bann stare, and again, as if by magic, George opened the door to allow him out of the room. He knew it had been a fucking idiotic thing to say as soon as the words left his lips, but it was typical Nobby, opening his mouth without engaging his brain. He shrugged. '*Sailor vee,*' he said to himself, not knowing why or what it meant, but he'd heard other people say it in similar circumstances so he thought it appropriate. He certainly wouldn't be losing any sleep over it.

'Mind how you go with that now,' advised George as he handed Nobby the confiscated carving knife handle first.

Nobby tucked the kitchen utensil inside his jacket and wondered if he'd ever have the bottle to use it. He supposed it all came down to circumstances. Defending your family, of course you would, no danger, and you'd use it to kill if necessary. But as a hazard of your job, like Spangla had obviously done, and maybe George, or even Royston and Mackie might be expected to do, he wasn't so sure. He'd been gobsmacked when Mackie had whipped out the gun with a lightning flourish and held it to the guy's head last Sunday, and like it hadn't been the first time he'd done it; the move had looked well practiced. Was it just a prop used to maximise the fear factor, or would he have pulled the trigger? Had he done it before? Were him and Terry parlaying with a bunch of cold blooded killers who slayed other human beings with a casual indifference on a Saturday night, then went to watch a bunch of thirteen year olds play football in the park on a Sunday morning? It all seemed a far cry from the good old days when he used to run with a bunch of like-minded herberts, eager to soften the skulls of a rival set of head-the-balls with the toe end of a Doc Martin.

Nobby thought of his mate laid up in bed, and supposed, whether he liked it or not, that Terry had joined an exclusive club, not by choice obviously. He assumed what he'd done hadn't been premeditated, but he had noticed how calm and composed he'd seemed about it all. No outward sign of remorse, no fear of the consequences. Maybe it was all still down to shock. Maybe the reality of it all would hit him in a day or two, or maybe, just maybe he remembered more than he was letting on and he actually enjoyed smashing the life out of his victim, maybe the experience afforded him a thrill and a satisfaction that he was too canny to admit to. It certainly hadn't fazed a nineteen-year-old Spangla, who had quickly embraced the feeling of power over life and had used it to his advantage over the years. Nobby imagined his partner prowling the streets of East Broughton clad in a dark overcoat and sporting a Charles Bronson tash, Terry the vigilante doing a Death Wish, ridding the community of evil. The image made Nobby chuckle to himself but something inside his head refused to dismiss the notion beyond all realms of possibility. It was just a crazy fantasy thought, but with somebody like Terry, you just never knew.

Nobby left the Duke and walked over to where he'd parked the car. It was still there, and remarkably, all in one piece. He put the key in the driver's door and all at once felt a tap on the shoulder. A bolt of fear shot through him like lightning. He tried to do a million things at once and succeeded in doing none. His car keys fell to the floor, and the knife he fumbled for tore through the cloth in his coat before becoming stuck and eventually joining the keys with a metallic clatter on the tarmac.

'Fuckin' 'ell, bro', chillax man, it's only me. Wassamarra wi' yer?' Royston stood back wide-eyed and with a defensive show of hands.

'Royston! You silly born bastard. What yer playin' at? You nearly gimme heart attack.'

'Easy, Nobby man, I is only lookin' after yer wheels, innit.' Royston bent down and picked up the knife while Nobby retrieved his keys. 'What th' fuck yer plannin' on doin' wi' this, bro?'

'I just brought it along for a bit o' protection,' muttered Nobby while relieving Royston of the weapon and trying to find a home for it back among the shredded innards of his coat.

Royston laughed. 'Protection from what, man?'

'I dunno. Muggers, druggies, psychopaths, crazy Albanians, idiots who creep up and tap you on t'shoulder.'

Royston was amused by Nobby's skittishness. 'You is a baphead, man. You is here at Spangla's request. What you fink gonna happen?'

'What? After last Sunday with all them shooters and dead blokes - you kidding? Christ knows what I thought was gonna happen.'

'Listen man, you has had more protection tonight than George Dubbya on a goodwill visit to Iraq, yer just didn't know it, is all. You was watched all th' way here, an' you'll be watched all th' way back home.'

'I'm not sure I like the sound of that either.'

Royston shrugged. 'Th' man don't take chances. When Spangla commits to sommink, he mek sure it done right. Attention to detail. Clean an' efficient. No room fer mistakes. That's why he is who he is, know what I mean?'

'So, you've been told to look after me car?'

'S'right, man, I is on motor watch duty, mek sure nobody steal yer wheels.'

Nobby's adrenalin levels were settling back to normal. He let out a sigh and the street lamp highlighted his expelled breath in the damp April air.

'So, where's Dirty Harry tonight then?'

'Who, Mackie? Ma nigga still on Jankers, man; confined to barracks after seven innit.'

'Oh, yeh, I forgot,' said Nobby, remembering Mackie's tag and the enforced nightime curfew.

'So?' asked Royston.

'So?' said Nobby.

'So, how'd it go in there?'

Nobby took a sharp intake of breath. 'Can't be divulging that. Private conversation between me and the Don; sworn me to secrecy.'

Royston sensed that Nobby wasn't taking the clandestine side to all this too seriously. ''S cool,' he said feigning disinterest, 'I understand.'

'Actually, I think I might have upset him a bit,' he confessed.

'How you mean?' Royston looked worried.

'I asked him if he still murdered people.'

Royston peered into Nobby's face under the poor street lighting to see if there was any sign that he was joking. The sheepish expression he got back told him he wasn't. 'What! What th' fuck yer say that for man?' the pitch in his voice rose.

'I dunno, it just sorta came out.'

'Just came out? Just came out?' The pitch rose higher. 'Der man pullin' up trees fer youse, fuckin' rain forests man, an'... an'...' Royston could hardly find the words. '...An' you go an' arks him that?'

Nobby shrugged unperturbed. 'Well, he virtually gimme his life story when I din't ask for it, so I din't think he'd mind. I was only being curious.'

'Lawwd fire!' exclaimed Royston, and then stamped around in a little circle all agitated. He seemed lost for words. 'I is lost fer words man,' he said, and then paced around some more only a bit more erratically. 'Speechless!'

Nobby watched him jig around with a curious but calm look on his face. Eventually, Royston stopped jigging and strode up to the big man; in his woolly hat he was almost as tall.

'You ain't takin' this shit serious, bro,' he said jabbing an accusing finger at Nobby's chest. 'This is your friend's, my friend's, our friend's dilemma we is talkin' 'bout here.'

'I know.'

'He could go to jail, man.'

'Ah, now, Spangla sez that's unlikely to happen if we stick to his plan.'

Royston paused, narrowed his eyes and at once began to understand the extent of Nobby's social gaucherie.

'Maan, after what you just arks him, he prob'ly on th' dog right now, "S'cuse me, mister Babylon, th' man yer lookin' for - one feller name o' Terry Gallagher - call collect, thank yer very much".'

'Nah, you're over reacting, we got on like house on fire.'

'Yeah? You best go home mek sure it not your house yer talkin' 'bout.'

'You know, the trouble with you lot,' said Nobby engaging gob before brain again. 'You're too fuckin' melodramatic.'

Royston became indignant. 'What yer mean, "*you lot*",' he said raising the pitch again. 'What's this "*you lot*"? Is we a different species or sommink? Or is it sommink to do wiv ver skin?'

Nobby groaned. The last thing he wanted was a heated confrontation on race, but he realised too late that last statement hadn't come out quite right. It was his turn to jab the finger.

'Now you know that's bollocks. You know I din't mean it like that. You're too sensitive is all I was trying to say.'

'I ain't too sensitive.'

'No? You just called Mackie "*ma nigga*" If I called him that you'd go up the fuckin' wall.'

''S different, man.'

'How's it different?'

'Is just a fing der brudders say, innit.'

'Yeah? Well t'brudders should know fuckin' better.'

'Youse don't understand…'

'Too damn right I don't understand,' interrupted Nobby. He'd picked up a bit of Terry's brusque debating skills and was going for it. 'One minute you're coloured and we're not allowed to call you black, next minute you're black and it's offensive to call you coloured. You never know where you are; it's like walkin' on fuckin' eggshells…'

Nobby wasn't expecting what happened next. Before he could continue verbally fighting his way out of a corner, Royston had rushed him, caught him off guard and off balance and had forced him backwards off the street and slammed him up against a shop door down the side of a building. Nobby tried to react and raised his arm to sling a punch, but Royston was surprisingly strong. He did his best to restrain the clenched fist that was doing its best to give him a good dig and clamped a hand over the gob that was beginning to roar with anger.

'Shut th' fuck up, man,' he hissed as Nobby's eyes began to pop out of his head. A moment later the lime green luminescent stripe of a police patrol car cruised past. It slowed almost to a stop outside the Duke of York, its two uniformed occupants having a good old nosey before leisurely turning down De Lacey Avenue and into the guts of the estate. Nobby's eyes had become fixed on a poster in the shop window, which declared *Had an accident? You could be entitled to compensation – Call in and see us – No win, no fee.* The moment had become a bit awkward as Royston's body remained pressed up against his.

'Royston, I never knew you cared,' said Nobby after he'd removed his hand from his mouth. 'Gerroff me, yer puff,' he added with a shove, knowing that a homophobic jibe wasn't as likely to offend as a racist one.

The two exchanged broad grins, the incident had diffused the situation but Royston soon got serious again.

'This is what it gonna be like fer th' next couple o' week 'till th' heat die down. Th' law already paid Mackie a visit - ain't caught up wiv me, yet.'

'What did they ask him?'

'Just the usual shit, where was he on Sunday, what was he doin', what had he seen, what had he heard. Arksed him a lot about what he was doin' up at Duane's on Sunday mornin'.'

'What did he tell 'em?'

'As likkle as possible apart from th' truf. Don't worry man, we is trained in th' art of th' police interview. We knows our rights better than they do. First fing Spangla teach us innit?'

'Why they call him Spangla?' asked Nobby curiously.

Royston told Nobby more of the legend that was Uziah Browne. How on his return to Kingston after his self-imposed exile as a teen-ager he was feted by the gangs who had been rival to the yardie boss he had executed in revenge for his father's killing. A myth had grown in his absence, and the gangs, who specialised in extortion and pro-tection, and were known locally as Spanglers, hailed the returning hero as king of the Spanglers, hence his adopted nickname.

'Yer ain't got to fink of him just as some big bad boogyman, yer naw,' warned Royston, eager to qualify the picture he thought Nobby might have got. 'He do a lot fer th' people in th' hood. Those o' his kind who is getting' a raw deal; those who is down on they luck, he mek sure them an' they kids don't go hungry. Anybody as in need o' sommink, anybody has a dispute wi' somebody else; th' people, they don't go to th' police, they don't go see yer councillor or no lame-ass M.P., they go see Spangla, cause n' they know he do th' business for 'em, they know they get justice, an' anybody step out o' line wiv his law get punished as he see fit, an' that how he earn th' respec' he have, know warram sayin'?'

'You make him sound like a proper Robin Hood,' said Nobby.

'Don't knock it man, no one forcin' him to do th' fings he doin' fer Terry. We tell him about th' fings you all achievin' wiv th' boys. Tell him all about The Albion an' th' strokes yer pullin' fer Duane, an' he like to hear that, sees it as a similar mission to his own, just tacklin' these issues from a different perspective is all.'

'Oh aye, rule by fear and murder's a different perspective alrate.'

Royston sighed with exasperation. He could feel another altercation coming on.

'Yer know sommink, mebee you is right; mebee th' trouble wiv us is we is too melodramatic. Well yer know what your trouble is, man? I tell yer, is you open yer gob wivout finkin' what you is sayin', innit? Mebee you has forgotten th' fact that Terry killt a man a few days back.'

'Self defence ain't murder.'

'Pshh. How you know it self-defence? You see th' back o' that guys head?'

'Oh, I see, so you think Terry's just gonna start on four guys for no reason? Even I wouldn't be daft enough to do that. Get real.'

'I hear what you is sayin', but the police already treatin' it as murder; it them he'd have to convince. Mebbe wiv Spangla's help he ain't gonna have to, mebbe then yer show th' man a likkle more appreciation.'

'I don't mean no disrespect,' said Nobby. 'I appreciate everything he's doing for Tel, but I can't make the connection between what *he* does and runnin' a kids football team, that's all.'

Fifty Cent warned Royston of an incoming text. It was a message from his boss.

'I gotta go; I been summoned,' he said snapping his mobile shut. 'I'll see yer Sunday. Don't hang around,' he warned, and with that he was off across the road, back to headquarters.

'Thanks for watchin' me car,' Nobby shouted after him.

'It's ma job, man,' Royston yelled back.

Nobby watched him disappear inside The Duke, realising he'd still only gained a small insight into his world. What did he mean, '*it's his job*'? He knew Royston was following Spangla's instructions, but what exactly was his job? What was it he and Mackie did through the course of a normal day? Did they have such a thing as a normal day? Did Spangla exclusively pay their wages? They never seemed short on expensive looking, if not garish, designer threads. And what of his boss? What had he really made of this self-styled paladin of the people and his D.I.Y. methods of social justice? The man was a walking, living contradiction, and Nobby's take on the guy, preconceived and newly formed, was just as contrary. He didn't know what to make of it all. These people lived in a world far removed from his own, and yet they co-existed barely a mile or so from each other albeit, seemingly, on an altogether different plane.

Thinking about how dragging a bunch of kids off the streets to play football had come to this, Nobby got into the car and started the engine. He thought back to that early summer evening in The Fusiliers and silently cursed Terry and his hare-brained ideas and crackpot schemes, but another part of him, despite what had gone down recently, wouldn't have missed the past ten months for anything, so much so that he was seriously thinking of taking his first UEFA coaching badge in the summer, if, that is, there was still a manager around and a team left to coach.

'So, I take it the pickup's blue now then, is it?' deduced Terry from the tale he'd just heard and the state his mate was in.

'Yep, midnight blue. She looks like a new motor,' said Nobby proudly.

Terry didn't share the same vision and wondered what sort of devastation his mate might have created while spraying the works vehicle. He leant over the bed to see what state the bedroom carpet was in but noticed that Jan had wisely ordered his boots off before letting him upstairs. The scented P.C.B's that were floating around the room as a result of Jan's de-fumigating session were irritating Terry's airways and he was suffering violent bouts of sneezing that were making him wince with pain and nurse his heavily strapped torso. The degree of sympathy shown towards his discomfort was only what he would have expected from his mate – he laughed.

Nobby watched his partner's face flush and eyes water with a big grin on his face. The fact that he was able to make fun of him, even as he suffered, meant that he knew he was going to be okay. Despite how he appeared right now, he looked and sounded a hell of a lot better than he had at the weekend. A hundred percent improvement, and whatever it was that the near future held, Nobby was showing in his own big, daft way that he thought things were getting back to normal. He was applying his own devil-may-care positive attitude towards it all. As in all things, Nobby lived for today, always looking forward, never back; what's done is done, forget about it, tomorrow presents a bright new dawn. Now, he felt was a time he could have asked Terry for more details surrounding last Sunday, get the low-down on what had really happened, but he wasn't about to press him on the subject. If Terry wanted him to know more, he would tell him in his own good time, no doubt, and that was good enough for him.

'Well, can't spend all day listenin' to you sneeze your head off, yer raspberry; some of us have work to do. Mrs. Sanderson'll be wonderin' where I've got to.' Nobby picked up the carrier bag containing his lunchbox, porno mag and dope and stretched, letting off two rasping farts as he did so. ''Ere, that'll cure yer sneezin',' he said wafting the noxious gas in Terry's direction. 'Pheww, pickled eggs.'

Terry groaned and buried his head under the duvet.

30

Detective Sergeant Ronald Patchett made himself comfy in the chair Jan had provided, and edged it as close to Terry's bedside as he could without actually getting in with him.

'Well, well. Oh dear, oh dear. What's happened to you then?' he asked with a slightly veiled hint of condescension

'Fell out of a tree,' Terry replied flatly.

'So I understand,' the inspector continued the patronisation.

What you fuckin' ask for then, silly cunt? Terry felt like saying but didn't.

'And when did this unfortunate accident occur?'

'Monday – Monday morning.'

'I see. Bit of a silly thing to do wasn't it?'

Terry wasn't even going to respond to that one.

Patchett formed a pained and puzzled expression. 'This might seem a bit of a daft question,' he said, 'but, what were you doing up a tree?'

A rake of responses flashed through Terry's mind but he settled on the most obvious. 'Pruning it.'

'Ahh…'

'I'm a landscape gardener, remember? Pruning trees is part of what I do for a living.'

'Quite, of course.'

'Dutch Elm disease,' explained Terry. 'Tree rots from the inside, can't tell there's owt wrong 'till it's too late. Hazard of the job.'

'I see. Looks like you had quite a nasty fall.'

'Smashed a couple o' ribs. Broke me thumb. One or two cuts and bruises. Wasn't a pleasant experience. Can't say I'd like to repeat it.'

'No, quite.' Ronald Patchett stared long and hard as if he was trying to find something in Terry's features only detectives can detect, but if he was, he couldn't. Terry's bad eye was swimming around behind his stitched and swollen lid hidden from sight while his good eye stared back impassively.

'Well,' he said at last, 'down to business. Seeing as you were unable to come to us, we decided to come to you.' He smiled like it was something he rarely did, and casually flipped open his notepad. It brought back memories of Sunday and Terry instantly felt depressed. 'We're keen to put this one to bed as soon as possible,' said the inspector flicking through pages. 'Just need to go through your statement once more.'

Terry sighed and endured the next half hour going over it all again. When Patchett finally appeared satisfied that all his loose ends had been tied, Terry ventured to ask some questions of his own.

'So, what's the finding, O.D. or foul play?'

The officer closed his notepad and leant back in his chair. 'Ever heard of crystal meth?'

Terry nodded vaguely.

'Crystal methamphetamine – Tina – Tweak – Ice,' said the Inspector putting great emphasis on each word. 'A bit like speed but ten times as nasty. In its most lethal form it can take on the properties of laundry detergent and lighter fluid. In and amongst the heroin, the coroner found a rather large quantity of the stuff swimming around inside Linda Caldwell'

'So, is that what she overdosed on?'

'Wouldn't say she overdosed as such. She had a massive coronary. Heart gave out before the rest of her vital organs; lungs, liver, so on.'

'What would she be taking that stuff for if she had her smack?'

'Probably coerced into doing so by a third party - person or persons unknown. We understand Mrs. Caldwell entertained male clients in a sexual capacity, more than likely in order to pay for her heroin habit. Heroin suppresses the libido; crystal meth liberates it. Apparantly Viagra can't hold a light to this stuff. Her punter must have been making sure he got his money's worth. Screwing somebody on smack can't be much fun. I suppose it'd be like copulating with a corpse - if you'll pardon the expression.'

Terry screwed his face up. 'How come she looked so disfigured, grotesque; almost inhuman?'

'Massive build up of gases and toxins in the body. Once the organs start to shut down, there's rapid decay. She'd have suffered severe convulsions, quickly followed by circulatory and respiratory collapse. It won't have been a pleasant death. The heart attack would have come as a blessed release.' Patchett told it like it was, without emotion in his own phlegmatic style. He'd seen enough of that sort of thing down the years, and his tone was discompassionate enough just to show the disgust he felt at some of the things he encountered in the course of his work. 'By the way, you'll be interested to know that we've eliminated Mr. Mackie from our enquiries. The tagging order means we can account for his whereabouts. Still need to speak to Mr. Morrison yet, but I'm sure that will be just a formality. Marcos Parlato.' He pronounced the name with overblown emphasis again. 'Ever heard of him?'

'No,' said Terry, 'should I?'

'Given the sort of circles you appear to be moving in, I thought I'd ask. Maltese, late thirties; dark, shady looking character.'

Terry shook his head. 'Never heard of him,' he said, realising by the description and the name that he must be referring to Caldwell's pimp cum dealer.

Ronald Patchett gave Terry a look that suggested him falling out of a tree served him right. He nodded, sniffed and tucked his notebook away in an inside pocket. 'Thanks for your time, Terry. I'm sure we won't be needing to bother you any further.' He stood up to leave the room. 'Oh, just one other thing,' he said on reaching the door. 'Where did you go when you left the flat on Sunday?'

'Home.'

'Straight home?'

'Well I'd missed me semi-final, hadn't I?'

'And you didn't see or come across anything on the way?'

'Like what?'

'Like witnessing a fight, a fracas; an assault?'

Terry shook his head. 'No.'

'It's funny,' said Patchett. 'A serious incident took place just around the corner from Cromwell House on Sunday afternoon around about the same time we were mopping up, a homicide no less. And you saw nothing, you say?'

Terry confirmed with another shake of the head.

'Very strange,' mused the policeman.

'How's that?' Terry asked.

'What? Oh, it's just puzzling that a young man, victim of a vicious and sustained attack carried out in broad daylight, and there doesn't appear to be any witnesses to it. People on the streets, house to house. No one we've spoken to saw a thing, you included. Odd, to say the least.'

'Sorry, I can't help you.'

'No. Quite…' Patchett paused and seemed to be taken up by his own thoughts for a moment or two before finally snapping himself out of it. '… You take care now,' he said with what could have been a degree of mock concern. 'Hope the ribs and the rest of it…' he said pointing around his own face. '…get better soon. And try and be a bit more careful next time.' He left Terry with a long, penetrating look that got deflected and returned with a smile teetering on insolence.

Terry picked up his book and tried to muster some interest to start reading again. His bedroom had been like Piccadilly Circus all day and quite frankly he was feeling knackered. He'd struggled to get beyond the first chapter, what with all the comings and goings, and his concentration levels weren't up to speed because of the day's revelations swimming around in his head. And when he heard the back door slam, followed by two familiar voices trading noisy insults, followed further by what sounded like two armies fighting their way up the stairs, he knew it was time to give it up as a bad job and abandon *Brave New World* altogether.

He threw the book to one side as the door flew open and Rory burst into the room like a cork out of a bottle, red faced and dishevelled, closely followed by his older brother looking equally as flushed and with a degree of agitation at having failed to get to his dad's bedside first. Rory flung himself on to the bed and Terry had to be quick to avoid damage to an area of his body that until now had remained relatively unscathed.

'Ooof! Steady on Bokanovsky, what's the craic?'

'Stupid little bastard!' spat Joe.

'Fuck off, numb-nuts!'

'Dickhead!'

'Toss-pot!'

'Cock-sucker!'

'Inch-knob!'

Joe flew at his brother and Terry had to virtually curl himself into a ball to avoid being hit by flailing arms and legs as the two of them went at it hammer and tongs across a crumpled mess of duvet.

'Woaah! Woaah! Steady on!' cried Terry helplessly but to no avail. Luckily, Jan had been hot on their trail.

'Pack it in the bloody pair o' yer!' she yelled storming into the room and tearing her squabbling sons apart expertly like the veteran no-nonsense arbitrator she was.

After almost four days, Terry was unusually buoyed to see his two lads, even though they were trying to knock seven lumps of shit out of each other. It was safe, it was familiar, it was bloody good to see, and although he'd come close to receiving a few more knocks himself, his warring offspring had brought a smile to his face, soon to be wiped off by his wife's glower. She hated it when she thought he was encouraging them. Against her better judgement, Jan had allowed the boys to go up together, thinking it might save argument as who got to see dad first, but it hadn't worked so she ordered Rory back downstairs.

'Why's it allus me? Why can't he piss off?' he asked sourly.

'Because you can't be trusted to do owt together without turning it into bloody World War Three.'

'He started it,' protested Rory.

'Nyaa nyaa-na-nit,' mocked Joe.

Rory aimed a savage kick but Jan saw it coming and quickly intervened, almost having her own kneecap smashed in the process.

'Ooh, you nasty little sod! Get down them stairs now!'

'S'not chuffin' fair,' he wailed, tearing himself away from his mother's restraining hold, 'he allus gets away wi' it.'

'You're both as bad as each other.'

'So why's it me has to go downstairs?'

''Ere, listen Podsnap, our Joe's got to get ready to go training soon,' mediated Terry. 'Why don't you go get your tea, then when he's gone it'll be just me an' thee.'

Semi pacified, Rory took his dad's advice, but couldn't resist a snarling parting shot at his brother. 'Turd breath!'

'Heyy!' said Jan.

'Fuck pig!' replied Joe.

'Heyyy!' said Jan.

Terry and Joe grinned broadly at each other as they listened to the berating and the backchat between Rory and his mam as they headed back downstairs. It was a bit of an awkward moment as neither of them were happy with the idea of hugs and embraces; the grins said it all anyway. Terry was eager to get the lowdown from last Sunday's game, he'd heard most of it from Nobby, but he wanted to hear it from his lad, especially about the last minute penalty that he'd stroked home to take The Albion into the County Cup Final. Joe was as eager to tell as his dad was to listen, but his old fella's wellbeing had to come first.

'How yer feelin' then, dad?'

'Ahh, not so bad; better than I was.'

'You must o' teken a rate smackin'. How high was yer?

'High enough to crack me ribs an' spoil me good looks.'

'You could o' killed yourself.'

'Aye, I could, you're right there.'

'No harness?'

'Don't tell Health and Safety,' Terry said sheepishly, while inwardly he was cringing at having to go through this whole sorry charade with his son, but he knew he had no choice, they couldn't risk taking any chances. They had to be meticulous. The story had to be solid and consistent and if that meant lying to members of his family, then that was the price he had to pay.

Jan had been great. She'd sat both lads down on Sunday evening and told them the truth about what their dad had witnessed up at Duane's that afternoon. He'd come home traumatised, felt unwell and had to go to bed. Then she'd had to sit them down again after school on Monday and had spun them the story of how he'd felt a little better come mid Monday morning and had decided to go to work against her advice and had ended up coming a cropper. They'd swallowed it, and she'd been telling the truth when she told them that the doctor up at the infirmary had said he needed rest and that's why she hadn't allowed them to see him till now.

'Was it bad?' enquired Joe tentatively, quickly changing the tone.

'Was what bad?'

'Yer know - Duane's mam.'

Terry sighed. 'Aye, it wasn't a pretty sight, son.'

'Peycos sez she warra smackhead.'

'Yeah, she had a drug problem you might say, but listen; don't be believing everything you hear. Don't go making it headline news everywhere. Let's be giving Duane a bit of consideration in all this. You understand?'

Joe nodded solemnly. 'What'll happen to Duane now?'

'I don't know. Kath's in contact with social services, no doubt she'll find out.'

'Can't he go live with her and Nobby?'

'I can't answer that one, fella.'

'Will he be able to play in the final?'

'Let's hope so, eh?'

'There were loads o' scouts there on Sunday.'

'Aye, so I've heard.'

'Fella from Blackburn was askin' about me an' Norbert.'

'Was he now? You'd best tell us all about it then, penalty King.'

Joe's eyes lit up at his dad's enthusiasm. But Terry was also thinking about the procession of club scouts that had to be pacified by Nobby's hastily thought up tale of last minute illness for the non-appearance of the kid that they had all really come to watch, wondering if any of them would be gracious enough to give him a second

404

chance. They only had one more league game left to play plus the final, and he wasn't sure at this stage if either he or the young Duane Geddess would be around for either of them

Joe cosied himself up on the bed and for the next half-hour or so, gave his own expert analysis on the semi-final encounter with The Panthers from Wakefield, along with a critical assessment of his own performance which he was careful not to be too modest about.

So, Nobby had changed the team sheet and had played Joe from the start. He'd had such a good game that Blackburn Rovers no less, had shown an interest. Terry didn't want Joe to get carried away by all that. Would the scout have asked about Joe and Young Nobby if Duane had been there? Probably not, but he was happy for once that his mate had defied him and had gone against his instructions. He listened with great pride as his lad described with unashamed glorification the build up to the penalty. How one by one his teammates' arses had fallen out; Slum, Rammer, Sully, and even Rigger their regular penalty taker had bottled it. He'd stepped up, and in the muddy, sticky conditions the penalty spot had been almost obliterated, and there'd been some dispute as to where the ball should be placed. The ref had been forced to pace out the required distance from the goal line. The delay had built the tension and the Panthers' goalie had done his best to put Joe off while all this had been going on, chelping in his ear hole and flinging mud about. Joe had remembered watching that documentary about the psychology David Beckham was supposed to use when he took free kicks. Positive thinking. Visualising the ball hitting the back of the net, picturing the scene over and over again. Single minded, shutting out all distractions. He'd wiped the mud-caked ball across his shirt before placing it with great deliberation, picking away any floating rogue bits of turf from where he was going to plant his boot. He'd taken three or four paces back, the heavy pitch sucking and squelching at his feet, wiped his hands on the back of his shorts, taken a deep breath, glanced up briefly at the target and the goalie who was trying to make himself large, arms spread wide, dancing from side to side across his line. The ref had blown his whistle and all he could hear now was the sound of his own breathing and the thumping of his heart. He strode up to the ball, almost casual, and stroked it low and firm with his instep. As in his mind, it fitted satisfyingly into the bottom right hand corner of the net with the goalie going the other way. He'd given the prone keeper a knowing little smirk before turning away to a feeling of immense relief and a fast approaching, joyous screaming mass of blue and white that he was about to be buried under.

Terry felt a pang of guilt at how he'd treated Joe after the Buckley game, especially after he'd had to endure the extra humiliation of the Lisa Boocock expose. At least favouritism was the one thing nobody could ever accuse him of.

'How's it going with Lisa?' asked his dad, 'I haven't seen her around for a bit.'

'Nah, she dumped me,' said Joe without a hint of self-pity or regret. 'Said I was too young for her.'

'Oh, sorry to hear that.'

'Ah, it's okay,' he said chirpily. 'She's right anyway. Don't think I was ready for a relationship. Sasquatch sez women complicate yer life. Boy, he was right about that. Don't need all that nonsense at my time o' life. It was affectin' me footie.'

Terry laughed and ruffled his son's hair. Joe appeared to be singing like a bird released. All that morose sulkiness that seemed to possess him of late looked to have gone, and his first real encounter with the opposite sex had seemingly left him relatively unscathed. He was at the start of a long learning curve where females were concerned, and Terry was glad that he'd seen the light for now.

31

It had been Terry's first outing since that fateful Sunday and the second funeral for all of them in just over a month. No one was there for Linda Marie Caldwell, sad to say, not even them. They were there for her eldest son, and any sadness they felt was all for him. Terry no longer felt hatred towards the dead woman, there wasn't any need for that now, it was a pointless emotion, and no doubt if he had been religious in any way he might have even offered up a prayer for her soul. And although he showed no sadness for her, there was an overwhelming feeling of depression and melancholy about the place, about the whole sorry proceedings. Maybe it was the thought of a hopeless life soon to be forgotten by all save for a young man who never refused to give up hope, who had futile dreams of a time when his mam would get better and all would be okay for him and his little brother. Maybe it was the thought of the cheap box and service paid for by the state, where God's representative donned his holy mantle and wearily went through the motions while Detective Sergeant Ronald Patchett lurked around outside in the shadows to see if any of Caldwell's old acquaintances cared enough to show. Terry knew he would have a long wait. He realised that if it wasn't for their own presence the minister would be speaking his few hollow words to an entirely empty chapel, and despite who or what she had been, maybe it did sadden him a little to think that no one on earth gave a fuck; no living relative, compassionate ex-lover, or so-called friends. It was a grim end to a grim existence. A life wasted and another sorry statistic. Paradoxically, there was still no sadness inside him for another such statistic; no thought for the illegal immigrant, the anonymous petty criminal who lay tucked away unclaimed in a morgue cabinet with a label attached to a big toe where the details remained blank.

Terry glanced sideways along the row where they were all seated: three faces, total strangers to the deceased, all staring impassively at the Co-op coffin, all lost in their own thoughts.

For Nobby, it brought back memories of his own dead mother. They were sitting in the same chapel where he'd said his last good-byes all those years ago, where he himself had become a teenaged orphan. He caught glimpses of her warm, loving smile that reminded him so much of his Kath. He saw that smile and those sparkling eyes worn down and dulled by the wearisome efforts of caring for his dying dad. Then he saw her in the coffin and a feeling that he hadn't had in over twenty years washed over him; that draining sensation that left you hollow and empty inside, that seemed to sap your spirit; the feeling of loss that, even after all this time, never really healed, never went away altogether. He wasn't one to dwell. He brought himself back to the moment with a deep sigh and counted himself lucky they were in the crematorium and he wouldn't have to endure the torment of standing over a hole this time.

Jan was also at another funeral, it was that of her husband. Just a few feet away she saw his battered and broken body lying flat out, cold and covered in a shroud. Crude attempts had been made to disguise his injuries. In death he looked hideous. She saw herself veiled, all in black, tearing at the box, wailing to the heavens, while her two boys, dazed and confused tried to hold on to her, calm her down. And, at the back of the chapel, four young men made obscene gestures, sneering and jeering in a foreign tongue. The images in her head made her shudder, and involuntary she squeezed the top of his leg so hard that it made him look at her inquisitively. He wasn't too much of a pretty sight at the moment, but he was still living flesh, and God was she thankful for that. She gazed at his face with an intensity that totally bemused him and vowed that she would never take him or anything else for granted ever again.

Kath's studied focus on the coffin was illusory. Her thoughts weren't with its contents, imagined or otherwise. She was waiting to see Duane again. She'd been in contact with Social Services and they had confirmed that he had requested to be at his mother's funeral. She sat still, trance like, as nervous and apprehensive as a child on its first day at school. She knew the circumstances were far from ideal,

408

but she couldn't wait just to see his face, to give him a hug and assure him everything was going to be okay. She hoped he'd been fostered with a nice family who were looking after him and giving him the love he deserved, but she secretly prayed that he wasn't getting too attached, or that the sordid death of his mother had affected him to an extent that he acted cool and distant towards her. All sorts of permutations and crazy notions were filling her head, and her palms were beginning to sweat.

Duane left the side of his social worker and walked slowly down the aisle towards them. He was wearing his dark grey school pants and a short black bomber jacket. He looked different, smart. Kath had only ever seen him in his WBA training top before because that was the only coat he'd possessed. She could tell he'd had a haircut, his dark, tight curls sitting close to his head. She stood and waited for him at the end of the aisle almost trembling with trepidation. As he got closer she could see he still had that air of fragile vulnerability that went everywhere with him. He looked up at her and with a faint hint of a smile fell into her embrace. A surge, not unlike a million volts of electricity shot through her, while Duane held on and fed off the love that was pouring out of her and into him, just like that Sunday when he'd trudged up all the way from the hospital in the bitter cold.

Nobby joined his wife and gently placed his giant hand around Duane's slender shoulders. He was soon joined by Jan and Terry, and the little circle of genuine love and affection was carefully observed by Duane's official guardian who was now standing a few feet away. The youngster indicated to her that he would like to sit with them and his request was granted with a smile and a nod of the head.

The social worker was the same woman who had made the house visit after Leo had been taken into care and who had taken such an interest in Duane's footballing activities. She sat herself a few pews back, and with Duane now warmly sandwiched between Kath and Nobby, focused her attention on them for the duration of the short service.

The whole thing went by in a blur for Duane. He wasn't listening to the bloke in the cassock, didn't understand the words or the sentiments. He'd never been in a building like this before and he didn't like it; didn't like the cold and echoing emptiness of the place. Didn't like and didn't understand the significance of its morbidness. Didn't like the look of the pine box that contained his mam or the metal bier that supported it or the maroon carpet on which it all stood or the large lit candles that eerily flanked it. He shut all that out. He was able to because it was easy for him. He'd had fourteen years honing the skill of closing himself off from the things he didn't like or were liable to cause pain.

He thought about Cromwell House. The stinking flat, his damp bed and the foisty, mildewed walls. No sentiment, just strange that he wasn't ever going to set foot in the place he'd known all his life and had laughingly called home. He thought about the little rituals, washing his gear in the kitchen sink, often in cold water when there were no electricity tokens and no money for the laundrette; fetching his mam's methadone scripts, running the gauntlet, dodging the attentions of Purcell, Wishbone and their cronies. Being forced to nick what he called luxuries from the Co-op down the parade: toothpaste, shampoo, bog roll. He certainly wouldn't miss any of that, but it was what he'd grown up doing; for him it was normal. The other stuff, the nastier stuff, he'd already tried to shut away. His mam was gone now, and all that badness she surrounded herself with had gone too. No more witnessing the screams and the assaults. No more having to barricade his bedroom door, and most of all no longer having to watch his little brother suffer. But they still weren't letting him see Leo. He'd asked and asked 'til he'd got sick of asking, but they'd always fobbed him off with some excuse. He sometimes cried himself to sleep if he'd been thinking about him too much and often found himself saying a little prayer to God, whoever he was, and had recently added his mam to those prayers. The guy up front was asking them to pray now, but he, for one, wouldn't be doing it here that's for sure. He knew he wasn't ever going to see his mam again, and if that was going to be the case with his brother, then he hoped that the family he was with were kind and were looking after him well.

Mr. and Mrs. Hutchinson were nice people, kind and friendly but a bit quiet and boring. He'd been with them for almost a week now but he was finding it hard to get used to his new surroundings. Their home was clean, and everything was so neat and tidy, so much so that it made him feel a bit uncomfortable. His room was spotless but it wasn't what he'd call a boy's room, nothing like Young Nobby's. The walls were decorated with old fashioned, lavender coloured, flowered wallpaper, and boring oil painted pictures of country scenes in gilt frames. Above his bed hung a wooden crucifix to which was nailed a yellowed ivory carved Christ, and on the windowsill a porcelain Madonna and child stood serenely on a circular crocheted doily.

He didn't ever want to appear ungrateful, but he was finding it hard to conceal his unhappiness. He felt so lonely. Mr. and Mrs. Hutchinson were nice people but they weren't Kath and Nobby Clarke.

The Hutchinsons had thought it inappropriate for them to attend the funeral, so Duane had come without them, accompanied only by his social worker.

After the service had ended, Duane, acting all grown up, made the introductions. Kath had a million things to put to the social worker, but the woman beat her to it.

'Can I ask you a question?' said Susan Burroughs before Kath could open her mouth and launch a string of questions of her own. 'Have you ever thought of adopting?'

Kath looked at her husband. He looked back at her. They looked at each other. Kath's face defied a hundred descriptions. She tipped her head back and began to laugh. Bitter mirth that grew and spilled out of her until it became long, loud and shrill, bouncing off the ceiling and around the walls of the small chapel, reaching a crescendo with a hysterical wail, much to the shock and open-mouthed amazement of all present, climaxing and breaking down into a descending pattern of shuddering sobs. The minister emerged from his vestry half dressed, astonished at what he thought was an outpouring of grief the like of which he'd never witnessed before. Nobby did his best to calm his missus down, hugging her close to him as he coloured up and before he made an apology in his typical clumsy manner.

'Sorry abaht that,' he said with his face the colour of beetroot. 'Decorators are in.'

'I beg your pardon?' said Susan Burroughs.

'Time o t'month,' explained Nobby awkwardly. 'She's havin' her periodical.'

32

'Hey up, chor, it's me.'

There was no mistaking Smiffy-No-Teef's hoarse rasp over the phone.

'Alrate Smiffy, what's up?'

'That fing we talked about. Might have a lead fer yer, charver.'

'Oh aye, what you mean, might have?'

'Well, I've been doin' a bit of investigatin', but I could only push it so far. Folk get a bit jumpy, start askin' questions as to why you're askin' questions if yer know wharra mean. Anyroad, vat fing yer lookin' fer, I fink I know where it is.'

'Go on.'

'Kellets.'

'Kellets on York Road?'

'Yep, vat's what me sources say, but I'm not hundred percent on vis one, so I don't want no come back if I aren't rate. An, if he has gorrit, he won't have it on display.'

'Thanks, Smiffy, appreciate that.'

'Just a word o' warnin', marrer. All my contacts are pretty good, but some were a bit cagey on vis one, din't really wanna know. Now, none o' vis is my business but summat tells me yer need to be careful. Zeb Kellet's no idiot. If yer go in actin' like you're ver filf you'll scare ver shit out of him an' you'll never get warrit is you're lookin' for - know wharra mean?'

'I do. Nice one, Smiffy, thanks for that.'

'My pleasure, chor, one good favour deserves anuver. You tek care now - oh, an' remember - we never had vis conversation, rate?'

'Rate.'

'Cushty.'

Terry wasted no time. The kids were at school, Jan was back at work and there was no one around to ask him where he was going or

413

what he was up to. He was going against Spangla's advice to stay out of East Broughton, he knew that, but he was on a mission, no time for procrastination. Thursday afternoon, wouldn't be too many people about, and besides he was bored silly having to stay at home. There was only so much reading you could do in a day.

Kellets was a long established but unbelievably tatty old second hand junk shop at the far end of York Road, sandwiched between a chippy and a former charity shop that now sat empty and half derelict. Out on the pavement, stacked tight together and linked by a heavy chain, was an assortment of bikes, garden machinery and implements, lawnmowers, strimmers, trimmers and chainsaws. Above the window was a crude hand-painted sign that declared: *We buy and sell anything.* Hanging inside the window were air rifles, fishing rods and all manner of innovative but hardly used exercise apparatus.

Terry stepped into the dingy, tightly packed Aladdin's cave that seemed to be stocked with everything but the kitchen sink, but as he gazed around fascinated, he saw that they even had a couple of those, too. The place had everything. The grimy shelves were stacked from floor to ceiling with TVs, videos, DVDs, hi-fi, car stereos, mobile phones. They even had MP3 players and the latest Ipods. It all looked as if it had come off the back of a wagon or out of a West Broughton living room, which, more than likely it had. Zeb Kellet had been done so many times for receiving over the years that the police had almost given it up as a bad job: in fact, he was so well known to some of them that they'd become regular customers; special discounts in return for hassle-free trading. Kellets was the last resort for punters when they couldn't move their goods around the pubs and clubs. Rock bottom prices and no questions asked.

Terry moved slowly around the limited floor space, taking it all in. He picked up a curious carved statue of what looked like a Greek God with an unfeasibly large penis that he was sticking up the rear of a naked, young maiden. He moved a lever at the base of the figures that made the well-endowed deity go through the motions, in and out, in and out.

'Warrisit yer lookin' for?' said a hidden voice. Terry jumped star-

414

tled and quickly replaced the statue. Out of the shadows from behind a cluttered counter emerged a figure, camouflaged chameleon-like against his ill-gotten stockware. He'd been sitting unseen, observing Terry from the moment he entered the shop.

Zeb Kellet was now in his early sixties, of average height and build; an unremarkable looking man apart from his pot belly and his Bobby Charlton head on which survived a few lank strands of combed-over hair. His grey stubbled face contrasted with his eyebrows, which were still dark and thick, and his eyes were set deep in their sockets, instinctively alert and full of mistrust. Over his shirt he wore an old knitted tank top, the front of which still bore the remains of one or two past cooked breakfasts. He was a grimy specimen and in total keeping with the shop. He took a pull on one of those slim panatela type cigars and blew the smoke in Terry's direction.

'I... er, I collect wartime memorabilia, and I wondered if you might have anything of interest.'

'Such as?'

'Well, what have you got?'

Kellet shrugged. 'There's a couple o' Nazi dress bayonets in t'window, ARP helmet, one or two gas masks...'

'I was thinking of items a bit smaller and of more value, like medals for instance.'

Kellet paused for a moment then shook his head. 'Nah, an't got owt like that.'

'Tch, pity. I was told you were the person to come and see for things more, out of the ordinary, shall we say.'

Zeb's eyes narrowed to slits. He wasn't falling for anything. He shook his head. 'Nah, sorry pal, can't think where you've got that from.'

Terry stared him out for a moment. 'Never mind,' he said eventually, 'I'm a collector you see, I'd have paid good money for the right object. Thanks anyway.' He turned to leave the shop.

'What, er, what exactly was it you were lookin' for?' The words *good* and *money* had soon changed Kellet's tune. He'd taken the bait, time to reel him in.

'A Victoria Cross.'

'An' you're a collector, you say?'

'That's right. I have four VCs in my collection at the moment; one from the Crimean War, where, incidentally, all the gun metal from the captured Russian cannons is used to make every Victoria Cross still to this day. One from the Indian mutiny, eighteen-fifty-seven to eighteen-fifty-nine. One from the Zulu wars; my most treasured, as only twenty three were awarded during the whole campaign, and one from the First World War. I was hoping to add to all that with one from World War Two. I suppose I'll just have to keep searching. Thanks for your time.'

'Er, hang on a minute...'

Terry turned again to see the pound signs rolling in Kellet's eyes. The greasy bastard snaked his way around his customer, flipped the sign on the door to *Closed* and turned the key in the lock.

'...Now yer come to mention it, I just might have the very thing you're lookin' for. You'll, er, forgive me for bein' cautious, but yer can't be too careful around here, I get all sorts comin' into this shop, if yer know what I mean.'

'I understand,' said Terry.

Result. He was convincing. He was good. He'd done his homework.

The sweaty shopkeeper lit a fresh celebratory cigarillo off the butt of his old one in anticipation of a big sale, and led Terry through a labyrinth of piled-high goods, into a back room where you couldn't move for stuff, where two ferocious looking German Shepherds, tethered together in a corner, leapt and strained at their chokers, barking out a savage welcome to the stranger.

'Shadapp!' shouted Kellet but the dogs took no notice. In another corner, on a table almost buried under junk, was a monitor with a split screen linked to multiple hidden cameras that kept an eye on everything. Terry took note. Edging their way past the pair of snarling canines, Kellet led Terry up a narrow staircase lined with dozens of boxes of lean, mean, grilling machines, faced with dozens of images of George Foreman grinning broadly at him as he passed. He took him into a room that Terry assumed to be the office. The place was still piled high with knock-off but there was a small clearing with a desk, a chair and an old green safe against a back wall. Kellet fumbled in one of the desk drawers for a key, then squatted down in front of the safe with his back to Terry.

'I'd been thinkin' about movin' this on,' he grunted and spluttered as he allowed his cigar smoke to float up into his eyes, making the juggling of combination numbers a bit of an effort. 'Thought about purrin' it on eBay but never got round to it.'

Terry's eyes flitted round the room until he saw the camera high up above the door. It was out of reach. They flitted around some more and he caught sight of an umbrella poking out of a Japanese style glazed plant pot.

'I've never really had a good butcher's at this,' continued Kellet as he struggled to get the tumblers to click. 'It's in good nick as far as I remember, ribbon an' everythin', still in its case.'

Terry moved quietly and swiftly. With the tip of the umbrella he nudged the camera up on an angle until it was pointing at bare ceiling. The safe door swung open and Kellet slowly grunted to his feet clutching the medal. There was no time to ditch the umbrella so Terry stood there striking a pose like John Steed minus the bowler.

Kellet didn't bat an eye. 'I can move them ten quid a chuck all day long,' he said, pointing at the brolly, 'fiver to you if you're interested.'

Terry nodded and put the brolly aside. He approached the desk, eager to view what he'd come for.

'Now, before we get down to business,' said Kellet sitting himself in his chair and placing the felt box on the desk, 'I know how much these babies are fetchin' as well as you do Mr. Collector. So if we're gonna be serious about this, let's dispense with any bullshit now. What d'yer say?' He narrowed his eyes to slits and blew smoke.

Terry gave a little smile. 'Let's see what you've got, shall we?'

Kellet opened the case and pushed it towards his client. As soon as he saw it a surge of something went through Terry's body, like he instinctively knew. He did his best to remain calm. He lifted the medal by its crimson ribbon and held it up to his face. 'How did you come by it?'

The vendor removed the panatela from between his teeth and shook his head. 'No, no, no, my friend, we don't ask questions like that. You're supposed to say, "Very nice, this is just what I'm lookin' for. How much d'yer want for it?" An' I rub me chin, have a bit of a ponder, say to meself, seems like a nice bloke, let's be reasonable, an' say, "Five grand ought to clinch it."'

Terry gave nothing away but another little smile. He knew that whatever was on the back of the V.C would tell him all he needed to know. He carefully turned it over.

It shouldn't really have come as a surprise, but it still shocked him to see that an engraving tool had been used to crudely deface the inscription. He tilted it towards the filthy window to shed a bit more light. The date of the act of valour in the centre circle was almost obliterated, but on the suspender bar he could still make out bits of name, rank and regiment. Whoever had commited this act of vandalism hadn't done such a good job. This Victoria Cross had been won by Herbert Johnson, there was no doubt about that. Terry put on his disappointed face and placed the medal back in its case.

Kellet looked up at him in anticipation. 'Well?'

'Sorry pal, it's worthless.'

Kellet almost choked on his cigar before spitting it out. 'Fuck off, worthless!'

Terry picked the medal back up and dangled it in front of him. 'It's been defaced, ruined. Whichever idiot's done this has rendered it useless. Without its history it's worth fuck all!'

Kellet snatched the medal from Terry's grasp and began frantically rubbing it. 'It's just a few scratches,' he said desperately. 'It can be restored. A bloke like you should be able to sort it.'

Terry turned to walk away.

'Hey, hold on a minute. Don't be in a rush. Three grand. Three grand an' it's yours.' Terry turned back and laughed in his face. 'Fifteen hundred quid; it's me last offer an' you're fuckin' stealin' it at that,' said Kellet starting to sound desperate. He held out the gong trying to tempt him back into the room.

Terry watched the slimeball nodding his head in encouragement like he was enticing a dog to come and get a treat. The contempt was building inside him and the flashbacks were starting again: Herbert's beaten and smashed features in the newspaper, the cowardly bastards laying into him, the wheelchair, the home, the funeral. He shook off the masquerade and became Terry Gallagher once more. He launched himself at the desk, snatched the cross and shook it in Kellet's face.

'It's already been stolen, you fuckin' idiot!' he raged between clenched teeth. 'Why d'yer think the inscription's been scratched off?'

'So, why should you care? Gerrit milled down an' scribe it again.' He was taken aback by the guy's sudden aggression. The bloke certainly didn't sound like a collector any more. He was starting to get worried. 'Second thoughts, I've changed me mind, it's not fer sale. I'll have it back.' He stood up and tried to grab the cross. Terry pulled it out of reach and roughly shoved Kellet back into his chair.

'What chance did you think you'd have of floggin' this, you dumb fuck? Registration. Authenticity. Verification. Certification. Proof of ownership. This is a Victoria Cross, not a fuckin' DVD player.'

'Why should you worry? Give it here an' then get the fuck off out o' my shop.'

'Oh no, you're not getting this back; this is gonna be returned to its rightful owner.'

'Go fuck yerself. You don't know where it's come from.'

'Oh, but I do.' Terry held the Cross so that Kellet could see it but not so near that he could make a grab for it from behind the desk. 'This was stolen in a house raid over eighteen months ago. Its owner, in his eighties, was beaten - badly beaten - and left for dead. He suffered brain damage, lived as a vegetable for over a year but eventually died as a result of his injuries.' He swung the cross by its ribbon into the palm of his hand and made a tight fist over it. He leaned in close. 'The case is still open. This is in effect a murder enquiry. The police are still keen to gather any evidence. I would say this is vital

419

evidence, and I would also say that you, Mr. Kellet, could be identified as an accessory after the fact, I think is how the saying goes.'

Kellet guffawed. 'Warra load o' bollocks. Listen, people mighta tortured an' raped for what I buy off 'em. Who gives a fuck? D'yer think I'm bothered? I buy an' sell in good faith, no questions asked. I've been in this game too long to worry about where me stuff comes from. You can pin fuck all on me, pal. Now, gimme back what's mine, what I paid good money for, then piss off.'

'Just how much did you pay for it?'

'Mind yer own fuckin' business.'

'I'll double it.'

Kellet guffawed some more. He shook his head with mirth. 'I don't know who you are, pal, but you crack me up, you really do...' he reached into a desk drawer and casually pulled out a gun. '...but I'm gerrin' sick o' listenin' to you now.' He stopped laughing and sat up serious. 'So, put the medal back in its box, turn around an' walk away, an' we'll say no more about it.'

Oh Christ, here we go again. Deja fuckin' vu, Terry thought to himself. He was getting a bit fed up of people pulling guns and pointing them at his head. This was all getting too much like an old Humphry Bogart movie. Half expecting Sydney Greenstreet and Peter Lorre to burst through the door at any moment, he sighed, transferred the cross into his left hand, approached the desk and made to lay the medal back in its case. Kellet had that sickly sweet grin of victory on his face. He puffed casualy on his cigar while Terry watched the barrel of the gun follow his every move. Shit or bust thought Terry. If Sam Spade can do it, so can I. With his right hand he heaved the desk backwards and upwards in one lightning quick move. The strike knocked Kellet back off his chair and as the desk landed on him two shots rang out and hit the ceiling showering him with a deluge of plaster and old black lime. Terry dived on top of the upturned desk. With the combined weight the edge of the heavy piece of oak cut across Kellet's potbelly and began to crush the life out of him. His face turned a peculiar shade of purple, he started gasping for air and his flailing hand relinquished hold of the gun. Terry stretched and

420

managed to pick up the piece with his left hand, the one that was still clutching the medal, while leaning across Kellet's throat with his right arm just for good measure. He scrambled to his feet wincing with pain. The move hadn't done his healing ribs any favours. He stuffed the medal in his pocket, composed himself and wondered what to do next. He had the V.C., he had the gun; he held all the trumps. Should he just get the hell out of there and hope for no comebacks? If Kellet was determined to get back what he assumed was his, he could face reprisals. It could shove him back in the limelight so to speak and Mr. Spangla wouldn't be too happy about that after all his efforts. The murder angle and involving the police hadn't fazed Kellet one bit. And it might have sounded stupid, but he would have genuinely thrown fifty quid at him to take the medal off his hands, walk away and say no more about it safe in the knowledge that Kellett wouldn't have forked out more than twenty-five quid for it in the first place.

The shopkeeper groaned and tried to lift the heavy desk off his gut.

'Don't move,' barked Terry.

'I can't breath,' rasped Kellet.

'Good.'

He would need the fifty quid and the rest in order to restore the medal back to its original condition, and Kellet wasn't exactly in a position to negotiate any more. Although he didn't feel too comfortable with the gun he decided to be Sam Spade once more and act the hard man.

Zeb Kellet lay flat out, covered in debris from the ceiling. He sounded as if he was having an asthma attack. Terry stood over him and loosly pointed the gun in his direction.

'I'm going now, and I'm taking this with me,' he said holding the medal out for Kellet to see one last time. 'You shouldn't ever see me again, but if you or anybody else tries to come after me, or it, I'll be back in your life in a breath. It'd be a shame to see an old establishment such as this go up in smoke. Do you understand what I'm saying?'

'Phhwwhrr…' said Kellet.

Terry put a foot on the desk and pushed. 'Sorry, didn't catch that.'

'Yerrss, yerrss!' wheezed the fence in obvious distress.

'Good.'

He spotted the felt case amongst the mess, took his weight off the desk and retrieved it. He carefully put the medal away.

Zeb tried to breathe a sigh of relief. 'Who the fuck are you, anyway?' he croaked. 'Who d'yer work for?'

Terry smiled. 'Ever hear of a gentleman goes by the name of Mr. Spangla?'

'Spangla!' the very mention of the name seemed to strike genuine fear into the prone shopkeeper.

Terry raised his eyebrows. 'Oh, I take it you've heard of him then?'

'Heard of him? O' course I've fuckin' heard of him. 'Why din't you say yer were one o' Spangla's boys? I coulda done yer a deal. All this coulda been avoided.'

Terry looked at the holes in the ceiling and at the mess he'd created in the already cluttered office, and at Kellet as he lay there huffing and puffing, covered in bits of plaster. 'Too late for that now,' he shrugged. 'You make sure you behave yourself and think on what I said. Talk to nobody about this.' He tucked the medal, now safely in its case, back in his pocket, went over to the window, opened it and dropped the gun into the alley below. 'You can let yourself up once you hear the door go and not before. Nice doing business with you.'

He left the room, shot down the stairs, past the pair of snarling dogs, through the shop, unlocked the door and went up the East Broughton street at a brisk pace. His heart was pounding, his ribs were sore, and inside his pocket he hung on tightly to Herbert Johnson's Victoria Cross. He'd taken a gamble using Spangla's name like that, but he fancied that Zeb Kellet would be sensible and keep shtum. He smiled to himself. It had been worth it. All he needed to do now was find a reputable jeweller, and get a forwarding address from the people at Garden Springs.

33

Kath Clarke hadn't been as positive and as upbeat as this in ages. It was as if Susan Burroughs had been sent from God. She was the sort of person who made all the noises in the right places; made things happen, got things moving. Now, every time Kath had the opportunity to speak to her she couldn't stop apologising for having lost it in the crematorium like that. Susan dismissed it with a laugh. She understood all about emotions; she was an observer, experienced in her work and she was good at it. She'd already spoken to the adoption agency, to the person who'd done their home assessment, and everything in the report had come back positive. They'd fulfilled all the criteria with only slight reservations on their respective ages. They'd been classed as suitable to adopt. It was like they'd cleared a major hurdle.

Susan had listened patiently and sympathetically to their story. She saw the genuine and unconditional love the Clarkes had for Duane and his little brother. She would do her best to fight their corner, but she also gave them the hard facts; it wouldn't be easy. The authorities still preferred to place children with would-be parents from the same ethnic and cultural backgrounds and if that meant keeping siblings apart, then so be it; that was official policy. The fact that Kath and Nobby were willing and hoping to give two brothers a loving home together might not cut it; it would have to go to a committee and they would have to prepare themselves for a decision that may well go against them despite all the positive facts and despite Duane's personal wishes. For Kath it was a no-brainer. Surely common sense would prevail in these matters – wouldn't it?

Duane's persistence, along with Susan's help, had at last been rewarded with an afternoon's get together with Leo. At Duane's insistence, Kath and Nobby had been invited along too, but it hadn't been met with approval from certain quarters down at Social Ser-

vices. Some saw it as bad practice and thought the whole thing coun-
terproductive. Susan Burroughs had asked certain dissenters along as
casual observers, but they had their heads full of doctrine. They
couldn't be swayed in the emotional round where they suspected that
the heart might well rule the head.

Duane spent the first hour with his brother on his own. During
that time he'd managed to teach Leo to pronounce his name as Dane
instead of Dede; not perfect but distinct and enjoyable progress. Kath
and Nobby had watched the interaction through a one-way mirror
and were enthralled. When, at last they were allowed into the room,
Kath was almost sick with excitement and trepidation. She wasn't
sure if he'd remember her, and from his initial reaction, she was
right.

Leo stared up at the two adults with his big, dark eyes and looked
a little worried. These weren't the people he'd been staying with, was
he being taken away again? He manoeuvred himself behind Duane's
legs and peered back cautiously but intrigued. Kath dropped to her
haunches, down to his level and softly called his name. He turned
away, more shy than scared. Then Kath remembered the treat she'd
brought along and dipped into her bag. She produced a bag of white
chocolate buttons and shook them tantilizingly. They'd been his favourites during her visits to the hospital, and as soon as he saw the
familiar packet his memory clicked. He came from behind his
brother's legs with a beaming smile on his face. 'Mam,' he said and
toddled towards her with his arms outstretched. Kath hugged him to
her like she never wanted to let him go. She'd been determined not to
get too emotional but she couldn't help it, the tears poured out of her.
The people behind the glass watched in silence. All but the hardest
and most heartless professional remained untouched by the scene,
even the big man had a lump in his throat and when Duane caught
his eye all he could do was give him his Stan Laurel smile and turn
away.

Leo loved a cuddle, God knows he hadn't had that many in his
life, but there were some choccy buttons being waved about a moment ago and he wondered where they'd gone. Kath opened the bag

for him and after he'd fished one out and popped it in his mouth he trotted off to show his big brother what he'd got.

'Can I have one, Leo?' asked Duane, and the toddler offered him the bag so he could help himself. 'Can Kath and Nobby have one as well?' he asked. Leo looked at him puzzled. 'Mam an' Dad,' he said pointing to the Clarkes unashamedly. They looked at each other, shocked at Duane's presupposition, but it brought a little smile to Kath's face; she liked the sound of that, it made her feel all warm and tingly. Leo happily approached them in turn and offered up his bag of buttons.

Kath couldn't keep her eyes off the little chap. He looked to have grown a lot since she last saw him. He presented a picture of health, happy and glowing. He was gorgeous. He'd also had his third birthday while in foster care, a date that would have gone unnoticed and uncelebrated like it always had if it hadn't been for D.H.S.S. records and the keen eye of a social worker. Linda Caldwell had never kept things like birth certificates.

They all spent a happy afternoon together. Nobby and Duane played *shots and in* with a soft football and two plastic skittles for goalposts while Leo chased after it, in and around their legs, giggling his head off, and Kath sat and watched with her heart singing. She didn't want the session to end, and when finally the two sets of foster carers came to collect, there was a heavy feeling of sadness all round. The time had flown by so quickly.

Kath said her goodbyes, determined this time to keep her emotions in check, at least until she got back to the car. She gave Susan Burroughs an almighty hug of gratitude and told her she'd never know how much today had meant to her. Susan said that from what she'd seen she pretty much thought that she did, and she promised to keep her closely informed of any developments.

Nobby politely said hello to the Hutchinsons. They offered a curt response and he got the distinct feeling that for some reason they didn't approve of him. *Fuck 'em,* he thought, as long as they weren't able to influence any decision over Duane he wasn't bothered, they could think what they liked. The youngster had called him Dad today and that was good enough for him.

Kath and Nobby Clarke walked to their car arm in arm. Happy, sad, elated, and exhausted, but above all eternally optimistic.

* * *

Terry had really been looking forward to this, his first training session in over a month and the penultimate before the cup final and the end of the season. One more league game left, away at lowly Mill Lane and a guaranteed third spot with a win. He wasn't up to doing any running around yet, but he couldn't wait to get back involved, keep a keen eye on all the lads, and make sure they were staying sharp and focused. He needn't have worried on that score; they were still buzzing off the semi-final win and seemed up for anything.

It felt great to be amongst it again. The pitch had held up well through the winter and Nobby had given it its first spring cut. Those familiar smells reached his nostrils and it made him feel good; brought him back alive. The aches and pains were beginning to fade and he was doing his best to forget about what had gone down these last few weeks. The clocks had gone forward, the nights were getting lighter, and the old pit arc lights had been stored away in Ginner's shed for the coming summer months. He felt as though he'd been away for ages, but the lads greeted his return as if he hadn't been away at all. One or two of them seemed to show a genuine concern for his wellbeing, asking him how he was, hoping he was feeling better, but most of them took the piss, said he was too old to be climbing trees. He laughed with them, took the stick; wouldn't have it any other way. He was back.

Colin the cat killer was enjoying himself in Mrs. Lightowler's vegetable patch, frantically scraping away at the hole he'd dug as if his life depended on it, a fountain of earth arcing into the air behind him, peppering the freshly washed white bedsheet and other sundries that had been pegged out to dry. The now not so crisp white bedding had already taken a couple of direct hits from the odd stray, muddy practice ball and Betty had had enough. She was about to go on the warpath. She emerged from the house screaming and yelling, brandishing a sweeping brush that she held menacingly aloft, bingo arms flapping and slapping in the breeze. She bore down on the surprised Boxer like Boadicea on amphetamines. Colin knew when he'd met his match and with a sharp defensive bark abandoned his excavation and swiftly leapt back over the garden fence.

What Terry hadn't been looking forward to on his first day back was another confrontation with Betty Lightowler. As Colin bounded past him he looked up to see Betty's formidable and angry form bearing down on him.

His diplomatic skills weren't having much effect, and when Nobby came blundering in, full of faux bonhomie he managed to set her off again. 'Nah then, Betty, I hope you haven't been attacking me boys and givin' yerself a thrombie.'

'Don't you chuffin' start, you bloody big lump yer.' She tightened her grip on the broom and brandished it like she meant business.

Nobby stopped dead in his tracks. 'Woah; steady on now, lass.'

'Steady on! Steady on! I'll give yer bloody steady on. You're a public menace. You want locking up the bleedin' lot o' yer.'

'Nay, there's no need to be like that.'

'Oh, is that right, Mr. Smart Arse? How'd yer like *me* to come round and throw shite at *your* wife's washing? I bet she wun't like that, would she?'

'Calm down, Betty love, I don't want to be having to call an ambulance.'

'If he tells me to calm down once more, I'll shove this brush where t'sun don't shine,' she said turning to Terry. 'Who's he think he is: Michael chuffin' Winner? It won't be me as needs ambulance, you mark my words.'

The three of them thrust and parried for the next ten minutes but no amount of patronising assuagement could pacify the woman. She was spleen-venting and no punches pulled.

'I'm on to t'council first thing in t'mornin'. I'll put a stop to all this, I'll have you lot off here if it's the last thing I do, you watch if I don't. I mek no wonder they're like they are,' she sneered hatefully.

'You're evil, the pair o' yer, and they're nowt but a bunch o' foul-mouthed little devils.'

They thought that last bit was a bit strong but Betty had seemingly browbeaten them into silent submission. She looked Terry up and down as if he were a giant turd. 'You,' she said, '*you* gerraway with bloody murder!'

Terry and Nobby looked at each other. Nobby quickly turned away. '*Many a true word...*' he said under his breath.

* * *

Mr. and Mrs. Hutchinson emerged from the car looking like they were ready to set off on a polar expedition. They were dressed up to the nines in all manner of thermal gear, as well as what looked like provisions for at least a month. It was the arse end of April, not even cold.

'I hope we don't get t'weather you're expectin',' Nobby met them cheerily, looking around to see if they'd brought a team of huskies and a sled and with only a slight smirk on his face. They'd obviously never been to watch a game of football before. His jocularity fell on stony ground.

'We weren't sure if we'd got the right place. You did say ten-fifteen,' Mr. Hutchinson observed deadpan, looking at his watch that showed almost half-past. Nobby wondered just what the criteria were for becoming a foster parent and hoped it wasn't the same for adopters - so bloody serious.

A few scouts had shown up for the game against Mill Lane, not as many as the semi-final, but representatives from Blackburn Rovers and Manchester City took the time to seek out Terry and introduce themselves. Observers from Leeds United, Sheffield Wednesday and Burnley were also present.

The game itself turned out to be very much a one sided affair. The Albion went one up inside five minutes and after that the goals flowed in at regular intervals. Nobby relaxed and enjoyed what was a warm-up for the final, a practice match in effect. The Mill Lane players simply couldn't get near or match the free flowng football that The Albion were now playing. It was testament to Terry's hard work and philosophies, but even when they were stroking the ball about for fun he was still pacing the line, barking out orders, making sure the concentration levels and the discipline didn't let up for one minute. They'd struggled to get a draw against this lot at home earlier in the season and, in the eight months since then, his lads had come a long way - a hell of a long way.

Duane, in his first game back, performed his magic like he'd never been away. Recent events hadn't affected him at all, in fact his play seemed to take have taken on a renewed vitality; freed and unfettered. He was a kid at the top of his game and, although the opposition was poor, those watching couldn't fail to have been impressed.

The six-nil scoreline at the end of the game could have been quite a few more had The Albion not taken the foot off the gas in the last twenty minutes. Duane had netted two, the second being an exquisite chip from all of twenty-five yards, having spotted the Mill Lane keeper off his line after completing a dazzling run from deep in his own half.

The scouts were queuing up, eager to speak to Terry and Duane at the end. They obviously wanted to see the youngster play against stiffer opposition and Terry told them they would hopefully get that chance in the County Cup final a week on Wednesday. Duane seemed a bit bemused and overawed by all the attention, even more so when most of the lads excitedly swarmed around him afterwards to find out what had been said. All this interest from clubs was great, but what mattered most to Duane right now was that he'd be allowed to travel back to West Broughton on the bus with his mates.

While he was chatting to the Youth Development Officer from Man City, a pair of eyes set deep inside the cave of a hoody gave Terry a dirty look. Mackie trudged by, hands deeply entrenched in his designer jeans pockets, the backside of which was somewhere down by the back of his knees. His body language told Terry that something, or someone, had obviously upset him. He hadn't been his usual animated self during the game, and hadn't even reacted when Duane

429

executed his wonder goal. Before they got back on the bus Terry pulled Flash to one side thinking he'd be able to shed some light.

'It's nowt to do wi' me, man,' said Flash defensively, 'I've not said owt to the sour-faced git; he's been miserable all day.'

Terry turned to the guy who knew him best. Royston looked harshly at the gaffer. 'Yer means ter tell me you ain't sussed why me man beefin'?' Terry shook his head. Royston turned away and made that clicking sound with his tongue. 'When's the final?' he turned back and asked.

'A week on Wednesday,' replied Terry not understanding the relevance.

'Wednesday *evenin*',' prompted Royston, 'seven-thirty kick off?'

The penny finally dropped. 'Ohh, shit!' said Terry.

34

To be an East Broughton postman you had to either be brave, incredibly stupid, or really strapped for cash. No other attributes mattered when you were the sixty-third sucker to do this round inside twelve months. That was an average of five point two five souls a month, just over one a week. A more alarming statistic was that forty-nine percent of all mail during that time never even reached its destination, most of it having been dumped by the beleaguered postpersons in question; not that the would-be recipients of what would have been bills, final demands, summonses, and CCJ's could have cared less anyway. The officers of what used to be called The Royal Mail were fair game to man and animal alike around here, and were usually only left to do their job in peace on giro day.

Postie number sixty-three shoved the morning mail through the Mackie letterbox in a screwed-up mess, like it had been delivered in nervous haste. In her dressing gown and slippers, and with a towel turban on her head, one of Mackie's sisters lazily came from the kitchen to retrieve it. She smoothed out the crumpled envelopes and went through the offers of cheap loans and credit cards with fantastically low APRs until she came across an official looking brown envelope addressed to her brother. She turned it over and saw the frank of the West Yorkshire Metropolitan Police. She tutted and took it into the kitchen to show her mam.

'Look like he been in trouble again,' she said tossing the letter on the table.

Mrs. Mackie frantically wiped her hands on a tea towel and snatched up the letter with a concerned look on her face. 'Lawwd, what th' bwoy gotten into this time?' She went to the bottom of the stairs and called up to her son at the top of her voice and at regular intervals for the next hour without response. After all this time, the letter had begun to bug her, so she snatched it off the table, stomped

431

up the stairs and burst into his semi-darkened room where she could just make out a *Tommy* hat sticking up above the duvet.

'Jerome! Jerome!'

Stifled grunt.

'I know you awake, Jerome, so stop ignorin' me.' She shook the semi-concious lump violently.

'Shit ma, what's goin' down? What's yer problem?' Mackie stirred from his pit agitated and with a sour look on his face. It was cup final day and he inteded to spend it in bed. He wasn't in a good mood.

'You my problem, bwoy. Tell me, what's this?' She waved the letter at him and threw it on the bed. 'An' why you go to bed in a hat?'

'It protect ma braids, innit.' He sat up wearily and rubbed his eyes.

Ma Mackie clicked her tongue, shook her head and folded her arms impatiently. 'Well?' she said eventually.

'What?'

'Aren't you gonna open it?'

'I could do wiv a drink o' tea, ma,' he croaked.

'Just open th' letter, Jerome.'

Mackie licked his parched lips, cleared his throat and nervously opened the letter, though why he felt nervous he couldn't say. As far as he knew he hadn't done anything wrong lately, or at least nothing that could have come to the attention of the police. He thought of the incident with Terry and the fugee, but if it had anything to do with that, the police would have been at his door with enforcers and Halligan bars, and not sending him letters through the post. He pulled the correspondence from the brown envelope and glanced up at his ma. Her standing over him like that didn't help.

Mackie squinted at the letter in the half-light and scanned through the blurb at the top of the paper: *Section 245A Criminal Procedure Act... blah, blah... Ref: RLO number 479001... blah, blah... Dear Mr. Mackie...* He read the rest of the letter to himself, much to the annoyance of his mother who couldn't contain her curiosity any longer.

'Well, what's it say?'

Mackie shrugged. 'Just sez to report down at central headquarters at a time of my convenience on th' fourth.'

'That's today,' she said after thinking about it for a while. 'Is that it? Let me see.' She snatched the letter and read it right down to the bottom where it was signed per persona on behalf of the Chief Constable, confirming what her son had said, but she still remained suspicious and gave him a stern warning. 'I hope you han't been tryin' to mek yer gran'ma wear that tag t'ing again ma lad...'

The West Broughton postman was a slightly different animal to his East Broughton counterpart, less nervous, a bit more reliable, and, on average having greater longevity in the job. The chap currently doing the rounds was even managing to whistle a happy little ditty as he worked his way down Ash Terrace. When he stopped to drop the daily load through the letterbox of number twenty-seven, Kath Clarke responded like one of Smiffy-No-Teef's greyhounds out of the traps when the odds were good, the way she had every morning for the last fortnight. On reaching the front door this time she stopped dead in her tracks. There, on the mat, as conspicuous as anything amongst the junk mail, was the one she'd been waiting for, staring up at her, thick and brown and official-looking, Department of Health and Social Security printed in black. She unfroze herself and, ignoring the rest, picked up the letter with a shaking hand. She walked slowly back into the kitchen as if in a trance. She stood there and held it up to show her husband who was in the process of downing his second mug of tea.

'It's here,' she said in a scared little voice that didn't sound like her own. 'This is it.'

'Open it up then, lass,' said Nobby.

'I can't. I daren't.' She started to tremble. Nobby quickly got to his feet to place a steadying arm around his wife and gently took the envelope from her. He gave her a reassuring smile and started to tear it open. She looked up at him, trying her best to feed off the optimism and strength that reflected in his face, but inside the big man, the c'est la vie, the que sera attitude that had always been a Clarke trait didn't apply this time, and before he read out the letter he did something he'd never done before in his life and that was to offer up a silent prayer to God, the someone or something he hadn't ever believed in, in the hope that they had been allowed the chance to offer a home and a lifetime of love to two special kids.

Phil Ashington's hands had gotten all sticky. Strawberry jam. It was all over the postcard he'd started to read. Flash didn't usually get letters; he wasn't on any mailing list, never got offers for credit cards or cheap loans. He wasn't on the electoral register, was unknown at the CSA and the Inland Revenue. Officially, he didn't exist. He was a non-person and that's how he'd engineered it over the years since he stepped off the treadmill, resigned from the rat race. He contributed nothing to the running of society and he asked for nothing in return, had never signed on, never begged for handouts, and the only thing in the world that could identify him was his passport, a necessary evil that allowed him his freedom of movement.

Phil's missus, hard worked and harassed, had gotten herself ready for work, the kids ready for school and the youngest ready to go to her gran's. She'd fed them breakfast, half of which the little one had managed to spread in her hair and on the letters and the postcard her mother had dumped in haste on the kitchen table while rushing to rescue another round of toast from being incinerated. She didn't have time to go through the mail except to gaze longingly at the letter that informed her she'd won a hundred thousand pounds in a grande prize draw that she'd never even entered, wishing if only it were true.

She was late again. She hurried the kids out the front door before shouting up the stairs, reminding her part-time fella to pick the kids up at half-three. It was the only chore she imposed on her man during his infrequent stays, but she felt she had to remind him every morning still, just in case. Oh, and by the way, someone had sent him a postcard from Ibiza.

Flash yawned and lazily spooned a succession of sugars into his pot of tea. He'd been doing a spot of DJ'ing while back in England, nothing at all lucrative, he didn't even have his own decks, but the gigs helped keep the wolf from the door. He'd just done a session in Huddersfield, hadn't got home till four in the morning and, despite the odd sherbet dab, he was still feeling knackered.

He took a long slurp and felt the tea do its job on the toxins and chemicals that were jiggling around in his gut. The postcard was from an old Trog mate of his who lived rough on the island. He read that he'd secured a pitch in Las Dalias, the hippy market at San Carlos. He was setting up a stall flogging objets d'art, weird artefacts and paraphernalia, and would he like to help him run it for the season?

Flash stopped yawning. He let go the postcard and licked his jam-sticky fingers. This was a job offer he couldn't refuse. In truth, it was exactly what he'd been waiting for. He liked Las Dalias; it was chilled out and steady. He'd grown out of the hedonistic scene that was so full of pushy wankers and gormless pill-heads nowadays; Manumission with its gyrating women in cages and the tedious Eden foam parties. There was no way he was going back to being a mule for the scousers, even though he knew that's where the money was to be made. No, this little number sounded fine and it had come along just at the right time. He'd been getting restless of late. He was getting sick of having to bum gear off people whenever he had a gig, and they had got totally sick of him. He suffered badly from SAD during the winter months, the short grey days and lack of daytime light making him miserable and depressed. In truth, he'd done well to last the past nine months without going mad or the wonderlust kicking in a lot earlier. He hoped he'd done right by the missus and the kids in the time he'd been home. Only she could be the judge of that, and judging him was a thing she never did. There wasn't any point. He was an enigma and a law unto himself. She'd got used to his ways, and the kids, as they grew up, were learning to have to do the same. At least he'd been there for his Billy; every Sunday without fail, even though for half the time his lad had been warming the bench. And his linesman duties were over with for the season now anyway. Only the Cup Final left to play this evening and they would have proper officials for that. He could sit back and enjoy it. No more trudging up and down the line suffering from trenchfoot in the depths of winter at places like Goit Stock. No more having to put up with the slings and arrows that came his way on the bus going to away games from a bunch of little fuckers who had no respect for their elders, especially the likes of Ginner, Peycos and Biscuit, who had always tried to tap him for some draw. He never knew if they were winding him up, or if they genuinely enjoyed a smoke. He wouldn't have put it past those three. But he'd always managed to resist their constant badgering. He could just imagine it, '*Tel, what's this smelly stuff Flash's given us? Sez if we tek it it'll mek us play better,*' stitching him up and right, Terry slinging him off the bus in the middle of nowhere and the whole of The Albion, snotty little faces pressed up against the windows pissing themselves, going mental as the bus drove off without him. He smiled to himself at the thought, but he knew it was the type of thing they'd have done given half the chance.

Then there was Mackie. Where their dislike for one another came from, he never knew. They clashed on almost everything. Poles apart, and you could be certain that whatever one of them did would be guaranteed to wind up the other. It was just one of those things. He didn't actually hate the guy, and maybe he could have made allowances knowing that the tag thing was driving him crazy and very often sent him into dark moods, but what the hell - touchy fucker. What Flash never knew was that on more than one occasion he came very close to having a loaded pistol pressed to his temple, controlled by one very itchy trigger finger.

Although November through to March in West Broughton wasn't a good place to be for Flash, either physically, or in his head, he'd enjoyed the Sundays with the lads. They had created the right sort of diversion for him. It had been good meeting up with Terry and Nobby again and listening to Nobby's crazy tales from the old days, not that he could remember half of them, too many brain cells obliterated in the interim. But now it was time to move on. He would take a leisurely trip down the travel agents this aft, book his flight, pick the kids up, and then get ready for the big game tonight. Flash had waved his last flag – for this season at least.

Joe was pestering the life out of his dad to let him have at least a glimpse of the new strip before he had to leave for school. Terry finally agreed to let him have a peek but only after he'd finished his breakfast and washed his hands.

The Nigel Adenbrook benevolent society had been at work again. A brand new kit just for the final, a proper kit, each item individually sealed and wrapped. Joe carefully unpacked a shirt and opened it up in front of him, rich, deep blue and alternating crisp, white stripe.

'Aww, smart,' he breathed, and held it close to his face to smell the newness.

Good old Nige. Once again he'd flourished the chequebook and pen as soon as he found out Terry and his boys had reached the final, and he'd even had the shirt's jacquard weaved just for the occasion: *West Broughton Albion U-14 County Cup Final* with the year underneath. And best of all, the kit had been ordered individually so that each kid had a strip that actually fit him. If this didn't give the lads the necessary pride and incentive, nothing would. The Smiffy-No-Teef, baggy, grey, knock-off outfit had been assigned to history, or more accurately, the dustbin, and Joe went to school with an extra spring in his step, eager to describe to the rest of them what they'd be running out in tonight.

Terry made a mental note to phone Mackie after breakfast. He'd been meaning to do so for the last couple of days, but for one reason or another he'd got waylaid. After Royston had made him aware of the cause of Mackie's sullenness Terry had got straight on the blower to the probation people and explained the predicament. They had told him only the Chief Constable had the power to make such decisions and that he should write to him in person. Not only had Terry done that, laying it on thick, explaining that Jerome Mackie was working over and above his community service by helping run a football team for deprived kids in an effort to atone for his past wrongdoings, but he'd followed up his letter with persistent phone calls to the Chief Constable's PA and secretary stating his case for the reformed youth, asking, pleading that they give urgent consideration with a view to rescinding the RLO, even if it be for this one special day only. They'd got fed up of hearing that Mr. Terry Gallagher was on the line again and had promised him faithfully that the matter would be brought to the Chief Constable's attention as a matter of urgency. He'd left it at that, careful as not to push his luck too far and hoped for the best. He hadn't told Mackie what he'd done, just in case nothing came of his petition. He didn't want the guy building up his hopes only to have them dashed and leave him feeling doubly distraught. He was beginning to think that had been a wise decision. It was already the eleventh hour, and if there'd been any good news, Terry would have expected an excited phone call from him by now. He'd done his best, there was nothing else he could do now except maybe drag the guy down to Central and kick up a stink. He knew he was unlikely to take things that far, stirring it up with the police with a well-known East Broughton bad lad in tow wouldn't be such a good idea especially in his situation, but he hated the thought of Mackie missing out on the lads' night of glory. He deserved to be there, and the notion of doing something drastic about it had kept crossing his mind.

Garthend United under fourteens were The Albion's Cup Final opponents. Terry knew very little about the team from the junior Carniege league except that they were odds-on favourites to win this one. According to Steve the Farshaw manager, Garthend United had a pedigree stretching back decades, at all levels, junior and senior. Their name appeared regularly on amateur cups and league title trophies, and they were often used as a feeder club for one or two league sides, even boasting a handful of players who had made it into the professional ranks over the years. Steve warned Terry that they would have already heard all about Duane Geddess and he could be assured that they would assign a couple of players to watch him

438

closely and take care of him if necessary. Terry had thanked him for the information but he wasn't going to worry too much about the opposition or what they had in store for his star man. Tonight he would be telling his boys just to go out and enjoy themselves, soak up the occasion. The result didn't really matter; their achievement as far as he was concerned was already complete. Steve had wished them luck and said he'd be there cheering them on, said he was particularly looking forward to watching Duane perform against what he knew would be a class side.

'That is, unless you're thinking of pulling him at the last minute with some mysterious injury like you usually do,' he'd laughed.

Terry didn't respond. '*If only you knew, Steve,*' he thought to himself, '*If only you knew.*'

The Farshaw manager wasn't daft. He'd gotten to know Terry Gallagher enough during the course of the season to realise all this *we're only here for the occasion* bollocks was just that. Of course the result mattered. He knew that Terry would be taking his warnings on board right now, making sure he had his own protection sorted out for his genius left-winger if ever it was needed.

Terry tried hard to convince himself that he *was* that person who hadn't fooled Steve for one minute. He really didn't want the result to matter, he'd even caught himself picturing the scene in defeat, and mouthing the different ways in which he could appear gracious. It just wasn't him, and the word certainly wasn't in the lads' vocabulary. They knew they were the upstarts of this competition; the underdogs, and that's just how they liked it. Gracious in defeat? I don't think so, because in their collective minds defeat wasn't an option. To them, winning this thing was the only possible outcome and they were supremely confident. Terry had given them that confidence; he knew that. He'd worked at it, they'd worked at it; they'd built it together and now they had the belief and expectation that he'd talked about tirelessly back in those summer months when they were just a rag-bag bunch of aimless little herberts, that assuredness, that almost telepathic understanding like the great Cruyff-Neeskens Holland team of the seventies he would tell them about. It was all down to him. So why all the pretend diffidence and constraint now? It was a safety net. There lurking in the shadows were the old demons still, skulking around, biding their time, waiting to pounce, that little old devil preparing itself in the wings, ready to dance a jig on his shoulder. After all that had happened to him, Terry was still scared of the fall. He was just one step away from glory and he was waiting for somebody to come along and kick the chair away. He was able to conjure up the visions at will; they came into his head thick and fast.

He could see them all being wiped out on the motorway, carnage on the M62 while on the way to the final. The special needs bus a twisted, mangled heap of metal, no survivors.

He could see the ref about to blow his whistle to get the game underway, then a tap on his shoulder and he turns to see DS Ronald Patchett with half the West Yorkshire Police Force behind him, telling him he was under arrest on suspicion of murder.

He could see Social Services running onto the pitch, sweeping Duane off his feet just as he was about to score the winning goal and take him away because his foster parents didn't approve. He saw the opposition pissing themselves laughing, and all the club scouts shaking their heads and returning to their cars.

He could see Zeb Kellet turning up on his doorstep as he was about to leave for the game and finding himself staring down two loaded barrels, a pair of snarling German Shepherds preventing escape and a demand for the return of a stolen medal - or else. He had to laugh at that one. *Pull the trigger mate, 'cos your medal's over ten thousand miles away,* only on that assumption he couldn't have been more wrong.

Terry jumped. He didn't believe in that sort of fate, but in cowardly fashion he didn't prevent Jan from answering the loud knock on the front door. She took the rather large pile of letters and signed for the airmail package that had arrived recorded delivery, wondering what on earth it was and who it could have come from. The postman went away up the path having now adopted a more *do-de-do do do* style ditty instead of the whistle.

The small package was addressed to Mr. Terry Gallagher, so it hadn't come to the wrong place, but it had been sent from Australia. Jan was intrigued. Among the letters she plonked down in front of her husband were a few envelopes bearing the crests of football clubs: Burnley, Man.City, Leeds. But what really made him open his eyes wide was the small airmail package.

'So, who do you know in Australia then?' she asked placing it directly under his nose.

'Caroline Goulding,' he said, already tearing at the well-padded parcel. Jan frowned like she'd heard the name but couldn't quite place it with a face. 'Herbert Johnson's daughter,' said Terry. 'We met her at his funeral, remember?'

'Oh, yeah. Why would she be sending *you* something from all that way?' Jan asked with the frown still on her face.

'Dunno.'

Terry recognised the felt presentation case straight away. He opened it. Inside was Herbert's V.C.

'What's that?' Jan asked intrigued.

'It's a Victoria Cross,' said Terry, realising he'd have a bit of explaining to do. 'It belonged to Herbert.'

'So why's she sent you it?'

Terry started to unfold a letter that had been wrapped inside the parcel. 'Well, actually I sent her it.' Jan's frown got deeper. 'Look, it's a long story,' he said looking up into her puzzled features. 'Let's see what this letter has to say.'

He opened up the pages to reveal the most beautiful copperplate handwriting. Jan perched herself over his shoulder and they began reading together.

Dear Terry,

I really didn't know how to start to write this letter, so I thought I'd begin by telling you about my dreams. Yes, I know what you must be thinking right now, but before you screw this up and throw it in the bin, I ask you to please bear with me for a while.

My dreams, or should I say, these particular dreams began soon

441

after our return to Oz, about a week or so after Dad's funeral. They weren't bad dreams; on the contrary, they were always rather pleasant if not a little puzzling.

In the dreams, which incidentally usually occurred two or three times a week, Dad would appear to me standing alone in a field of long, lush, grass that was being waved about in a gentle breeze. Sometimes he would be far away, just a figure in the distance. Sometimes he would appear standing in the middle of the field, and other times he would feel really close, so close that I could almost reach out and touch him.

In the dream I would try to speak to him but try as I might, nothing ever came out. In the end he would sense my frustration, put his finger to his lips and smile. It was like he understood, like he was trying to reassure me that everything was all right. Often he would turn and walk away into the distance, at other times he and the dream would just fade. Whichever way the dream ended I would always wake with a feeling of peace and contentment.

After a week or so of this same recurring theme, one night, all of a sudden Mum appeared. I hadn't dreamt about her for years. She stayed in the background at the far end of the field just watching and waiting. Although she came to the dream regularly after that, she always remained in the distance as if she was waiting for Dad to come to her, just patiently waiting.

I didn't have a clue what any of it meant, and because none of it was disturbing in any way I never tried to interpret or analyse. I never even bothered to tell Michael. Then, one night around a month ago the dream took a bizarre twist. – Please don't think I've lost my marbles when I relate this next bit, but this is exactly how it happened and now I'm glad I've been given the opportunity to write it down.

*Dad was there as usual, and as far as I can remember Mum was doing her waiting in the background. The crazy bit is **you** were stood alongside Dad as large as life. I know we have only ever met briefly just the once but it was definitely you. This time the dream was anything but pleasant. Although nothing bad actually happened, I had an* overwhelming sense of foreboding. It's the only word I feel can describe it, like someone, somewhere was in mortal danger. The details are all a bit vague now, but I remenber that all of a sudden you weren't there anymore, just Dad left alone in the field with Mum waiting for him as usual. I remember trying to speak again and this time the words came out precise and clear. I asked Dad where you'd gone and he told me that you'd had to go back, that it wasn't your time yet. I tried to ask more questions but something seemed to stifle my desperate search for answers. Dad just put his finger to his lips and smiled again.

I remember waking up in a panic, bathed in sweat. I resisted the urge to rouse Michael although I was desperate to tell him what I'd just dreamt and the awful feelings that had accompanied it. He'd been working so hard of late and was in surgery the next morning, so I went to the kitchen to get a drink of water, calm myself down and try and make sense of it all.

I was restless and didn't sleep much for the rest of the evening, and all next day I couldn't get you out of my mind, so much so that I seemed to spend my time at work in a constant daze; I even had people come up to me and ask if I was okay.

Still with me?? You must think I'm mad. Anyway, after that the dreams suddenly stopped, just like that. Nothing, or at least nothing I could remember on waking. Then, only last night, Dad came to me again, but now he was a young man, and in uniform. He looked so healthy and smart, and I remember an overwhelming feeling of joy and pride wash over me. He didn't say anything, just gave me his usual smile only this time he added a wave and a wink before he turned to walk away. He strode through the long grass towards Mum who had begun to walk towards him with her arms open wide. They met and embraced in the middle of the field and over his shoulder she looked up at me and smiled as well. Then they turned and walked away hand in hand.

I woke up briefly to a tear soaked pillow before falling back into the deepest sleep. This morning I awoke feeling totally at peace with myself. It has been the most beautiful autumn day here and I went to work with a renewed appreciation of all that was around me.

When I got home this evening my neighbour came round with a package for me that she'd signed for. I saw that it was airmail and had a U.K. stamp on it and thought that it must be something of Dad's that had been left at the nursing home that they'd thought important enough to send. Imagine my surprise when I opened it to find the Victoria Cross and your accompanying letter.

I don't really know what attachment to my dreams and you and the medal I'm trying to make here, and you might declare me crazy insane for thinking it but I do strongly feel some sort of, how can I put it? Some kind of link, some kind of connection, be it spiritual or whatever. Don't get me wrong I'm not particularly religious and I certainly don't make a habit of going around trying to talk to the dead, but what I do have is an open mind, and for me, these events for want of a better word, didn't just happen as a coincidence. What they did happen for, I'm not sure; I'm still trying to work that one out; maybe a warning, maybe a message, maybe a lesson, who knows? The dream in which you appeared left such a profound effect on me, and at the time I remember feeling quite fearful for you.

I trust all is well with you, your letter didn't mention otherwise; nor did you say how or where you acquired the medal. No matter I'm sure you have your reasons. To be honest with you, I'd forgotten all about it, in fact I think I only ever saw it once or twice as I was growing up; Dad very rarely got it out or had it on show, and he certainly never talked about it, not in my presence at least.

I'm looking at the cross as I write; it really is in excellent condition and the inscription on the back looks like it could have been done yesterday. It's strange to think that I grew up all the while not realising that my Dad was a hero, but in my eyes he'd always been one regardless of what he did during the war. It's funny how people tended not to want to talk about their exploits after those dark days, and Dad, in that respect was no different, too many painful memories I suppose, but judging from your letter you seemed to have had the knack of prising stories and anecdotes out of the likes of Dad and his mate Stan during your sessions down at the club. It's sad in a way

444

that following generations are ignorant or don't seem to care about the sacrifices these men, boys even, made for us all back then. So it's warming to know that there are still one or two people around like yourself who hold a genuine interest and appreciation.

The dream last night was so vivid I'll never forget it as long as I live, but I know that I'm unlikely ever to have those dreams again; don't ask me how I know, I just do. And if they were meant to be some kind of lesson, then I'd like to think that I'm already learning. When I met you on that cold and windy day in the churchyard I knew I was looking into the face of a good man. Again, don't ask me how I knew that, I just did. I know that you must have gone through an awful lot of trouble for this, and it was such a fantastic gesture, I can't begin to tell you how much I appreciate it.

All the cherished memories of both Mum and Dad are safely stored away in my head and in my heart; I don't need anything else now. I'll never forget what you did for my father, so I'm returning his medal, his Victoria Cross as a gift to you on his behalf. I'm sure; absolutely certain in my heart of hearts that this is what he would have wanted.

You're a fair bloke, Terry Gallagher, as they say around these parts. God bless. I'll never forget you.

Yours truly,

Caroline Goulding.

Terry was speechless. He blew air from his cheeks and looked up at Jan. She'd also been lost for words apart from the odd '*Bloody hell*' that she'd uttered at a couple of bits in the letter.

Terry didn't know what to think, especially about the dreams. He had to admit it all sounded a bit weird. He nervously fingered the medal while a voice in his head kept on repeating, '*You're a good bloke – You're a good bloke…*' Then the phone started to ring.

'You *have* got a bit of explaining to do, haven't you?' said Jan as she went to answer it.

Terry placed the medal back in its case and silently begged the voice to go away. He made a grab for one of the envelopes, the one with the Leeds United crest on it. He started to tear it open when a flash of vivid blue appeared outside the window. The new colour on the old pickup was going to take some getting used to.

He heard the driver door slam with a familiar knackered rattle. His mate Nobby came running down the path like a fourteen year old.

Jan picked up the phone. 'Oh, hi Kath,' he heard her say in the background.

Something told Terry Gallagher it was going to be an eventful day.

THE END

About the Author

DERRYL FLYNN GREW up in a northern coal mining town in England during the fifties and sixties. He studied Film-Theatre & TV at Bradford College of Art in the early seventies where he developed a passion for writing drama for screenplay and radio. His debut novel *The Albion* was first published in 2008. *Scrapyard Blues,* is his second novel.

Derryl lives with his wife, on the edge of the moors and just a spit away from Bronte country (not a good idea if the wind's in the wrong direction) where he continues to work on his third MS.

Scrapyard Blues

by Derryl Flynn

Sex, drugs, and rock 'n' roll. How did one crazy night of excess end up with 25 years behind bars?

Convicted for the brutal murder of an ex girlfriend, JD Smith is back on the streets a bitter and broken man. Now in his fifties, the once good looking, carefree, former musician in a post punk R & B band is left to reflect on the bizarre events that led to his long incarceration without right to appeal, where, despite maintaining his innocence, all the evidence continues to point to his guilt. Out on licence, Jack Smith is determined to find the real killer and bring them to justice. But before he can pursue the quest to clear his name, he first has to assuage the demons that reside inside his head and haunt his nightmares; rid himself of the darkness that continues to taunt, torment and test his sanity. Other distractions come in the shape of a sultry female lawyer whose practice methods aren't always entirely ethical. And a trip to India in search of an elusive butterfly, the daughter he hasn't seen since she was two. Mistrusting of a legal system that has already failed him, Jack decides to take the law into his own hands, but unbeknown to him, someone else is on a mission to catch a killer...

Scrapyard Blues is a pulsating story of one man's quest for redemption and reconnection with a life lost.

"Scrapyard Blues is a gritty yet uplifting tale of redemption, renewal and perhaps most importantly self-discovery. Derryl Flynn has captured the pathos of 'The Shawshank Redemption' and the verve of 'Get Carter'. Not only is the tale beautifully told, but a bluesy backbeat permeates the writing from start to finish, ranging from slow, brooding delta to hard-driving rock. I had tears in my eyes when I got to the last page and that is the finest compliment I can pay."
Terry Murphy, author of *Weekend in Weighton*

GRINNING BANDIT BOOKS

A word from our sponsors…

If you enjoyed *The Albion*, please check out these other brilliant books:

Rupee Millionaires, Kevin and I in India, He Ain't Heavy, He's My Buddha, Ginger the Gangster Cat, and *Ginger the Buddha Cat* –by Frank Kusy (Grinning Bandit Books).

Weekend in Weighton by Terry Murphy (Grinning Bandit Books).

The Ultimate Inferior Beings by Mark Roman (Cogwheel Press).